DELIVERER

C. J. CHERRYH
DELIVERER

DAW BOOKS, INC.
DONALD A. WOLLHEIM, FOUNDER
375 Hudson Street, New York, NY 10014

ELIZABETH R. WOLLHEIM
SHEILA E. GILBERT
PUBLISHERS
http://www.dawbooks.com

First Printing, February 2007.

1 2 3 4 5 6 7 8 9 10

DAW TRADEMARK REGISTERED
U.S. PAT. OFF. AND FOREIGN COUNTRIES
—MARCA REGISTRADA
HECHO EN U.S.A.

PRINTED IN THE U.S.A.

DELIVERER

1

Morning—a very early morning, with the red-tiled roofs of Shejidan hazed in fog, presenting a mazy sprawl in the distance beyond the balcony rail. A definite nip of autumn edged the wind that swept across the table and flared the damask cloth.

Ilisidi, aiji-dowager, diminutive of her kind, and very frail, seemed little affected by the chill. Bren Cameron, opposite her at the small breakfast table, swallowed cup after cup of hot tea and tried to still his shivers.

The dowager, seemingly oblivious to the slight breeze, slid several more eggs onto her plate and cheerfully ladled on a sauce Bren would never dare touch.

They were without bodyguards for the moment, or, rather, their respective bodyguards were sensibly standing just inside, out of the wind. The balcony was high enough and faced away from likely sniper sites, so that here, at least, one had no reason to fear bullets, assassins, or remnants of the recent coup and counterrevolution.

"Lord Tatiseigi will go home soon," Ilisidi said conversationally—one never discussed business over meals. This was a social remark, ostensibly, at least.

"Indeed, aiji-ma?" They had come here from Lord Tatiseigi's estate, which had suffered extensive damage in the fighting, damage ranging from its mangled hedges to an upstairs bedroom missing its floor. It would not be a happy homecoming for the old man . . . though it was a triumphant one.

"He has so many things to arrange," Ilisidi said. "Carpenters, plasterers—stonemasons." An egg vanished, and Ilisidi rapped the dish with her spoon. "Do trust the white sauce, nand' paidhi. Have the fish. You look peaked."

Frozen was nearer the truth, and sauces were a minefield of alkaloids delectable to atevi, and potentially fatal to humans, but Bren obediently slid a little of the fish offering onto his plate, and spooned white sauce atop it, a sauce kept hot, despite the bitter gale, by a lid and a shielded candle.

The breakfast service was silver lined with hand-painted porcelain, hunting scenes, each piece exquisite and historic. Everything was historic in Ilisidi's apartment, which no rebel hand had dared touch, even when everyone had believed that Tabini-aiji was dead and Ilisidi was unlikely to return from space. Tabini had lived, and she had returned, and those who had thought differently were, at the moment, running for their lives.

Bren himself had a small guest quarters within Ilisidi's domain, inside the Bu-javid, that massive city-girt fortress which housed no few of the lords of the Association. Herein, inside a building that loomed above the city of Shejidan, resided the aiji himself, the lords, the officials, besides their offices, the legislature and their offices—the complex sat atop its hill in the ancient heart of the city. The fortress and the city, not to mention the continent that spanned half the world, were newly back in the aiji's hands, and they, Bren Cameron and Ilisidi and their respective bodyguards, were newly returned from their two-year voyage, dropped down to the world in support of Tabini-aiji. The two of them had come down from the sterile security of a steel world, where the only breezes came from the vents, to this balcony, where nature determined the temperature and the breeze, and Bren found the change of realities—and the intervening few days of revolution—both exhilarating and a little unreal, even yet. The paidhi might freeze and shiver, but this morning he enjoyed the sensations, the sight, the tastes— the very randomness of things.

Not too much randomness, thank you. The random shooting had died down in the city. The Assassins' Guild had sorted out its internal affairs and begun to function politically, which meant more stability, enforcement of laws and, indeed, elimination of certain individuals bent on civil unrest. As a result, they two, and the rest of the country, could draw an easier breath, and sleep at night in relative confidence of waking up the next morning: Bren personally welcomed that sort of scheduled regularity, even bloodily achieved.

"Tatiseigi will go home," Ilisidi reiterated across the rim of her teacup, "and I shall go with him. He will need our advice."

Significance penetrated the shivers. "One understands, then, aiji-ma," Bren said. "One will make other arrangements immediately."

"Arrangements are already made for the paidhi-aiji's residence." Ilisidi's cup touched the cloth and a servant appeared, to pour more tea. "Nand' paidhi?"

Tea, she meant. Bren set down his ice-cold cup and the servant whisked another, steaming hot, into its place, before pouring. "Thank you, nand' dowager. May one ask—?"

"Tatiseigi will inform you of the details himself, doubtless, or at least leave a message, but he intends to make his own apartment available for the paidhi's use . . . under current circumstances."

"One is honored." Thunderstruck by the old man's action was more to the point. Tatiseigi's apartment was, indeed, where he had once resided, in Tatiseigi's long absence from the capital, and he had once thought of it as home; but a good many things had intervened—a very great many advancements, and a great many violent things. He had dealt with Lord

Tatiseigi, who did not approve of humans, or televisions, or any other human-brought plague on his traditions, and who had housed him in the meanest rooms in his great house on his return from space.

And Tatiseigi was willing to invite him back? One would be very glad to believe that the old man had suddenly suffered a complete change of perspective about humans, had determined that he was an admirable and acceptable being.

Or the sun might rise in the west. The old man had something up his sleeve, surely. "One is extremely honored, nandi, and I shall express it to him."

"Understand, this residence would remain available in my absence . . ." Ilisidi ladled sauce onto fish. ". . . except, one regrets to say, my grandson, who finds his personal residence greatly disturbed, has set eyes on it."

Disturbed was an understatement: Tabini-aiji's personal apartment had been a battleground during the coup: certain of his servants had died there, blood stained the carpets, there had been a fire set, and certain priceless artworks had been damaged or stolen. The premises was under thorough restoration and examination for security problems.

Meanwhile the paidhi's own apartment, on loan from the Maladesi, had been a case of don't-ask on his arrival: a clan of difficult man'chi, claiming to be distant relatives of the Maladesi, had occupied it, had been instrumental in getting access to that floor during the aiji's entry into the Bu-javid—since they had taken out political rivals, supporters of the other regime, in the process—and in point of fact—the aiji had not found it politic to toss them out of the residence, never mind the fact they had jumped themselves to the head of a very long waiting list for Bu-javid residency . . . it was a mess, it was an absolute mess, and the end result was—the paidhi had no apartment until the aiji finessed the Farai out of it. And the aiji was too busy finessing his own living quarters to worry about the paidhi-aiji.

"So Tabini will lodge here," Ilisidi said, "while the aiji's official residence is restored and renewed. Tatiseigi, for his part, is very anxious to get back to Tirnamardi and assess damages there. It seems a convenient arrangement, that the paidhi should lodge in the Atageini apartments."

Which meant that the Farai were either persons that Tatiseigi of the Atageini would not invite—possible: they were southern, not high in Tatiseigi's favor at the moment—or the Farai were still barricaded into his apartment in hopes of getting concessions out of Tabini.

He was still amazed at Tatiseigi's hospitality toward him. "Dare one ask," he began cautiously, "whether this gracious gesture was his lordship's idea, aiji-ma?"

Ilisidi chuckled and lifted an eyebrow. "We did suggest it . . . considering my grandson's impending residency here, and considering our assistance in the Atageini defense, which has indebted Tatiseigi, when he will acknowledge the fact. In very fact, *our* attendance out at Tirnamardi will prevent another sort of disaster. Tatiseigi *will* bully the artisans. The artist he most wants will certainly quit if not kept in good humor, we well know. So we will be there to prevent the old fool from threatening the man's life."

One could only imagine. Ilisidi was in for a lively stay under Tatiseigi's roof.

But to have something like his own quarters again: that was glorious news. He was delighted. But on a second thought, he was not the dowager's only guest, and that other individual's security was a matter of deep concern to him. "And is Cajeiri going to Tirnamardi, too?"

"No." A sip of tea, and a thoughtful frown. "No, my great-grandson will stay here, with his parents. That will be safest.

Far too many things in Tirnamardi invite his ingenuity. And best he have time with his parents in exclusivity, to allow bonds to form . . ."

He ventured no comment at all, nor deemed it proper. Hundreds of years humans had been on this world, and as long as there had been paidhiin—interpreters and intercessors between atevi and humans—and as close as he had gotten to the culture, atevi had still kept certain things unsaid—as was their custom, to be sure. Certain things were either never commented upon, a matter of good manners, or remained entirely outside the realm of the paidhi's dealings, and the bringing up of their children was a major zone of silence: neither Banichi nor Jago volunteered information in that regard, and when he had asked, Jago had professed ignorance and indifference on her own part . . . a clear enough signal it was not a topic she favored.

But he wanted to know—not only professionally: since he had taken up dealing with the boy, for two significant years of his life—since he had acquired an entirely unprofessional fondness for a boy he in no wise wanted to damage or misdirect, he wanted to know.

The dowager only added, "We have cared for him too long. His sense of association needs time to form naturally, and in appropriate directions. This is his chance, in a field of diminishing chances, and best take it."

Sense of association: that emotion atevi felt that wasn't friendship, or love, those two most dangerous human words. What Ilisidi referred to as diminishing was the opportunity for Cajeiri's forming his own sense of attachments, which constituted an ateva's internal compass in relationships, a feeling central to a healthy personality. A human could only ask himself how wide a window of opportunity a child had, to begin to form those necessary—and reciprocal—bonds, and if there was a point at which that window shut, after which they were left with one very confused young boy.

Certainly the ship where Cajeiri had just spent the last two years had held no youngsters of his own species: more, it had contained far too many opportunities to form ties to the human population, youngsters who used the terms *friend* and *birthday party. . . .*

"Should I seek residence entirely elsewhere, then, aiji-ma?" he asked. He was through eating. The portions were far too much for his frame. The warmth the food and the tea provided was fast fading, especially in the contemplation of a separation from the household. "Should I take myself and my staff down the hill to the hotel—or perhaps all the way to my estate for a time? I could conduct certain business there quite handily, aiji-ma, if more distance would—"

"Our compliments to your sensitivity and grace, nand' paidhi. No, that will not be necessary. We are confident that a removal down the hall will suffice. My great-grandson still needs your advisements, and your good sense. We should not all desert him at once, and doubtless—I have absolutely no doubt at all—he will attempt to contact you, whatever the difficulties. One also foresees he will attempt to politic with you *and* his father, playing one against the other: you know his tricks far, far better than my grandson. A surrogate for his father—oh, indeed, you have been that, paidhi-aiji, over the last two years. One rather assumes that you have formed some sort of bond to my great-grandchild as well."

"One must confess it, aiji-ma, one does feel such a sentiment."

"Well, well, one must necessarily let that association grow somewhat fainter, particularly for public view. I have spoken to my great-grandson regarding this. And to my grandson. One trusts the paidhi absolutely understands."

Indeed. He was saddened to have it confirmed it had to be.

But Cajeiri had had far too much to do with humans, the last two formative years, between six and eight—and now he well understood that if the dowager needed to back away and let the boy form ties to his parents, then he had to back away and let Cajeiri become what he had to be, to be adult, sane, and healthy—not to mention heir to his father's power, ruler of the atevi world . . . aiji of the *aishidi'tat*, with all *that* meant. Aijiin didn't form upward attachments, or they abandoned them increasingly as they grew up: the boy he saw as just a boy was, if he was ever going to rule, going to have to change—would have to drink in other people's manchiin like water, and attach himself only to his inferiors.

Would have to become cold enough, calculating enough—to rule, to judge, to administer. To be impartial in decisions, reasoned in debate, and ruthless with his enemies, as enemies not only of himself, but of the people he represented . . . it was not a mindset a Mospheiran wanted to encourage in a child, but it was what Cajeiri was supposed to become.

So they had come back to earth in various senses. The change had to come, and for the boy's own psychological health, the right signals needed to run down the boy's nerves, and that set of instincts needed to find answers that a human just couldn't give him . . . not and produce a sane ateva.

At least, he thought, this time someone had warned the boy ahead of time that his life was about to be jerked sideways. Cajeiri wasn't going to like it. That was also part of his mental makeup: he defended himself, oh, quite well.

And for good or for ill, he told himself, waiting for the dowager to finish her last cup of tea, he wouldn't be totally out of reach, *when*, not *if*, the boy needed him.

Great-grandmother, a Stability of One, was having breakfast with the Lord of the Heavens. That was marginally more fortunate to say than to remark that Great-grandmother and the

Lord of the Heavens were having breakfast, an Infelicity of Two. There was, of course, a compensatory flower arrangement on that table on the drafty balcony, and the bodyguards, five in number—only Jago had come with nand' Bren, which was odd—made a Felicity of Seven. . . .

All of which was to say that Cajeiri was not invited to that table, but he was sure it was not just the numbers. He was sure it meant the grownups were discussing him, because it would have been a great deal less fuss over all to have provided him a chair at the same table and made felicitous three, would it not?

As it was, he had a quiet breakfast with his bodyguards, Antaro and Jegari, who were brother and sister, and only a little older than he was. They were Taibeni, from the deep forests of the slopes of the Padi Valley, and they were not at all accustomed to city manners, so it was a relief to them, he supposed, not to have to stand in the hall and try to talk to the likes of Cenedi, Great-grandmother's chief bodyguard, or Banichi or Jago, who were Bren's, and terribly imposing—Banichi was actually a very obliging fellow, but Jegari was quite scared of him: that was the truth.

His guard liked the informal ways of Taiben. He, on the other hand, was accustomed to servants at his elbow, oh, indeed he was. He had grown up first with his mother and father, in the most servant-ridden place in the world, and then with great-uncle Tatiseigi, who was a stickler for propriety, and finally with Great-grandmother, traveling in space with nand' Bren, in a vast ship far too small to hide him from proper manners. It was first from Uncle Tatiseigi and then from Great-grandmother he had learned his courtesies: they were very old-fashioned, and insisted on the forms even if they secretly didn't believe in the superstitions. He had been locked up in Great-grandmother's apartment for two years on the ship, and she had made sure he would be fit to come back as his father's son and her great-grandson—his left ear had gotten positively tender from all the thwacking.

He had left the world when he was six. He was now in that awkward year before nine, that year so infelicitous one could not name it, let alone celebrate its birthday in any happy way. That was very bad fortune, since it was the only birthday he had had a chance to have with his new associates on shipboard— Great-grandmother had finally agreed he might have a small celebration, and then he had not even gotten that much, because of the crisis—because they had plunged right down to earth on the shuttle, leaving all his shipboard associates behind and spending the next number of days getting shot at . . .

Well, except he had gotten to ride in the engine of a train. That had been exciting.

He was very precocious in his behavior and in his schooling: nand' Bren said so, so he was already as good as nine, was he not?

He could speak Bren's native Mosphei', as well as ship-speak. He could speak kyo, for that matter, which only a handful of atevi or humans could do. He had learned to ride and shoot before he went into space—well, he could ride, at least: he had learned to shoot on the ship; and Great-grandmother had taught him how to write a formal hand in all the good forms and made him memorize all the lords of the Association and their rights and duties . . . and proper addresses . . .

So he was really not too uncivilized to be at their table, was he?

He was not yet fluent enough in adult Ragi to dance across the nuances, as Great-grandmother called it. Using it could still get him into embarrassing trouble. And it was ever so hard just to sit and listen when really interesting questions were bubbling up into his head.

But he could at least parse everything that was proper at that table. Bren, a Stability of One, he most-times referred to very properly as Bren-nandi. Bren's guards were, together, Bren-aishini, not just *aishi*, the association of Bren-paidhi, and his guards were *aishishi*, meaning the protective surrounds.[1] So, there! He could handle the basic forms of the adult language and remember to put in the compensatory numbers—that was at least sure, and people did use the easy forms, well, at least they did informally, or when they were pretending to be informal, which was a layer of pretending which he understood, but *he* was not supposed to use it with adults or he was being insolent . . .

How could one learn the whole nuance of adult Ragi if no one would ever talk with him?

How could he be i-ron-ic if people only took him for a baby who used the wrong form because he had not a clue?

He wanted company other than Great-grandmother's staff. He wanted people he could surprise and make laugh.

He missed Gene and Artur, his ship-aishi (one could not call them aishini, or at least one had certainly better not do it in Great-grandmother's hearing.) He had gotten more used to young humans than he was to atevi over the last two years, and

---

[1] A note from Bren's dictionary: The number of a noun or verb is always considered In-Its-Environment, which means the *kabiu* of the item is subject to the surrounds and Number Compensations such as seating and arrangements. This is complex enough. Rendering human views in Mosphei' contains words with sentiments strongly reflecting human emotions—for example: "motherhood" and "friendship." To give equal expression to an ateva speaking Ragi, which contains constructs for his own biological urges, any accurate translation of his thoughts into Mosphei' must, for the human hearer, create special forms to note the mental direction of those feelings. For example, Ragi has "respect" in general but also specifies "familial-respect" or "aiji-respect" or "newly-met-stranger-respect," each of which evokes feelings which resonate through the ateva psyche. Ragi is meticulously specific in many sensitive terms in which a human, reading the translated words, must struggle to remember contain emotional impact at all. A mentally healthy ateva feels, in saying, for instance, "aiji-respect" as powerful a sense of emotional bonding as a human would experience in saying, "my dearest friend" and "my own front door . . ." The central difficulty of Ragi translation rests in the fact that while specific words can be translated, the human brain hearing them, unless cued to do so, does not readily attach sufficient or correct emotional subtext. Numerically auspicious and inauspicious aspects present yet another subtle resonance, sometimes a presentiment of luck or foreboding.

still found it strange to look across his own informal table and see two dark, golden-eyed atevi faces, so earnest, so—

That was the heart of his domestic problem. Antaro and Jegari felt man'chi toward him, a sense of duty and devotion so passionate it had drawn them away from all their kin to live in a city they hardly understood. It had brought them to risk their lives for him on a dangerous journey, with people shooting at them, and he knew he should feel a pure, deep emotion toward them in turn—great-grandmother had said on the ship that he was in real danger of never developing proper feelings, which would be a very unhealthy thing; and that once he was back in the world, proper feelings would come to him, and that what he felt toward his *aishini* would be ever so much stronger than anything he had ever possibly felt toward Gene and Artur, because that feeling would be returned . . . in ways Gene and Artur could never return what he needed.

But on that point everything broke down and hurt, it just outright hurt, because Gene and Artur did care about him, in their human way, and he knew they still cared—in their human way. He knew they had been hurt when he left—they must have hurt the same way as he hurt, and no one would acknowledge it.

Aishimuta. Breach of association. Losing someone you never thought of losing.

Losing someone you could never even explain to anyone, someone that no one else thought you could care about . . . there ought to be a word for that, too, even worse than aishimuta. He had never thought he would lose Gene and Artur. He had been so confident he could just bring them home with him when he had to go down to the world, and that sensible grown-ups would, with no problem at all, agree to the idea of their living with him.

That had been juvenile thinking, had it not?

And once their coming down to earth had fallen seamlessly

into place, so his plans had run, of course he would bring Gene and Artur to his father and his mother and tell his parents what wonderful associates they were, and how clever, and unusual, and all those things, and the whole world would understand it was a wonderful arrangement. He would have Gene and Artur with him forever, the way his father had nand' Bren to advise him about humans, and everything would be perfect and happy.

He had been a fool. Great-grandmother had not quite said that word, but he was sure she had disparaged his plans in private and spared him her opinion, only advancing that argument that there would be someone who would appeal to him when he reached home, and that he would know that person, or those people, in a situation that felt right. According to her, there would be no question what he felt . . . all the things everyone told him he would feel . . .

And for one moment, he had almost had it. When Antaro and Jegari had declared for him that day in the forest, with so many dangers around him, he had accepted it—he had been surprised by their gesture, for one thing, and he had believed that something special would flash down from the heavens or something—he didn't know exactly what. But he was open to it. He had tried.

But he still waited to feel it take hold of him.

Now he felt uneasy in his connection with Antaro and Jegari, who had done so much for him. It was true they were comfortable companions and he felt at ease with them. He knew what their expressions meant as if he had known them all his life, and he could guess what they were thinking with fair accuracy . . . that was something. They were faces like his own, black, golden-eyed, and naturally subtle around strangers. They were not at all like aboard the ship, where no one stood on ceremony—where he could all but hear Gene shout down the hall in that reckless, wonderful, irreverent way, "Hey! Jeri!"

He was Jeri. He had been delighted to know it was a proper human name, too, the way it was a proper atevi one.

And oh, he missed that voice, and that irreverence, and that sense of fun. And he felt so guilty and ashamed of himself for it. Antaro and Jegari were a steady warmth, not a spark and a flash. They never offered a really wicked glance, the way Gene would look at him to let him know some adventure was brewing and they were about to risk trouble. Jegari and Antaro would ask, cautiously and solemnly, "Do you think your great-grandmother would approve, nandi?"

And that was the way his life was supposed to be. Solemn. Cautious.

Well, he supposed he had had adventures enough for one year at least, riding on mecheiti and buses and trains and being shot at—he had shot a man himself, because he had to, to save their lives, but he had no wish to remember that part, which was not glorious, or an adventure, or anything but terrible. He thought it ought to have changed him—but it was mostly just not there in his thinking.

Certainly a lot of people had died. That had been horrible, too. And he knew that just the journey had changed things around him—more, that it had changed him in ways he was still figuring out.

But the thing that really hit hardest was how close he had come to losing everyone he really knew and relied on . . . the last remaining: Great-grandmother, and nand' Bren, and their aishini. All his associations in the whole universe were, if not broken, at least stretched painfully thin, and people wanted to shove others at him, fast, while he was alone and desperate. That was a nasty thing to do. A few meant well—Great-grandmother, and nand' Bren. But lords were all but battering at the door to introduce him to their own children, and he just would not see them: Great-grandmother at least supported him in that.

He had learned that not everything was that sure in his life: that was the second lesson he had gotten on this voyage. Having lost the heavens, he had come within a breath of losing everything that was ever going to matter on earth, too, and right now he was stranded with no chance ever to get back to the heavens, because the shuttles were not flying, and might never, if certain people had had their way. It had been close, on that score, but great-grandmother and Lord Bren had taken precautions, and the shuttles were being protected—for which he was very grateful.

In recent days he had been alone, and scared of being alone, and of dying alone, although dying was something he still could not quite figure out—how it was, or how it worked. And he had met Jegari and Antaro, who had some promise, if they weren't so rule-following.

And they were going to get the shuttles flying again, so there was still hope. . . .

But he was not supposed to think about Gene and Artur coming down here, and worse, he had to face the possibility they might not ever be able to. Now he understood how very politically difficult it was going to be, to bring humans anywhere near him, and how people would be watching him and suspecting him. He saw how people all over the world had blamed nand' Bren for everything that had gone wrong, which was just unfair, but that was how people had wanted to think, because it was easier to blame humans for everything that was the matter, and now for people to blame any association *he* had ever had with humans for any peculiarity *he* would ever have or any bad thing *he* ever did—that was just wrong. It was wrong, and he could not go for years being good. It just made him so mad he could just—

But one could not. One had to be calm, and act like an adult to get one's way. And most people were coming to a different opinion about nand' Bren, now, so maybe the trouble would die down.

But it could take years.

Great-grandmother had told Uncle Tatiseigi that he had had enough association-separation in his young life so far; and great-uncle Tatiseigi had argued he had come out of it perfectly fine for a boy in an unfortunate year of his life. Uncle Tatiseigi had told Great-grandmother he was not unbalanced in his head: that much was nice of Great-uncle. But then uncle Tatiseigi had added that he certainly would have been unbalanced if he had stayed in space much longer, that there were clear signs of improper thoughts, and it was a damned good thing he had come down here among *real people*.

That had made him mad, too, but that was Great-uncle.

And at least he knew his elders worried about him, and great-uncle did sincerely worry that he had grown up under questionable influences. The problem was, Great-uncle had very firm opinions about what was right for him, and unluckily for him, Great-grandmother and Great-uncle were not that far apart in their arguments. Uncle Tatiseigi would like him never to mention humans again. Great-grandmother wanted him to give up even thinking about Gene and Artur, and she was hoping, too, that he would forget about them coming down to earth, ever.

And years and years could pass, and they might quiet down about bad influences, but that would be long after he had grown up sane and normal and Gene and Artur had turned into human adults he would never even recognize if he saw them.

That hurt. That thought already wore a deep sore where it lodged and was not going to heal, because he never intended to let it. It made him resolve one thing, that the moment he did get any power, he was going to bring anybody he wanted down to the earth and keep them there.

Ripping him away from every association he knew . . . was that not damage to his psyche, too?

And if it did hurt him, and everybody knew it, why did

familial-adults he trusted keep doing this to him? Why did they think it was for his own good?

Because he had to rule the *aishidi'tat* when he grew up, that was what, and there had been a war, a stupid, long-ago war, and that was why he could never be too close to humans. That was why everything bad had happened.

And something in him wanted to explode whenever he thought about it, but he could never let his upset show, because that would absolutely assure he never got power.

He would not have chosen differently for his life than Great-grandmother had done for him this far: he never would have missed the voyage with Bren and Great-grandmother, he never would choose to miss knowing Gene and Artur—

And he was absolutely sure that the adults who had combined to make his life miserable in his homecoming did not really have him particularly in mind when they did it—that was what Great-grandmother would say: she had said, word for word: *No one is thinking too much about you, young gentleman. There are larger things at issue. If my distressing you were at all personal, you would have no confusion at all about the fact.*

That was the truth. He was quite sure of it. And he was disabused—Great-grandmother's word—of any notion that the world was going to change its ways to accommodate him. He had imagined being his father's son would mean being rich, and happy and getting just about anything he wanted.

His father, it turned out, had to make compromises, and the world was complicated, and no, he could not even *ask* his father for what he most wanted.

All his rank thus far had done for him was to see everyone he attached to had to leave him alone for his own good, because they weren't perfect enough, in the opinion of his great-grandmother or his great-uncle, or even, in Bren's case and his uncle's and his grandmother's, because they were important and busy and had no time to bring up a boy. His father had welcomed him, hugged him close, looked him in the eyes, and straightway gone off to talk to people about an assassination in the south; his mother had hugged him, remarked how he had grown, patted his cheek, and gone off to talk to Uncle Tatiseigi and the lord of the Ajuri about where they were staying and how they were going to deal with Lord Bren's apartment.

He knew, because Great-grandmother had told him, that being aiji was necessarily a lonely job. He already knew that ruling the *aishidi'tat* meant owing no aiji-respect, only collecting it from others—he had made a start with Antaro and Jegari—and if one was born to be aiji, one had different sorts of emotions from the rest of the world. One was just peculiar, compared to other people. He would be sitting someday at the top of a pyramid of man'chi, and getting it all, but needing to dispense, well, very little, in an obligatory way, though Great-grandmother told him that a wise aiji was as good as he knew how to be or people left him in short order, the way they had left Murini.

So he could have a few people close to him, but mostly he had to deal with everybody equally and impartially . . . because that was good, and it kept everyone happy. Favoring certain people was a bad thing. If one was aiji.

Was he that peculiar-minded? He had no idea. Loneliness sounded—well, boring as well as painful. He had no way to tell if it meant something else to other people.

On the ship he had been amazingly safe, and comfortable, and could do almost anything he liked when he was off with Gene and their other associates—and was that not having power, even when he had to worry about getting caught? It was never serious. Nobody died. Nobody even got hurt—well, much . . .

Here he had to slip about to do the least little thing, and invent somewhere to have been, if he was not where someone expected him. Overall, it had been so pleasant up there, being attached to people. There had been endless things to do. There had been surprises, and plans and plots.

Now he had won the place he was supposed to have . . . and everything had changed for the worse. He was bored and irritated most of the time he was just with Jegari and Antaro, bored and lonely when he was by himself. Great-grandmother no longer gave him his daily lessons. She forgot he existed.

He was a prisoner, was all, not even invited to breakfast on the balcony.

He pushed his plate back. "Nadiin-ji," he said to his young bodyguards, "I have no appetite. But one has no wish to worry Cook. Will you make it disappear?"

"May we ask, nandi?" Taro asked, the sister of the pair.

A deep sigh. And two devout faces stared at him, concerned and with their own world out of sorts, because he frowned at them and said he was out of sorts.

He saw how the atmosphere was of his own making. He decided it was time for a supreme effort, and that he was going to break several rules at once.

"I shall talk about Gene and Artur," he said solemnly. "About the ship. About how we lived aboard."

"We will be glad to hear," Jegari said earnestly, as if Jegari really were glad, even relieved. Antaro's face brightened, too.

"I might have an egg or two," Cajeiri said. Having made up his mind to talk, and having met actual enthusiasm for a change, he found something of an appetite to go with it.

He had shared tea with a kyo, a being neither Taro nor Jegari could imagine, even having seen pictures of that event. He could tell them about that association.

He had done so very much in his young life, and to have Great-grandmother telling him—but not directly ordering him—to drop all his former associations . . .

Well, but it was just *stupid!* Breaking with associations was *not* his value in the scheme of things, was it? Had not Lord Bren said that? Had not Great-grandmother and Great-uncle agreed? He mixed most of the continent in his bloodline, and it had turned out the lords were considerably wrought about that, each vying to claim a share of him for their province, their people. They all thought those connections he had were a good thing.

So, and had he not gained human associates, including Lord Bren, who advised his father. He was never going to give Lord Bren up, was he? Did not Lord Bren serve his father, and his father approve him?

So he could make these two who were so devoted to him understand how that was, and maybe get them to stop objecting about the rules.

He decided, he was not going to sit on his hands—Bren's word for doing nothing. He was not an island. He was not born for that. He connected everything. Was that not why everyone who wanted the *aishidi'tat* to survive—had cheered him in the streets when he came here?

"Gene and Artur were my associates during the voyage home," he began, attempting cheerfulness toward two maddeningly attentive faces. He decided to be patient. Great-grandmother had taught him to be, and thwacked his ear when he fidgeted. He decided to fight with words. Lord Bren had taught him that. "Gene and Artur and Bjorn. They made fortunate three." That hurt to think of, because, up there, they still would be fortunate three, without him. Gene had somehow invited Bjorn into the group. Or Bjorn had added himself, and confused him, since he had known his great-grandmother would disapprove. "I said Irene should join us because it made us five—though humans hardly think in numbers. They were born on a space station we never even knew existed, a few years ago . . ."

*   *   *

"A number of matters have to be attended to," Ilisidi said to Bren, and spared a glance up. "Are you chilled, nand' paidhi?"

"Only a little, aiji-ma. Please, finish your tea."

"Well, well." She poured her cup, and by gesture, offered the same to him, from her own hand, in this breakfast with few servants.

"Honored, aiji-ma." He took it, and warmed his hands and scalded his mouth with the first sip.

"Bitter?"

"Hot. Heat is welcome."

"Well, well, but I shall be leaving the Bu-javid. Things must be said while we have the chance, nandi-ji. The repairs of Tirnamardi are one thing. The repairs to the fabric of the Central Association—those are far more urgent."

"Indeed. Whatever you wish said, or done, aiji-ma, I shall do."

"There have been too many assassinations in our absence from the world, even into the East. Lord Mesi is dead."

That was a neighbor of hers, in the Eastern Association, her distant home.

"One regrets to hear it."

"Poisoned. And he was such a careful man."

"One urges the dowager take very great care at Tirnamardi. We already know its risks."

"Disaffection in the district. A house neighboring the Kadagidi. Not to mention marriages across that border." Of which Cajeiri's mother's relatives in Ajuri clan were several key ones, nominally interested in mending fences—and likely to make approaches, honest or otherwise. Ilisidi pursed her lips, the cup stayed on its way to her mouth. Her gold eyes darted a sharp glance aside to the doorway and back. "Tatiseigi asked remuneration from my grandson for the damages to the estate. He will get it. He will be quite astonished."

So Tabini himself was going to foot the bill for the battle. Or the national treasury was. "It seems just," Bren said. "But the province at large suffered, too."

"A people as stubborn and prideful as their lord. They will wrangle over compensatory damages and ask funding for repairs. That is not the compensation my grandson proposes for them."

"Not industry."

"Never." Amusement crinkled her eyes. "No. The Atageini have no bent for factories. Nor would Tati-ji ever accept it. But developing the hot springs at Comei . . . public baths there will gain money and trade, and preserve the natural environment. It was our suggestion, to my grandson."

"An excellent notion." It truly was. He knew the area, a set of terraces and hot springs, natural and beautiful, but almost inaccessible. They only had to get a rail line through Tatiseigi's estate—and he began to see that Tabini had another motive in mind besides gratitude: they had tried to get that line through for the last fifty years. Putting it through near Comei—that was brilliant. Tabini hadn't dropped a stitch.

"Beyond this," Ilisidi said, "the recovery of one bus from the Taiben woods . . . that will mollify the transit authority. Recompense to various districts for wear, tear, and damage to the trucks and buses: my staff is making a list. The monetary damages will be dealt with."

She was a force of nature.

And she would be leaving the capital soon, to find her own way back east, to her own holdings, after her sojourn with Tatiseigi. So he imagined. He would miss Ilisidi. He had lived so closely with her and her staff and Cajeiri during the voyage that he had, yes, dammit, regarded her as family—he had lost his own mother in parting with the world, and it had been too natural during those two years to fall into Ilisidi's orbit. It was an emotional attachment that would shock and amaze the dowager.

Time, he thought, to cut those bonds. Might it be his own too-frequent presumptions on her society that had driven her to take refuge elsewhere?

But she knew what was right to do, and she was self-protective, and protective of the boy. She had the right instincts. She surely saw that those bonds needed to be cut, and national politics as well as the welfare of the boy himself was the urgent reason for doing it now, as painlessly as possible.

Wise Ilisidi, he said to himself. Wise. Even kind. Ilisidi had found so delicate a way to manage, had arranged all the details, and set up a plausible situation which would help the boy through it and wean them all apart, their little family that could only have existed in the human geometries of shipboard living. That this departure to Tirnamardi was just the natural, convenient progress of things . . . he by no means believed it.

The breakfast invitation was the last he would have of her company for a while, he became sure.

"Well, well," she said, pushing back her dish, "best break this up before you freeze, nandi."

"Then I must say good-bye to you, aiji-ma."

"Oh, indeed, not quite good-bye, paidhi. Join me for dinner this evening."

He might have stopped in rising, ever so slightly, but he covered his dismay with a bow—or thought he had.

The dowager smiled beneficently.

The party, he well knew, was a company of Easterners arrived yesterday, to meet the dowager, to felicitate her on her return, and probably to deplore her recent associations . . . meaning humans, shipboard and current.

And she wanted him there tonight, when he had intended to have supper in his rooms, troubling the staff as little as possible and giving no intimation of his presence in her household.

"I shall, then," he said, his heart beating just a little faster. He searched her face, the flick of a glance, for motive, or hint, or warning, and gained nothing at all. "Honored, aiji-ma. Indeed, I am honored."

"There was no place on the ship we could not go," Cajeiri said. "Well, except onto the captains' deck, or into a few such places, but we knew every passage, even between decks, even the dark, cold places, where you could almost float when you walked."

His audience followed everything with rapt attention—gratifying. Jegari and Antaro were older and taller and stronger than he was. It was hard to feel in charge when one had to look up constantly. But at the moment, he felt embraced, and felt their loyalty about him, solid and good and steady.

He could hardly help it. Wicked ambition took over. His next sentence was: "We need to know this place that well."

A spark leaped up in that placid, absolute devotion, the same little spark he had seen leap up under fire in Tirnamardi—in two young bodyguards who by no means knew this place, this huge single building. Was ignorance and fear of this great house the reason they had been so subdued, so absolutely, deadly earnest and spooked by every noise? They had known their deep forest. This stone place had different rules, and they must be more lost than he was.

"Yes," they said, almost as one, seizing on what he said. And he immediately had second thoughts: he knew the hazards of what he proposed, and knew, too, what these two were not—Guild, for one: Assassins' Guild, the way bodyguards were supposed to be, and their pretending to be would not sit well with those who were. Pretense was no longer a game. Not in the Bu-javid's nervous corridors—where there might well be people bent on killing. It might get them into dangerous trouble.

But neither was it a game, that he needed to have his freedom, and he needed to have knowledge of his surroundings, in case some intruder got into Great-grandmother's apartments, or met them in the halls. They had to know the escapes and the secret ways, and these existed: he knew they did—they had used some of them to get into the Bu-javid alive.

"There are wires," he said. These two had seen the effect of wires, that could be set ankle-high, nearly invisible, that could take a foot off. It was one of the deadliest traps the Guild used, and there were wires guarding the aiji his father, and guarding lords, and various other sensitive places throughout the building. He knew that just on a reasonable guess, because he knew the resources of the Guild that defended them.

"We know wires," Jegari said cheerfully. "Taiben has them."

They would know other things, then. That was good. His father's hunting lodge had been a major security installation in Taiben province, and the Taibeni had maintained it until the coup . . . so they were not ignorant in that regard.

And after Murini took over, the Taibeni had served to protect his father, as woodland rangers . . . and they had shuffled here and there about the province, eluding Kadagidi attacks and returning attack only when they picked the ground and the odds. They might be wide-eyed and quiet, these two, and spooked by shadows, but that was because they did notice things. They were quick and they might be clever—once they knew facts to work on.

They had to find out how things were set up, that was what, and that included even the Guild's security precautions, so they could move in safety. If they were his substitute for Gene and Artur, and this was where he had to live, well, freedom to come and go would fix a great many things. On the ship, he had had the computers on which to look things up, and they had had the intercoms at every turn, and the back passages and service accesses and crawlways to enable quick movement and secret meetings. The Bu-javid was absolutely riddled with passages on its lower levels, and had no few above. During the fighting, at the very time he had been running for his life and climbing stairs until his stomach hurt, he had seen the pipes and the conduits that ran right along overhead and all around them on the walls, and he knew that where those conduits and pipes disappeared and appeared again for water lines and vents, there would be access panels, valves, and interrupts of some kind. That was the way plumbing and electricity worked. There had always been access panels on the ship, and there had to be such here, unless one wanted to chisel through a wall to get at something stuck in the plumbing. And that was just too stupid. It was not the way clever builders would do things.

"We need maps, nadiin-ji," he said. "And we can draw them, for all the servants' halls."

"We can indeed do that, nandi," Antaro said.

"But no one should see you at it."

Jegari touched a finger to his head. "We remember forest paths. There is no difference, nandi. All we have to do is walk through and then draw the map when we get to the room."

He was perplexed suddenly. He found he had no Ragi word for *service access*. He thought, sometimes, in a mishmash of Ragi and ship-speak. "Panels where you can reach wires and pipes."

"Entry plates, nandi," Jegari supplied.

"We have to know where all those are. Those should be on the maps. I know how to wire things." He was very proud of that. "And I know about—the things you turn like faucets, to shut water off . . . what do you call the things that shut off pipes?"

"Valves," Antaro said.

That was still a Mosphei' word, by the sound of it. Ragi had borrowed a great many words from Mosphei', so nand' Bren had told him, even for things like plumbing, which atevi had had a long time before humans dropped down to the world. His head was stuffed with new information: he met strangeness on every hand, all the hours of the day, and he was determined not to forget his lessons from shipboard. He was determined, now that he thought of it, to draw every passage on the ship, from memory, with all the accesses they had used, he and Gene, and Artur, when grown-ups tried in vain to find them. And then he intended to do the same for the Bu-javid.

There were bullet-holes in the hallways here in the Bu-javid. People had died out there, and his father's staff had been murdered in his apartment without even a chance. Here the back ways could very clearly be important. If he knew them, he said to himself, he could get himself and Great-grandmother to safety. So anything was justified, so long as he was careful, and kept his notes secret.

"And we need to get into communications," he said. "If it were the ship, we could just listen in. We need to learn how the phones work, so if we want to know something, we can learn it."

"Security will surely catch us at that, nandi," Antaro said with a frown. "They can tell if we tap a line."

"How?"

"One by no means knows how, nandi, but they will know."

"We need to know how they know. One could ask our security that. One could find a clever way. Or one might find a manual. Is there a library, do you think, nadiin-ji?" He had no idea if there was a computer library here in the Bu-javid, the way one could call up files on the ship, but it seemed reasonable that people would want some sort of reference near, and the Bu-javid certainly had every other amenity. Downstairs, when they came in, there had been records strewn across the floor. Those had to sit somewhere . . . records of all sorts. Books. Maps. Charts. Diagrams.

"There is a library," Jegari said. "There is a great library, nandi."

"A very famous one," Antaro said. "But one has no idea where in the building it may be."

"*I* can find out," Cajeiri said in every confidence, "and they will lend books to *me*. My father will approve my study. Study always looks innocent."

"Can one be certain," Jegari asked carefully, "that this inquiry will not bring trouble on you, nandi?"

"I have no such fear," he said, and indeed, had none at all, and quickly changed the subject. A servant had just come in. It was that woman who always smiled at him and made smiling look like a chore. Pahien was her name. She belonged to the staff here. And he detested her. "Eat the eggs, nadiin-ji. Quickly, before I have to."

The servant had brought a message cylinder, a silver filigree one, proffering it in a small silver bowl. It was, Cajeiri saw, Great-grandmother's personal message cylinder. And he did not think it portended anything good. Great-grandmother rarely sent him messages, and they were usually social, but often a reprimand, sometimes a very scathing reprimand. He was prepared to control his face, and hoped to the depth of his heart they had not just been overheard in what was a very important scheme.

There was, the message read, a party tonight.

And he was invited. His heart leaped up.

But it was a dinner party for lords out of the Eastern Association.

Well, that was not good news. It was no one he knew. Probably nobody in all the world he knew would be there, except Great-grandmother and Cenedi and his men, and security would be on strictest duty, which meant Jegari and Antaro had to eat later and stand behind his chair. He would have to dress in starched lace and sit on display, like a porcelain on a pedestal, and be perfect and still while people stared at him.

It was just gruesome. It was not at all what he called a party.

Everyone would talk past him, or expect him to perform, or ask him cleverly worded questions about things Great-grandmother would not want him to talk about and then smirk if he proved too clever for them.

"I shall answer, nadi," he said to the maidservant, who took the cylinder and the bowl away and would return with his own plain message cylinder and appropriately sized paper and pen. And then she would stand by and stare at him while he wrote.

On the ship he could have called Gene on com and asked whether they might have pizza.

But even on the ship, he would have answered Great-grandmother with a carefully written message, and that message would say, inescapably, in very proper script, "One will be extremely honored to attend the formal dinner this evening at sunset, esteemed Great-grandmother. One is gratified by the invitation."

2

The paidhi's quarters within the dowager's apartments were, indeed, a little cramped for the burgeoning piles of documents and letters which had been pouring into the paidhi's nonexistent office since their arrival in the Bu-javid. Citizens had complaints, felicitations, and earnest queries as to whether, for instance, the station was the agency which had sent down the mysterious capsules that had been rumored landed in the remote north.

Probably they had done so, was the short answer. But Bren had no personal idea what these mysterious landings portended, whether such packages were dangerous, or observational, or just what the station might have had in mind. One could note that they had been landed during Murini's takeover, when the station had every reason to mistrust the situation. But the station had neglected to mention the existence of such things when they had passed through—admittedly in haste—and he had no information for the recipients of such landings. He could not say whether they were dangerous to approach, and now everyone was looking for such items in their bean patches and hunting areas. It was hard to tell a farmer just to be patient, with an unknown thing sitting in one's orchard, with a parachute draped over the fruit trees . . . that was one photo he had received, and yes, if he were the orchard-keeper, he would be understandably perturbed.

He had those inquiries—and letters from a handful of persons seeking appointment. He had a dinner invitation for five days from now from the Lord of Dur, who wished, with the mayors of several coastal towns and villages, to host a celebratory banquet in the paidhi's honor. Even five days from now was still early for too provocative celebrations of the defeat of certain powerful interests—the relatives of whom were still at court. Human influence at court was a touchy topic in many quarters, and it was a delicate matter to accept or refuse the honor, not least because he owed Dur considerably, and might be expected to reciprocate with some signal favor to that district that he could bestow in turn. And he had no way to swing that influence, nor ought he to try . . . not being atevi. That was one thing riding the back of his mind.

For another matter, he was reluctant to bring Dur in as egregiously supporting the paidhi before he was entirely sure the paidhi had a future in his present post. Politics might yet have him replaced, at least as related to his current status as the aiji's personal interpreter. Tabini-aiji still favored him, and Tabini's word was ordinarily law, but there was contrary pressure from a number of disgruntled southerners (granted that, as the source of the recent coup, they had limited expectations of being heard, and some of them were lucky to be alive), but there was, in fact, an alternative. Yolanda Mercheson, over on Mospheira, had held his post for the last two years. Yolanda had rather walk barefoot through fire than come back to the mainland, and only wanted to get back to orbit; but that had no place in the calculations of atevi who would cheerfully see Tabini divorced from the adviser many blamed for economic troubles. There were, for that matter, certain people who wished the paidhi dead, so Yolanda would have to come back.

So he hardly knew what to tell the good people of Dur about the dinner.

He passed through his little sitting room, designed for a guest, not a full-fledged office, on his way to the bedroom, and rang for the servants. Jago had gone on to her own quarters, adjacent and down the short inner corridor. This was a safe place. There was hardly any safer in the entire continent.

That fact did not, however, protect him from the towering stacks out there. At the very least he had to answer his hourly-growing backlog of letters and queries, some of them from very serious people with very difficult questions.

And in the meantime, he had to prepare for a series of legislative hearings on the restoration of the regime and the distribution of appointments. *He* would sit on several of those legislative committees, whose work was waiting, pending location of various people who had fled the capital to save their lives.

He had another set of inquiries of lesser import, including requests for interviews, and several requests for commemorative notecards from well-meaning individuals.

And meanwhile various people ambitious to gain space within the Bu-javid saw no reason to allot any precious room to a human official.

He had sent a desperate request in for proper offices downstairs in the Bu-javid, and if he could locate enough of his old staff to start sweeping up the debris of data and records, he might start his own work with skilled help—he hoped the specific office space he requested would be a reasonable balance between security and modesty.

Top priority on his agenda—he had, sometime in the next day or so, to get a call through to the island, to the President of Mospheira, who, thank God, happened to be his old bureau chief, Shawn Tyers. The atevi Messengers' Guild, in charge of all mainland communications, had concentrated its repair efforts on land lines and claimed the big dish at Mogari-nai was near resuming service.

Once that was up, the continent would have communication with the station in orbit—and calls could be relayed with a great deal more reliability to the island. But there had been, all along the coast during the troubles, a perfectly adequate unofficial radio network. He had, yesterday, sent a report to the Messengers' Guild and requested the transmission of the bare facts to Shawn by means less publicly known: *we're alive, we're safe, Tabini's back in power.* It was the sort of wide-open communication that anyone could read—and he was sure that spies of every sort had; the Messengers' Guild was a little looser in its membership than was the Assassins' Guild—but if Shawn failed to know they were back in power, Mospheiran agencies were completely asleep at the switch.

For formality's sake, he had said: *We're alive and safe. The aiji is back in authority over the mainland.* And then the key part of the message: *Tell Jase and Yolanda that the shuttles on the mainland are in fairly good condition, and the pilots and crews have survived—they're going to have to catch up in training and service, but we are in far better shape than we dared hope. . . .*

Maybe Shawn knew, being in communication with the station. Maybe not. So they proceded a lot in the dark about what this side and that knew. It had been five days since the shooting stopped. They had had time to do a bit of mopping-up, some of it bloody, and they had done a bit of repair—and now messages flowed. Air service resumed, though it was sporadic. The trains ran. True, the Assassins' Guild had its own wireless network—and that functioned . . . but one did not ask to send even official messages through those channels. One just did not. The Guild did what the Guild did.

The dowager's servants arrived to take his coat. He assumed a lighter one, and went back to his makeshift office. The servants offered tea, which he declined, having had tea up to his eyeballs. He sat down at his desk, shifted papers into stacks he mentally tagged "critical," "dire," and "maybe in a few days."

Jago returned, and stood, immaculate in Assassins' black and silver, looking particularly inscrutable at the moment.

"These visitors of the dowager's tonight will certainly be spying on us," he remarked, making a slight guess as to what occupied her mind.

"One assumes so, nandi." She would have heard every word that passed between him and the dowager, so there was absolutely nothing he needed to tell her about the invitation, or about the impending move. She would be with him tonight, at that table, parsing every lifted eyebrow and watching every dish that came and went—even in this household.

But she had been alone this morning, extraordinary as that was. Her partner had not been with her; nor had Tano or Algini.

"What *is* Banichi's business this morning, Jago-ji?" he asked. He had not had time to ask before now, at a place and in a privacy from the dowager's servants. He had kept assuming Banichi would turn up, but he had not, and when he had reached the dowager's vicinity, the numbers of the dowager's guards had turned up compensatory. That was mildly troubling. But asking what Jago had not volunteered seemed to require some little space for communication, a commodity which had not been available yet this morning, nor on the walk back. Now the servants left. In those diminishing footsteps, they had perhaps five minutes of sure privacy.

"He was called to the Guild, nandi. Tano and Algini are with him."

He had somewhat concluded that. And more footsteps passed the open door, and diminished in the distance.

"They may not be back this evening," Jago added, entirely gratis, once those footsteps were gone.

He returned a worried stare, wondering what she was trying to tell him in that further, unsolicited information. It was unusual that Banichi stay that long at a Guild meeting, but at this juncture his Guild was in turmoil, Guildsmen had died, and one suspected there was a thorough shake-up going on, even yet. His own staff, particularly Algini, as it turned out, was very high up in that secretive guild—so if Tano and Algini were with Banichi, he felt a little better about the situation, but he hoped Banichi was not in some difficulty for actions he had recently taken in the paidhi's cause . . . and he hoped that Algini himself had not seen his position weaken. Guild infighting was scary beyond all comfort. "If Banichi needs your support," he began.

"I am not to leave you, nandi-ji," she said.

"Nevertheless . . . one could promise to lock oneself into the bedroom and not come out until you get back. If Banichi needs you, Jago-ji, that is *my* priority."

Solemn as she was, a ghost of a smile crossed her lips. "And what would you do about the dowager's dinner party?"

"Hell," he said in Mosphei', which she also understood perfectly well. "But I personally value Banichi's safety, nadi-ji, and yours, above any protocols."

"I am assuring that safety, Bren-ji, by staying here. I by no means trust these dinner guests."

The dinner and the dowager's motives for asking him were not the main area of his concern. But it was certainly a valid concern. The guests had come from the eastern half of the continent, Ilisidi's home territory—and come in a time of unrest. He very vividly remembered a broken arm and a very rough few days, early in his tenure, both thanks to Easterner politics, not to mention having been deliberately poisoned by the great lady who was his host. "I shall stay as close as I can to plain tea and bread tonight, Jago-ji. I shall be extremely discreet and stay entirely out of trouble, I promise you. I do remain extremely worried about Banichi."

"Spare your concern for him, Bren-ji. He would wish you to have your mind on business. And one is assured the dowager's cook will take pains to provide you a safe dinner at the dowager's table. Only mind anything passed to you. Do not take such favors from any hand but the dowager's staff."

Atevi thought alkaloid poisons quite flavorful, hence their prevalence in sauces, in particular. Atevi cooks in the dowager's employ knew he had special considerations in that regard, and no, he had no desire to offend the hard-working cook, or the devoted serving staff.

"Well, then one will rely on the cook. And on you, Jago-ji. And Banichi."

"Indeed, Bren-ji."

He thought, and he delayed the question, and then he asked it, Guild secrecy or no: "Dares one ask—are they voting tonight, Jago-ji?"

Jago's face went instantly impassive, remote. "The paidhi-aiji might not be incorrect to surmise so."

Enough asked, enough said; she breached her Guild's rules to advise him. Lives and fates were being decided tonight. The Guild, having had a crisis in leadership, was electing a new Guildmaster, he very much suspected, and whether the previous Guildmaster had actually lived through the coup, he was unable to determine—nor would he press Jago on the point.

So it was far more than window-dressing that kept Jago close by him tonight. It was a very dangerous time, an unhinged evening for everyone who sat in government, and the paidhi-aiji, the aiji's human translator, was one of the most conspicuous targets of discontent in certain quarters—the human translator being a safer focus of discontent than the aiji himself. There was some word in servants' gossip that the old Guildmaster had returned to the Assassins' Guild, but in what condition or capacity, outsiders still did not know. Granted the first piece of gossip was true, there was also some hint he might step down soon.

And by what Jago hinted, he must have done so—if he was alive, and not merely represented by the action of a proxy.

"I have letters to write," he began to say, and intended to invite Jago to sit and relax in his room while he worked, since she insisted on watching him; but at that moment someone rapped at the outer door.

Jago went immediately to investigate, and he followed at a more leisurely pace, into his makeshift office, in time to see one of the dowager's men hand Jago a silver wire basket of cylinders.

She set it on the table and shut and latched the door.

Messages. Letters. Half a dozen of them. He uncapped the most tempting, a plain steel cylinder, a case such as the Messengers' Guild provided for unjacketed phone messages, and drew out the little roll of paper. He was hoping for word from the island.

It proved to be a message not from the island, however, but from his estate. His major domo there reported the staff in high spirits at his return, and the whole seaside community—a small village attached to the lodge—putting things to rights. They hoped he would visit his estate soon. They promised his boat was now in good shape despite, their words, "an untoward incident during the troubles." And, indeed, Moni and Taigi had quit the employ of the estate some lengthy time ago. Why did the paidhi inquire?

Because Moni and Taigi had shown up here and gotten through security, was what. Perhaps they had returned to him in some sense of man'chi, perhaps not. He had ordered them released, to go where they liked. Where they were now was a matter his staff knew. He didn't ask—yet. So many things were uncertain. So much suspicion had fallen on old acquaintances, a great deal of it perhaps undeserved. The fate of those two—or their potential shift of man'chi—worried him. The two had served him well, years ago. He had thought so, at least.

He did long to see his coastal home, where he so seldom set foot that he knew it was inexcusable extravagance to maintain it, for his own sake; but closing that establishment would throw all those good people out of work and depress the village economy. The whole district relied on him, and took pride in his prominence at court. He was indeed their lord, more than he was Lord of the Heavens, that ostentatious title Tabini had bestowed on him. He had responsibilities there, not least among them to see Moni and Taigi settled, somehow, if he could get all his staff back, and find the resources to do a reasonable investigation. And he owed all those many people, those very good people, in his district.

Truth be told, his little estate was the home he had thought about when he was in space. It was as much of a home as he had nowadays, apart from the Bu-javid—since he had no home left on Mospheira. His mother had been the focus of his visits, and now his mother was gone, his brother Toby divorced, and he had lost track of all his old University contacts, the people who had worked with him, and worked for him. A man destined to be paidhi was all job, no social life, and it had only gotten worse. Now not even his brother's house offered a refuge for him on the island any longer.

Well, there was that, and the fact that Toby had taken up with the one woman on earth he most wanted to avoid . . . even that tie was in jeopardy, and that troubled him.

And, more troubling, Toby was out at sea on a boat that hadn't put into any port, not since he had used Toby's help in his return to the mainland, in a maneuver that might have brought Toby into harm's way. If that boat had gotten to any port, he had no message from his brother yet—but the lines had been down; and, well, failure to phone—that was an old pattern with Toby, too. Likely Toby, hearing that Tabini was back in power, as the rumor likely was over there, had just concluded he had no more part to play and had settled in with Barb, never even thinking of a phone call. Toby cherished his private-citizen status. He didn't insert himself into international agendas.

Well, well, but Toby would surely report in once he could get a convenient and routine message to the mainland. He was all right.

And as far as losing contact with Toby over Barb, hell, if Toby and Barb did make a couple . . .

If they did, hell, sure, he'd invite them to his estate.

No, he wouldn't. He didn't want Barb making a play for him, was what. And she *would*. She hadn't omitted to do that on the boat crossing the strait—he'd had a damned uncomfortable feeling about what she was doing.

Damn and damn. One more connection with humanity starting to fray . . . and he'd let the connection go cold before he'd hurt Toby. The last family connection he had, and Barb was in the middle of it.

But what could he expect? Go off to space for two years . . . and the world just got along, was all. He'd become a ghost, a revenant, in the spaces he'd used to call home.

His home here in the Bu-javid—well, that was gone. He was upset about it: he was still trying to track various of his staff, scattered to the winds in the troubles.

But nand' Tatiseigi's court residence had suited him before, and would suit him again, and it was a handsome offer from the old man. He did hope that Tatiseigi would leave the staff intact rather than remove them with him to his provincial estate—he truly did like the staff of that establishment, supposing that Madam Saidin was still in charge, and more, that staff knew him, knew all his ways. In all the changes, he had learned, it was the staff that made a place home, and if the Atageini staff should have been broken up in the troubles or pulled home to Tirnamardi with Lord Tatiseigi now, leaving him the furniture, but not the soul of the place . . .

A sigh. Well, if that happened, he would have to be writing to the coast to pull people in from his estate to serve in Shejidan . . . and that without even visiting it, without even taking a tour on his boat. That would be a terrible reward, would it not, for the people who had risked their lives to save that tranquil nest from armed rebels? He honestly didn't see how he could do that without at least visiting and praising their efforts there. He had to go do that, as soon as it was safe to travel. As soon as he got Banichi and Tano and Algini back.

And had he not promised Cajeiri one day to go sailing?

They'd made plans for that trip while they were in the intervals of folded space, on the ship. Cajeiri, his young eyes shining, had said that if he could learn to handle the yacht it would show him something about big ships.

He'd laughed, then, imagining the boy's next outrageous ambition—in those innocent days before they'd gotten home and found the world in chaos.

But they'd set it right. They'd begun to, at least. And that promise ought to be kept.

Now, with Tabini back in power, and a flood of letters from returning loyalists reporting the slow restoration of order, he did look to keep that modest promise—to the boy, and to Jase, too, for the long-postponed fishing trip. It would be good for his soul to do that. He could combine Cajeiri's trip, maybe, with the needed courtesy call on the estate. The staff would be thrilled to host the aiji's son—and it would be some promise he could hold out to the boy when he left the premises.

"Nadi," he wrote to the old man who cared for his estate, *"please express my gratitude to the staff, and accept my most earnest sentiments. . . ."*

He plowed through more messages, mostly from department heads, felicitations on his survival, reports on where the scattered directors of agencies had fled, measures they had taken for the security of their staffs, occasional, probably very sincere apologies for having worked with the new administration—assurances they had only been waiting for reversion back to legitimate authority, and preventing damage to equipment or records by remaining at their posts.

"The paidhi-aiji is extremely gratified by your message," he wrote to each, with suitable variations for circumstance, and filed the details away in memory.

He had gotten through a small stack of such messages when one of the dowager's servants, Pahien, appeared in the doorway, reporting that he had a phone call—the staff, she said, with just too lively a curiosity, believed it came from the island.

He leaped up, went out and took the call, in the dowager's well-appointed library, hoping—

Hoping it was Toby.

"Hello?"

"Bren. Delighted to hear your voice."

"Mutual." A disappointment, but not a deep one. Not Toby. An official call, and welcome. Shawn Tyers, his old boss. The President of Mospheira.

"I got your message. My staff's been trying everything but rocket launches to get through to you. How are you?"

"All in one piece. All of us are." Damn, he hadn't known he was that worried over Toby. But he was. He tried to re-sort things in his head, bring up the things he needed to tell Shawn. There were details he wished he dared give, specifics on who was where and in what degree of stability, but giving them over the phone was roughly equivalent to shouting them in the public street.

More, if Shawn had been using unorthodox methods to get to him, the Messengers had not gotten them to him. And he took *that* mental note, intending to refer a complaint through channels—the Messengers' Guild had roadblocks somewhere in its structure, purposeful slowdowns, he strongly suspected. And he did *not* trust them . . . nor, he thought, did Tabini.

He retained, within his computer, the means to reach into

the island secure network—if he had been able get a stable and noise-free connection, but his line to Shawn was far from noise-free at the moment, and he wasn't ready to risk too much verbal frankness, not yet. No details.

And Shawn seemed to observe equal caution. *"Tell me all you can. Are you safe?"*

"We're certainly in far better shape than we expected—the people have backed the aiji, the dissidents have fled without too much fuss: comfortable and secure here. The shuttles—the pilots and techs have saved the manuals and hid out. They're coming back—some in transit at the moment. It's going to take a while to get the shuttles flying again, but we're in good shape there, comparatively. The University is back in operation; we didn't lose the books." The Astronomer Emeritus, Grigiji, had come into the fray with a handful of his faithful students. Grigiji and his entourage were currently resident in the hotel below the hill, with a fierce group of the coastal folk of Dur around them for protection . . . the hardiest Assassin would hesitate at that much trouble; and students who had carried away the precious books were filtering back to the University, with classes due to resume within days. "We've been promised full service on the dish in another few days . . . I'll leave that to the Messengers' Guild. But I've been trying to get through from my side." He tried to sort his scrambled thoughts into order, trying to think what Shawn most needed to know, besides the restoration of Tabini's regime and the good news about the space shuttles. The connection cracked and hissed, and might go down at any instant. "How is it aloft?"

"The station reports all the refugees are now aboard the station and the new tank is functioning—they're holding for another few months with no problems at all, but they're sending down an order for fruit candy as soon as we can deliver it."

It was code for hurry-it-up, he understood that—four-plus-thousand new residents, refugees from the remote depths of space, dumped onto a station already short of supplies. That was a worry—but the wording was worth a laugh. He could actually laugh, now, if shakily, hearing Shawn's voice. So much suddenly seemed possible again, including getting ahead of the mess. But the hissing on the line had increased.

"Shawn, I'm afraid I'm about to lose you. Tell my brother, will you?" It went against years of discipline to give way to personal matters, but he couldn't stand it. "Personal favor, Shawn. I haven't heard from him. Can you find out if he's all right?"

The faltering line went completely dead, then, on one personal item he desperately wished he could learn—and before he was sure Shawn had heard him.

But the phone had worked, and he'd gotten through to Shawn, at least, and Shawn had been aware of where they were. He was vastly relieved to have that, just to touch the island and to know things were well there, that the shuttle and crew that had brought them to the planet were still safe, that everything he relied on that wasn't in his power was secure . . . and that the informal network of coastal radio and spies was still operating.

He flashed the receiver, got the operator, and decided to press his luck on that personal matter, while the Messengers' Guild was having a moment of efficiency. "This is the paidhi-aiji. Please restore the connection to the Mospheiran operators."

"Nandi," the reply was, deferentially. "We shall try. Please wait."

He waited. And waited. And waited.

"This is the Port Jackson service operator," a human voice said, through static. *"How may I help you?"*

"This is Bren Cameron, calling from the mainland. I need to reach Toby Cameron, either by ship-to-shore or residential phone."

"Which do you wish, sir?"

"Try one and try the other. The boat name is *Brighter Days.*"

"You have a bad connection. I'm not hearing you. Please re-dial."

"I'm calling from the mainland, for God's sake! This is the best connection available. I need to reach Toby Cameron, ship-to-shore or residential. On the *Brighter Days.*"

"You'll have to contact the marine operator for ship-to-shore," the reply came back.

"Then call his residence, please." On the verge of swearing, he gave the old number, the personal number that ought to stay valid for life, clenched and unclenched his fist the while. "This is an emergency."

"Yes, sir." Blandly, as if sleepwalking. The woman still didn't know who he was, or where. Not the brightest light in the phone service, Bren was sure.

Clicks. Silence. More clicks. He bit his lip and waited, but the phone did ring. And ring. Toby's voice came on, making his heart skip for the moment, but it was only the answering service, saying Toby was on his boat and could be reached via the Port Jackson operator.

He tried to get the operator back. The connection cut out.

"We have lost connection to the island, nandi," the atevi operator informed him regretfully. *"Shall we continue to try?"*

"Attempt to reach Toby Cameron on ship-to-shore, boat name *Brighter Days.*" He gave the name in Mosphei'. "Advise me when there is an answer—at any hour you receive it. This is an urgent personal matter." He was trying to persuade himself his sudden attack of anxiety was only that. It hadn't been so many days, and it was unreasonable suddenly to go feverish with desire for news, but the momentary thought it might be Toby calling had just taken the lid off his anxiety.

Which was stupid of him. Toby might have stayed out at sea awhile, attempting to pick up shortwave transmissions, looking for information. Or if he had come back to shore, he probably was camped out on his boat in some harbor, even at Port Jackson, ready for a call to go pick his errant brother up off some beach on the mainland. Toby would very likely do exactly that, and maybe not communicate with Mospheiran authorities for fear of having the navy step in and take the job away from him. He'd be ready for one phone call, the same phone call he was trying to get through to him.

Toby was all right. He had to be all right. It could even be a weather delay. It had rained, hadn't it? So there'd been weather at sea.

He desperately hoped Shawn had heard his last statement in that call and would check up on Toby, which would bring down the whole Mospheiran navy into the search, for sure, but dammit, he wanted to know, and he wanted to know now. He wanted someone looking out for Toby, when he couldn't go do it himself.

He'd ask Shawn in the next call he made. Maybe by tomorrow the communications would be a little better. The Messengers were working on it.

Frustrating. But that he had any phone contact with Mospheira at all was a great improvement over yesterday . . . a relief not just in his personal level of anxiety. Peace between the mainland and Mospheira rode a little easier now that Mospheira had been made officially certain Tabini was back in power, and the station could start making preparations to make drops of supplies and personnel on this side of the straits—if that had to be done—to help them get the shuttles flying . . . because the station, in turn, depended on the shuttles getting foodstuffs up to them.

"Shall we continue to try the contact with Toby, Bren-ji?" Jago asked from the door.

He hadn't even realized she was standing there. The servant had departed.

"Insofar as you have time," he said, "yes, nadi-ji, pursue it with the Messengers' Guild. I have some concern for him. One cannot understand why the Guild cannot come up with one clear line."

"Yes," Jago said, receipt of an order.

"Is there news?" he asked. She had that manner about her.

Jago came all the way in and shut the door. "Tabini-aiji's choice of bodyguards is under Guild dispute at this hour. The western and northern members want their own members near the aiji. The aiji has selected only Taibeni clan. This does not please the south or the Padi Valley. This may go on some hours. One believes the aiji will have his way, particularly as the last choice was not trustworthy."

The chief of Tabini's guards, Ismini, was dead, with two of his men. Another had gone south, which said something. The surviving heart of the usurping regime was in the south, on the verge of eradication—politically struggling for what scraps of power it could get back, and damned cheeky to be asking anything.

"There was some notion," Jago said, "of myself and Banichi being called to that post. We have refused, Bren-ji. Banichi has refused a direct request from the aiji's staff."

He didn't know what to say to that. Tabini's safety was paramount. But losing Banichi and Jago to Tabini—he didn't know what he would do, and yet he couldn't refuse the order to give them up, either.

"We would not consider it," Jago said, "and the aiji has graciously backed us in that determination."

He owed Tabini for that one. He ever so greatly owed him.

"If it were advancement for you," he said, constrained to think of their side of the situation.

"No," Jago said, flatly, and simply walked out on the discussion.

Offended? He earnestly hoped not. But when he found her a little later in her quarters, she seemed content and rather smug.

Preparations for the formal dinner still did not produce Banichi, nor Tano nor Algini. So it was an Infelicity of Two, himself and Jago, unless one counted them each a Stability of One—Bren personally chose to do so.

Given any choice at all, he would have declined the honor of dining with people he knew wished him dead. But his appearance surely had its purpose. It was difficult for the aiji-dowager to hide his presence in her household: that he resided here was a matter widely known in the Bu-javid, and it was not the dowager's nature to hide any controversial fact, not in the least. Her neighbors from the East surely knew her ways, her inviting him was a statement on her part, and the wisest thing he could do, he was firmly convinced, was to keep his expression pleasant and his mouth generally shut.

So he gave himself up to the dowager's domestic staff, bathed, dressed in his courtly best, braided and beribboned—he insisted on the white ribbon, the paidhi's neutrality, rather than the black of the Lord of the Heavens, that title with which Tabini had attempted to put a human of no house into the ranks of the great houses. That distinction had been useful in dealings on the station. It was not useful here, and certainly not among conservative Easterners.

"Nawari will accompany us tonight, nandi," Jago informed him. That was one of Ilisidi's young men, a member of the dowager's own bodyguard, a very reliable man, and it improved the security, besides improving the numbers. "The young gentleman will also attend," Jago added. And then dropped the bombshell: "So will the lord of the Atageini."

God. Lord Tatiseigi. Preeminent lord of the Padi Valley, in the central regions of the West, and an old flame of the dowager's—in any sense, Tatiseigi was certainly an odd and volatile inclusion in tonight's invitation. But Ilisidi and Tatiseigi had become thick as thieves since Ilisidi's return from space, and perhaps the dowager meant her Eastern neighbors to see that she had strong allies in the West, that her power was increased, if anything, since Tabini's return to power . . . and to make one additional point that if they shared her dinner table and sought her favor, they had to share it with her intimates and behave themselves.

It was like a great deal else Ilisidi did: difficult to parse, and covered with thorns. Tatiseigi's presence would not please the East, though in conservatism, they hardly had him outdone. More, he had to wonder if Tatiseigi knew that the paidhi-aiji would be there, or if Jago had gotten the full story of the dowager's dinner party even from Nawari: Ilisidi's guest lists could produce very uncomfortable surprises. Her sense of humor was not what other people called amusing, particularly when someone pushed, and he suspected it was in full force tonight.

Jago appeared, sleek, black-clad, and armed, at the very moment they needed to depart. Nawari had showed up at the door, likewise elegant, a handsome young fellow—all Ilisidi's "young men" tended to that description, besides their other qualifications.

From there it was a short walk to the dining hall—and despite coming from within the apartment, he was not the first or even the second guest to arrive: Lord Tatiseigi was already there, his arm in an elegant brocade sling. Lord Tatiseigi had been wounded in recent action, and was quite proud of himself. Cajeiri was there, attended by two Atageini men in Assassins' black, as well as the Taibeni youngsters, the latter in genteel court dress . . . rumor would tell the Easteners who and what the two anonymously-dressed young people were: not Guild, but certainly self-appointed bodyguards to the young gentleman—from a clan not highly approved by the Atageini, who asserted *their* close kinship to the heir . . .

"Nand' Bren!" Cajeiri said brightly, rising from his chair and bowing—due courtesy for a young person to an elder, but a little out of precedence. Bren managed a courteous, quick bow to Lord Tatiseigi, and had a nod from him, before addressing the youngster.

"One is honored, nandi." One saw the white token at the place opposite Cajeiri, and next to Lord Tatiseigi—and above the places designated for their guests. It was *not* where the paidhi would have chosen to sit . . . certainly not above a trio of Eastern guests. And one had an immediate intimation that the dowager was up to something.

"One is *bored*," Cajeiri complained, as he began to sit, but at that exact moment the Easterners showed up, a commotion at the doorway, with their own clutter of bodyguards and only the colored markers to tell *them* that they were sitting below the paidhi-aiji at the table.

And just then, thank God, the dowager and her guard entered by the other door. Bren reached his seat, but remained standing. So did Cajeiri. Lord Tatiseigi—senior, elderly, and injured—made only the most perfunctory gesture toward rising, but received a small motion of the dowager's hand, making even the effort unnecessary.

There were grim bows from the Easterners, and a lingering, frowning glance at the two Taibeni, as the dowager introduced her great-grandson, then Lord Tatiseigi—an impassive politeness on both sides, while Ilisidi beamed; and then smugly introduced the paidhi-aiji—"Whom *surely* you know, nandiin."

As if anyone could mistake him. The looks shifted his direction went a shade darker, and Bren chose to ignore the fact in a small, respectful bow—but not too deep a bow.

The Eastern glower turned to stony smiles and polite bows, however, as their regard swept back toward Lord Tatiseigi and their hostess.

Cheerful lot, Bren said to himself, and realized he had himself physically braced, as if shooting might break out at any moment. There was a godawful array of weaponry on every hand, openly visible on the varied bodyguards, that was certain. Only the Taibeni youngsters stood in civilian dress, stiffly polite.

Ilisidi provided the names in their acknowledgment: Lord Caiti, Lady Agilisi, and Lord Rodi—Caiti was youngish, broadfaced, a surly customer. Agilisi, a thin, stylish woman, was expressionless, which never boded well among atevi. And Rodi, as plump as atevi came, eyed both the Atageini lord and the paidhi-aiji with a biding frown.

Neighbors of the dowager's estate of Malguri. Not the best sort of neighbors, Bren decided. And his chair was not too happily between Lord Tatiseigi on the right and Lord Caiti on the left. Never would he have thought to find Lord Tatiseigi the more comforting presence—but at this moment the old man was a haven of courtesy and kindness. Cajeiri was across the table, between his great-grandmother and Lord Rodi, a perfect model of young gentlemanliness and current Ragi fashion. It was chilling, the grim look on that young face when no one was addressing him: it transited to perfect affability and a spark in the eyes as quickly as ever his father could manage, as his great-uncle Tatiseigi addressed him and asked whether he had seen his mother today.

Little politician, Bren thought. Never mind "little" was as tall as he was.

"No, Great-uncle," Cajeiri said quite cheerfully. "One is certain she is busy."

"The boy does not reside with his parents, 'Sidi-daja?" Rodi asked Ilisidi bluntly.

"My great-grandson resides with me, at present, nandi, and has over the last two years," Ilisidi said.

"For security," Rodi pursued.

"Indeed, nandi," Ilisidi said. What *that* extended exchange meant Bren had no idea, since dinner service began, the servants moving in, and conversation contracted to requests for the sauces, compliments for the cook, and, thereafter, discussion of the weather and the plane flight the lords had had, coming west.

Ilisidi did regale the company with an account of the weather on the coast and in the midlands and inquired after their estimates of the coming winter—suitably tame topics for dinner, notably boring, as Tatiseigi, a font of past meteorological data, somewhat tediously compared notes on recent winters with Lord Rodi's recollections, two gentlemen living on one side of the continent and the other, and gave his theories about the predictive qualities of early leaf-fall. It was actually the bright spot in the dinner: the two seemed to warm to one another, seeing they shared similar views.

Cajeiri ducked his chin and smothered an occasional yawn over the vegetables. He perked up at dessert, however, and took a second helping.

Bren had one helping of the custard, and rather hoped to escape before the brandy. He looked for chances. But there was absolutely no breath of a gap in the proceedings. It was outright impossible to present his excuses and leave when the dowager seized him by the arm and asked, "And have you been able to reach nand' Toby today, nand' paidhi?"

She knew the answer to that question. He'd bet his coastal estate on it. Jago had been using her staff's equipment, no doubt of it. "Regrettably I have not, aiji-ma." As he found himself steered for the sitting room. "Though I am indeed pursuing it."

"So. Well, well, my staff will keep trying, too, nand' paidhi, in all good will." This, as they passed the door into the more intimate setting. She turned and made an expansive wave of her cane, all the while maintaining her grip on his arm. "Lords of the East, share a glass with us, and my great-grandson will of course have a lighter refreshment. The paidhi-aiji has very graciously agreed to stay with us for the social hour. Do not hesitate to inquire of him or us, gentle neighbors." She at least released his arm. "And how *are* affairs in the inconvenient snowy heights, Lord Rodi?"

Brandy made the rounds. Bren knew the server, at least, would be careful of his sensitivities. He took the glass and intended to claim a seat unobtrusively in the corner near the door, but:

"We are bored, nand' Bren," Cajeiri remarked, at his elbow before he could achieve his objective. "Where is Banichi this evening?"

"A necessary meeting," he said, and had a sip of brandy standing. "He will be back soon, young sir, so I am promised."

"There was an assassination this evening," Cajeiri informed him cheerfully. "A Talidi lord. We forgot who."

Jago had not told him that news. Possibly, considering the boy's sources, even Jago had not heard it yet. "Was there indeed, nandi?"

"Yes, nandi," Nawari reported quietly from behind his shoulder. "Lord Eigun is dead."

Eigun was a disagreeable man, a man he personally wouldn't miss, though he was sorry for the news, on principle. Rodi seemed pleased, however, and he passed it on to Agilisi, who outright asked the dowager the details as everyone settled to enjoy their brandies.

"Cenedi-ji," Ilisidi said, and Cenedi, her head of security, stood forth in the gathering and gave the more particular details: Eigun had been returning from a trip to the southern islands, probably fled there for his safety during the upheaval of the aiji's return to power, and had returned too soon. It was doubtless Assassins' work, a neat shot out of the morning dark. There were no other fatalities in that household, and no one knew whose order had sent the Assassin who had done it—if it wasn't the Guildmaster's own order, or a Filing approved by the Guild—likely not a recent one, since the Guild had been obsessed with its own upheaval in recent days—but the Bujavid records were in a thorough mess, under intensive review. It was a nightmare, that there might be Filings floating around as relics from the former regime, with Assassins engaged, and Tabini's administration as yet unapprised of their existence.

Not even mentioning the occasional in-clan assassination, when man'chi had broken down.

"Well, one happy event for our visit," Agilisi said, turning a dismissive shoulder: there was insouciance in her tone, outright rudeness to her host, and arrogant disregard of other possible opinions or allegiances present . . . when it was very likely Agilisi had no intimate knowledge of western connnections.

"We never met him," Cajeiri remarked, frowning. He had walked over next to Bren, with his fruit juice, and a small mustache of it on his lip. "Was he indeed a bad man, Great-grandmother, and should one indeed be glad?"

There was a very uncomfortable moment. The boy had learned his manners on the ship, where he knew the undercurrents to a nicety. Here—was another story. But he had just rebuked the lady and deferred to the host with an accuracy that made Bren's heart skip a beat.

"We hardly knew him," Ilisidi said smoothly, and redirected. "Does the paidhi-aiji happen to know his character?"

A chance, a palpable chance to salve the Eastern lady's provocation and the heir's jibe with diplomacy—or to provoke the lady in a way that would be very unprofitable to the dowager's relations with her neighbors.

And, professionally, he gave a shrug and avoided eye contact with the Eastern lady, answering the dowager's question in a deferential way. "Having been absent so long," he said softly, "we find ourselves inclined to reserve all judgments: recent events have reshaped allegiances. The paidhi-aiji would far rather consult those who might be better informed."

"And who would those sources be?" the belligerent lady asked, ignored. "What authority does a human ever consult?"

Now he had to look in her direction, and bowed, politely and respectfully—before firing back, softly: "One consults the aiji-dowager, of course, nandi, in all matters."

"Perhaps," Lord Caiti said, out of the breath of shocked silence that followed, and gesturing with the empty brandy glass in his hand, "perhaps the paidhi will elucidate on matters he should indeed actually know something about: machines from the heavens. What are they, and what business do they have settling on our land?"

Landed in the East as well? That was news. And it was not a polite question, not the way it was stated.

"One has had rumors likewise from the north," Bren said smoothly. "Any such landing in the East is news to me, though certainly not out of all possibility."

"As if it were nothing? We have destroyed them where found! We assure you of that! And in the north as well? What are we, raining infernal machinery from that pernicious station?"

"My office must confess ignorance in the matter, Lord of the Saibaitet Ami. Our passage through the station at our return was much too rapid to gather all details of what the station lords have done or caused to be done during the dowager's absence, but one assures the gracious lord that if there was such a landing within his district—"

"Repeatedly!"

"Then I can only surmise the intention was both benign and possibly of service to you, if indeed, the package came from orbit and was intended to be set where it came down."

"You impugn our common sense? What do you take us for?"

Bang! went that formidable cane. "Caiti, Caiti-ji, the paidhi-aiji is telling you what he knows, which is, we assure you, no

more nor less than what we know: that fools in the south instigated all manner of trouble in our absence, that murder was
done under this very roof! That Lord Tatiseigi's neighbor, who
has been repudiated by his own clan, has acted quite foolishly,
and that the paidhi-aiji, Lord Tatiseigi, my grandson, my great-
grandson and I have all spent so much time being shot at
that we have not investigated strayed items dropped from the
station—as the very least of concerns in Shejidan! These things
were parachuted down possibly to reconnoiter, possibly to
map, who knows? The installation at Mogari-nai is under repair and we are unable as yet to inquire of the station aloft
their reasons for such landings. But we assure you the station
acts consistently in support of Lord Geigi, among others, in
any such mission undertaken to the mainland, and subject to
his will. Lord Geigi, whom we left in authority on the station
is still in power on the station, was never overthrown in the
general disorder here in Shejidan, and he to this hour enjoys
great authority over any such operations aimed at the planet,
let me assure you, Lord Caiti. I certainly hope you have not destroyed some installation which would have monitored rebel
aircraft encroaching on your province. That would be a misfortune."

"I have every right to destroy whatever foreign object falls
on my land! Whatever foolishness you pursue here in the
west . . ."

"Pardon me, nandi." A high and indignant voice intervened.
"This is my great-grandmother's house, and," pointing at what
Caiti held, "that is her brandy glass."

There was stunned silence. Then Agilisi outright laughed,
and Rodi smiled, silently, behind his hand.

Caiti looked at the offending glass as if he hardly knew
whether to fling it at the floor or set it conspicuously on the
side table. Security all around the room was braced, hands not
moving, but close to it.

"You trust my brandy," Ilisidi said quietly. "As indeed by my good grace you may, Caiti, you scoundrel, and you know you may trust our brandy and our opinion. Rodi and Agilisi at least have no doubts of my intentions, nor have deserved to have. You share my hospitality with the paidhi-aiji and my hot-headed great-grandson, and of course you have questions in our return to the world, but grant we have moved with too much speed to pause for detailed briefings. Tati-ji, we ask your indulgence for our esteemed neighbors: they know us; we know them, oh, intimately. Patience, I say, Cai-ji, and do sit down."

"Disagreeable woman!"

"Dare you?" Tatiseigi broke in, dignified and lately glorious in battle. "Dare you insult your host, nadi?"

Oh, it was about to get bitter. "Nandi," Bren said, concentrating his gaze on his waterglass, "do allow the aiji-dowager to make peace, one most earnestly entreats it."

There was an audible huff of breath, but the old man sat down. Cajeiri went to stand by his great-grandmother, right by Cenedi, and entraining his own unofficial security as he did so.

"Now, now," Ilisidi said, reaching for the boy's hand. "Defense is unnecessary, Great-grandson. These are my neighbors, my esteemed neighbors around Malguri. They are inclined to speak bluntly, but they are not fools. Caiti has been a valued associate in prior years. And—" The latter in a low voice: "remember what is done here, in your own time."

"Ha," Tatiseigi muttered, with a look like a jealous lover. He positively youthened as he glowered at the three Easterners.

"Foolishness, foolishness," Ilisidi said. "Let us have a civilized agreement, shall we? As for Lord Bren's presence, it now seems very wise to have asked him to favor us with his attendance tonight. Would you not agree, Bren-nandi, that whatever was landed in the East was likely done with Lord Geigi's consent? And Lord Geigi is out of the Coastal Association, long correspondents of the East—an old, old alliance, his with Malguri."

"If the ship-aijiin acted otherwise and failed consultation with Lord Geigi, it would breach all manner of agreements," Bren said, "and I would be obliged to carry strong words to the ship-aijiin in protest. I hardly believe they would have done so. But even if there had been some misunderstanding, take reassurance in this, nandiin. Two ship-aijiin have returned to the station aboard the ship that brought us, and they are extremely well-disposed to the aiji-dowager and her interests, having spent two years in her close association. The third, Ogun-aiji, whatever he may have done good or ill in his administration of the station, must now account to them for all he has done in their name, and I have no doubt he will do so."

"So there is disagreement in the heavens, and they drop machines of war in my woods!" Caiti cried.

"Nandi, one is certain that there will be adequate explanation and accountability for any actions taken in the aiji-dowager's absence, to your ultimate satisfaction. And one is equally certain that none of these actions were aimed at all at seizing advantage for the ship-humans, or aimed in any wise at securing a foothold on the earth. One is very confident that any machines dropped from the heavens have been in support of legitimate atevi authority, most probably to secure communications for the aiji's forces when he might need them."

"Communications to do what?" There was no polite address. It was entirely rude. "To make us a battlefield? No aiji of the west has ever set foot in the East."

"No such thing, nandi, but the ship-folk will have wished to preserve your ability to contact the aiji's forces, should hostilities break out. One is most regretful that such a gesture could have been misconstrued."

"Misconstrued!"

"Nandi." A tap of the dowager's fingernail against the

empty brandy glass, a clear, crystal note. "One may not lay the deeds of the station in the paidhi's lap, certainly not if you wish his good offices to lodge inquiry on your behalf."

"We expect an explanation." There was a small silence, and the old lord muttered, "Nandiin."

The plural was generic. It did not necessarily include the paidhi. But it might. It did not, however, properly respect the dowager.

No sense pushing it, Bren said to himself.

"Doubtless," he said, "we will learn the answer, once communication with the station resumes—which it has not, nandiin, so whatever the station-folk have dropped, they have not activated, or we might not have these problems in reaching them. One rather thinks they have not activated them, in deference to the dowager's efforts and the aiji's return to the capital. They would not wish to offend sensibilities."

It was not a damned bad speech, impromptu as it was. Its numbers were convolute enough to keep the restive Easterners calculating and digesting the information for a few heartbeats at least.

"Well," Agilisi said with a ripple of thin, manicured fingers, "well, well, accountability in the heavens. That would do a great deal to settle our stomachs." She finally sat down. So did Rodi, and Caiti settled, still frowning.

"Sit down, Great-grandson," Ilisidi said with a little pat of her hand on Cajeiri's, which rested on her chair arm, and Cajeiri finally went and took the chair by Lord Tatiseigi. A servant quickly offered him a refill of fruit juice. The servants moved in general to pour more brandy on the situation, and for a moment there was an easier feeling in the air. Caiti took a very healthy dose of brandy—whatever its effect on his common sense.

"Well," Caiti said then, "well. Machinery falling out of the heavens. High time the dowager attended to her estate. When *will* you visit us, 'Sidi-daja?"

"Oh, soon. Soon." Ilisidi took her own glass, refilled. "Those who thought our being sent to space was our grandson's means of being rid of us were quite wrong. We are *back*, nandiin-ji. *Believe* that we are back."

"Oh, there were far worse rumors than that, 'Sidi-daja," Rodi said. "There were immediate rumors you were being held prisoner in Shejidan or on the station, there were rumors that the humans on the station had joined Murini, or that you had long ago died in space and no one would confess the fact, while humans corrupted the aiji's heir."

"A pretty fantasy," Ilisidi said, and smiled. Her eyes did not. "Surely Murini hoped so. But we thrived. We succeeded. The aiji's heir is quite uncorrupt. He rides, he shoots, he ciphers, and he is conversant in the machimi. And here are three of my neighbors come to threaten our glassware and wish me a fortunate homecoming. What could we lack? But where are Ardija and Ceia tonight?"

These were two other districts of the East, major holdings not represented here: Ardija was actually closer to Malguri than, Bren recalled, Caiti's holdings at Torinei, in the Saibai'tet Ami.

"We came in respect of the aiji-dowager," Caiti said flatly. "We chose to come."

"Well, well, and Lady Drien of Ardija and Lord Sigena of Ceia did not. Ah, but perhaps they had a previous engagement."

"One doubts that," Rodi said under his breath.

Ilisidi nodded sagely, contemplatively. "Your attendance at our table confirms my judgment of you. We shall not ask about Sigena. We are not on the best of terms. But our neighbor Drien? I am somewhat disappointed in Drien. One would have expected word, at least. Can *kabiu* have failed her?"

There was a restless shift, not quite glances exchanged, but uncertainty.

"We do not judge, nandi," Rodi said. "But we are here."

"Guard yourselves, the while, nandiin," Ilisidi said. "Households returning are just now settling, and the capital is still in turmoil. One should take great care, coming and going to the hotel tonight. As for that scoundrel Murini, Tati-ji, have you any recent information?"

Tatiseigi cleared his throat. "Reports state he has landed in Talidi. Who knows, now, with this assassination? Perhaps he is behind it. Perhaps he will move on, fearing retaliation. We have *not* heard word of Lady Cosadi, who has dropped entirely from sight."

"Perhaps the aiji is already settling old scores, nandi," Agilisi remarked.

"Not quite yet, nandi-ji, in her case," Ilisidi said. "One believes she is hiding. And you will find no one in the north will mourn Talidi moving against each other. Murini himself may not survive this settling of old scores—if he is not behind it; and if he is, then one may lay odds others will deal with him without the aiji's turning a hand. There will be a certain repaying of old debts all through the south. I should not be surprised. I should not be surprised if Lady Cosadi now finds Murini an embarrassment. But clearly she will not live long, and her own followers may be thinking of that. Twice spared, twice made a fool of in her choice of causes, and I believe my grandson is entirely out of patience. Others certainly may be."

Fruit juice *was* a treat after their long voyage, on which even tea had run short. Cajeiri sipped it the way the adults did the brandy, out of the special glasses, as he kept a careful watch on Lord Caiti, and nand' Bren, who had answered the Easterners' bad manners very sharply and very correctly. Greatgrandmother was keen-edged tonight: it was something to watch.

Reminding Lord Caiti who provided the drinks had been a

good touch on his own part, too. Cajeiri was very pleased with himself, and with the way great-grandmother had taken it right up. She had already told him about Caiti: more mouth than thought, Great-grandmother had said, and she was right. Rodi was smart, and said very little. Agilisi was probably the one to watch in this set, and just occasionally she looked curiously distressed, as if she was not entirely happy with the evening.

The people they talked about—Sigena was to the west of Great-grandmother's estate, and a perpetual problem. Drien was closer, and more so, being upset about some old land dispute right on Malguri's edge. Drien was great-grandmother's youngest and only surviving cousin, and her not being here tonight had certainly raised great-grandmother's very ominous left eyebrow. He wondered if these three had known how to read Great-grandmother's expression—it had left him a little confused.

They were all Great-grandmother's neighbors, and their numbers, combined with Great-grandmother alone, were not felicitous—they would have been felicitous, had Lady Drien come, but they added badly, without, and cast the balance-making to Great-grandmother's good will, to make up the rest of the table. So she tossed in not one, but three of her own asking for dinner; that saved the felicity of numbers, but he thought the visitors might have hoped for his father and mother and him to be sitting here instead of Lord Bren and Lord Tatiseigi.

So they were surprised to find Lord Tatiseigi, who was too *kabiu* to quarrel with, more *kabiu* than they were, if it came to that, in their coming here all but demanding a dinner—the proper thing to have done would be to write from the East hinting they wanted an invitation: *that* would have respected Great-grandmother's rank, but they had not done that. And they kept calling her not nand' dowager, but 'Sidi-daja, which was about like yelling "Hey, Gene!" in Great-grandmother's hallway. Great-grandmother said they were both more *kabiu* and less respectful of western offices in the East, but that seemed pushy of them, especially considering they were pushy in coming here.

So if he read the clues, it was not a happy meeting, and Great-grandmother had shoved her closest associations and particularly nand' Bren right in their faces. That was the way Gene would express it, and it fit. Right in their faces. He liked that expression.

And they were powerful, all three together, but they were not that important in the affairs of the *aishidi'tat*. Lord Sigena had been, but he was not here. Drien had *kabiu*, but not a great force. It was a dispute in the East whether it was *kabiu* to have Guild, which was a western institution; but Great-grandmother had, and for that reason a lot of the East walked very quietly where Great-grandmother was involved. How dangerous those bodyguards over there were—he would pick Cenedi and Jago over all of them together, he was quite sure; but alarms were still ringing, in the barbs flying back and forth, and he sipped his fruit juice and kept trying to add things in his head, who was barbing whom, and most of all why Great-grandmother put up with it.

Because they were neighbors? Because they were all Easterners?

He had memorized all the provinces and their lords, all the provincial estates and the holdings in all the *aishidi'tat*, including the Eastern districts in which Great-grandmother's heredity meant property, and rights, and obligations that stretched on into very long ago, until he yawned and Great-grandmother thwacked his skull and asked him to recite it all back. Great-grandmother had thumped the details into his head over two long years, along with the machimi, a grasp of poetry, and the laws of inheritance, property, and bloodfeud.

He knew he was actually very, very remote kin to Lady Agilisi. He was not sure he liked being. And he was more kin to Drien, whose absence Great-grandmother found interesting.

And the news about machinery dropping out of the sky onto Lord Caiti's lands, that had been an exciting point, and he wanted to know more about it. He had ached to inform Lord Caiti he was a fool for breaking what was probably very valuable and useful equipment, but Lord Bren had handled the man well enough.

Now it was just talk. And talk ran down to actually polite discussion over the third round of brandy, naming names, some of which he knew. They talked about Malguri, which was Great-grandmother's estate, and she was glad to know it had not been bothered during Murini's rule.

So was he. He had never been there. She had kept promising him—or threatening him with a year there, where she informed him there was no television at all. He thought it would be interesting to see, but he wanted not to be left there.

So, well, grown-ups were in charge of the evening, and there was more and more talk, and things grew boring.

Then deadly boring, as they got down to babies and births, which he tracked, because he was absolutely certain Great-grandmother was going to ask him. He had to memorize who was related to whom, particularly those that were related to him, and he tried.

But the back of his thoughts took comfort in the fact underlying all this conversation, that the guests were leaving Shejidan in four days, going back across the mountains, and he really, really hoped there would not be another dinner party before they left

More boring things. He watched their security, wondering what they were. At the very last moment, arriving for the dinner, Great-uncle Tatiseigi had provided him two Guild Assassins that loomed over him and Antaro and Jegari. He had left them both in the outer hall, but they would be coming and going in his apartment, and he really had no choice about it if Great-uncle was going to insist. They were Atageini: they were substantial protection, Great-grandmother had said this evening, making it fairly clear he had to take them, and he had gone so far as to mutter that none of Great-uncle's men had done very well about defending them this far, which his Great-grandmother called ingratitude and impudence, and said he should never, ever say that to Great-uncle.

So he had to thank Great-uncle for sending two people he had as soon not have spying on him.

Because he was sure that was exactly what Great-uncle was doing, and Great-uncle had picked this evening to slip them into Great-grandmother's household. They were nowhere near as good as Banichi and Jago, and they were probably not happy to be assigned to him, either; they were glum fellows, in their middle years, and had no sense of humor, if looks said anything.

More, they were Atageini, and Atageini were not on good terms with Taibeni folk, not for centuries, and the recent alliance had done nothing to patch up personal feelings. They clearly looked down their long noses at Antaro and Jegari attempting to protect him, not only because they were not really Guild, and Guildsmen took a dim and jealous view of non-Guild trying to do their job, but also, he strongly suspected, just because they were Taibeni. Antaro and Jegari had gotten respect even from Lord Bren's staff. Banichi and Jago had said, had they not, that they were very brave?

He feared he was losing certain elements of the conversation. He tried listening and remembering, but it was just more names that meant nothing to him. He had a notion he could ask Great-grandmother later and get a long, long explanation which he *would* have to remember.

And he intended to find every excuse to leave the Atageini guards standing in the hall at functions like this, until they got the notion they had to please him in order to get permission to do anything else.

If they got bored enough standing in the hall, they might go back to Great-uncle and beg off. Then he could talk about them with Great-grandmother and maybe get rid of them altogether. That was a plan.

He could get Antaro and Jegari into the Guild; they could start their schooling. Banichi said they could, and he would back them. And that would mean they would be gone some of the time, and the Guild had a lot of things to decide before they got around to two youngsters from Taiben, but it was going to happen, was it not?

But that might mean he had Great-uncle's guards on his hands all the while they were in training, which could be years. And years. And years.

That was just—Gene would call it—*gruesome*.

He would still have them stand in the hall, until they knew to take his orders.

But Antaro and Jegari had to go to the Guild. They were not cut out to be domestic staff. He knew that. They were rangers . . . well, they had been trying to be. They knew guns, and hunting, and tracking . . .

"Well," Great-grandmother said, in that particular way that made all her guests know that the social hour was about to end—and he paid attention. It was very effective, that *well*, and had to be a particular tone, with the look and the attitude. Cajeiri had practiced it himself in private.

Great-grandmother, however, wielded it with expertise and her guests never dared take offense. She simply said, "Well," and in due time the guests got up and finessed their way to the door as if they felt apologies were due on their part for leaving: it was very curious how that worked.

And it came very welcome.

He got up, too—Lord Bren found his way out, and Cajeiri decided there was no particular reason to bother adults with a good night. He was only wishing he could shed his lent Atageini clan bodyguard with a similar lack of offense. "Well," would not be adequate.

But he ever so much wished he could have somebody else.

"Jeri-ji," Great-grandmother said.

"Mani-ma." He bowed, offering that intimate address. "Excuse me." He had been caught inattentive. He had no wish to be found at fault, and bowed again to Lord Tatiseigi. "Greatuncle, thank you very much for lending staff this evening. I will return them with profound gratitude when things are settled."

"They will remain here," his uncle said dourly, with that lack of address only acceptable when one confronted a child. "Your mother will call on them at need, with her own staff."

"Yes, Uncle," he said, wondering what his mother's need of staff had to do with anything, but uncle could be at least as indirect and as scheming as his great-grandmother.

"Patience, Tati-ji, patience. We have not yet told him," Great-grandmother said.

"Told me what, mani-ma?" They had drifted out into the hallway. All the bodyguards were standing around them, now, those he wanted, and those he did not, not to mention Cenedi and Nawari, and Antaro and Jegari, and he really disliked that tone of voice everybody was using—had he daydreamed right through something important to him?

"You will keep your current rooms," great-grandmother said. "But I shall be leaving before daylight, to spend time at Tirnamardi, so we will say our good-byes now, young gentleman. When you wake, your father will be in residence, with staff you may not know—expect strange faces, but reliable persons. My caretaker staff has their orders to stay near and identify them to you during the transition."

His heart had picked up its beats, faster and faster, and shock and anger first cooled, then heated his face, all in the space it took mani-ma to assault his whole life and his plans and dispose of them in a single, ridiculously easy stroke.

It was absolutely necessary, dealing with Great-grandmother, and in front of Uncle, to maintain iron composure, and he managed it, short of wind as he found himself: a grown man had to manage that rush of heat and anger, cool it to a faint, easy breeze, and keep his voice absolutely, absolutely steady and pleasant. That was what Cenedi had said.

"But, mani-ma," he said, "When did you decide this?"

"Oh, over the last several days." His great-grandmother touched his cheek. "We have enjoyed a most remarkable adventure together, have we not? Now it is extraordinarily important for the heir of the *aishidi'tat* to learn from his father, and understand the things his father and mother can teach him. I have business to care for, as you heard this very evening. So do you. Your business is to learn. Your father and your mother need a residence, as they have been most uncomfortably camped in inadequate quarters, and they have accepted our hospitality here. There is hardly room for your father's affairs and mine under one roof, so we have accepted your great-uncle's very kind invitation to visit in Tirnamardi, and you, Great-grandson, are to stay here and get acquainted with your father."

Disaster. His father hardly paid attention to him, except naturally as his heir, and his mother had concern for him, but no great care, either. And both of them were more concerned with keeping him safe and contained and completely out of their way. He had no great resentment for their dealing with him: he entirely understood that they had abdicated his rearing to Great-grandmother, but she could not just walk off and leave him with Great-uncle's guards. They wanted him to find man'chi for his father. Well, he did have. He was perfectly fine in that regard. His father was the authority. He was willing to say so. But nobody cared what he thought.

"Will nand' Bren be here?" That was his last hope, his one appeal to his personal needs.

"Nand' Bren will be moving to your great-uncle's apartment. It is considered," she said in that voice with which she made implacable pronouncements, "that you should have a period of dealing only with atevi, learning the things your sojourn on the ship could not teach you. You know you need that time. You know why, and you may immediately erase that frown, Great-grandson."

"But—" he began.

"There is no 'but,' Great-grandson. People are watching you at every turn. Be seen to be your father's son, as you ought to be. You will see us again, in good time. It will not be for that long. Surely one can trust your discretion."

"One can trust. If I were on my own—" He leaped to the next foothold, the only possibility that offered relief. "I had my own place at Tirnamardi. Surely, mani-ma, I might have my own household . . ."

He had mastered the anger, at least: and he would not let mani-ma embarrass him in front of Great-uncle and his own staff, who stood nearby, witnesses to the scene. She let a little well-guided astonishment lift a brow, now, that, in itself, enough to make him think, for one terrible moment, that she might still say something to make him out a fool. Great-grandmother's wit was quick, and lethal.

"Your managed your own suite, yes, Great-grandson," she replied to that doubtful argument. "For the few hours you were in it, and with Lord Bren's staff coming and going. But that brings us back to the fact your father and mother have nowhere proper to live at the moment. Their apartment needs renovation, the Bu-javid's undamaged suites are all occupied, and the primary purpose of our removing to Tirnamardi is to afford your parents suitable quarters."

So he would pass under his father's authority, and his

mother's, people who hardly knew him, who had last seen him when he was a baby. His composure wavered dangerously. He fought to recover it, knowing Great-grandmother was about to walk away and end all discussion. "But," he said, the solitary word he could muster on the instant, and then sucked in a deep breath and made his best try. "Mani-ma, may I just go to Tirnamardi with you and Great-uncle?"

"You have parents, Great-grandson, and all eyes are on your behavior. Persons will wish to know the source of influence on your behavior. I have had my time. Time now for your father and mother. And the demonstration needs to be public."

"They hardly know me at all, mani-ma!"

"And you hardly know them, Great-grandson. Time to remedy that. Man'chi must settle where it should. Lord Bren must resume his duties. I must attend my own business. You, as your father's son, have so many things to learn. See to it you do. Your father thinks quickly, and the *aishidi'tat* as it exists is his creation. You will do very well to learn what he thinks, and what your mother thinks."

That was the problem. And Great-grandmother ran right past it. "They by no means know what I think!"

"One is certain your thoughts will be of interest to your father once you prove yourself to have worthwhile actions."

"Will you tell him so, mani-ma?"

"We have already told him so. Convincing him of that is your job, great-grandson. He has faults of his own: impatience and temper, infelicitous two. These should not become your faults, mind you. He has virtues: cleverness, a keen sense of opportunity, and courage, fortunate three. Profit by them. Avoid the one and imitate the other. They are both in your blood: deal with them."

"One had far rather be in Tirnamardi! Or with Lord Bren."

"Yes. Clearly. But that is not what you have. And one is hardly surprised at your reaction. You are afraid of your father. He makes you afraid."

His chin lifted, betrayal of emotion. It was involuntary.

"Ah," she said. "We offend you. You think nothing can frighten you."

"No, mani-ma." He scrambled to recover, and turned the argument completely end-first, as mani-ma had demonstrated, oh, very often. "You do not offend us."

"Us. Us, is it?"

"We learn from you, mani-ma. But one must agree this is a very bad surprise."

"Tell us that when you meet us next." The cane rapped the floor. "Infelicitous reversal. You have missed several points."

His face went hot. "I have not!"

"Are you my great-grandson?"

"I certainly am, mani-ma." Her subtleties hammered her opposition: few grown-ups wanted to trade words with mani-ma. One had to add up the things she never said as well as those she had, and think fast, and still be respectful; and he knew what point he had failed to answer—the point he had not wanted to consider. "And I will show my father." He took a great risk, and left an infelicity, a proposition unresolved, just as mani-ma would do when she meant to provoke someone to ask, *"What?"*

The network of lines about Great-grandmother's mouth, that map age had made, could be either hard or amused, and it was not, at the moment, amused. But he stood fast, and composed his face as well as he could, waiting for her to ask the mandated question. Or otherwise comment.

"Indeed," Great-grandmother said, and the dreaded eyebrow lifted. "Pert, are we? Your father will certainly see our influence in that. We are not certain it will please him."

"I am not certain I shall please him, mani-ma," he said. "Perhaps then he will send me to Tirnamardi."

"He certainly will not, since I will not permit it, and he certainly should not, with the whole Association watching and judging you. It would be no favor to you were he to do that, Great-grandson."

"Perhaps I shall go live in space with Gene and Artur."

Foolish provocation. He knew it the instant it slipped out.

"Do you imagine," Great-grandmother asked him, "that that course would not require you to grow up? Do you imagine that the changes now proceeding in you would inexplicably cease, and you would be forever a little boy? I assure you, Gene and Artur are growing up. Are you?"

"One has already grown, great-Grandmother."

"You have reached an infelicitous year," Great-grandmother said sharply, "and yet show promise in it. Your arguments have improved, but do not yet convince us. Learn from your father, boy. Then argue with us again."

He was dismissed. He was left with no recourse but to bow, and watch mani walk away ahead of Cenedi, a straight, regal figure, walking with small taps of the dreaded cane, with great-uncle Tatiseigi at her side and both their bodyguards behind. His staff, his own and Great-uncle's spies, had seen and heard everything: staff witnessed everything, and one was obliged to be dignified, even while losing badly and being embarrassed and treated like a child.

He remained upset. He was not fit at the moment to discuss matters. He walked down the short hall to his own suite and cast Great-uncle's two guards a forbidding look as they attempted to go in.

"Wait here, nadiin," he said, assigning them to stand at the door. It was only Jegari and Antaro he admitted to his rooms; and pointedly he shut the door and glared at Pahien, who, across the hall, had started an advance on his door.

The Taibeni pair had gained a certain wisdom about his moods. They went and turned down his bed, and quietly prepared his closet, choosing his wardrobe for the morning, doing all the things Pahien did, and said not a thing in the process.

He was not in a mood to sit down and talk with them and not in a mood to go to bed. He stalked to his desk and looked through his books, and looked at his unfinished sketch of the ship. That made him think about Gene and his associates up above, and made him think about being happy, which he was not, at the moment. Not at all.

He knew what he was. His parents were an Infelicity of Two and he was a Stability of One. He served the same function with his great-grandmother and his great-uncle, to keep them united in peace. He had served that function with Lord Bren and the kyo, and very many other people, and he had wished someone else would take that job—but he was clearly stuck with it. That was what Gene would say. Stuck with it. That expression meant very many different things in Gene's language. One was stuck with something. One stuck with a thing.

Mani would say everything fluxed and changed, and very few things stuck together, unless there was One to make them stand still. A Stability was a valuable thing to be. Everyone wanted a Stability. It was when it stuck to something else isolated and became an Infelicity of two that it began to be in trouble.

Baji-naji, mani would say: fortune and chance: flux. Everything shifted, or the numbers would hold the universe from moving, and the ship could never move through space and people who were wrong would never change their minds.

He detested numbers.

But he had to acknowledge he was probably stuck with Great-uncle's two guards.

At least for a while.

And mani had come out of that meeting with her anger up, and that was why she had been so blunt and so unobliging.

He should have seen it. He had not. Fool, he had been, to talk to mani when she had just had to deal with rude people in the salon. She had been on alert, and that had been an infelicitous moment to go on with that conversation. He should have asked to talk to her in the morning, but now she had closed the subject and taken a position.

He had to learn. He had to learn not to walk into such arguments, and to pick felicitous moments. That part he agreed with. He had seen enough fighting to give him bad dreams at night. He had seen people die. He had probably killed someone, which he tried not to remember, but did. And he knew people here on the planet wanted to kill all of them, and that he was obliged to be smarter than most boys.

He was obliged to grow up faster than most boys.

And then people would see what he was.

A Stability could become an Aggressor, quite as well as a Support. He wished people really *were* afraid of disarranging him and disturbing his life. No one believed he was a threat—well, his father's enemies might, but people in his household called him a Stabililty. He had rather be an Aggressor, at the moment.

But Bren-nandi said no. Bren-nandi had told him it was better for an aiji to prop things up than to knock them down. Murini was the sort who had knocked things down, and look what it had done, and how badly he had ruled . . . and everybody wanted him dead. Build. That was Bren-nandi's advice.

But he still wished he had his father's power to break heads of those who had hurt his family. If he were aiji, if he was his father, he would be thinking about that. So was mani thinking about it, and he was well aware that was why everybody was too busy to talk to him as if he had any worthwhile ideas of his own. Mani was more Aggressor than Stability, and she was One, was she not?

But she had dinner with disagreeable people. She was polite. She found time for them, and smiled, even when it was a political smile.

And she had invited Lord Bren, when people there were not well-disposed to him. Why?

She was either a Stability or an Aggressor. Bren-nandi was always a Stability. One could feel the flux settle, when Lord Bren took hold of a situation.

That was a sort of power, too. That was a great and valuable power, was it not?

Nand' Bren knew his timing to the finest degree. Nand' Bren spoke, and even his father changed his mind.

So it was not just Aggressors who changed things, was it?

Something occurred to him as he fingered the sketch of the ship and thought about Lord Bren and great-grandmother.

On Bren's advice, his father had agreed to have atevi go into space. It was his father who had had all the factories built which built modern machines. It was his father who had used television to reach the outlying villages and towns and kept the *aishidi'tat* informed. It was his father who had seen that if the humans failed to get their affairs in order and establish a stable authority up in the heavens, then disorder would spread in space—and that had led everybody to discovering the trouble at the far station, and rescuing Gene and everyone, and meeting the kyo, and learning about that danger in time to do something. And it was his father's decision that they were building another starship, one that would belong to atevi, and maintaining an atevi authority on the space station, and using all manner of technology . . .

So his father might be an Aggressor—aijiin were that. But his father had wanted nand' Bren's influence and mani's both to instruct him in his growing up. His father had gotten him and mani out of the reach of Assassins, seeing danger coming. His father was behind all sorts of change and technology which had brought on the trouble. So his father took chances.

And valued technology. And nand' Bren.

So it was not like arguing with uncle Tatiseigi, who deplored everything new just because it was new.

So living with his father was not quite like being in Tirnamardi.

Mani had said there should be no televisions under her roof. Where mani came from, in the East, things were very *kabiu*, and proper, and people were more interested in the traditions, like Uncle Tatiseigi.

But if Father were running the apartment, well, he could just possibly ask for a television, and maybe a computer, could he not—he could tell Father how he had learned to use the computers on the ship and he needed to keep his skills in practice, and he could tell Father how he needed books. There was the whole human Archive, over on the island, or at least up in space, on the ship, if he could get it. And that would bring movies. He ached to have movies again.

And there was a world of things on the ship that were just more convenient, that they could set up, like the kind of communications he knew Banichi and Jago and Cenedi and Bren himself had brought down in their luggage—

Communications which had proved so much better than Uncle's, and saved their lives, besides. His father would not disapprove of that. His father might be impressed if he knew his son could use computers as well as he could. His father would think it was a very good thing for his son to have learned.

Things could be different with his father in charge.

Not to mention Father might let him fly with Dur's son in the yellow airplane.

Father was very close with Lord Bren, so he would be seeing Bren often, too. That was not so bad. If Bren was staying in Great-uncle's apartment, that was just down the hall.

And if his father gave him computers and keys and permissions and the like, so might his mother, who might be easier to approach in some respects. Then getting places and getting information might be a great deal easier. His father would be the one to approve his going to the library, and "going to the library" could cover a lot of territory, besides that he would bet the library Jegari and Antaro had talked about had more than one door.

So it was not quite that he was about to be locked into an apartment with his father and kept like a prisoner. He was gaining access to someone who could get anything and do anything and get any book and any key in the world, if he could practice Bren's kind of skill and just use his head.

That was one point in its favor.

Having those two Atageini bodyguards watching him and reporting to his mother and to great-uncle Tatiseigi—that was a problem.

But he could get past problems. He could depend on Jegari and Antaro for anything.

He drew a deep, deep breath, contemplating his sketch of the ship.

Now that he thought about what his father could do if he wanted to, this could work out. It could very well work out.

3

Breakfast, and Banichi was back—just after dawn, a towering and unexpected shadow in the dowager's inner hall. He stopped, he gave a sketchy bow; Bren did, on his way to the dowager's table.

And kept at bay the human desire to fling arms about his bodyguard, in sheer relief.

"One is extremely delighted to see you, Nichi-ji." Ever so properly. "One is ever so greatly relieved."

"One is extremely delighted to be back, nandi." Banichi looked uncharacteristically tired, and was a little hoarse—one could imagine long talk, or loud talking, both unlikely in Banichi, but it had been an extraordinary week.

"Did Tano and Algini come back, too?"

"They are still at the Guild," Banichi said, drawing that opaque curtain on all information within that organization, and telling him no more than that. It was worrisome. He wanted the rest of his staff back, with all his heart he wanted them, and considering Algini's high rank in the Guild, he was by no means sure he would get them back. But he had Banichi safe and sound, and equally important, Jago had her partner back. Both facts made him feel ever so much happier in the start of a chaotic day.

"Do go rest," he said. "The dowager's staff is packing and moving for us, with help from down the hall. I don't know if you may have heard." It was almost impossible that Banichi had not picked up, from Jago, if no one else, that they were changing residences, but he delivered the information himself, for courtesy. "We are to remove to Lord Tatiseigi's apartment this afternoon, but no one will disturb your sleep, on my explicit order, and one is certain the dowager will concur."

"Indeed," Banichi said, for once evincing the need. "I shall do that, Bren-ji. And I am thoroughly briefed. I will be awake by noon, when your security will gain advance access to the premises ."

"Go," he said, and Banichi disappeared, with one more duty in front of him—getting them in there, and coordinating with Cenedi. He knew Jago would refuse to leave him unattended for an instant, and with Tano and Algini still—engaged—at the Guild—it was all on Banichi.

He had seen nothing of Jago since they had waked, however, in these safe halls: she was closeted with the dowager's security so far as he knew, doing everything alone, at least as the sole representative of his own staff in the transition. There were matters to be arranged with the place he was leaving as well as the place he was going: passwords to be changed, keys to be traded, God knew what else.

But Jago knew Banichi was back, and that it would not be all on her. Banichi would have advised her first of all, and he would be linked in by electronics at least the moment he passed the front door. So his personal world was knitting itself back together. Banichi was coming down off that state of high alert that had occupied his staff ever since their return—or at least he was relaxing enough to admit he needed sleep. That was good to see. And he very much preferred Banichi's parting "Bren-ji" to "my lord."

He felt easier in body and soul, despite the disarrangement of the impending move. He returned his attention to his unanswered correspondence, composing on the keyboard, where erasure did not mean throwing away a piece of tangible paper that could then fall into wrong hands—and where he had an automatic copy of his exact words. Even carbon paper was controversial modernity, in very conservative households, and worked exceedingly poorly with calligraphic pens, to boot— but at the moment he had no staff to turn it into proper handwritten text, and he could work very much faster on the computer. He answered the inquiries from Patinandi Aerospace, and also from the Ministry of Transport, assuring the latter that he had communication with the scattered flight crews—the truth: they were in the "answered"' stack, and, being sensible people, would get their typescript quickly.

Most of all, he hoped Algini and Tano would show up soon, and his whole world would steady on its axis if he had some word from his errant but probably safe brother.

The dowager was in the process of leaving; he intended to go say a formal farewell, but wanted to stay out from underfoot otherwise. Lord Tatiseigi had left his apartment at the crack of dawn, witness the fact that his own staff, namely Jago, was beginning to get contact down the hall in that other apartment. He had no idea how soon after the dowager's departure Tabini would arrive here—or whether Cajeiri would come to wish him farewell as he left the premises. He dreaded that scenario. On the one hand it hardly seemed such an occasion, considering he would be only down the hall, but the change was far greater than that in the boy's already unstable life, and he hovered between fear Cajeiri would pitch a fit and fear that he would only sink into quiet unhappiness.

Damn, he would miss the boy's frequent company, probably more, he told himself, than the boy would end up missing him. He at least hoped that would be the case. In the welter of arriving stimuli, in the sudden plethora of atevi to deal with as the boy settled into court life, ideally young nerves would discover the stimuli that made them react properly—that was the theory behind the dowager's decisions. The boy, educated in space among human children, would find more and more atevi associates, discover them much more to his own comfort, and become, in short, whatever a normal atevi boy ought to be. . . .

Which was not—the dowager was absolutely right—*not*—snuggled too close to the paidhi-aiji and passionately addicted to pizza and ancient movies from the human Archive.

He did interrupt his work to bid Ilisidi a brief farewell—she must have bidden farewell to Cajeiri already, since the boy did not appear. He asked Jago to order flowers sent to the dowager's household staff, and more flowers to the staff of Tatiseigi's establishment, and went in person to thank the cook in particular for his skill and courtesy in avoiding poisoning him; and he also thanked old Madiri, the major domo attached to the apartment itself, for his devotion. Madiri looked to be in the final stages of collapse; he had the aiji's household about to move in, and had Cajeiri in his charge in the meanwhile. It was not an enviable position, and he accepted thanks in a distracted series of frenetic bows, then rushed off to investigate a crash in the hallway.

It seemed a good thing for the paidhi-aiji to disappear back into his office. He attended to his correspondence and did the requisite courtesies for the staff as people became available. And by noon, indeed, Jago turned up paired with Banichi, looking much less grim, and reported everything ready for his occupancy down the hall.

He signaled his departure to the staff. He rather expected Cajeiri to come out and bid him farewell when he stood at the door, at least, but there was no such appearance. He only repeated his courtesies to Madiri and thanked him for his assistance with baggage and the like, and walked out, a little worried for the boy, a little distressed, to tell the truth.

It was a short walk, the move down the hall; he personally carried nothing but his computer, Banichi and Jago nothing but two very large bags of what was not likely clothing.

And, except for the worry nagging him, it felt like the settling-on of a well-worn glove, walking through that familiar door and finding that, indeed, Madam Saidin and staff members he knew were lined up to welcome him.

"Nandi," Saidin said—a willowy woman of some years, an Assassin whose working uniform was graceful brocade and whose principle defensive tools were her keen-eyed staff.

"Nadiin-ji," he said, using the warmly intimate greeting on first arrival, for her, and for the staff. They bowed—mostly female, and impeccable in their attention to the floral arrangements in the foyer, the priceless vases on their fragile tables beautifully arranged, incorporating his flowers, his colors, as earlier they would have been all the Atageini lilies.

He felt immediately at home in this place—home in a sense that he had not been since his return from space, living on the dowager's tolerance. He allowed himself to be conducted on a brief tour of the thoroughly familiar rooms, every detail evoking memory and very little changed from their state when he had last been in residence, unchanged, down to the precise placement of vases on pedestals, the display cases in the parlor, the little set of chairs—well, little on the atevi scale. There was a tea service beside flowers in the library, where he had loved to spend his idle time.

The immense master bedroom was ready for him, the bed with its historic hangings, its tall mattress piled high with comforters and pillows, and again, a vase of flowers. There was the luxurious bath, with its deep black-marble tub, fire-hose water pressure, and steam jets at one end—silver-fitted, of course.

He was toured about the well-stocked kitchens, introduced to the cook—a man who had worked with Bindanda, and who was doubtless very competent and knowledgeable about his requirements. Cuisine was one area in which Tatiseigi's household excelled, and this man was very anxious to demonstrate the new containers of human-safe ingredients he had acquired precisely for him.

Never mind they were, to a man (or woman) Lord Tatiseigi's staff and no few of them, likely down to the cook, were members of the Assassins' Guild. That was more or less common among lordly establishments in the Bu-javid and round about, where assassinations were a threat. Never mind that he suspected Lord Tatiseigi had invited him to resume his residency in these historic and museum-like premises so that he could have better current information on him and on the aiji, who might presumably invite him and confide in him, than for any reason of personal regard. But that was very well. It was a place to be.

So here he stood. He had absolutely nothing to hide from Lord Tatiseigi, and knew that being spied upon by such a pillar of rectitude and tradition had a certain benefit: other eyes would see that he had nothing to hide, since he was willing to be minutely observed by the staff of this Padi Valley lord. So his residency had value to him and to Lord Tatiseigi alike, and indirectly, to Tabini and the *aishidi'tat*.

The tour concluded, praise and felicitations duly delivered. It was, finally, bliss to sit in an armchair he had once regarded as his, and sip a very delicate tea in a room little changed from simpler times—times when he had only had to worry about the political annoyance of certain regional forces, never seeing where that annoyance could lead. In these very rooms, he had contemplated the situations that had allowed Murini of the Kadigidi to survive, and finally to ally with the south—it would have been hard to see that unlikely alliance coming, still less to imagine its world-shaking effects, but he certainly wished he had done so.

Regrets, however, were only useful as instruction, not a dwelling place. He had to observe with a little greater suspicion, was all, and he had to go to Tabini with his suspicions: he had once held certain observations private, fearing the atevi answer would mean, literally, bloodshed. But at a certain point he had changed his view. He saw Tabini's opposition as likely to commit more bloodshed than Tabini, and moreover, against thoroughly undeserving people. That was the deciding point for him. But he remained doubtful that he ought to advise on such matters, where he lacked an internal sense of how the chemistry ran. He wished he had been a little less morally sure, back when there had been a chance—and knew how to be morally sure in the other direction that he was not losing touch with his own, admittedly alien, instincts.

He received a message cylinder which had chased him from one residence to the other. It brought good news, that his clerical staff had received approval for its old offices, which were to be refurbished on a high priority. His old staff was setting up preliminary meeting space in the hotel at the foot of the hill, vying with various other offices attempting the same. And—to his great relief—records were reappearing, being checked in and stored safely at a secret location, before their restoration to the refurbished office. Staff had stolen them away to safekeeping, and now brought them back.

He answered that letter immediately, and sent expressions of gratitude to his office manager. Thank God, he had some means of retracing his steps through correspondence: he might have records of what had been agreed and what was not. And with certain of the lords, this was a very good thing to know.

"I have one lingering concern, Saidin-nadi," he said to Saidin, who dropped by to assure herself that her new charge was well-settled. "If there should be a message or a call from the Presidenta of Mospheira, I should be waked at any hour, and also if there should be any word from my brother Toby or his companion Barb. He assisted us to reach the mainland, he is somewhere at sea, we think, and my staff is still attempting to locate him. He speaks a few words of Ragi. Whoever might

handle a call from him should ascertain his welfare and his location, if safe to do so . . . You understand."

"We shall certainly do everything possible, nandi," Madam
Saidin said, with a little bow of the head and a level look afterward. Even Guild resources would not be off-limits to this lady:
she was a very potent ally. "We remember nand' Toby well, indeed, and we shall gather whatever information we can."

He so hoped Toby was being sensible with that half-kilo letter he'd given him in file: it was in most points the same report
he'd just given the atevi legislature—he'd given it to Toby
when there was a real chance it would be the only copy to survive. Now that the report was public, the danger of having it in
his possession had gone, but Toby might not know that. He
hoped Toby would just go into port soon: he surely had to, to
resupply—there was a limit to how long he could stay out.

And then Toby would check his messages and call him,
please God, quickly.

He answered two more letters, with that element of worry
gnawing away at his stomach. If Tabini-aiji were not busy and
distracted, and if the atevi navy was not concentrated down
south trying to assure the nation stayed intact, by rounding up
Murini's southern partisans, if all that were not true, he'd put
in a plea for a full-blown coastal search from this side of the
water.

He did put in a query to the atevi weather service, which he
sent with staff, to inquire about maritime weather over the last
week. It was, the report came back, calm and clear in the strait
until midweek, then overcast and colder.

Some time later he heard an unbidden and familiar step
enter the room: he knew whoever-it-was. It was absolutely certain in his mind even before he turned his head that the someone who had entered was part of his household, but it was
neither Jago nor Banichi; and he was a little surprised and very
relieved to discover it was Algini padding in—but solo.

An uncommonly resplendent Algini, leathers polished and winking with silver. "I am back, nandi."

"One is extremely gratified, Gini-ji." Algini and his partner Tano were the ones he most feared he would lose in the general shake-up of allegiances and revisions of duty as the Assassins' Guild sorted out its internal business, and he still feared Algini had simply come to collect belongings and offer his regrets. "We are very glad to see you safe. Is everything all right?" He added: "Are you staying?"

Algini was very, very high in the Guild, as he had discovered.

But was that a pleasant expression he saw on Algini's face? Algini was not a man who outright smiled often. And, yes, that was indeed a smile, a faint, even gentle one. "It seems that we are now without official employment, nandi. Tano suggests we would still be welcome here."

He was utterly confused, and shoved his computer aside and got up to meet what was officially now a mystery. "Of course you are welcome here, Gini-ji, you are both very welcome— how can you doubt it? Are you in some difficulty with the Guild? One is not obliged to say, but if you are in any danger, this house is always yours, no matter the difficulty, and we will sort it out."

"Nandi." Algini's face took on great earnestness, and he bowed. "Nandi. By no means. We are yours. We now have no other man'chi, and we are very content with that situation."

So, so much passed under the surface of the Guild, never admitted to outsiders; but one had had the strongest indication in recent days that the Guildmaster had died.

So perhaps that had freed Algini and Tano from the clandestine service to the Master their Guild forbade them ever to admit had existed. Or perhaps they weren't free even yet. Maybe they were going under still deeper cover. Maybe there was a new Guildmaster by now, who gave them such orders; but that was no matter to him. He trusted them, whether or not Algini was telling him the whole truth now. If, by some remotest reason they could not be trusted, he had every faith Banichi and Jago would have disputed their being here; and emotionally, he could never believe they would defect from him; logically—logically it was his business to remember he was on the mainland, and lives depended on his judgment. But not these two. Never these two. On some matters, a sane man just stepped over the cliff and trusted.

"Welcome," he said wholeheartedly, ever so glad to put logic in second place. "Welcome. Do Banichi and Jago know you have come home?"

"They know, nandi," Algini said.

"Bren," he said. "One prefers Bren, in private. One is ever so glad to have you back."

"Indeed," Algini said, with another low bow. "Bren-ji. Tano will be here soon. Tell him immediately that you know. It will be clear to him, and it will save him worry. Meanwhile there is equipment to move."

No hour off for rest or socializing. "Yes," he answered, that atevi absolute, and Algini bowed and left to that duty.

So his little household had survived intact. He settled in his chair again and a sigh went out of him. He found himself increasingly happy in the situation.

And in a little time Tano came in, bowed, and said, "My partner has reported?"

"He has. You are very welcome. Exceedingly welcome, Tano-ji. He said to tell you I know."

A sober nod. The flash of a shy smile, a little amusement. "We are very content," Tano said, and then: "There are boxes to bring up, nandi. Algini and Jago need my help."

"Go," he said, and Tano went to see to business, likely the installation of lethal protections all over the apartment, but that was all very well; his household drew its perimeters, and more than any electronic system—all his people were here. He felt safer, in an emotional sense, than he had been under the dowager's roof, and he worked with a certain lightness of heart he had scarcely felt since they had entered the capital.

He finished his session with the correspondence, or at least, reduced the stack considerably, being now in a fine and communicative mood. He reassured ministers of various departments that he would hear any request fairly and with understanding for the actions taken under the previous regime. He scheduled his priorities: certain committees had to meet soon to resume close communications with Mospheira and the ship; certain others had to assess damages . . . granted the phone system and more, the earth-to-orbit communications, were patched up.

In the several days since the fighting, in a situation changing literally by the hour, the hasdrawad and the tashrid had passed through a period of sticky-sweet interregional cooperation, but that was over. Now regional interests shouted at each other in separate committee meetings. The lords of the south protested they bore all good will to the returning regime, but that they could not locate Murini, who had unaccountably taken to sea in a boat which no one admitted giving him, and as for Lady Cosadi, who had aided him, she was nowhere to be found. There was no particular destination available to Murini from that coast, and one was a little suspicious that there really was no boat. Everyone hoped that, by now, there was no Murini, either, nor any Cosadi. Embarrassing leaders had no grave markers.

That was as much as to say, the provinces of the south no longer wished to carry on the fight with the northern provinces as the odds now stood. They were anxious to reconstitute their positions on committees in the national capital and to mend matters enough to get their voices heard in the process of reconstituting Tabini-aiji's authority, since that was the authority they were going to have.

It was the paidhi's one chance, in particular, to try to approach these southern representatives, when their fortunes were at the lowest ebb, and try earnestly to mend some of the problems that had started the rebellion—without, need one add, antagonizing those provinces that had stayed loyal at great risk and sacrifice. Unfortunately, most of the southern representatives were as hostile as they had ever been to human influence, merely biding their time and hoping he would, oh, take a fall down the stairs, so they could support Tabini-aiji with much better conscience.

Jago came in to report a member of his coastal staff was inbound on the train, hoping to deliver a detailed report to him on affairs at the estate, and possibly bearing some message from Lord Geigi's nearby domain: that message, if actually from Geigi's estate, might be a little more urgent than an accounting of the silverware. Air service was still spotty, mostly due to a tangled-up refinery dispute, but coming back on schedule, and the gentleman, unable to get a flight, inconvenienced himself greatly.

"One will be extremely glad to see him," he said, and since her hand was on the arm of his chair, he touched it, and gained a glance of those golden eyes, a little acknowledging flicker, and a curve of very familiar lips.

"Things are falling into order," he said, which, in Ragi, amounted to a sense of "taking the course the numbers allow."

"The paidhi is master of his own suite, now," she said, "and can order privacy as he wishes tonight. His staff is very sure he will be safe."

He looked up at Jago, saw the mischief in her look.

The night seemed suddenly much too far away.

4

There were two days of such bliss, after shipboard life and their stay in various residencies where there was no privacy. The move had restored a sense of calm and ordinary safety. The staffer from the coast turned up with a neatly written chronicle of affairs there and on Geigi's lands, wished to confirm local staff appointments, and wished to relay to Lord Geigi, the first that anyone could reach the space station, that his niece wished to marry. There was no deeper crisis from that quarter, only an assurance of things restored to order—besides the delivery of a suitcase of valuable items which had been rescued from the paidhi's apartments, including several very welcome pairs of boots—and the advisement that certain national treasures, including, of all things, the carpet from his study, were to be found at his estate, and could be returned to the Bu-javid in good condition. The gentleman also reported two assassinations at which no one was surprised, likely not even the victims, who had abused the coastal villages where they had asserted authority on Murini's behalf. The gentleman returned on the following day, after a very pleasant dinner as the paidhi's guest, and went back with the paidhi's request to keep a sharp eye out for Toby's boat.

The Bu-javid over all assumed a quiet sense of order, a quieter, more formal environment than he had experienced in years—no human neighbors, no crisis of supply, no disputes with human passengers . . .

But, somewhat to the paidhi's disappointment, no Cajeiri. Tabini had moved in, and the whole hallway was under tight security. There had been no invitation into the household, which was in the process of setting up and settling in. There was no knock at the paidhi's door from that quarter, not even to deliver a message cylinder.

At times, in the intervals between official letters arriving, the apartment seemed deathly, even ghostly still, a silence broken only by the quietest of steps and the hushed voices of servants going about their business as atevi servants did, most times by that series of back passages which only servants used. Doubtless, down the corridor, Cajeiri was recounting his own adventures to his parents, living with them, sharing staff, and, one hoped, developing those relationships needful in a young gentleman and particularly in the aiji's heir. Cajeiri was not, Bren imagined, without the company of the Taibeni youngsters, who would entertain him and restrain him from ill-advised projects. Inquiries proved the lad was spending a certain amount of time in the Bu-javid library . . . so he was getting out and about, but there was still, and now worrisomely so, no visit.

There was, at last, however, a small contact. One of the solemn Taibeni youths showed up at the door and presented a message cylinder—very formal and proper—which Madam Saidin had a maid carry to the study.

Esteemed paidhi, the enclosed miniature scroll said, straight to the point. *Please use your influence with my father and mother and explain to them that we have greatest need of a television. Please point out that it is educational. We are otherwise well and hope that you are also well. We wish you would come to dinner, but my father has to ask you.*

Well, Bren thought. That was interesting.

There was a postscript, in passable ship-speak, with the letters mostly facing the right direction. *If we had a televizion we could see news and pictures about the other provinces. This would be educationish. Also if you have any movies on your computer or can get some, We would be very pleased. I am drawing a map of the ship. Sincerely, Cajeiri.*

The little rascal, Bren said to himself, at last smiling.

And he instantly understood about the map: the boy didn't want to forget the place he knew best, now that he had come down to this world where he should have been at home, and wasn't. It was sad, in a sense, and entirely comprehensible, and no, he didn't think it would be politic to provide movies to the heir.

He wrote back, in courtly Ragi: *One will find an occasion appropriate and suggest these things to your father the aiji. One is extremely gratified to know that you are well and interested in educational experiences.* He daren't write: I miss you. He wrote, instead: *One has wondered how you fared and one is very glad to hear such favorable news. Please convey our respects to your father and mother and be assured of our lasting good will.*

Flat and formal, as it had to be—with just a little warmth. He did miss the boy. He sealed his own message cylinder, and hoped that Tabini would not take umbrage at his sending a reply to a minor child—assuming Tabini had any notion that the boy was sending out messages of his own. Atevi were protective of their children. They *didn't* deal with non-household adults on their own. He didn't know why he had expected anything different than a very proper, very *kabiu* situation for the boy under his parents' care.

Drawing maps of the ship. Remembering the associations there. He sighed, and spent a moment or two retrieving those mental files of his own, his own cabin, filled with those silly spider plants, plants that grew another foot and exploded into streamers of young every time the ship transited folded space . . .

His surroundings here were all gilt and golds, white and porcelains, the colors of the Atageini. Ancient hand-knotted carpets, the upholstered curves of furnishings were all larger than human scale; he tended to use footstools and other means of letting his feet rest somewhere solid, one of those habits so engrained he scarcely thought of it these days. It was like being a permanent child, with, however, adult respect. Which Cajeiri no longer got, poor lad.

His surroundings here were Banichi and Jago, Tano and Algini, and Madam Saidin and her Atageini staff. If he wanted something, it appeared, or if he wanted to know something, Jago ferreted it out. He controlled his surroundings as Cajeiri could not, any longer. No computers, no network. No television.

Most of all, his time began to slow from the frantic career it had observed since they had landed. It had only been a few days. It felt like forever. And he planned on cultivating that leisure. He feared time passed much more tediously for the boy. There was absolutely nothing he could do, not while matters were delicate, not while human intervention could only make matters worse.

But the very next day a second message came, this one from Tabini himself, and not contained in a cylinder: Tabini's new chief bodyguard, Jaidiri, came to Banichi, and informed his staff that the aiji wanted to meet the paidhi-aiji in private conference in the afternoon. It was not a brusque or alarming order: it came through polite channels; but it was scarcely time enough to get ready, and not quite time enough to marshal his thoughts on various topics.

Madam Saidin's staff, by dint of hard work, had the wardrobe in excellent order, and recent days had let it multiply, with the welcome additon of dress boots that fit, that most difficult article, thanks to Tatiseigi's staff, and shirts with the fashionable amount of lace, not to mention ribbon that wasn't tattered and warped.

"One wonders, nadiin-ji, if this summons regards Cajeiri's letter," he said to Banichi and Jago as they exited the apartment.

"Possible, nandi," Banichi said, and added, "things have been very quiet."

It had been quiet within the committees, within the court sessions, which he had not attended. Atevi were busy reconstituting their own channels of communication and influence. The lack of requests for the paidhi's offices limited the number of reasons Tabini might ask to see him, unless his attendance was suddenly important.

He did long to see the boy. He wondered if Cajeiri might be there—ready to embarrass both of them. That could be unfortunate. For both of them.

Or it might be there was news from the mainland, or more, from Toby. Jago had been tracking communications and making daily inquiries regarding Toby's whereabouts, as yet turning up nothing, and that worry constantly gnawed at his stomach. Surely it was not bad news. Tabini would not have called it an interview if that were the case. And Jago would have known before anyone, and told him.

They presented themselves at the door of the dowager's apartment, entered, and Banichi and Jago, by protocols, let him go on alone into the little drawing room beyond, guarded only by the aiji's people. It was a house to which they had man'chi, and in which there was every presumption of safety.

"Aiji-ma." Bren bowed to the ruler of the atevi world, who sat quite easily and informally, in a chair next to his grandmother's vacant favorite chair, and acknowledged the greeting with a casual wave of his hand.

"Sit, paidhi-ji."

Paidhi-ji. The intimate address. So he was not in towering disfavor, at least. Bren chose his frequent place in this room, a brocade-seated, spindly side chair, and waited while Tabini ordered tea from the servants, that lubricant of all social dialogue.

"Be at ease," Tabini said, which surely meant it was not bad news in the offing, so he felt free to draw an easier breath. "You cannot think, nand' paidhi, that your actions are in any sense disapproved. You should by no means seem so ill at ease."

Did it show that badly? He tried to settle. "One hopes that this is the case, aiji-ma," he said, "but it was a long voyage, and the *aishidi'tat* has seen a great deal of disturbance in the interim."

"This report of yours," Tabini began, and Bren's pulse picked up. He had been trying to get that report read since they had landed: a very lengthy report, it was, a very detailed report, in its whole, and he had made a summary of it for Tabini's convenience, but even that had seemed too difficult, in the hours immediately after Tabini's return. "I have read the long version," Tabini said. "Our son did not exaggerate his part in matters."

"He hardly needs do so, aiji-ma," Bren said. "He was very much in the midst of things."

"Oh, he is in the midst of most things," Tabini said with a laugh, and Bren found a quiet smile.

"That he is, aiji-ma, but profitably so during the mission."

"He sent you a message, so we hear."

That was a question. "He did, aiji-ma." He took a chance on Tabini's mood. "He pleads for me to intercede with you for a television."

"The scoundrel!"

"The paidhi-aiji is requested to present the very best case and to say that it would be educational."

"We have no doubt," Tabini said, and the ghost of a smile played about his stern mouth, even reaching his eyes. "Well, well, perhaps." The servant arrived with tea, and served him and Bren. For a moment courtesy required silent appreciation, which Bren paid with a nod.

"Indeed," Tabini said. "And this report. This report, paidhi-aiji."

Bren's pulse renewed its pace. "One absolutely stands by its conclusions," he said. "The kyo will surely visit the station, aiji-ma, and they must see order and stability when they arrive. They were much taken by your son and your honored grandmother, for his youth, forthrightness, and enthusiasm, and for her age, authority, and wit. They do not understand the arrangement that allies our two species, but they are intrigued by the fact we are diverse species in close association: this offers them hope for their own affairs, which have not gone at all well in this regard."

"In the case of their aggressive neighbors."

"The trouble may well lie with them, aiji-ma: that is one possibility. It may lie with their neighbors, or in the way the kyo proceed with problems. In our cooperation, we presented them a model of a different way of dealing, when they had no hope of other outcome with their own neighbors. They were impressed that we finessed the problem of the hostile station in a relatively quiet manner, which they did not foresee happening. They place as great a value on precedent as atevi place on numbers: what has been done once is what is done thereafter, and change in their expectations of a situation comes exceedingly slowly—not because they are stupid, aiji-ma, but because their concept of precedent frequently diverts them from constructive risk. We have shown them other modes of behavior than they expected, and they now, I suspect, have had their confidence shaken in regard to their own decisions regarding powerful neighbors. They wish to understand if their conclusions about us are correct and if the reality here is as we represented it to be—they correctly understand that it is one thing to theorize peace, and quite another to obtain it from rival masses of people. Precedent is so very important to them in securing peace within their own population, based on their traditions, and yet they see us as stable, inventing our way through problems; and they are curious and a little fearful that we will do unpredictable things. It is very much in the interests of this world, aiji-ma, that they respect us and view us as potential allies. To put them off now will not increase our chances of impressing them: on you, in fact, and on your holding office, depend the chances of peace in the heavens. The paidhi very strongly recommends we make peace with this group, aiji-ma."

"And thereby alienate their enemies?"

"We cannot reach their enemies, as yet, aiji-ma, and hope never to see them, if the kyo deal reasonably with them as a result of their contact with us. They are our buffer. I know there is a risk, a very great risk, but we must decide on some posture toward the strangers: it was not by our invitation that they will come here, but by their own insistence and assumption. On the one hand one does not see any way to prevent their visit, and on the other, one may see advantage in acquiring their respect. We are involved in their affairs not by our own choice, but because humans who were related neither to Mospheira nor to the atevi built a station in their territory without permission. Their view is that atevi are the real authority, and have exerted it with Mospheira and with the ship-folk to retrieve this illicit settlement. This is, is in their view, impressive, and while they do not grasp that the ship-humans do not represent other humans, it is useful for them to conceive now that the station-humans have come peaceably under ship-folk authority, and that ship-folk are allied to atevi. It creates, at least, a perfectly valid interpretation of the situation, and produces at least an expectation on their part that we will deal rationally. The ship-aijiin will not dispute our dealing with the kyo, since their affairs concern their ship and its fueling, and they readily admit they lack expertise in negotiation. Certainly Mospheirans will not dispute it, since they have no grasp of affairs outside the earth's atmosphere. So the kyo will seek contact with your representatives, and you, aiji-ma, will govern negotiations and influence their next moves. As they by no means wish us visiting their planet, I do not think it likely they will ask to descend to this one: symmetry plays a large part in their thinking, and this is a trait which can be reconciled with atevi philosophy—I strongly resist the word 'reciprocity' as inviting a parsing of numbers that will only confound the issue. 'Symmetry' is the word that will best translate. One has tried to create a small, carefully limited vocabulary with the kyo, and to agree firmly on the words we do share."

Tabini's eyes—their shade of pale gold was quite remarkable and unnerving among atevi—flickered in deep thought. He was not a traditional thinker, but he was no headlong fool, either. If he had been the enemy of humankind on the planet, humanity would have been in very dire circumstances, indeed. As it was, he saw humankind as a personal advantage to his power.

And right now, Bren suspected, the keen mind behind that pale gaze was laying one or two plans he would not mention to the paidhi-aiji at all, to deal with contingencies which the paidhi-aiji and his grandmother might have failed to foresee.

Fear had not been part of their relationship, however, not before he left, and he refused to have it become so, now. He trusted this man—would trust him even if Tabini found it necessary to go against him and send him back to the island as an encumbrance to his future plans. The greatest fear he had had until now was that Tabini for some reason might refuse to read the report he had spent two years composing, and now that Tabini said he had read it—that was enough to produce relief in a great many senses. The paidhi had done all he could do until Tabini gave him the authority to act, and Tabini was, at the moment, thinking about next steps. He had every confidence he knew exactly what was going on in Tabini's mind, at least in this one narrow regard.

"Symmetry," Tabini said, and nodded, still thinking. Then he frowned, as definite as a total change of topic. Tabini repeated: "And my son did not exaggerate."

Total, but not quite.

"He did not, aiji-ma, if he said that he was very instrumental in gaining understanding of the kyo and their language. He has an unexpected gift in that regard, a facility with languages not uncommon in the young, but very uncommon in the intelligence he applies. He speaks the kyo language as well as I do, which is to say, imprecisely, but he communicates, aiji-ma. His youth engaged these foreigners' interest, and moreover proved our peaceful intentions, since one gathers they do not bring their young or their elders near a conflict. They were, in a word, engaged with him, and regarded him highly as a symbol of hope. If their representatives do come, aiji-ma, as they will, one urges that their request to see him should be granted. They will wish to assure themselves he is well and that his father is a person in authority as we claimed, and his appearance will have a powerful effect."

Again, a slow nod. "Indeed."

"He spent the return voyage practicing and increasing his command of their language, aiji-ma, besides the lessons the dowager taught, in geography, law, and manners. He has prepared himself."

"And does this fluency include Mosphei'?" Tabini asked pointedly. "We have heard the name 'Gene' on several occasions."

Bren's face went hot. He hardly dared break with that stare. "Indeed. One was aware of the difficulty developing—not as aware as perhaps one should have been. One has now been informed he was at the age of social attachment: one did not entirely grasp the potential of the situation, and therefore failed to prevent the contact."

"His great-grandmother would have been the one to prevent it. We have discussed the matter. She deemed the association with these children better than no association: that is a point worth considering. And *we* knew he might reach that age during the voyage. We deemed his situation in the heavens was better than the risk of assassination on the ground. That he should survive, unassailable by my enemies, was important to the existence of the *aishidi'tat*."

So Tabini had indeed seen upheaval coming—upheaval possibly to be triggered by the departure of the ship from orbit, in the mistaken apprehension of Tabini's opposition that his most fearsome allies had left him unprotected. That had been a point of curiosity, and the swiftness of the popular reaction once the ship did return suggested even that the heir's return, unassailable, and his daring landing, and his advance across the country, had done a great deal to support his father's return. A grand gesture, an unexpected stroke revising the numbers—the psychological impact of Murini-aiji being caught so entirely flat-footed had been no small part of their victory, and Tabini's sense of timing in pressing right into the heartland had been absolutely dead on. He had sensed the movement of the wave sweeping the country without entirely absorbing where it was going, or how devastating it might be when, in two days flat, Tabini carried the capital.

The numbers had shifted. The trend had changed. And Tabini had not been able to do it until the key items of his own numbers, protected from the coup by distance, had reassembled and started moving.

At that point, Murini had started to topple.

Interesting, looking at it from the inside.

"About a television in his great-grandmother's apartment," Tabini said, "—we remain doubtful. We resist his notions of bringing this Gene down to earth. We further hope our son will not demonstrate his command of Mosphei' for the news services. But, over all, well done, paidhi-ji."

"One is grateful, aiji-ma, knowing one's great shortcomings."

"Nandi," Tabini said sharply, "you will sit in the legislature in all the honors of your lordship, should you choose."

Tabini would back him that far, and ram his presence as a lord of the *aishidi'tat* down the throats of senators jealous of their ancient prerogatives. He quietly shook his head. "I shall not vote, aiji-ma, nor attempt to hold a seat there. I cannot advise impartially, if I vote, nor can a human decide matters for atevi."

"Better than some who hold that post," Tabini said, though clearly he was not put out by the refusal. "But your ministerial rank and your lordship stand. I am adamant on that matter."

"Not to any detriment of yourself or the people, aiji-ma. One would not wish that."

"What great reward would you desire for yourself, nand' Bren? What could we give you? A television?"

He laughed a little, and then thought of one thing. "Word of my brother, Toby, aiji-ma. He has not reached the island since he brought us to the mainland. That is my greatest personal concern."

"My grandmother told me so. So, indeed, has my son. Both have requested a search. It is already in progress."

"Then I shall be patient as well as grateful," he said, indeed grateful that those two had set it so high in importance. And that Tabini had. He was better-cared-for than he had known . . . than perhaps even his staff had known, though he was not sure on that point. "Thank you, aiji-ma."

Tabini looked at him a long, long moment. "That you have no permanent residence in the Bu-javid is more than an injustice. It is our personal inconvenience."

It was well-known there was no space for new families. Residency in the Bu-javid was the most jealously guarded of privileges . . . and he had had such a place, which now was bound up in politics—a difficult matter, with several deserving houses wanting the honor and the space and a touchy one already fighting for it. "Even if it were possible, I would not violate the precedences of those waiting for room." He attempted a modest joke. "There would be Filings, and there are already so many, aiji-ma."

Tabini laughed outright, but briefly, not to be diverted. "We will consider the matter—should Lord Tatiseigi return to court. As, who knows, he may, soon. You would not be averse to resuming the Maladesi residence once that matter with the current residents is sorted out . . ."

"I would not, aiji-ma, or any other the aiji might deem just, but—" What in hell were they going to do with the family who had occupied it? Was Tabini proposing to add that household to his list of enemies?

"But there is the present solution," Tabini said, "until Tatiseigi returns. We take it you are comfortable in your current situation."

"Very much so, aiji-ma."

"Then we shall let it rest for now." Tabini's conversation thereafter bent to administrative committees and details, current matters under investigation, inquiries on communications with various committee heads.

That Cajeiri had not interrupted the audience was both unexpected and somewhat disappointing—he hoped the boy was not forbidden to see him. He supposed Tabini was bearing down on protocols, and needfully so, and no, his son should not come bursting into audience as he pleased. It was a new and rule-rimmed existence Cajeiri had entered.

So they drank their tea, and settled several committee matters. Bren asked no questions about the boy, nor had any answers volunteered. Tabini, he concluded, had taken his son back, as he ought, and Cajeiri was, by implication, no longer the paidhi's business.

He took his leave, finally, taking with him a small folio of important papers which were part of committee agendas with Transportation and Commerce. So his wild days were settled, now, and it was back to committee meetings, tedious oratory, and something of his old function. It seemed forever since a committee meeting had occasioned a rush of adrenaline. He wasn't sure he could still muster it in such an instance.

And, damn, he'd rather hoped to see the boy before he left.

Nand' Bren had left, before ever Cajeiri had heard he was on the premises, and Cajeiri knew, after dealing with his father and his mother, that complaints about the matter after the fact would find no sympathetic ear at all.

No matter he was angry enough to fling his stylus at the wall—he restrained himself from doing that, and discovered that the very deliberate act of returning his stylus to its box and straightening his paper on his desk likewise rearranged his temper into more potent order—a temper stored up, filed, labeled, and ready to access when it counted.

With that small angry treasure on an otherwise bare mental shelf, he called a servant—*not* Pahien—to call his great-grandmother's chief caretaker, the older man, Madiri, who had the premises under his care, and a small staff at his disposal. He could have gone to his father's major domo, or his father's servants, or his father's bodyguard: but these new people that had come in with his father, in the way of servants new to their posts, would run somewhere higher up for instruction, possibly all the way to his father . . . no, Madiri was definitely the way to go.

"One is greatly distressed, nadi," he began his protest, "that my great-grandmother's staff, knowing my association with nand' Bren, did not inform me he was here."

"One assumed," the good old man began, but it was unnecessary to listen to his lengthy protest.

"We know," he interrupted the man, "and entirely understand your position, nadi. But they are all new, and have no concern for our wishes. We were not even thought of, one is quite sure. Where is my staff at the moment?"

"Your senior staff, young sir, is attending your wardrobe, I believe, and changing the linens." Senior staff was the pair of personal servants lent him by great-uncle Tatiseigi, more spies, he was quite sure, to go with the bodyguards he had from both Great-grandmother *and* Great-uncle. Not to mention the domestic staff, that opened drawers and went through his spare shirts—and everything else. "Your senior security, young sir, is absent at a general Bu-javid security briefing." *That* was the pair of his great-grandmother's own, Casimi and Seimaji, honest young men he honestly *would* rely on for safety—and rely on to tell his great-grandmother every time he sneezed, too. They made incomplete four, counting Uncle Tatiseigi's two, which, with him, and counting also *his* two young attendants, made fortunate seven, his *aishishi*. But Casimi and Seimaji agreed with Great-uncle's pair much too often. If he had to have anybody of Great-grandmother's guards, he would wish for Nawari, who had a lively sense of humor—but Cenedi took him, and put grim old Casimi in charge. It was maddening.

Then Madiri added, almost as an inconsequence: "The young staff is still absent, one believes, also on some sort of errand: they said it was on your behalf."

Getting supplies from the town, that was the story. He had sent them there himself, and that had been unlucky coincidence, because if they had been here, he would have known Bren had come in, no question about that.

"My father's staff, being new in their posts, has to ask permission before granting me anything, and that takes far too much time, nadi. You know very well what my great-grandmother allowed, that I should be allowed."

"One must protest, young sir, that there is no authority in my hands to admit or fail to admit . . ."

"There was no question of admitting anyone yourself, one protests, Madiri-nadi, but simply to inform us of persons coming and going, persons I may know. My father and mother are too busy even to think to inform me, and it would look very odd, would it not, for them to be sending staff to me at every moment? They will not regularly consult me. One must rely on Great-grandmother's staff, who one thinks should attend to me far better than these new people. We were greatly embarrassed to have failed to greet nand' Bren. We were set at extreme fault."

The man looked chagrined at the accusation and flattered by the grant of responsibility, however strangely that combined. And everything he said to the old man was fairly close to the truth, however slightly re-aimed and refined to have his way.

"So the young gentleman will wish to see nand' Bren at next opportunity."

"Indeed, nadi, we wish to see nand' Bren, or our cousins, or Great-grandmother's staff, or nand' Bren's staff, or any people we *know*, nadi-ji. We are shut in. We are a prisoner here. We are desperate, nadi, to see people we know. We are so lonely, nadi! Papa-ji hardly means this to be the case. But he is busy. He is always busy. We have only you, nadi."

Exactly the right nerve. The old man nodded sympathetically and bowed. "One hears, young sir."

"One will remember such a kindness," he said, meticulous in the manners Great-grandmother had enforced with thwacks against his ear. "Thank you, nadi."

"Indeed, indeed." The old man bowed again, and went away at his slight signal—as slight as his great-grandmother's: in fact, precisely hers—he had practiced that little move of the fingers, with just the right look. It worked.

So he was still angry, and absolutely certain his father *had* perfectly well thought about him during Bren's visit, and decided not to tell him, because he was not to be that important in the household, nor should think it for a moment—but he had at least done something about getting information.

He longed desperately now for Gene, for Artur and Bjorn and Irene. He missed racing cars with Banichi or studying kyo languages with Bren, who could always make him laugh. His heart would widen just at the sight of Sabin-aiji, or Jase, or Nawari—or Great-grandmother or even Great-uncle, for that matter. He longed for anyone more than the staff that soft-footed it around him, delivering food or drink or just maddenly hovering, ready to pounce and pick up things he might drop. He was not altogether overstating his case with the old caretaker. It was driving him to desperation. He hated the hovering of servants. He hated Pahien standing outside his room just so she could dive over and be the first there, any time he needed anything.

He hated most of all being shunted aside and told he was a child.

Most of all—loneliness, after being in the center of things, was entirely unjust, and such injustice—hurt. Hurt made him sulk.

And sulking only worried the servants and brought them to hover around him. Especially Pahien.

So he did as Great-grandmother had instructed him and sat straight and kept his face composed, struggle as he had to just now. It was, she would say—he could hear her voice, and almost feel the ping of her finger-snap against his ear—an excellent lesson for him. He should be grateful to be inconvenienced.

The hell, nand' Bren would say. The *hell*. He could hear nand' Bren say that, too, under his breath—esteemed nand' Bren, whose face showed absolutely every thought, and who laughed so nicely and who was angry so seldom—he so wished Great-grandmother had sent him to live with nand' Bren and his staff. *There* were people with a sense of humor.

But he was obliged to get acquainted with his parents, who elicited his stories at supper, and seemed to appreciate them—they mostly laughed in the right places—but some things clearly failed to amuse them at all, and occasionally when he thought something should be funny, or impressive, he saw definite signs of their disapproval—disapproval of him, of his experiences, and his enthusiasm for human things, over all. Mani-ma had warned him, and now he understood: he had to keep certain things to himself, and not talk about them.

He went back to his diary, which he kept in ship-speak, in the ship's alphabet, and which he trusted no one could read except maybe his father and his father's security—accordingly he kept it locked away in a secure place, along with his kyo studies, and his pictures, the ones he had drawn and the photos from the ship, which he had gotten from Bren's report.

He would meet Prakuyo an Tep again, so he hoped. And once they had the link to the ship running, he wanted to download some tapes he knew the ship had, so that he could practice his kyo accent.

Once that link was running, he most of all wanted to talk to Gene—but he was sure his father would not approve that conversation, especially if it could become public.

Everything going to and from the ship ran through the Messengers' Guild: that was the problem. The Messengers' Guild had not been the most loyal of the Guilds during the trouble, and his father mistrusted them. So if he was going to talk to Gene, he had to think of ways to do it in some secrecy, or at least in some words nobody else could understand, and he was thinking on the problem.

This residency with his father was a test of character, mani-ma would say. Well, so it was. Perhaps it was also a test of his ingenuity and resolve. Was that not part of his character? If he and his personal staff—Antaro and Jegari—had succeeded yet in penetrating the communications system, he would have known Bren was coming.

But that failure of information had turned up a flaw in their assumptions: proper invitations did not come through the phone system, but in writing, by way of that small silver bowl in the foyer, to be hand-carried by staff, or, between closest allies, simply given verbally from staff to staff: that was a problem to penetrate.

That meant someone had to be stationed in some position to overhear what was going on—or there had to be a microphone, and there had to be loyal staff to monitor it, the way they had had in the security station on board ship—he did not think he and his young staff could manage anything that elaborate, not past real Guild.

But he had been used to that system on the ship. Security staff had always been sitting there in one little room full of equipment, doing things that had been a mystery to him during the first half of their voyage—but not after he had seen them in action in a crisis. That station had been aware when any door had opened, and when anyone left and whether they had come back safely—and they had learned to get by it, getting out. There was, in fact, exactly such a station in manima's very apartment, right down the hall, where now his father's people were in charge—it was very great trust for mani to let his father's very new staff handle that equipment. And that might *even* argue that mani had gotten one of her own people into his father's staff.

Probably she had. He *bet* she had. Such things certainly went on, as Uncle had wanted him to have Atageini among his guards, not trusting the Taibeni, oh, no, not with centuries of bloodshed between Atageini and Taibeni. And then mani had gotten her own two guards in because she wanted to watch the ones Uncle sent.

And *that* meant if he was going to get information and get

him and his staff in and out past his father's security, he had to figure on Great-grandmother's staff and on Great-uncle's, too—but they would be busy watching each other.

He was supposed to be learning. He certainly was.

Getting information out of his father's security station, which was always manned, meant getting it out on two legs. And that meant getting Antaro or Jegari or someone into position to find out things. Antaro and Jegari's age, and most of all their status as non-Guild, made that all but impossible. And if they were to take Guild training, which Banichi said they could do, that would take them away from him just when he needed them desperately.

Damn, Bren would say. That was no good.

Freedom such as he had enjoyed on the ship was going to take some work. Phone-tapping could be useful, but it never would give them things that flowed on the house system, he was sure of that.

But he had not set everything on that plan. He was working on other projects, and Jegari and Antaro had in fact slipped out on his orders—to all appearances, they had simply walked out, on the legitimate excuse of visiting relatives in the hotel down at the base of the hill. And because he was sure at least Great-uncle's people were watching his staff for misdeeds (Atageini never trusted Taibeni) he had told the two of them to get their cousins to go out shopping down the hill. And they were to bring back ordinary things like clothes to wrap the electronic items and tools they needed and were going to buy at the same time. It was amazing how hard it was to get a simple screwdriver in this place.

He, meanwhile, was mapping out the pipes and conduits, and doing it mostly in his head, because Uncle's staff was large-eyed, and, he suspected, reporting everything.

Perhaps Uncle's staff reported he was a zealous student, spending a great deal of time in the library—where staff did let him go with only Jegari and Antaro in attendance, because the apartment and the library were in the same secure area.

Perhaps the librarians reported he had a fascination with engineering and history. Both were true, so far as the plumbing and electrification of the Bu-javid went. He had pulled down every book on the building's history he could find, there being no manuals to show how things were now. There had used to be a gas system, but it was disconnected. There had used to be fireplaces, but they were in disuse, and many had been walled up, their flues—that was the word—still there, sometimes converted to bring in fresh air to the ventilation systems, but often just remaining hollow spaces behind masonry or panels . . . which was why certain places were spying-spots, and you could hear things that came through the old conduits: a number of these had been filled in, and people who worried about security worried about those things.

The history of the Bu-javid was, in fact, a long, long chronicle of modifications and reapportionment of space. The kitchens had lost their hand-elevators when one had been used in the assassination of a lord of Segari, a hundred years ago. Now food came up by the main elevators. The stairs that servants used, some of which did interconnect, or had used to interconnect, had also used to have guards.

Now the various establishments in the building all had security systems like the ship. Also servant passages no longer interconnected with those of allied staffs as they once had. Such connections were bricked up, but they were still only a wall away in some cases, and if they had been reestablished in certain instances, no one outside a given household would likely know it until that apartment came up for reallocation. To this day, there was officially no interconnection between apartments . . . that anyone admitted . . . and there definitely was, if one read the records for hints. He had tried to explore all of the servant passages, but there were doors that locked, and one supposed it was part of security—but *he* had no key. That was inconvenient. There were stairs that went down a whole other level, and met a door, and he had no idea where that went. *That* was locked.

It was, of course, safer to have both guards and electronics. And it did seem that industrious security might have installed modern listening devices right at those points where passages had once connected. Some such devices the ship used had been very sophisticated at picking up conversations much farther than anyone would think. He would bet, in fact, that some things his father used would make it a good idea to do any verbal scheming well away from the Bu-javid.

But he was teaching his staff kyo and Mosphei' for communication emergencies. He knew some of the Guild handsigns, and taught them. Antaro and Jegari had other signs they had used in hunting. They were teaching him those. They had their own language.

He was personally, too, getting much faster at skimming text in Ragi, in his library sessions: Antaro and Jegari scanned things so slowly and methodically—but he could find the word "passage" or "stairs" or "water" with one glance at a page.

It was curious, was it not? The word for electricity was that for fire in a wire. It was curious that the word for pump was really two words that meant stream and lift. Humans had given their technology to atevi after they had lost the War of the Landing, step by step, so as not to disturb the economy or wreck the environment, but atevi had not brought the human word across with any item until just very recently, when a few Mosphei' words had begun to describe things like computer parts.

Interesting. Interesting. That change had happened during Bren's service as paidhi. Bren had changed things, and let that happen, and the whole world had sped up.

And it had all happened during his father's regime. Never

before. The technology had come in so fast, with computers and spaceships and all—it was like Cook's bread when the yeast set to work. It was one little bit, and then it was huge, all of a sudden.

If Uncle Tatiseigi had been aiji instead, no Mosphei' words would have gotten in at all, but his father had let it happen, and let technology just explode all over the place, because humans were taking over the space station and if his father had not gotten atevi their own shuttles, and trained the only pilots, humans would run everything up there. Now they shared the station with atevi, and atevi were even building a starship of their own.

But the changes down here in the world had upset a lot of people like Uncle Tatiseigi, and Murini had gotten a lot of those upset people together, particularly from the south and among Uncle Tatiseigi's neighbors, to overthrow his father.

And what did they think they were going to do, then? Break all the computers and turn off the televisions? That would upset everybody else, who were not happy with southerners running everything.

Mostly the overthrow had let Murini sit in Shejidan and take revenge on his enemies before they got to him. Murini had never built anything or done anything good.

So the moment it was clear Great-grandmother was back from space and his father had help enough to take the government back, everybody ran out in the streets and cheered.

Who was related to whom had been a lot of boring lessons on the ship: it had gotten very interesting since they had landed, and he started wondering why his father let certain people get away with having supported Murini, while others ran for their lives.

His pocket dictionary showed hard use. He chased words through the thickets of very thick writing, sometimes looking up every major word in a sentence. But he learned what things had used to be true and where they came from. He filled long, boring hours with chasing needful words and following one word to its associates.

He found out how everything was put together—not just the pipes and wires and the servants' hallways.

He found out what people on staff were likely to inform his father on him, and who might have a sense of humor.

And he swore to himself that there would come a day very soon when he found out events like Bren's visit . . . oh, *well* in time to turn up uninvited.

5

The paidhi's office had not quite opened its doors for business, down on the lower tiers of the Bu-javid, but electronically speaking, it had come alive last night, and Bren was ever so delighted to see it happen. The walls still smelled of fresh paint, the plaster was cold to the touch, still curing, but twenty-one computers were busy receiving polite messages from the provinces and the city, and a youngish set of technicians at another bank of computers, five in number, was busy feeding in every rescued file from the computers which Murini's zealot reactionary supporters had destroyed—a destruction, one secretary informed the paidhi with immense satisfaction and amusement, well before Murini's sole computer expert, a man with unfortunate southern connections, had had a chance to investigate them. Murini, who had a smattering of computer knowledge, had been beside himself.

But even so, the paidhi's departing staff had wiped the disks clean before the zealots ever got there, with only two exceptions they could not reach, and those two computers Murini's thugs had very obligingly not just bashed, but blown to small bits. At the very least, the number of people who could have become targets of Murini's enforcers had diminished by thousands with that single blast of a grenade.

Meanwhile the loyal staffers of the paidhi's office, carrying the storage media, had headed for remote areas. Some had gone fishing. Some had gone to powerful relatives, persons too highly placed to fear Assassins and too secure to regard any demand to turn over a member of their households. Some staffers, of lesser families, had simply slipped into allied households and vanished from all notice, retiring to family estates in the highlands or the isles. For every staffer there was a story, and some of them were epic. Bren heard one after another, while pizzas, sent up from the kitchens, disappeared. Meanwhile the computers kept blinking and restoring and storing.

"One is deeply moved," he told the company, in a lull in serving and drink. "One is profoundly, forever bound to remember your actions. Within the year, the regime standing firm, one would wish to have all these adventures committed to print, with suitable protections for names that might not wish to be too public, and set in the library to be part of the history of the house. Above all the aiji should be informed what a brave and clever staff honors the paidhi-aiji with their service. Thank you. Thank you. Thank you." He bowed three times, to the whole staff, all around, who demonstrated great pleasure.

It was a happy gathering. The computers digested the flood of letters that came in to the paidhi, letters to be catalogued and answered, ranging from schoolchildren's inquiries to matters of state. He had used to do it all by hand. And it had used to come only by post, taking days. Now it was minutes. They had yet to receive the physical mail, which would arrive in sacks and on trolleys, he was quite sure, excavated from post offices that had been physically shut down.

He enjoyed a piece of pizza. Banichi and Jago, on duty, declined to eat in public, but he shared lunch with all the staff, some of them eating with one hand and punching keys with the other. He had already told Madam Saidin that the refreshments in the office would constitute sufficient for the day— please God they had ordered enough food, as fast as it was disappearing. The capacity of some of these computer workers for food and drink was astounding.

Nuggets of information arriving amid the general flow of congratulations, he had received substantial letters, welcome news of escapes and survival among the Manufacturing and Transportation staff, news of associations that had held fast despite Murini's hunting his people—there had been six of his personal staff brought to trial and one imprisoned. That man was released, recuperated, and on his way by train. Kinships, marriage ties, on-job associations, and all sorts of obligations—and his staff's understanding of what records were precious. The University had suffered the most, and had been the target of immediate armed raids, but the students had gotten warning, as it turned out, from the paidhi's staff. Consequently, the students had walked out with their library and the papers. Communication between his staff and the pilots at the spaceports had outright saved the *aishidi'tat*'s records and research in that area . . . not to mention lives. These people were heroes—every one.

"Nand' paidhi." One staffer came to him earnestly with a printout in hand, and bowed. "The Messengers' Guild reports that Mogari-nai's link has just gone up. It expects contact with the station at any moment."

"Excellent!" he exclaimed, absolutely delighted—it was something he had hoped to hear for days; and now—*now* that the messages were beginning to flow unchecked, the Messengers' Guild managed to get the dish up. *Something* had gotten their attention: he was not so uncharitable as to think they had been waiting for some more *atevi* request from members of their own Guild. "Excellent, nadi!"

And in that selfsame instant of triumph, he noticed an anomalous sight in the doorway, a smaller than average anomalous sight: *Cajeiri* had turned up, with his two young bodyguards.

Cajeiri had spotted him, too, no question, but made no effort to come his way.

He went to Cajeiri instead, a matter of precedences. The young rascal bowed, and he bowed. "Welcome, young sir," he said. He had not invited the boy. It might have been the aroma of pizza, or the gossip of staff which had drawn him, and by his manner, the boy knew he was trespassing, junior lord of the *aishidi'tat* or not. "One certainly hopes your father knows where you are."

"Oh, we're at the library," Cajeiri said pertly, and in Mosphei', in a room where rudimentary knowledge of that language was not that rare. "We heard there was pizza. We haven't had pizza since the ship."

We in this case embraced only the young rascal, not his staff, who probably had never had the treat. "Well, you and your staff are welcome to share, young sir." He persisted in Ragi. "Some people here can understand Mosphei', you may know. And how are you faring? Are you doing well with your parents?"

"One is bored," Cajeiri said in flawless, adult Ragi. "One is very, *very* bored, nandi."

Banichi and Jago had noticed the boy's presence. The whole room had noticed, by now. The party had greatly diminished in noise and impropriety, and hushed all the way to silence as Bren looked around at the staff.

"This is nand' Cajeiri, the aiji's son," Bren said, fulfilling clear expectations of some sort of ceremony at this arrival. "He has come to felicitate the staff on its survival and is somewhat fond of pizza."

Faces lit in relief and gentle laughter. There were bows all around, and with the instincts of a consummate politician Cajeiri happily bowed back and beamed. Banichi and Jago stood in close attendance. The Taibeni youths had come in, and stood shyly by, looking entirely uneasy.

"Indeed," Cajeiri said in his high, childish voice, and in the children's language. "We are very pleased. Thank you, nadiin."

This pleased everyone. Smiles broke out, and the staff—the office was already well-stocked with stationery and other supplies—came to beg a ribbon and card for the office, that genteel custom of seals and signatures as mementos of an official contact . . . "Which we would frame behind glass for the office, nandi."

"I have no ring," Cajeiri said sotto voce and still in the children's language.

"One may just sign and use the office seal," Bren said. "It will be perfectly adequate for the purpose, young sir."

"Nandi," Cajeiri said with a nice little bow, and the staff happily scurried about getting the wax and cards and ribbon— there was even available the black-and-red ribbon of the Ragi atevi as well as the white of the paidhi: the office, dealing as much as it did with protocols, had prepared for all ceremonial eventualities. There was a coil of red wax, there were embossed cards, and Bren, on inspiration, ordered out not just a simple card, but a large sheet of paper vellum for the signatures and seals of everyone who had come in. He signed it himself, and Cajeiri did, as well as signing personal cards. The office had lost most of its framed commemorative cards in the organized vandalism that had hit the former premises, except those that had returned with returning staffers, and now the office had a new start on suitable items to hang, an honor for the place and the moment that cheered everyone.

In the midst of it all, a Messengers' Guildsman showed up at the door, officially to report Mogari-nai's dish was indeed functioning and the link was indisputably up. The paidhi could speak to the ship above at his leisure and at this very moment.

"We are very grateful, nadi," Bren said, and nothing would do, in his staff's opinion, but immediately to link up a phone, hush the tumultuous party, and indeed, to formally salute the station staff aloft, the entity with whom the office had been in frequent communication, in the name of the paidhi, before the

troubles came on them. There was quick consultation on felicitous wording of the formal statement.

The Guildsman, personally put on the spot, saw to the link,
and set everything on speaker, so that the whole hushed room
could hear the staff at Mogari-nai, out on the coast, actually
complete the link to the space station.

"This is Alpha Station," the human voice came back. *"Is
this Mogari-nai?"*

The office director leaned close to the mike, and said, in
passable Mosphei'. "This is the office of the paidhi-aiji in Shejidan, rejoicing to resume communications with the office of
the station-aijiin. Stand by, Alpha Station, for the paidhi."

Cheers broke out, as the acknowledgment came back, and
fell away to an excited hush, as Bren moved close to the mike.

"This is Bren Cameron," Bren said, leaning near. "Alpha,
hello."

"Bren," another voice said delightedly.

A smile broke out on Bren's face when he heard that: he
couldn't help it.

"How are you?" that voice asked him.

"Jase." He lapsed unthinkingly into ship-manners, then
bounced back to Ragi, which Jase understood. "One hardly expected one of the ship-aijiin to be standing by, nandi."

"This is my watch," the voice came back with some mi-
nuscule delay. *"They warned us the link was going up, that
they were going to contact you. They've been stuttering off
and on all this watch. So how are you? Are you safe? Is everyone safe?"*

Bren switched to ship-speak, for confirmation. "I'm in the
middle of an office party, at the moment, celebrating getting
our records back—which we're doing. We're putting things
back together as fast as we can. The aiji is back in office, the
bad guys are on the run, the trains are almost on schedule, and
the airlines are back in the air. How are you, up there?"

"May we talk to him?" Cajeiri asked, leaning close, and yelled: "Hi, Jase! Hello!"

"*Hello,*" the informal reply came back, startled. "*Nand' Cajeiri?*"

The boy was on his own agenda. Bren edged Cajeiri back a little. "You can see," he said, preempting the mike, "that we're in good shape here, hale and well. How are your supplies holding out up there?"

"*Oh, we're surviving, but we're getting damned tired of fishcakes. We're in contact with the island. They're prepping the shuttle there. They're telling us the other ships survived. Is that true?*"

"Survived, but need extensive maintenance and checks, and likewise training time for the crews—they're coming in, and unfortunately the simulators didn't fare as well as the shuttles themselves. A few personnel are taking stock, going through checklists right now, and we can get flight programs and such from the island, even use their sims, I'm sure, if we have to. We don't have an initial flight date. It may be a couple of months yet, but we will fly."

"*That's great news,*" the answer came down. "*Really great news. We wish it were tomorrow, but that those shuttles survived, that's a real bonus.*"

"How is Gene?" the youthful voice shouted past his shoulder.

"*I'm sure he's well,*" Jase answered him. "*No great problems in the population. We're well fed, well housed, and settling in.*"

The ship crew settling into the station was probably at about the same state of organization as they were, settling into the Bu-javid, Bren thought, living out of baggage and trying to find their records. Thousands of refugees from the far station had to be fitted into quarters, and a handful of malcontents had to be put into very secure confinement. The station had already been short of supplies when its population had doubled—with, thank goodness, spare supplies from the ship itself—and order and supply was probably balanced on a knife's edge now, until the shuttles started making their regular flights.

"We're going to get essentials up there on a priority," Bren promised him. "Start making your shopping list. Get that to my staff here as well as over to Shawn. We'll compare notes and get the number one shuttle going with a full load of the most critical."

"*Wonderful news,*" Jase said. "*Don't worry about us starving. The tanks will keep us going, and we're careful with water, but we're not short. We're tracking a near-Earth iceball we're pretty sure we can nab, give or take a month, and that will set us up much better, in that regard.*"

"Good, good," Bren said.

"*We'll set up a contact schedule,*" Jase said. "*There are some technicals we need to advise the aiji about. Measures the station took while we were gone, some satellites we deployed during the difficulty.*"

Well, that might explain certain complaints. "We have reports of landings."

"*Unmanned ground stations,*" Jase said. "*Those are separate. I gave your staff a parting gift. Rely on them.*"

Bren shot a look at Banichi and Jago, who stood near each other, not far away, their faces completely uninformative—

So maybe it wasn't something to discuss even with this entirely loyal staff, and in front of a trio of youngsters who weren't a fraction that discreet.

"I'll ask, then," he said, taken aback—as he was sure Banichi and Jago were, since that had been one of the ongoing puzzles of the new administration. "It's good to hear your voice, friend."

"*I've been worried about you,*" Jase said.

"Mutual." So Jase was safe. There had been no riot among the four-thousand-odd stationers they had just installed in a station with limited food and water. But with Jase reporting in safe and secure, his other personal worry, Toby, came back to him with particular force in the moment. He didn't intersperse personal crises with official ones, not if he could help it, but Toby had deserved official attention, dammit, some gratitude for his part in things—and communication was still newly restored: his present recourse to the ship and the island might be more than spotty in days to come. "Jase, you haven't heard anything from my brother Toby, have you?"

A pause. *"I know his location."*

My God. He was ordinarily cautious. He'd tumbled into this one in front of a room of witnesses, the way he'd just done about the unauthorized landings. He blurted out, nonethless: "Is he safe?"

"Tyers knows. Can you ask him?"

Shawn Tyers. The President. He'd asked Shawn to find out. And Shawn had been in contact with the ship. He was numb with shock and—he thought—relief. And there was the Messenger standing by, who might or might not penetrate deep ship-speak slang. He had just blown cover. Not badly, but enough to say Toby was in play, and Shawn knew.

"Is he all right?"

"He's safe."

So Toby was listening, he thought. Still on duty. His heart was pounding. The wretch hadn't just done one mission for the government: he'd posted himself offshore to relay information. And now that he'd just blown his cover, Toby had urgently to be reeled in. "Thank you, Jase. Thanks."

"I'd better let you go," Jase said, *"and go report. We're at shift-change. Sabin and Ogun will want me to stay hello on their behalf."*

"Hello back."

"Can you say hello to Gene for me?" Cajeiri asked, bouncing into mike range.

"*I shall, young sir.*" The last came in Ragi, and Cajeiri—there was no restraining him—looked at least mollified.

"Please let him call me, Jase-aiji!" Cajeiri cried.

"Thank you, Jase-ji," Bren said.

"*Take care,*" Jase said, without answering the juvenile request, and the contact went out. The room broke into cheers, after its breathless silence, staffers delighted to have another demonstration that essential systems were working, and the Messenger looked absolutely relieved that it had gone without glitch—in itself, encouragement to believe this was an honest man—though one could not but think this was the one mission in all the continent that the chancier leadership of that Guild would want in the hands of a man of their own. He didn't trust him. Not for a gold-plated instant.

"Your leave, nandi," that man said, bowing. "I shall report the contact a success."

"With my gratitude," Bren said. "With utmost gratitude to your Guild. Wait." They had all the appurtenances of ceremony, and wax was still ready. He signed and sealed cards for the occasion, one for the Messenger and one for the Messengers' Guild as a whole, before the Messenger left their company, an official sentiment of thanks and a memento of the occasion. The network was back up, communications were restored with the space station and the ship, and most of all with Captain Jase Graham, who had just told him what Toby was up to—and he could just about guess where Toby was—

—keeping absolute silence and quiet in a zone Bren particularly knew, a little triangle where there was no regular shipping, where fishermen generally didn't venture, it being inconveniently far from various villages—and where Toby might even have been somewhat in intermittent touch with his own estate staff. His estate had supplied themselves during the troubles by fishing those waters.

The Messenger left, an honest man or not, he had no way to

know, maybe quite smug in having been respectfully received, and bearing his report. It was a damned mess.

And the phone lines were still down and the radio was a security risk; and if he told Toby to get into port at his estate, now, today, and lie low, he would have told the whole Assassins' Guild Toby was out there, which could mean a race or an ambush. He was a fool—he had been elated, and off balance, and Jase had tried to warn him off, hadn't he? It was Jase who'd used common sense, not he.

Meanwhile Cajeiri stood there, eye to eye with him, looking both defiant and hopeful. "One would wish, Bren-nandi, to call Gene on the radio."

Cajeiri, among other distractions, had not behaved well, had not behaved well in public, what was more, and now compounded matters by his behavior. It was not for the paidhi-aiji to discipline the aiji's heir, and Cajeiri knew that, too, knew it damned well, and pushed—hard.

Bren stared him straight in the eye and said, on the edge of his own temper, "Ask your father for such permission, young sir."

"You know what my father says." The latter was in Mosphei'. By now, clearly, the whole room knew the heir was fluent in that forbidden language, a matter the aiji had somewhat hoped to have less public. There lingered a stunned and uncertain silence in the merrymaking.

"I do know the aiji's opinion, as happens," Bren said, keenly aware, as the heir himself seemed to have minimum regard of the witnesses. "I also know that words on the wind do not come back."

Cajeiri's chin lifted slightly. That had been a quote from his great-grandmother's repertoire; and the boy surely recognized the reprimand.

"These are, of course, the paidhi's loyal staff," Bren said in ship-speak, "and loyal to your father and to you as well. One asks consideration for *them* in that regard, young sir. Because they are loyal, their restraint and their secret-keeping should not be abused. Nor can any of us vouch for the Messenger, who just left."

Did just a hint of embarrassment touch that prideful young countenance?

It might be. It was a reprimand as graciously delivered as the paidhi could manage, and the paidhi did not ask the respective bodyguards to manage the situation, nor dismiss the party, nor lodge a complaint with house security, or ask for the arrest and detention of what might be an honest man of a troublesome Guild. Cajeiri could figure, by now, that he had been rude, and excessive, and beyond indiscreet. In an atevi way, Cajeiri was privately adding the numbers of the situation. He certainly had gone blank-faced.

"Indeed," Cajeiri said, that immemorial refuge of atevi caught short of words. He gave a slight bow, sober and restrained. "We thank you for the hospitality, nand' paidhi, and felicitate you on the occasion."

The memorized phrases, the precisely memorized phrases: Cajeiri had been able to lisp that formula, more than likely, when he was five.

"One owes an apology, nand' paidhi," Cajeiri added then, the courtesy his great-grandmother had thumped into his skull. It seemed sincere. Certainly it was public.

And it just could not pass without comment. "Young sir," Bren said, as severely as he had ever spoken to the boy, "speak to me later."

"*When shall I, ever?*" A little uneasy conversation had resumed in the room, staff attempting to resume the party, but everyone went silent a second time at that sharp young voice. Even Cajeiri seemed taken aback by the resulting silence.

So. And was that "*when* shall I?" the source of the misbehavior? Resentment for desertion, a wicked, childish prank suddenly spiraling into the spite and full-blown anger of a young lord?

"By my will," Bren said in measured tones, "certainly you may call me whenever you will, young gentleman, and whenever your father allows. I have missed you very much."

Cajeiri had his mouth open for some other tart remark. He shut it, looking as if he had just been hit in the stomach.

"Nandi," Cajeiri said then, and bowed, and left the office, drawing his two mortified Taibeni companions with him.

He had not suggested the young rascal visit him. He had challenged the boy to summon *him* through his father's front door—which was exactly the situation: thorny, difficult, and not the paidhi's to mend. Cajeiri might just have figured it out.

Oh, doubtless there would be storms once Cajeiri reached the privacy of his father's apartment. Bren felt, rather than saw, Banichi's close presence, and Jago's, supporting him.

But there was more than one crisis going on. He tried to regroup, knew he urgently needed to do something about the situation he had just put Toby in, being an utter fool—since hostile clans knew the shipping lanes just as well as the rest of them. In the subsurface of his mind, he wished he had dealt otherwise with the young heir, maybe drawing the boy out into the hall to have that last exchange with him. It had been, God help him, public. In front of the whole staff. Yes, he had tried to get Cajeiri to deal in private, and yes, Cajeiri had kept after him—but was he, like Cajeiri, eight-years-old? He had been psychologically pressed, dealing with someone at eye level, but it was an eight year old boy, for God's sake. What else was Cajeiri going to do but throw all his ammunition? And now he had gotten rattled enough to breach security, risking his own brother's life. And he had put his staff in a position, besides . . .

Besides this deliberately provocative turn in the boy, who was no saint, nor had been on the ship. But there Cajeiri had kept to pranks, not such deliberate misdeed. He was no longer in any authority over the boy, and the boy was acting out with a vengeance. It was not a pretty character trait the whole office had just seen, and it was not private: it had public implications, in the fitness of the aiji's heir and the dowager's teaching, and he himself had not come off with any credit in the business.

"We have to reach Toby," he said under his breath to Banichi and Jago, looking all the while at his office staff, who still stood thunderstruck, caught between pretending they hadn't heard and the respect they tried to pay to his distress and embarrassment.

"Nadiin-ji," he said then, and gave a sober little bow. What did he ask them? For discretion on a private matter? His own staff were devoted to him, and it would insult their man'chi to imply they would talk. Did he plead that he had lost his focus and that the boy was having a tantrum? Both were evident enough. "Thank you very much. The message contained excellent personal news. My brother is found safe, and his location must be kept secret. One has every confidence in this company."

There were bows. One could have heard the proverbial pin drop. Acknowledge that the heir had been a brat?

There were some things atevi did not mention. Children were one of those topics, a private matter, intensely so.

"Please," he said, with a broad gesture, "this is a celebration, and with every reason to celebrate. Continue, please, nadiin-ji. And thank you."

The room collectively drew a breath. People moved from where they had rooted themselves, and refilled cups and opened pizza boxes.

He refilled his own cup, trying to seem casual, wishing it were stronger, and turned from the watchers to Banichi and Jago.

"I should have applied the brake on the young gentleman at

the very first," he said under his breath. "One entirely misread him, nadiin-ji."

"He realized he was in the wrong," Jago said.

"The witnesses have children of their own," Banichi said. "Even his father has had to restrain that one in public. And we have just contacted Tano, nandi. We will find nand' Toby. We are moving on the matter."

That was a vast comfort on that front. On the other— "What we lack is the dowager's stick," he said shakily, and drew grins from both of them, which afforded the large room encouragement to more noise. The air in the room lightened perceptibly.

"He goes about the halls with only the Taibeni," Banichi said under his breath. "Which is not good, nandi. One has no idea how he has shaken his guards."

"They told me they were at the library," Bren said. "He has abused a parental permission, one suspects."

"He has deceived his father's staff," Jago said. "This is not a small matter, Bren-ji. His security needs to know exactly what he has done, and report it to the aiji."

"Indeed," he said, and was not surprised when Banichi named himself to go, and likewise to consult with Tano on the other matter. "Do, nadi-ji," he said, and Banichi left on that dual mission.

"We no longer live on the ship, nandi," Jago said.

"No, we do not," he said, aware they were still under furtive observation by the staff . . . and being aware, he turned from Jago and picked his individual, his advisor in correspondence protocols, an old man many times a grandfather. Idly wandering over into converse with the old man, he remarked, "The heir misses his great-grandmother, misses my staff. Hearing of a party, the boy hoped, one believes, for a few guests here his own age."

He did not mention that the heir of the *aishidi'tat* had

formed strong associational bonds to a human, never mind he had quite publicly and vehemently attempted to contact a human aboard the ship, disregarding all protocols with a ship-aiji in the process. And never mind he had never heard of an adult party with children in attendance. It was a foolish excuse he had uttered. His mind still racketed back and forth between the mainland and the ship aloft. Here and there. Now and then.

So, unfortunately, must Cajeiri's. The boy was eight. How was he to know what the world's customs were, regarding parties?

"One entirely understands, nand' paidhi," the old man said in low tones. "A nameless year, a difficult age. And the boy has been right in the thick of the trouble. He doubtless has assumed a certain maturity of expectations."

That was certainly one way to put it.

"He accompanied us," he agreed, "through gunfire, explosions, shelling . . . all directed near him. At a certain point, we had to restrain him from rushing to our rescue."

The old man laughed gently, perhaps taking it all for exaggeration. It was not.

"A bright and excellent young man," the old man agreed. "The *aishidi'tat* will be well led, in his day."

He had several virtues, did the protocol officer. He was dignified, he expressed himself well, and he was very willing to spread his tidbit of information at least among staff. As diplomacy went, it was a little like painting, starting with the black and the white of a situation, adding a little color here and there, until the disastrous image revised itself.

He only wished his gaffe with Toby's situation could be so readily patched. He imagined hostile Assasssins moving at high speed, seeking to reach those waters.

On the sea, however, he would wager on Toby's side: Toby

handled that boat with great expertise, and would let no one near him that looked in the least suspicious.

"Banichi has overtaken them, and has them under personal escort, nandi," Jago said, meaning the boys. "He will speak to Casimi and Seimaji."

Those were the boy's proper, adult, and Guild security—the ones the young rascal had escaped. The discomfiture of Guild members was profound, even life-threatening. The Assassins' Guild did not accept excuses.

"I shall owe my own explanation to the aiji," Bren replied, not looking forward to that, either.

Jago looked no happier in that prospect than he was. But, he said to himself, thank God Toby was accounted for—damn him. Toby couldn't let it go, couldn't just go back to port—he'd probably already had his understanding with Shawn Tyers, no less, the President of Mospheira, that day that he'd showed up at the hotel, and he hadn't gone back to the island after landing his errant brother and his party on the coast, no, he'd simply sailed south to waters he knew would be close to information, trusting no one with his position, and hanging about the coast, ready even to intervene, it might be, if things had gone badly in their return to the continent—relaying news reports while he sat there, and ready for a pickup.

And Toby wouldn't know now that his brother had just made him a target. Maybe at this point they just ought to use the radio, blast out a warning to Toby to get out of those waters, now—it would set the hunters on his track, no question, but Toby with that advance warning could elude most threats.

Except it wasn't some random lunatic with a cranky motorboat they had to worry about. What might go out would be much better equipped, much faster.

Near his estate; he had his own boat. If he could get out to the coast on a private flight, pretending an oddly-timed vacation, he could be there in two hours, could sail out and personally tell Toby to go home . . .

No. His going to the coast would draw every assassin in the region precisely in that direction. And Banichi had already talked to Tano—had alerted him to something, and would probably meet him with plans the moment he had delivered the boy to his father's door upstairs. Something would be done, something far more efficient than he could manage.

God, he had to keep his mind on present business. The secretary in front of him had presented him a complex proposal about the priorities for answering secondary correspondence, and he had only half heard it. "Indeed," he said, foreseeing no possible damage from the order he had just half-heard, and, rattled as he was, he was willing to be obliging to his patient staff. "That seems a good idea, nadi."

There was just too much coming at him. He had lived aboard the ship in a stultifyingly quiet routine, and now every unattended piece of his life seemed to have come loose and careened out of control. He had heard from Jase, who desperately needed him to get the shuttles flying, and meanwhile the station had launched equipment toward the planet without advising him, or, possibly, without advising the legitimate aiji—possibly aimed at Murini, but violating several treaties in the process. Toby was found, doing something entirely logical, but out of reach and unaware his brother had been an oblivious fool. Cajeiri had run amok, and the aiji and the dowager were going to get that report before sunset. He wanted to seize every stray piece of his life, set it firmly in separate chairs, and keep everything still until his brain caught up to speed, but he foresaw that was not likely to happen.

What in hell was the matter with him? Cajeiri had blown up under his care, and he had lost his focus entirely. Surrounded by computers, he had outright forgotten he wasn't on the ship, in that limited environment, with limited enemies. So, perhaps, had the boy. And that had fixed the rest. That just could not happen twice.

He drew a deep breath, tried to center his thoughts on a staff resuming their good time, and wished for the second time he dared take a cup of something rather stronger than tea.

6

"Toby, Jago-ji," Bren said, broaching the topic again the moment they were done with the festivities, out the door, and on the way back to his own apartment: "What are we doing?"

"Banichi will have moved on it, Bren-ji," Jago said. "He has not informed me of the details, but he is on his way back to the apartment."

The Guild used verbal code on their private communications. One could wonder what the day's code was for "the paidhi has been a complete fool," or "do not trust him until he has recovered his good sense," but Jago walked along with him at deliberate speed, took the public lift with him, and so up to the main level where they took the restricted lift homeward, into the elegantly carpeted hallway with the tables, the priceless porcelain vases, the portraits, and the seasonal flowers. It was a place restored to *kabiu* and tranquillity. It soothed, it advised, it warned.

They passed the aiji's temporary residence, where the aiji's guards stood. They went on to their own quarters, on the opposite side of the hall and down some distance, where the only one on guard was Banichi, a looming shadow by the door.

They entered the apartment together, and Bren surrendered his formal coat to Madam Saidin, who took one look at their faces and asked no immediate questions. Her staff provided him the less formal house coat, and immediately, at her signal, left them in discreet silence.

Even so, he waited until they had reached the study and shut the doors.

"One is extremely distressed," Bren said, "to have been an utter fool, Banichi-ji. The Messenger's presence—"

"That man has passed clearances to deal with the aiji's messages," Banichi said. "But we take nothing for granted, Bren-ji. Your boat is awaiting orders. Tano and Algini are already at the airport. Our immediate plan is for them to go out and bring nand' Toby in to your estate quietly if at all possible, and not have him exposed in the long crossing."

He drew an easier breath. "Nadiin-ji, words cannot express—"

"Tano and Algini will use the young aiji's fish for a code word."

That lethal catch of Cajeiri's, that had flown all about the vicinity on a wildly swaying line. Only someone who had been on that deck would know that reference.

"Excellent." Tano and Algini could function in Mosphei', at least, and he hoped *fish* was among the words they knew: Toby's grasp of Ragi was limited. But he was immensely relieved, all the same.

"We updated the estate staff's codes four days ago," Jago said very quietly.

And they could communicate with less prospect of having their code cracked. Such efficiency was like them. He could only wish he had matched their precautions.

Soft-headedness. Too much reliance on staff to think of things. A steel environment that simply didn't change, while the universe ripped past at mind-blurring speed.

"One is immensely grateful," he said. "Well covered, nadiin-ji. Well covered."

Jago quietly poured a brandy at the sideboard and offered it to him.

He took it. His lapse had taken his innermost staff down to

two, again, and settled work on their shoulders. He owed it to them to sit down and accept that they had things in hand.

"Sit with me," he asked them, "if I have given you the leisure to do so, nadiin-ji."

They settled, Banichi with an unreadable expression—one had the faintest notion it was tolerant amusement.

"Brandy if you wish," he said.

"We remain on duty, Bren-ji," Jago said.

"And I have immensely complicated your problems," he said. "You know where he is."

"With reasonable accuracy, given Jase-aiji's information," Banichi said. "But well that we do know, and well that we move quickly. We shall reach him, Bren-ji. We shall use every persuasion to bring him to the coast."

"Every persuasion," Jago echoed, meaning, he was sure, a modicum of force, if need be, to overcome Toby's presidential orders. Toby knew Tano and Algini, once they were face-to-face. He would trust them. So it would be all right—better that they learned where Toby was than to let some dissident faction find out and set out after him, them and Toby none the wiser: seeing what Banichi meant in that *well that we do know*, Bren let the brandy warm his stomach, and let go a pent breath.

"One trusts," he said, "one trusts, then, that everything possible is being done. My gratitude, nadiin-ji, my gratitude to Tano and Algini, and please express it to them, if you can. One also understands," he added, because the amount of distress his security would bear if anything did go wrong at this point was beyond easy expression, "one clearly understands that Toby's position is fraught with hazards by no means within our control. Baji-naji, we will win this throw."

"We are closer," Banichi pointed out, "than any potential enemy in the south. And we have the estate staff already at hand."

"True," he said, and had a second sip, feeling better. "What a morning, nadiin-ji! But the young gentleman is behind doors, we are fairly well toward reaching my brother, and one is extremely glad to have the dish up again.—May one ask, nadiin-ji, what Jase-aiji meant? What is this, dropping equipment?"

There were looks, a little reserve. That was unusual.

"Are these things the paidhi-aiji needs to know?" Bren asked, "And are these matters the aiji himself does not know?"

"Possibly he does not," Banichi said judiciously. "We do not know, ourselves, the nature of these devices dropped. The equipment came with Tano and Algini. We have carried it throughout, but not turned it on—on their advice, not relying on any outside gift, and not having any assurance of all its capabilities, in the haste of our departure, and in an uncertain situation. We do not trust without knowledge."

"It is much the same as location on the ship," Jago said, "but we are told they can locate a position for the user anywhere in the world, relative to a map. If it had seemed useful at any point, for the ship to know precisely where we were, we understand we might have provided that location. But we never used it. We have no knowledge how they have tracked Murini, or if they have means to do so, but until we have heard nand' Jase's voice, we have had no assurance how things stand aboard the station, or whether nand' Sabin has resumed authority. That is the sum of it, Bren-ji. Since we have never doubted where we were, we have never used them."

Understandable that his security, with enough on their hands, was not relying on some untested system handed by authorities aloft . . . not when, until now, they had had no way to be sure who was in charge up there.

"Are they with you now, nadiin-ji? Or did they go with Tano and Algini?"

"Tano and Algini have two. We have three."

Three. "And the landings?"

"We have no knowledge of those," Banichi said, "nor have

Tano and Algini mentioned any such thing, Bren-ji. We do not believe they would have failed to say if they had any such information."

Considering the sieve that was Tatiseigi's security net, and the way their communications had fed into the enemy's, entirely understandable his security had wanted to trust only what they knew . . . knowing there was very little the station could do to assist them, without some dramatic action that might scare off the people that were moved to rejoin Tabini-aiji. . . .

Thank God they hadn't dropped anything in on Tatiseigi's estate. Half the force gathered there would have run for the hills.

But they were a different issue than this equipment Tano and Algini had brought with them . . . like the locators they'd used on the station and the ship.

The network that would have to support it—if not the landed devices—was a staggering implication. Satellites. A grid all over the globe.

"Do you suppose Presidenta Tyers has such devices provided him," he asked, thoughts cascading through his mind on various tracks, "and that he provided the same to Toby? Were we tracked?"

"Certainly we did not have any knowledge of it," Banichi said, "but did not the Presidenta have access to the shuttle crew? Clearly, he might have received such equipment at that time, and he might have had some understanding with nand' Toby—which we were not told, for reasons of security."

"If the Presidenta involved my household in some dangerous enterprise, he could have told me," Bren muttered, and added: "But so could my brother have told me, nadiin-ji."

"Toby-nandi surely knows what you and we would say to his involvement, Bren-ji," Jago said, not without dark humor. "But one doubts he would be dissuaded by the Presidenta or by the paidhi-aiji."

It was true. It was damned well true of Toby. "Well, so, what are these things, 'Nichi-ji? Entirely like the locators?"

"A network, nandi, and since communication with the station requires somewhat more power than our ordinary equipment provides—one does conceive the notion that these reported devices dropped here and there by parachute may be connected to this system, perhaps supplying power to transmit."

"Communication without Mogari-nai. But no vocal capability."

"One suspects, at least, that the system is more than reception . . . since they claim to know where nand' Toby is."

"Curious. And I was not to know."

"One believes, Bren-ji, that there was some amount of secrecy connected to its usefulness," Jago said, "perhaps that it is something already known to Mospheira, about which they might have advised us—but we received no information there, either. Tano and Algini themselves suggested we refrain from using them—*they* foresaw a certain doubt about the station-aiji and the ship-aijiin, whether we might rely on them."

Guild reticence. Guild suspicion. Some third party gave them equipment, and damned right they weren't going to use it unquestioned.

But there were those who would.

"If Tyers has it, the island might manufacture it, given *their* communication with the station has never faltered." The picture began to come clear to him, that Shawn's administration might well have had a global mapping project going with the station, at least from the time the *aishidi'tat* fragmented itself and Tabini left power . . . Shawn, damn his hide, had been tracking things, had *been* in close communication with the station, and had neglected to discuss that system with his former employee—namely him? Ogun had provided his staff with the equipment, maybe not telling *Shawn* that they were doing it? And Shawn didn't tell *them* if they were being tracked from orbit, given the things might be two-way?

Oh, things were in their usual tangle of suspicion.

Trust had broken down completely, was what. Bet on it. Murini had been in charge, at that hour, and Tabini's retaking the capital had not even been on the horizon when Tano and Algini had come into possession of these tracking devices. Shawn might have assumed they were going to set the dowager and the boy in the aijinate. And damned sure Shawn had sweated when they'd crossed the water and stayed untrackable.

He understood why his bodyguard hadn't wanted to turn the equipment on—with all it potentially connected to. He wasn't that anxious to use it himself, not utterly understanding what it did, or who it informed.

But if Toby was on the system—somehow—

And if Jase was in a position of authority up above and Ogun was playing straight with Jase and Sabin—

"Pacts," he said, "pacts apparently exist between Shawn Tyers' government and the station. They've permitted the installation of this equipment. Tyers very likely knows. And the station possibly violated secrecy in giving these units to Tano and Algini—considering the mess we were going into. Considering that the dowager *might* end up ruling the *aishidi'tat*, with whom it could be argued certain treaties had been trampled on—the station did not want us to feel betrayed by this system. And Shawn, for whatever reason, would not breach security to inform us this was going on—possibly because he thought he was doing enough putting it in Toby's hands, possibly against agreements he had with the station, perhaps otherwise. *Toby* didn't tell us, because Shawn had asked him not to. He *is* the Presidenta. He would have argued with Toby that it was best I not know—because *he* was asking Toby to undertake a second mission he had no wish for me to know about.

And Tyers may or may not know you have that equipment now. One would expect he does know—if Jase has been telling him all he knows. But Tyers may *not* have the capacity to track—if it exists. That ability may reside only with the station, from their vantage, with their receivers."

"Humans," Banichi said dourly, "can be puzzling."

"No man'chi, nadiin-ji. Toby knew I would argue to the contrary. And Toby wished to do this, for his own pride."

There was no atevi word for a person who would step outside man'chi, defy a prestigious relative, and seek personal risk because he'd been waiting for a chance like that all his cautious life. No word, but *Toby*, damn it all.

So neither the station nor the island had been idle while the continent had been under Murini's rule—they'd been working hand over fist to do something. Those landers out there were for *something*, and there were satellites up there tracking them—had to be.

And if local farmers took to hacking up the mysterious landers with axes—that was not a desirable situation, either—no knowing what contamination they might let loose, for one unhappy result. But there were others possible. Deaths. Resentment. Suspicion—that he had to answer, somehow, when neither the station authorities nor his former President had leaped to provide him answers.

He had an inkling what the mix was that had given his bodyguard pause—the certain sense there was something human going on, and that if they just didn't turn the damned things on, they could postpone upsetting the paidhi-aiji and adding one more vector to the problems of the *aishidi'tat*. Just settle it on the atevi plane, first. *Then* let the paidhi-aiji take on the foreigners . . .

Let the paidhi-aiji get the truth out of the station-aijiin.

Let Tabini sit in authority again, and let the world get back to normal.

He intended to have more information, from Shawn and from Jase, that was dead certain. And he wanted Toby safe, and if the station's little secret project—spread all across atevi skies in a plethora of foreign numbers—could get Toby back to shore in one piece, good.

Another sip of brandy.

He was going to have to explain it to Tabini, this business of foreign equipment parachuting into local fields and frightening the wildlife. He was going to have to say that this had gone un-mentioned for days, and there were installations from space dropped all over the continent, for unknown reasons.

More, he was going to have to explain to the superstitious and the uncounted atevi institutions that *humans* had divided their world in *numbers*. God help him.

"Did they mention anything else it would be useful for me to know, nadiin-ji?"

"That was the sum of what we were given, Bren-ji," Banichi said. "We all kept it close. It was my own decision. It seemed a possible point of controversy, in certain quarters."

Understatement. And he was, Banichi had always informed him, an absolutely wretched liar, by atevi standards.

"Perfectly understandable," he said. "It *is* understandable, 'Nichi-ji: by no means trouble yourself. We both agree I do not lie well."

Banichi gave a visible wince. "Indeed. All the same—"

"No fault, 'Nichi-ji, no fault at all."

He so rarely scored one on Banichi, and the brandy had made itself a warm spot, in a confidence that, however tangled the skeins of information around him, he had finally begun to get a real sense of what had been going on—what had been going on all during the time that Yolanda Mercheson had run for her life and the station in orbit had started cooperating closely with Shawn Tyers on measures they could take to pro-tect their assets.

The Treaty of the Landing had taken a beating during the last decade, but it was still what kept humans and atevi trusting one another enough to keep out of each others' affairs, and out of each others' territory. It was the basis of peace and order. And the station and Tyers had had something going that hammered it hard. He didn't think Tyers would in any wise contemplate invading the mainland. Human agents on the mainland would be a little damned conspicuous.

But Mospheira might have contemplated bringing Lord Geigi and his people down in the one shuttle they had left in orbit, and letting *Geigi* go after Murini.

Now there was a thought.

Well, thank God it hadn't gotten to that. Thank God Tabini had stayed alive, and the relative framework of the *aishidi'tat* had bent, but not broken.

A close call. None of the alternatives had been good ones. But if any had been put into play, one hoped Shawn would call them off quickly, so they could all pretend nothing had ever gone on.

And if Toby *and* Tano and Algini had locators, they stood a good chance of finding each other in all that water. Dared he think that?

He hoped so. He fervently hoped so.

Delivered to one's own door by Banichi.

Escorted to one's own chambers within those doors by his father's bodyguard, and watched like a criminal. Cajeiri was disgusted.

He had been so close to reaching Gene. He had talked to Jase-aiji, and when he had, all the memories of the ship had come flooding back, the very textures and smells and the details, down to the ribbing on the lights and the pattern of the floor tiles—suddenly, in his mind, he had seen Gene's face, with his pale skin, not unpleasingly brown-speckled across the

nose, his eyes, a remarkable muddle of gray, green, and blue—
his hair, which was brown and dark, and curled generally out
of control— He had already begun to lose the details he tried to
hold in his head, but they were back, now. Artur's face,
narrow-nosed and with a chipped front tooth—Irene's, dark as
an ateva, but brown, and eyes darker than her face, scarily
dark, full of thoughts—

Golden eyes around him, now, two sets of purest golden
eyes, worried-looking. Antaro and Jegari seemed sure they
were at fault, which was absolutely stupid. It was stupid the
way everyone down here seemed anxious to sop up blame
when he did anything at all. For a moment overwhelming
anger welled up in his throat, anger enough to strike out and
break something, but mani had taught him better, so he
choked it back.

Oh, he had anger enough for a sharp word to his father's
guards out there, but mani would do far more than whack him
on the ear if he let fly. If mani-ma were here, which she was
not. She had deserted him, given him up to his father. Everyone had deserted him, everyone that he actually wanted to be
near him, everyone but these two, who sat staring at him as if
at any moment he would have some incredibly brilliant answer for their collective embarrassment.

Banichi had not had two words for him, beyond the fact that
he was delivering him to his father's care, and that he was not
to be out and about in the future without Guild in attendance.
It was absolute disaster.

And Jaidiri-nadi had shown up in person to take custody of
him, and he was sure Banichi had gone back down to the party,
where he would inform nand' Bren the *boy* was back in his
room, under guard.

It had been fun down there until—

Until the business with the phone call, and he had brushed
past nand' Bren, and pushed right in front of Bren's staff—he

knew better, but he had done it, and he knew he had gone far past even nand' Bren's patient limit. He knew what mani-ma would say about what he had done. He had known it before he did it. But the bitter truth was—he had assumed he could get away with it. He had pushed too far, and Bren, Bren, that he relied on for patience, had turned him in.

And that was that. He all but shook from anger, in the realization that from now on he would be watched—lucky if he could get out of his room, let alone the apartment. It was not fair. Nothing was fair. Nothing in his life was the way he wanted any more, and now Banichi, of all people, who used to play games with him, had turned on him and told him not to be out without real Guild in attendance, and Bren-nandi was furious, and probably would talk to his father.

And Jadiri was absolutely furious. He had gotten past Jaidiri when Jaidiri was in a meeting with staff, he had planned it that way, and now Jaidiri knew it. Probably Jaidiri was in a great deal of trouble with his father, new in his job as he was: Jaidiri was professionally embarrassed. His new servants, Uncle's people, too, were embarrassed. Everybody was upset with him, because everybody was going to get into trouble for letting him get outside.

Well, so was he upset, but nobody cared that he was upset. Nobody at all cared what he thought. Mani-ma went away with Uncle, and Bren moved out, and his father and mother had seized control of him, but just installed him as one more obligation on their busy schedules. They paid no attention to him except at dinner-times, when they spared an hour to talk to him.

Damn, damn, *damn!* He would say the word and nobody cared to stop him. Nobody cared at all: they just shoved him in a room to be let out only for supper, and they embarrassed him in front of Jegari and Antaro.

He flung himself down at his desk and picked up his sketch

of the ship and flung it. Papers scattered, and Jegari and Antaro were too wise to move to pick them up. He wanted to rip things in shreds. And they just stood, part of the disaster, finding nothing at all they could do to help.

"One desires some of that cake from last night, nadiin," he said finally, which gave them an excuse to leave, as they could do and he could not: they could pass the guards at his door without being tracked—even if nobody gave them keys, such as *other* guards had. They could at least go out and do something useful. He remembered the cake from last night's supper. He had liked it. He wanted some sort of comfort for an upset stomach. He wanted meanwhile to calm down and use his wits. He could hear mani-ma telling him that he was a fool when he was angry and nobody wanted to take orders from a fool.

Maybe they could filch keys. It was not like keys on the ship, which were cards if they were not personal codes or thumbprints: they never had figured how to get by the thumb locks; but the Bu-javid keys were metal, and people carried them, and might be careless if he kept his eyes open.

He could all but see the passages on the ship. Gene and Artur, and him, with their breath frosting in the light Gene had, and Gene saying, "We can go wherever we like. I know how."

He picked up his own papers off the floor. He straightened them into order, and tried not to choke on his own breath.

How could he have forgotten any of the details that had just come back to him? How could he have forgotten details about Gene? His own memory was fading in this place, after hardly more than a handful of days, and he might forget other things, important things. He might start speaking only Ragi, and lose a lot of his ship-speak, if he was not careful.

That was the plan, was it not? This was such a different place, and the things he forgot were the very things the grownups wanted to take away from him. That was what they were doing—taking things away piece by piece, so he would forget, and be what they wanted. . . .

Well, he would refuse to forget. He made a little note: he drew a pathetic little figure beside it, that was Gene, and gave it dark hair. He wished he could draw better. He would draw his room on the ship, just the way it was, with the simple little bed, and the bath, and the things he had had in the cabinets, things he liked, which he had not been able to bring down with him—he'd just packed a few changes of clothes, was all, but everything he had up there was still up there, over his head. . . .

And it would be for years, as far out of reach as the moon.

Even the moon was a place, when they were up there. The earth was somewhere else. Everything he knew was different up there. It was wider. Warmer. It had nooks and levels and places he could explore or just sit for hours without guards breathing close behind him.

He missed it all. He missed it terribly.

He drew Artur and Irene, stupid, simple little figures, just to remind him of the details he had gotten back.

And with a knock and a rattle at the door, Jegari and Antaro came back to the room accompanied by one of the under-cooks— of course it would never be just a piece of cake they got—no, no, it was one of the cooks, who personally served him tea, juice, and a generous plate of the requested cake. He found it unappetizing now that he had gotten it with such a fuss, but he insisted Jegari and Antaro share some with him, and have some juice, and they seemed happier because they thought he was. The cook took the dishes, and left the three of them alone again.

At least the shakes had stopped, and Cajeiri finally found it in him to apologize to them.

"One is very sorry, nadiin-ji, for getting you in trouble."

"We would wish to take the blame, nandi," Antaro said.

"You shall not! I shall tell my father it was my idea, and it *was."* His anger rose up again, and he remembered what mani-ma had said about orders from fools. "But we did find out about the dish, and we did talk to Jase-aiji. So we gained something."

"Indeed," Jegari said faintly.

"Jase-aiji is an ally of nand' Bren," he informed them, "and used to live here on earth. He parachuted down. He was lucky to survive. Then he flew back with the first shuttle. Nand' Bren and he are very close allies. And Jase-aiji keeps his word. He will talk to Gene, and Gene may well send me a message when Jase-aiji calls nand' Bren back. So it was not a failure."

They looked impressed with that reasoning, and he felt comforted by the look on their faces. Most of all, when he thought of those familiar names, the ship became a place again, in his head, and would not immediately go away.

When you have atevi around you, mani-ma had said, you will find their actions speak to you in an atevi way. You will find a degree of comfort with them that you will not find with your human associates. You will see.

He had not believed that prediction, not for a moment. But, truth be told, there *was* something that tugged at his attention when he faced Jegari and Antaro, the same way that when mani-ma spoke, or when his father or mother did, his own intentions slid, and his insides wanted one thing and his head wanted another.

But a third thing, inside him, resisted any trick that was going to separate him from his earliest real associates, and that part he clung to, reminding himself that he was not an infant, to be distracted from his intentions by some bright bauble, or a diverting voice. *Forgetting* was what the adults all planned for him, and it was too bad Jegari and Antaro had fallen right into that plan of mani-ma's: they deserved an untainted connection to him, but he was never quite sure that someone had not put them up to their sudden declaration of man'chi, be it an ambitious father, or the lord of the Taibeni, or mani herself. . . .

Which was so wretched and horrid a thought it stained everything and made him angrier than he was.

He was not happy, being pulled in that many directions, but it was what it was, as mani herself would say. And he would not just sit down and react like a baby. He had his ship-plan. And he remembered, and he knew now the trick was to think of the names and the faces and remember everything they had done. Every night before he went to sleep, from now on, he would put himself back on the ship, face-to-face with those he knew were loyal to him for no reason but their own choice. Anything else was suspect, since it came to him with increasing force that if someone wanted him to do things, and here he was, because of his age, all ready to open up to the first ateva who just happened along into his life . . .

Well, someone as clever as his great-grandmother and his father would make sure their own people came along and got next to him earliest of all, would they not? And other people were ever so eager to shove their offspring his direction. It was like one of those movies, where people wanted to marry off a daughter, only he was the daughter, and it was not marrying, it was much more serious: it was getting into his man'chi, forever, which just made him mad. And if he ever found out Antaro and Jegari had been pushed into it—he would be furious. Not with them. But with someone.

So there. He had figured that out almost from the start. He had recovered from the first astonishment that Jegari and Antaro had joined him, and they were well-intentioned, and good, and he was sure it was a safe enough connection for him to have, and a natural and useful one: the Taibeni Ragi were relatives, after all, and it *was* a way of making sure Great-Uncle Tatiseigi could not claim him exclusively—Uncle was at odds with the Taibeni, and the other way around, which meant he was the point at which they had to make peace, to deal with him: it was good for both sides, he thought, and they could not have stood off the Kadagidi without both sides working together.

But it meant that he was on his guard about guards and servants any other relative appointed, and he was entirely on his guard about the ones Uncle gave him, and he certainly wanted no one from his mother's Ajuri relatives.

If there was anybody under the Bu-javid roof he truly trusted, it was nand' Bren: Great-grandmother said nand' Bren had no real feelings of man'chi, but she had said, too, that what Lord Bren had in him was something else, a human thing, but steady, and centered very firmly on certain people. One could never predict entirely what he would do, but one could rely on it to be in certain people's interest, sometimes entirely against their will.

So, well, was that not like Gene? Great-grandmother relied on Lord Bren, and while Lord Bren did things that just set uncle on edge, he was still reliable. Safe. Connected. Why was it not the same as man'chi?

But oh, he wished he had not showed out so notably at Lord Bren's party. Most of all he wished that Lord Bren had not gotten angry with him. He had deserved it . . . he just had not expected it, because it took a lot to make Lord Bren angry.

And maybe mani-ma was right and nobody but another human could understand what nand' Bren thought, but surely Lord Bren would understand better than anyone how he felt about his associates up on the ship. Lord Bren knew that strong feelings could exist between humans and atevi: he knew Lord Bren slept with one of his own staff, which was, he suspected, completely scandalous, even if he were not human—everybody tried so hard to pretend it was not going on, but it was, and he had never dared ask Great-grandmother whether *she* thought that was all right.

Now it might be forever until he could ask her questions like that. He certainly had no intention of asking his parents, or of letting on that he even knew it went on. He did at least know that such a relationship with staff had gotten past great-grandmother's very close scrutiny, and he had at least an inkling that Great-grandmother and Cenedi had a close relationship, too, whether or not it was proper. And he was certainly not going to mention that relationship to his parents.

He was not moved to have such ties himself down here on the planet. He hoped he never would be, well, not for a long time, because that was one *more* person who would try to complicate his life and tie him to earth. But he was sure if there was anybody as lonely as he was, it had to be nand' Bren, who was different from everyone around him, and if Bren needed to sleep with Jago, or Great-grandmother needed Cenedi—that was all right, if it made them happy. When they were together, they were—really together. Happy. He could feel it. And he had had just the littlest notion how it felt to be that connected—before Jegari and Antaro, and before they all had to leave the ship, and before people started shooting at each other, proving only that atevi could be just as stupid as the humans they had rescued out in space. And it all was designed to mess up his life, which had been as happy as could be up on the ship.

He had not even the ability to call outside his room, now. Communications were just . . . backward . . . on the whole planet, except the Assassins' Guild, and maybe over on the island. The net they had used on the ship did not even exist on the planet. It certainly ought to. If he had Gene, and they had computers, it *would* exist in short order. . . .

Except nothing connected to anything, and why it failed to connect was something he could find out inside an hour—if he were connected to a library. It was all just disheartening.

He thought about it, and thought through the things he knew how to do, and finally inquired, via Jegari, through his uncle's guards outside, whether his father would see him alone. Well, *one* of his two guards would go to inquire: they were cautious.

But: Yes, the answer came back, after a lengthy wait.

In the meanwhile, in all hope, he had had Jegari bring out his best coat—he immediately put it on and lost no time at all. He exited his rooms with his own guards, swept up the one of Uncle's security who had delivered the message, and who escorted him as far as the door where his parents' security waited.

His father, it turned out, was having tea with his mother.

He had rather have dealt with one at a time, but in the terms of his query—he supposed it counted as *alone.* He covered his dismay with a little bow, and in great propriety, waited for a signal. His mother gave it, and he came to them and presented himself with a second little bow to his mother and a third to his father.

"Well," his mother said, reaching out for his hand. He gave it, and she straightened his already straight cuff—he was absolutely certain it was straight—and patted his hand as if he were a toddler. "What occasions this finery, son of mine?"

His mother very well knew he had just gotten caught in the halls. He was absolutely certain of it, and his father sipped his tea, not quite looking at him. His planned approach began to fall apart, if his father was going to let his mother deal with him, and particularly if he was due for a punishment.

"One greatly regrets, honored Mother—" It was Great-grandmother's best manners, her most precise formalities. "One regrets a breach of propriety, Mother-mine. And honored Father." Another bow, difficult with his hand imprisoned, and he looked the while at his father, trying to judge his reaction. "One had come to pay respects to nand' Bren in his office, and when nand' Bren reached the ship by radio—it was exciting. Everyone was excited, and one very regrettably made a misjudgment, a great misjudgment. Nand' Bren will not complain, but it was a great embarrassment."

"What precisely did you do?" his father asked, looking straight at him, and gave a hint of that expression that terrified councillors.

But he was ready for it: he had assumed his most sober face. "One interrupted the paidhi-aiji, honored Father, when he was speaking to Jase-aiji: I spoke to Jase-aiji myself. I know him very well, honored Father. It hardly seemed rude at the moment. It was, however, a great misjudgment."

"And what was the nature of this address?"

"I sent a small courtesy to my associates, to say that I am safe and well. They must be worried."

"Indeed." His father's *indeed* could wither grass. "And a ship-aiji was to deliver this message in person?"

"Jase-aiji knows me very well, honored Father, and may well do it very quickly, by computer. And one was in all courtesy required to assure my associates of my safety. If I could send a letter up—"

"The welfare of the station and the ship are dependent on the slender resources of Mogari-nai, and my son wishes to send letters."

"But the transmission of letters is very fast, honored Father. A whole library could go right in the middle of someone talking, and the computers would never even slow down at all. I used to write every day, everyone does it, on the ship—letters go back and forth all the time, sometimes just a word or two."

His father lifted both brows. "In which language, son of mine?"

Caught. "In Mosphei', honored Father." And he was determined not to look guilty. "You surely know Mosphei'. It seems useful to know."

His father's expression changed not at all. "And you are in the habit of sending such personal letters?"

"Everyone does, honored Father! The system has all sorts of traffic. Even the lights going on and off are on the system. It just goes so fast no one notices. Computers are like that. Jase-aiji knows it would be no disturbance at all for me to send letters—if we could write back and forth, it would make me ever so happy, and I could find out things that go on in the station—that would be useful to you, would it not? And the computers would never slow down at all, never. The ship-folk send hundreds and hundreds of letters all day long, even silly one word letters, and the computers never blink—the lights go on and off and the air moves and everything runs without a mistake, all while thousands of letters go back and forth in every watch and everybody talks at once—just as if everyone were sitting in one room. And if one is asleep and not able to receive a message, it sits and waits for notice."

"This seems quite a wonder," his mother remarked into the silence that followed.

"We could have such a thing here, honored Mother! *We* could set it up if we had only a few computers. And it runs so fast! If I had had the system with me in Tirnamardi—"

"Uncle Tatiseigi would have had a seizure," his father remarked.

"But if I had had it, honored Father, we would have been able to send letters as fast as a phone call. Just like that, only to hundreds and thousands of people at once. And we could have gathered even more people!"

"A few computers," his father echoed, so far back in his train of thought that he had to blink to remember what he had said.

"Well, and one needs the connections between them, honored Father. But it takes hardly anything at all to run it, no extra power, and computers run so fast they always have time for letters or even whole conversations—they hardly notice at all while they do other jobs."

"Indeed," his father said, but this time it was not the withering version. In fact, his father had leaned a little his direction, and his eyes sparked with a faint interest. "One imagines the ship system my son used must be much more advanced than we have here."

"But we could do it here, honored Father! We could connect up the mail and the phones and the security systems and the servants and everything just like theirs, and once you have the computers talking to each other, it goes far faster than phones, because if you call someone, you have to say hello and they have to say hello and you have to talk through the courtesies, but these are just pieces of information, just sitting there waiting for you, just the things you need to know. And they fly from computer to computer as fast as thinking. Mani-ma said there was a rudeness about it, but if one's staff does it, then the servants can throw out the silly bits and find the important things. Mani's staff did, and *her* staff sent back and forth to Lord Bren's all the time. The Guild does it. One is very certain the Assassins' Guild does it."

"Interesting."

It was close, so close. He had his father's attention. He plunged ahead. "If I could get Gene to get the manuals—he could just send them down to me by Mogari-nai, and once we had the manuals, we could set it up with just two or three computers, and then we would hardly need the—Messengers' Guild."

"One is certain the Messengers' Guild would be gratified to think so."

"But, well, they could find something to do. They can run computers."

"Gene is this young associate of yours on the ship."

"He is extremely reliable, honored Father."

"And he will somehow find the ship's manuals and give them to us without the paidhi's intercession? Remarkable, this reliability."

"Everybody has the manuals, honored Father, well, the ordinary ones . . . One can even use the computers to read their own manuals."

"And you can read them that fluently?"

He was caught with his mouth open. He shut it, and bowed. "Yes, honored Father. I can."

"And in which language does my son habitually speak with Gene?"

Deeper and deeper. And a lie would come out to his discredit, at the worst possible time. "Whichever one seems to fit, honored father."

"Ah," his mother said. "So Gene speaks Ragi."

"A little. Just a little of the children's language."

"And you," his father said, "speak the ship-language *and* Mosphei' and this alien language, too."

He bowed respectfully. "Yes, honored Father. Expediency."

"Expediency. What a precocious choice of words."

"Mani would say that. But she taught me, honored Father."

"Well, well, two years in her care, and one is hardly surprised at such thoughts."

"I ever so need to maintain these associations with the ship-folk, honored Father. *You* have nand' Bren, and his advice. I have Gene."

"A person untested and unadvised."

"He will grow up, honored Mother. And so will I!"

"And you wish to slip a personal letter through this wonderful system," his father said, "of *course* with a ship-aiji's permission, asking that technical information be sent down—with or without the paidhi's intercession?"

"It would be absolutely no inconvenience to the system, honored Father. And nand' Bren would approve. And it is honorably owed that I present courtesies to Gene-nadi. I had no proper chance even to speak to them when I left."

"Them," his father said. It was a question.

"Gene, and Artur, and Irene, and Bjorn."

"The convenient number of a personal guard."

"They were that. They were, honored Father. They would defend me."

"They are children," his mother said.

But his father gave a small wave of his hand, which he dared hope was indulgent dismissal, *with* permission. "Compose a letter. Nand' Bren must approve it before sending. You will *not* ask for the theft of manuals. You may ask nand' Bren what he will request for you, in that line, and what nand' Bren approves may go out. *Only* what he approves may go. Is that clear? He is the paidhi, and he must rule on technological matters, even when we see ways around his authority. You will need his favor, and *he* will need my permission as *we* need his assent to obtain such books. That is the way the world turns. See to it."

"Shall we have computers, if one can get the manuals, honored Father?"

"Ask Bren-paidhi, I say! Deal with him!"

Did his father already know how angry Lord Bren was with him, and that he had somewhat skirted the truth in that matter? It was possible. It was also possible that particular complaint was still to blow up as badly as it might. It was probably *not* the time to ask for a television.

"Honored Father." He bowed. "Honored Mother."

"You will not leave these premises without senior security," his father said. "Deal with Lord Bren as best you can."

"Yes, honored Father." Another bow. One to his mother. And a retreat without argument. He had learned that with Great-grandmother: if one had gained something in the exchange, it was not time to risk losing more than one had come in with.

He exited with his tidbit of permission and walked, head high, back to his own rooms, collecting his two implacable Atageini guards *and* Great-grandmother's two men, and Antaro and Jegari fell in as he went. Antaro and Jegari he bade come inside, and left the other guards standing at the door, if that was where they were determined to stand, in a household guarded by his father's men, and all sorts of other precautions. *He* was what they were watching, not protecting his personal premises from intrusion. If there was intrusion, they were likely the ones committing it—which was the unfortunate difference between here and the ship.

Antaro and Jegari were too polite to ask what had just happened or how the interview with his father had affected their fortunes. So he told them. "I have permission to write a letter to the station. The misfortune is that those two outside have to go with us *everywhere,* nadiin-ji." He was bitterly upset and tried not to let it affect his voice or his manner. "They are upset with us and now my father has said they have to be with us. So they will go with us to the library. I think my father has heard another story of where we went today."

Their faces were duly sympathetic. "These guards outside our door are men are in your great-uncle's man'chi, nandi. They do not favor Taibeni."

"They do not," he agreed glumly, thinking that if he were clever he might still get out the door alone, but he had better make it worth it. In an otherwise idle portion of his mind, he wondered how Great-grandmother would deal with the situation if he and his staff simply went down to the public train and showed up at the Atageini station.

More to the point, he had to wonder how his father would deal with such a slippery move, and he did not think the outcome would be good.

Tano and Algini were on the next air cargo flight to the coast—Jago was in touch with them, and she would, Bren was sure, tell him if there was any glitch in their plan. Tano and Algini would reach the coast, the local boat would get him to the yacht, and they would go with the party from the household to make absolutely certain they could find Toby out at sea. They had the best of chances. The best of equipment, that was certain.

Bren rested on pins and needles the while.

And in the meanwhile, since a note had arrived from the aiji, he was already scheduled for a special meeting with Tabini before supper—God, there went the schedule. The note did not give the reasons of such a summons, and that meant having all his mental resources in working order. The occasion of the office party had at least gotten the staff together, and now the party-goers were at work restoring order in the premises and cleaning up the last of the crumbs, so that was handled . . . he had meant to go back, but postponed that.

By tomorrow, the office would be in full swing, and he had set its number one priority as getting communications established and bringing the shuttles—in some measure the paidhi's particular responsibility from the beginning—up to operation as soon as possible. That had become the paidhi's responsibility in the first place because building the shuttles had meant coordinating an immense volume of cross-cultural communications, and (which had never been the paidhi's responsibilty, but which had become so) getting the secretive and jealous Guilds and various legislative departments into communication with each other.

And Mogari-nai was talking. The station was talking to departments again—granted the link stayed up. Tabini might want to get straight what the station had to say.

And for his own agenda, the earthbound Pilots' Guild had to reestablish its training facilities, the technical branch of the Mechanics had to establish its space operations offices and get credentials in order. All of it, what little he had begun to heave into motion, had been on his shoulders until now. Now he had a thousand hands, a hundred small offices in communication with his staff. And it was not at all excessive for the task.

The whole space services system had to be repaired, from manufacturing and testing upward . . . and his staff, who had done the bulk of the translations, now had to get those manuals and the people trained in the professions reunited, not to mention printing copies of the manuals and training and checking out any new personnel they had to hire—and then double-checking to be sure what was agreed upon to do had actually got done. Equipment had to be checked, down to the smallest detail, and materials and spare parts had to be found, a great deal of it unique to the shuttles, which meant a supply reserve of less than ten, down to spare bolts and cover plates, if they were lucky. The inventory system had gone into chaos.

There had to be staff lists, at the companies that manufactured the parts. There had to be copies of the agreements and specifications. All, all this complex business meant finding experts scattered to the winds . . . and being sure they were loyal, which meant, though reluctantly, engagement of the Assassins' Guild, with its investigative expertise at finding out man'chi, estimating relationships—he doubted there was a single individual inside the program who had wholeheartedly supported Murini, but that confidence did not extend down into, say, the third marriage of the financially troubled factory worker. That depth of understanding was easily the province of the Assassins, who could gather up that sort of information as readily as asking the local membership.

And it all had to be done. They had a station up there depending on resupply of critical things the planet provided, and they had a space program to get running.

But they could not make the same mistakes as they had made in the past, to so trample on certain regional jealousies as to create uproar and protest. There had to be an oversight committee, someone to investigate the validity of complaints and mediate where mediation would serve.

And it was not precisely the paidhi's job to suggest to Tabini that he hear regional complaints the paidhi saw fit to bring to his office, but he felt constrained to try, if the opportunity presented itself. Damned sure few other court functionaries had the gall to broach the topic.

With Tabini, there was quite often no round of tea before talk. One went into the room and delivered information, answered quick questions, heard the aiji's instructions and bowed one's way out. The aiji's schedule would have the aiji awash in tea if he were not, to a certain degree, abrupt and untraditional.

Today, however, there was tea offered, setting a genteel pace for such a private meeting. And a cup of tea provided time enough to recall the heir's invasion of the party, the problems he had presented the aiji's house, and the various reasons the aiji might have for a summons of the paidhi-aiji which did not involve the paidhi's agenda with the space program, his office, or the location of his missing brother. One waited for the aiji to declare the subject of the meeting. And waited, until the tea ran out.

"My son," Tabini began ominously, and then took an unexpected curve . . . "suggests we link computers together, for ease of communication within the household, and one is not certain how much farther. He believes he can do this if he has certain manuals he declares to exist on the ship."

Bren drew in a breath, thinking rapidly, and finding himself at the edge of a cliff, and not at all the cliff he had planned. "To do that, aiji-ma, yes, he indeed has the skills do it, given computers with the capacity to connect. The aiji knows we do this in a limited fashion. But to establish that link for personal communications the young gentleman envisions, in the fashion the young gentleman has been accustomed to use on the ship—the changes the space program has brought would be slight, compared to the changes such a system would bring, implemented in full. And I must say, in all good will, aiji-ma, the regions are distraught enough—"

"Name these changes."

"Speed of information would increase. So would proliferation of bad information and rumor. Speed of daily events would increase. Secrets would travel down paths that would proliferate by the hour and change in retelling. The giving of decorous invitations and messages would meet the same challenges the custom encountered in the introduction of telephones. Communication would become more abrupt. And less formal. I cannot immediately foresee all the changes such a system would bring, but I advise against it, aiji-ma. Given the upheavals already troubling atevi life, I very much advise against opening that particular door for the young gentleman, no matter his frustrations with the pace of things. The ship operates entirely on linked computers. If one wants something, one does not go to a master of craft; one requests a computer to act, and the computer figuratively opens a book in some library and makes that information available instantly. It can contact another computer and has a message waiting for some associate the moment he sits down to use the machine, much like the message bowl in the foyer. But it leaves no papers behind. And it is subject to misuse. A skilled operator can reach out and affect a system half the ship away, or gain a key to one he is not supposed to enter. Security becomes a major concern."

"My son," Tabini said, and sighed, chin on fist. "My son, one fears, wants to recreate the ship."

"He will adjust his thinking, aiji-ma. He understands the ship very well, but he is only beginning to meet the world. The *aishidi'tat* must not see the heir as providing a more rapid pace of change than his father has done."

Tabini gazed at him a long moment in silence, with that remarkable pale stare. "Perhaps we erred not to keep him here with us. But one does not know how he would have survived, where we have been."

One could only guess what territory that covered: the aiji's survival had been a hard struggle, one that had left its mark on Tabini—he was harder, leaner, his eyes darting to small sounds. And he had grown more reticent, if that was possible.

"What he has learned on the ship, aiji-ma, will benefit atevi all his life—if these things are wisely delivered."

"Are they true things, paidhi-aiji? Are they truly profitable? Or are they like this computer system, fraught with immeasurable problems? And can the paidhi explain to the child why this should not be undertaken?"

It hit him with peculiar force, that question. No, it was not possible to explain such things to a boy who saw only the ship, and who had not truly met the world such things would disturb. The father might have met the problems inherent in hasty change; the son had yet to know there *were* problems.

"I shall at least try to explain to him, if the aiji wishes."

"Perhaps he will listen to you."

That was equally troubling, such a request from Cajeiri's father . . . who was accustomed to obedience from strangers. Not to have obedience from his own son—

"He will more aptly listen to Banichi, aiji-ma. And Banichi can say things very simply: I think he will say that if the young gentleman does such things it will create a great deal of bother *the young gentleman* will have to deal with."

Tabini had not smiled often since his return. This smile began subtly, and became an outright laugh as he sat upright. "The paidhi has a certain insight into my son's thinking."

Tabini remained amused, and the slight smile lightened everything. It was a vast relief to find communication opening up, both of them finally seeming on the same wave length about risk and change, and with something like the old easiness coming back to their conversation. Things southward, Bren thought, must be going well—the mop-up of the rebellion was proceeding. And things with the boy must not be all that bad: certain families might be disturbed to know their offspring was somewhat self-centered and not quite thinking of their interests so much as his own ambitions. But a future aiji *was* somewhat self-centered.

"Well, well," Tabini said then, leaning back and seeming to have recovered his sense of humor. "So the dish at Mogari-nai is up. And Jase-aiji speaks to my son in front of your staff . . . I have had the transcript." A small wave of his hand dismissed any report on the details. "And Toby-nadi is found. This personal news surely pleases you."

"Immeasurably so, aiji-ma." He was so relieved he only then recalled that the whole conversation, ergo the transcript, had been in ship-speak.

"Amazing feat," Tabini said, "to locate a specific boat, in so much water."

"Your staff may have told you, aiji-ma—" Straight to the one piece of news he must not seem to conceal—nor had he any such intent. "The ship established much more precise surveillance over the world during the disturbance. It has—I surmise—established numbers for the entire planet, in a gridwork of precise coordinates. It dropped ground stations—*these*, I have discovered, are the mysterious landings in the reports: I believe they must be communications relays, but I am far from certain, or whether they are even connected to this mapping system. I am seeking clarification on that point—I am not familiar with the details of the technology, and it was not sent through my office." And dared he tell the rest, the precise location of persons available with the equipment his staff carried?

A world where hiding became impossible, where, first of all persons, *Assassins* were in possession of such devices, starting with his own staff? It was another earthquake of information as profound as a computer web, and Jase had blithely handed the technology to his security staff without consulting him.

But then, the station had deployed its mysterious ground-based devices without consulting Murini, either . . . and God knew what *they* did.

"Aiji-ma, my own staff carries certain items related to that technology, which they were given on the station, and I have only just been apprised of the fact. We rushed from the ship to the shuttle, with very limited time to settle certain matters. I did not approve. I have the greatest misgivings about that technology existing down here."

"Down here."

"On the planet, aiji-ma." So profoundly his view of the universe had been set in the heavens, not on the planet where he was born. He had to re-center himself in the planet-based universe. He had to make certain other mental adjustments, urgently. "I think it may possibly constitute a very dangerous development—useful to the Pilots' Guild, but as worrisome in the hands of the Assassins as the computer link in the hands of the public. It will possibly give precise locations of anyone who has such a device on his person. It can inform anyone who carries it precisely where he is, on a map. Useful—but fraught with possibilities."

"Interesting," said the most dangerous schemer the *aishidi'-tat* had ever produced. "Indeed, interesting, paidhi. Is there any means of detecting this technology in operation?"

"Anything that transmits, I would suspect, can be detected by the right instrument, but this location device primarily receives, one assumes, and it is something outside my expertise. I ask the aiji not to reveal its existence to the Guild at large. I am sure of my own staff, that they will not reveal it, and I may have to order it suppressed, even destroyed—but numerous installations fallen from the heavens and sitting in vegetable fields across the aishidi'tat are clearly within general notice."

Tabini smiled, this time with darker humor. "Tell me, paidhi-aiji, is my son expert in this technology, too?"

"This, one doubts the young gentleman has theorized, since he has never been that far lost—aboard the ship. But we did track him—in his wanderings aboard. He may know this."

"A wonder," Tabini said, and the smile generously persisted. "Ask your sources these details, paidhi-aiji, and report to me. Should we worry about the ship-aijiin's motives in bestowing this technology on the world?"

"I think they originated this notion in support of your administration, aiji-ma, or I would be exceedingly alarmed. I believe that they planned to turn this system over to you, if they had been able to find you in the first place—which I think they could not, since you had no such device. I think it was done to be able to point to precise spots in the world and track events, and to report to you where your enemies were. The station's ability to see things on the planet is very detailed. This system helps describe the location of what they see. The world is now numbered and divided according to their numbers, and one does not believe this would comfort the traditionalists."

"Indeed. And by this they have found your brother." Tabini stretched his feet out before him, seeming thoroughly comfortable. "The lords will assemble for ordinary business; committees will enter session. Your office is functioning. You are seeking to reestablish the shuttles."

The summation. Change of topic. Or introduction of another one, which might wend its way back to the first. "Yes, aiji-ma."

"A very reasonable priority. But what will the shuttles bring down to us when they fly? More of these mysterious landings? Technology in support of these devices? Persons? Ogun-aiji has been in charge of the station during the ship's absence, and we have had no contact with him for an extended time. One has not had great confidence in Yolanda-paidhi before that: her man'chi, so to speak, is still not to us, and not to this world, and one has, while finding her useful, never wholly understood her motives. She has been resident on the island, in daily communication with Ogun-aiji, receiving orders from him. It seems possible Ogun-aiji's intentions might also have drifted beyond those we understand."

"It does seem time to ask Jase what these items do, and to have a thorough account, aiji-ma, of what sort of machine they have dropped from orbit. There seems no great harm intended. I still believe these devices were intended to support your return—" "

"Or support Mospheira in an invasion?"

His pulse did a little skip. "One doubts Mospheira would be willing to undertake it on any large scale. Operatives, perhaps. But that my staff did not find any opportunity to tell me—Tano and Algini had the devices, and had them before my return. Unfortunately—they are in the field at the moment one would most want to ask them questions. Banichi does not know."

"Guild reticence, perhaps."

It was a proverb, that the Guild never admitted its assets, particularly in the field. In that light it was entirely understandable. If there seemed an advantage in having it, hell, yes, Banichi would take it, and settle accounts later. As he had. As Tano and Algini had. Whatever Ogun had been up to, Ogun had not cut his on-station staff out of the loop. There was that.

But coupled with the landings, and who knew what other changes . . . Tano and Algini had given him no explanation, presumably had given Banichi and Jago none, nor any to Cenedi, as he concluded.

"The aiji is justifiably concerned," he said, "to find they have sent technology down here that my office would not approve. The paidhi is concerned. My on-station staff knew things that were not communicated to me. This is all I know, aiji-ma, and one is distressed by it."

An eyebrow lifted. Some thought passed unspoken, behind that pale stare. The aiji said: "The paidhi's office will report when there is an answer. And this time I will receive the note."

Reference to a time when absolutely no message of his had gotten through, officially speaking. The gateway to communication was declared officially open again. At least that, even if the aiji held some thoughts private.

And he had a job to do—reins of power to gather up, fast, before Ogun's unilateral decisions—and the questions proliferating around these foreign devices landing on the mainland—did political damage to Tabini, or societal damage to the atevi. Whatever atevi got their hands on—they were damned good at figuring out. And that might already be in progress, in some distant province, if not directly at Tabini's orders.

He had done enough, himself, casually letting the aiji's heir get his hands into technology unexamined in its effects. Of course there was a network. Wherever there were computers, there was very soon a network. Small-area networks existed within offices, small nets had aided factories, had shared data within departments. There was the secure net over on Mospheira. And if Cajeiri could get adequate communications and a computer equipped to communicate, God knew what he could get his hands into, and God knew what mischief he could proliferate.

But what the heir had experienced as ordinary on the ship didn't just link departments to libraries: it spanned every activity on the ship. It embraced that whole world. It gave access everywhere, if one knew the keys. Cajeiri hadn't seen it as essentially different from ordinary on the station, which had been his second home, during the awakening of his mind to the outside world.

So an eight-year-old boy had come out of that environment and wanted to replicate that convenience in the world he had just re-entered. And Captain Ogun, in charge on the station, and finding the planet going to hell under him, had wanted to know where everything in the world was, at the flick of a key. Proliferation of satellites aloft—he strongly suspected that, after what Banichi had told him about the system. Ground installations of unknown capacity.

Seeing all these things, even Tabini, who had alarmed and unsettled his own generation with his penchant for human technology, Tabini, who was still sponsoring the building of a second starship—even Tabini saw reason for unease in this development, even while he was figuring out what he himself could do with it.

Do your job, paidhi. Advise us. Tell us what to do now. What about this notion of Ogun's?

It seemed a damned good question.

7

A teacup suffered in the aftermath of the interview: Bren was very glad it was not one of the historic good ones, but the carpet in Lord Tatiseigi's study certainly was a historic good one, and he had no idea how he had overset the cup, but there it lay, in pieces. He owed a great apology to Madam Saidin.

She looked at him curiously, then ordered it removed and a new one provided, while servants mopped and cleaned the carpet.

"I was distracted," he confessed to Banichi and Jago, who had come to see what the stir was that had relocated him and his computer to the library and brought such a scurry of activity into the study. They both looked at him a second or two longer than need have been, so that he felt exposed and disturbed and realized he could not be not utterly honest in his answers.

"Tano and Algini have reached the coast, nandi," Banichi said quietly, "and are heading out on the boat."

"Excellent." That *was* a certain relief, to know things were proceeding in that regard. To lay hands on Toby would at least let him trust that part of the universe was stable, if nothing else was.

"Is it worry for nand' Toby that distracts you, Bren-ji?" Jago asked him, lingering after Banichi had left on his own business.

"Perhaps," he said. "Worry for him. Worry for the boy." No, dammit. She deserved the whole truth. "Worry for the packages Ogun-aiji has decided to drop across the landscape . . . one earnestly hopes you have not revealed to your Guild the existence of that equipment the ship-aijiin gave you."

"No, Bren-ji," Jago said, and that *no* patched another hole in his universe, the fact that he had been afraid to ask where, in the scheme of things, their loyalty had necessarily come down on the question of illicit human equipment—whether it would be loyalty to their Guild, which on an ordinary day trumped every loyalty they owned, even to the aiji above all—or whether they would give it to him and his office, which properly ought to regulate things that came from the heavens.

"This is a dangerous thing, to have such power to locate individuals," he said. "It is worrisome. And it does not come without a great increase in orbiting satellites." The servants arrived in his new refuge, with a fresh pot of tea, and a new cup, which they offered. "Thank you, nadiin-ji. One hopes to keep this one intact."

"We understand," Jago said, not about the cup.

"What we taught the boy when he was in our care," he said when the servants had gone, "was not all he learned on the ship. His enthusiasm for innovation, for electronics—for all these things—he has brought with him. One did not fully grasp the extent of his ambition—or his researches, or his command of written ship-speak. The more one attempts to restrain him into the model of—one assumes—an ordinary young gentleman, the more he resorts to stratagems and technologies he learned on the ship. He has no concept of the planet, no understanding of the complexity of its systems, or its history. The War of the Landing means nothing to him."

Jago shrugged and arched an eyebrow. "He will learn."

"One wonders if Jaidiri-nadi—" This was Tabini's new chief of staff, a sturdy, bright fellow. "—is up to the challenge he has. He cannot possibly understand what he is dealing with, or what the boy may think of."

"Jaidiri and his partner," Jago said, "have just had their own experience with the boy, in his escaping their watch. They were greatly embarrassed—and not to be caught twice, one thinks. They are not stupid men."

"One would think not," he agreed. No one could be stupid, who protected Tabini-aiji; but learning to anticipate what Cajeiri might be up to was another matter. They had had two years to experience the boy, Jaidiri and his team had not. They were Taibeni, and had, at least, some advantage of communication with Cajeiri's young attendants, who they might hope would inform them of the boy's truly dangerous notions; but one wondered if the new security team, considering southern Assassins, had remotely appreciated the difficulty the young gentleman posed.

"We have warned them," Jago said ruefully. "Now, indeed, one hopes they do understand the problem. They have not to this hour set up their own surveillance within the apartment: that proposal is creating a disturbance with Madiri's staff, who wishes them to use Cenedi's arrangement, but the matter is under discussion." Madiri was the caretaker of Ilisidi's domain, doubtless Guild, and no one to be trifled with, nor was his immediate, and younger, staff.

"So argument exists."

This prompted a laugh, a dark one. "Argument would be a mild word. Phone calls have flown between the Bu-javid and Tirnamardi. Cenedi is sending a team back here to investigate what the new men wish to install."

"Jaidiri is new to his rank," he observed in some alarm. "And at odds with Cenedi?"

"There is rancor in several households," Jago said, glancing down, and up again. "Various man'chiin are vying for positions within the aiji's household. The aiji would, by his will, choose only Taibeni, if he were deaf to objections. The aiji-dowager would wish him to choose at least two from the East. The

Atageini of course want a foothold within his guard. The Ajuri
are pressing for Ajuri clan to serve at least on domestic staff,
and also to have a post with the young gentleman."

He hadn't realized that little Ajuri clan had their bid in. He
knew that others, notably in the midlands and even in the
west, were trying to get members at least into domestic staff.
Where clan members were in service, information necessarily
flowed, and domestic voices, however discreet and respectful,
could still insert a judicious opinion or two into the aiji's ear.
Such influence was beyond a valuable resource: it was reassurance for the several clans who had been attempting to straddle
the political fence during Murini's takeover, a redemption for
them—and a damned great security risk for Tabini if he let certain clans into his immediate staff—or onto his son's or his
wife's. But conversely, he didn't want to alienate them and
make those fence-sitting clans consider other self-protective
actions, either.

"More to the point," Jago said in a very quiet voice, "The
Easterners who serve the aiji-dowager are *not* well-disposed toward the Ajuri, a historical issue, relating to numerous insults,
and have no good feeling about the Atageini's competence to
participate in the dowager's level of security, this on recent experience. In particular, this opinion has profoundly insulted
the Atageini staff, and there is now personal rancor between
the major domo and the young gentleman's two assigned
guards, from among the Atageini—who are not welcomed by
the Taibeni youngsters, either. Now that Taibeni are guarding
the aiji himself and have begun giving orders in the household,
the ferment has markedly increased, and one perceives the
Atageini guards are attempting to politic with Madiri's staff."

He had felt a certain strain there: he had put it down to the
extreme exertion of recent days and the stress the aiji's new
staff must place on security. He had not, however, twigged to
the strain of the caretaker staff and the dowager's own security

against the intrusion. The Easterners must not relax their guard during the dowager's absence: that was a given—and they had to contend with a new power structure around Tabini and a formative one around the heir—not to mention, one supposed, the presence of Lady Damiri, who was Atageini-born and had suddenly ambitious Ajuri relatives, bringing along staff members of those two clans. It was not a pretty situation—amusing on one level, but posing a security risk in the diversion of attention and the slowdown of communication; and if Cenedi, who never left the dowager unattended, was coming back here to see to the matter, the tension must be epic—tastefully managed as far as outside visitors were concerned, but absolutely epic.

Under said circumstances, the aiji had to be particularly upset at his son's faring about the halls without escort—the Taibeni youths hardly counted—which only pointed up the inability of the wrangling staff to manage one eight-year-old boy. The boy had found the security lax enough to let him get past it. That was not pretty, either, and likely furnished ammunition to the anti-Taibeni staff against the aiji's guards.

"Banichi," Jago informed him, "has ventured to attempt to mediate within the household, and it was then that Cenedi decided to return, at least long enough to communicate directly with Madiri."

Meaning a call had likely gone from Banichi to Cenedi, with or without the aiji's knowledge, telling him to get here—leaving the dowager at Tirnamardi, something Cenedi would be very reluctant to do. "A disturbing situation. One hopes Banichi has not gotten himself entangled." Meaning *his* whole household, which was encamped in an Atageini apartment.

"He hopes the same," she said. "But it is by no means easy to balance political considerations with security considerations—there *are* no nonpolitical choices of Guild to serve in the aiji's personal guard, under these circumstances, and cer-

tain influences are fighting hard for position—not even to mention the recent events within the Guild."

That Jago even alluded to that meant that there was a serious question in that quarter. And "serious" with the Guild
meant serious. "Is there any chance the household is already
compromised?"

"That is Banichi's great worry, nandi. You stand in an
Atageini house, guarded by a staff more affiliated with Tabini-
aiji; the aiji is guesting in an Eastern house, bringing in Padi
Valley staff to guard his son and balance the Taibeni influence,
not to mention the Ajuri setting up a fuss about the Taibeni. Ilisidi is hosted in the Padi Valley, conducting politics within
the recent borderland of the disturbance, while applicants from
her province in the East are dividing their efforts to gain her attention, and scurrying back and forth between her staff here
and closer influences, like Cenedi, in her immediate entourage. The Easterners have delayed their flight home. And
the dowager and Lord Tatiseigi hosted the new lord of the
Kadagidi at a banquet last night."

"The Kadagidi." Murini's own clan, which had attempted to
disavow Murini in his fall from power. And the very clan that
had been shelling Tatiseigi's estate. They held a dinner party?
Good God. "With the aiji's knowledge, Jago-ji?"

"Very possibly," Jago said. "It may be the particular reason
for her sudden choice to sojourn at Tirnamardi, precisely to
reestablish ties with that clan and forestall a Kadagidi approach
to the Atageini alone, or worse, forestalling the Kadagidi from
continuing rancor and another attack on Lord Tatiseigi—who
does not view the Kadagidi favorably at the moment, new leadership or not. You see how it is, Bren-ji, and why this is a very
inconvenient time to have Cenedi separated from the dowager's guard over a spat between factions. He will have sharp
words for the dowager's caretaker, one fears, and sharp words
for the young gentleman."

"One can see why," Bren said, and it was a difficult call, where to apply sympathy—to Ilisidi's caretaking staff, who viewed their standards as under assault, housing the aiji's very modernized staff, or to the aiji's newly-constituted Taibeni bodyguard, who had come under political attack from every quarter but Taiben, and whose young senior, Jaidiri, had just made one glaring mistake, in relying on Cajeiri to stay behind family doors like any other atevi youngster.

It was not a happy situation, and both sides owned a certain amount of fault in the general disturbance. So, indeed, did Cajeiri for exploiting it, but anger was in the ascendant there, too, one had seen that: anger, boredom, and a passion for things that had once been allowed and were never going to be allowed again.

"It is an entirely unfortunate situation, Bren-ji," Jago said. "One protects the paidhi-aiji. This is the most we can do."

She looked so tired. He said, quietly, "If we can rely on Madam Saidin for my present safety and comfort, Jago-ji, one wishes you personally do so, and take a little luxury for yourself. You and Banichi—indeed, Tano and Algini, too, have rested far too little in far too long. Efficiency, Jago-ji. Efficiency surely depends on rest. And will we not encourage Madam Saidin's staff to feel trusted, if we trust them?"

She cast him a troubled look. "There have been changes at every level of the Bu-javid, Bren-ji. Your staff needs to know what these changes are, where they are, and who is now attached to whom. Our return, aside from the aiji's, is one stone into an already troubled pond."

Not alone the new people, but the new alliances were in question. Under what doors the connecting threads now ran was a mystery even to his staff. His staff was consequently pursuing everything, reweaving the informational web that had once been second nature to them—before they had spent two years and more in space and gotten entirely out of the loop. The fact they had lost their residence to an interloping southern clan, of all things, the Farai, who could not be dislodged, or whom the aiji did not dare dislodge, considering the instability in the South—was a disturbing situation, and one they viewed with indignation.

"I do promise," he said, "to keep a certain prudence in my own contacts, and I solemnly swear I shall in no wise attempt to elude my senior staff, not even for a party."

A grin, a decided broad grin from Jago.

"And nand' Cajeiri is no longer within your personal responsibililty," he added pointedly. "It is impossible for you to track him or to be responsible—or even to feel you should have known where he was."

"True," she acknowledged, and let go a little breath. "One has acknowledged it, indeed, Bren-ji, but the habit is strong."

"Relay the same to Banichi. He has hardly stopped moving long enough for me to speak to him."

The smile reappeared, though subdued. "He has had certain responsibilities outside the house, Bren-ji. But those will soon cease."

"May one ask?" If it was Guild business, the answer would be no, she could not say. If it was the aiji's—

"He has pursued certain inquiries regarding the aiji's recent staff, approaching those who would not divulge privileged information to Jaidiri. Jaidiri was too proud, too confident when he arrived, too prone to consult only his own associates and this offended certain persons. This is changing. Jaidiri has now requested assistance, and is making respectful contact with those persons of the service staff. Banichi has provided a more auspicious beginning and has pursued those reconnections, and the security questions."

No wonder Banichi seemed to be burning the candle at either end. Tabini-aiji might outright have drafted him back into his service; but hadn't. And in some sense of debt and common-sense efficiency, Banichi was doing as much for the aiji as could be done from within the paidhi's household. He must be doing a fair job of knocking heads together, by what Jago reported. Jaidiri was a proud young man. And Banichi must have had serious words with him about the heir's escape.

"One understands, Jago-ji," Bren said. "But rest. Do rest. And get Banichi to rest."

And with that parting shot, he took his leave, headed back to his reports and his papers in his study.

He had supper with his security staff that evening—Banichi, whether on his advice or not, finally took the time for a leisurely dinner, and that pleased him.

And when he had gone to bed, Jago came into the room, and undressed and settled in with him, very welcome company.

"We have had a message couriered from Tano, Bren-ji," she said, as she settled. "They have report of a possible sighting. They will not communicate with us again until they have gotten nand' Toby back to the harbor."

"Excellent," he said with a deep sigh, and rolled over and put his arms around her, his head against her shoulder. Her hands moved. He enjoyed an interlude of very pleasant forgetfulness, of quite reckless abandon—the sort of luxury two years in space had afforded them. Their two-year plethora of safe and secure nights had gone. Very few nights since had been safe, and fewer had been private, and they both took advantage of this one, until he quite slipped away from all awareness.

He was deep in a peaceful sleep when the light unceremoniously flared overhead. He flailed his way half-upright, and saw Jago on her feet.

"The heir is missing, nandi," she said straightway.

"Missing." His heart thudded. A midnight trip to the library? "Banichi?"

"On his way to the aiji's residence," Jago said, and grabbed her shirt from the chair.

"This is too much." He rolled out of bed and snatched up his clothes—he could be useful, he thought. He and his staff had experience tracking the young miscreant. Two years of experience. And the aiji's residence was their destination: he needed clean clothes. He found them himself, in the bureau and the closet, and dressed as fast as he could pull them on.

Midnight excursions. Where?

God, had the rascal decided to leave the Bu-javid? Go down the hill to the hotel, where his escort's relatives stayed?

Decided to go find his great-grandmother—all because he was in disgrace with his parents?

"One only hopes he has not gone down to the hotel," he said, and added, "or the train station."

Jago shot him a look at that last, and zipped her jacket shut. She came immediately to help him with his necktie. That froth of lace could *not* be left dangling, not if the building were afire—

"He might have gone to the Atageini," he said, on a breath expelled as she finished a hasty, expert knot. "Is there word from Banichi?"

"No," Jago said. She had the com in her ear. And was buckling on her sidearm. By now there was a light outside the door, the whole household waked by their stirring about.

"Let us go," he said, trying to still his frantic heartbeats, while every instinct he had said go straight down to the train station, to the cars that came and went in the night, supplying the Bu-javid, carrying away its unwanted elements. But that was not where protocol dictated. That was not the source of information. Things had best go in order. The train station had its own guards. And a train could be stopped with a phone call. The thing was to find the boy quietly, and not publicize the latest escapade to the national news services. "Let us find Banichi, Jago-ji."

*   *   *

Bodyguards clustered about the aiji's outside door—Taibeni, the lot of them assembled, and grimly unwilling to let anyone else in, if the door had not opened from inside. Banichi, in contact with Jago, met them there, with two of Cenedi's men— and Banichi's face was completely grim as he nodded a signal to go aside for a moment, beside an ornate table and a mirror.

"Antaro was found unconscious on the lower level of the servant stairs," Banichi said, "and Jegari is not found at all."

"God." That in Mosphei', under *this* roof. "The aiji?"

"Safe," Banichi said. "The aiji's staff was caught entirely unaware, Bren-ji."

"But how could they be?" It might be a Guild question. But it was incomprehensible to him. "Who could get in? *What* lower level, nadi-ji?"

"Staff is suspect. Cenedi has arrived in the midst of the search, and he has entered the aiji's drawing room, but the dowager's motives are in some question in certain quarters and the Taibeni security does not want him near the aiji. Weapons are at issue. And there is within the servant passages, Bren-ji, a door which leads down to a private escape, two floors below."

"Good God," he said, hardly able to get a word out. He felt literally sick at his stomach. "*She* would never attack Cajeiri, of all people." Even granted, in atevi politics, the aiji-dowager might remotely, conceivably, have motives against her grandson, her great-grandson was already hers.

And a Taibeni struck down? Was it window dressing? His just-sleeping brain was skipping all over the map. Had Taibeni Ragi made some move against a half-Atageini heir—of their own blood?

"We concur," Banichi said, regarding Ilisidi's lack of motive. "But the aiji's staff has cast suspicion in a wide circle, even to the paidhi's household."

Us? Bren wondered, in utter shock. Me?

"Outrageous!" Jago said, with a hand on her sidearm.

"We are officially believed innocent," Banichi said, with a nod toward the shut and guarded door, behind which the aiji and Cenedi were in conference. "Sensible conclusion, considering we, of all possible suspects, have nowhere to put the young gentleman. The Bu-javid, meanwhile, is in lockdown."

Lockdown was one of those ship-words his staff had appropriated. "The train station as well, nadi?"

"Trains are being stopped and searched, nandi."

Trains were not all that left the Bu-javid, meanwhile. Nor was there any way to look into every apartment in the Bu-javid. Ancient rights. Ancient prerogatives.

And meanwhile the heir was in mortal danger, and the damned Taibeni, hot to prove their own competency, were pointing fingers at *his* apartment—an *Atageini* apartment, to boot.

" 'Nichi-ji, please gain access for us. We will see the aiji."

"Yes," Banichi said, and was off like a shot, while Jago stayed by him, glowering at everyone but Cenedi's men—there were Taibeni, there were several just arrived Bren didn't know, and he didn't trust any of them, not at this moment. If violence had gone after the aiji's family, his own household might be a logical next target, and his bodyguard was literally scattered from here to the coast. Jago stood her watch close at his side, a looming and baleful presence.

Certain looks came back at them, too, from the aiji's Taibeni guard. If no less than the aiji-dowager was suspect in some eyes, much more so must be anyone housed with Tatiseigi, who had his own ambitions for the boy—but he refused to doubt Madam Saidin and her people, down the hall, absolutely refused. His own immediate and reasonable suspicion was Tatiseigi's neighbors the Kadagidi, Murini's clan—the source of all the recent troubles—and Tatiseigi's recent guests, at the estate.

Had the dinner party been only a diversion, a means of turning suspicion for what they intended? Had they gotten into staff somehow—God, even in the Atageini Guildsmen the boy's great-uncle had lent for his defense? The Kadagidi clan, unfortunately, was centuries interwoven with Tatiseigi's, by kinship and favors given.

And that historical fact could have suspicion falling on Cajeiri's own mother, Lady Damiri herself, and particularly her maids, who were right under Tabini's roof at the moment. The maids and staff that attended Damiri indeed might have a motive if the name of the game was another overthrow of the aiji her husband, this time with the half-Atageini heir firmly in their own hands.

And never leave out the Taibeni themselves—who hated the Atageini. Tabini's bodyguard were new men, Taibeni, like Cajeiri's young staff, but, no, one of that clan had been left lying unconscious in a passageway. Taibeni kidnappers would not have injured her and left her there, surely not, nor would her brother Jegari, under any reasonable circumstances, have betrayed his young lord—he just could not believe it of the boy. The aiji's new guard, Jaidiri and his men, might turn into prime suspects—but never those two youngsters, not unless there was some completely hidden connection that no research had turned up, some man'chi undetected, that caught even atevi completely unawares—

God help them all, he thought; they might well be on the verge of a second coup, this time to set up a regency for the underage heir, or possibly to dispose of an heir with unwelcome blood connections: either was possible, and there were all too many people in the *aishidi'tat* who wished the paidhi dead right along with the current administration.

He could not think about that. That danger was not even a consideration in the need to get the facts straight and most urgent of all, to find the boy and get him back.

Banichi had gone into the drawing room where the aiji was.

He came out again. "Come," he said, and brought them both with him into the study, where Tabini and Damiri stood with Cenedi. Both were engaged with Jaidiri and Madiri in very heated conversation. The nature of it all Bren could not immediately figure, except, from Jaidiri's side, it regarded incompetence, a designation which one feared meant the dowager's domestic staff. Madiri looked as if he had something caught in his throat and wanted to spit it.

"The dowager knows no such thing," Cenedi said strongly, "nor has she any knowledge. She is in the air at this moment, on her way here to answer her grandson's questions in person— if we can get clearance for her plane to land."

The latter with a burning glance at Jaidiri.

"She will have it," Tabini said with a dismissive motion of his hand.

"Aiji-ma," Jaidiri began in protest, and Cenedi cut him off short.

"We have three planes aloft that took off before anyone ever shut down the airport, gods less fortunate! We have trains moving, we had simple trucks coming and going for the better part of an hour before we had a report, let alone put up barriers. *I* have had time to get here on a scheduled flight, and what other trucks have now gone to outlying airports or train stations? No one knows!"

"That is being answered," Banichi said somberly, as Tabini glowered and Damiri simply paced the floor, her arms folded and her lips pressed to a thin line.

"Aiji-ma," Jago said quietly, arriving inside, and bowed, and came close, bowing again. "The young gentleman's escort, Jegari, has just phoned from the airport. He lost contact with the kidnappers there. He hoped he could stop them taking off, but two of the three planes had left the ground before he reached the airport security office, the third shortly after. There was no stopping them, aiji-ma. They are in the air."

Damn, Bren thought. From there—south? It was a disaster.

"The Guild has grounded all other flights, aiji-ma," Jago said.

"Too damned late," Damiri said, from behind Tabini's chair, the first words she'd uttered.

"The boy followed them?" Tabini asked sharply. "How?"

"One is given to understand," Jago said, "that he escaped at the airport. He has not reported the identity of any aircraft. Guild is questioning him at this moment, aiji-ma."

"The airport and these planes leaving may have been a diversion," Jaidiri said from the side of the room. "They may have deliberately let the Taibeni boy escape, to give out that news."

Jago had her own electronics, was into the information flow within the staff, clearly, and still listening with one ear, her finger pressing that unit close. "The boy jumped from a moving truck. Cajeiri is now alone with these people and unconscious, as Jegari last saw. He observed their truck go toward the freight depot as he was trying to reach an office." A pause as she, and by his look, Banichi, both listened to what was apparently an ongoing account. "The boy said he knew the men, aiji-ma. He had seen them in the apartment, as the dowager's guests—"

"Caiti," Cenedi said sharply.

"Easterners," Jaidiri muttered, as Cenedi's back stiffened.

"The aiji-dowager is approaching the city," Cenedi retorted, "and has no part in this. Her relations with Caiti are not close. Where was your staff, nadi?"

A sore point, clearly. "Men of yours as well, nadi."

"Drugged," Banichi said shortly. "The heir's entire guard, nadiin."

"Except the young attendants," Jaidiri muttered.

"And *who* carried away my son?" Damiri asked sharply. "Who, on this staff, nadiin, drugged Guild security? *And why is no one preventing that plane from landing in the south?*"

*   *   *

The silence persisted a few beats. Nobody knew the first. Nobody had the resources for the second. Nothing outflew an airliner. Ground resources in the south were scarce—not non-existent: scarce, and difficult to contact in a secure mode.

"Banichi, Cenedi-nadi," Tabini said, and beckoned them close. "Nand' paidhi." Tabini beckoned to him.

He had not expected it. He went, and he bowed, and knelt down by Tabini's chair, in intimate hearing. And what the aiji's guard thought of this conference one could only imagine: the man must be seething.

But then Tabini said, "Jaidiri-nadi," and beckoned that man to join them. Jaidiri did so, a stiff, disapproving presence.

"The culprits are likeliest Eastern," Tabini said, "and our position is that we will not negotiate with them in whatever they demand. If my grandmother goes East, nand' paidhi, you will join her."

"Yes, aiji-ma."

That the kidnappers were Eastern was certainly the most logical assumption in the current situation—and Tabini's position was the only position he could take in the situation. Both Tabini and his grandmother had to maintain their grip, and after them, that boy, and, no, Ilisidi might actually have done in a husband and maybe a son and might conceivably be aiming at her grandson, Tabini, but the boy she alone had raised—

God, had *that* been part of Tabini's motive in sending his son *and* Ilisidi on that voyage? To forge *that* sense of connection, that unbreakable man'chi? To make his son and heir safe from his own great-grandmother?

The mind jolted absolutely sideways, when it needed desperately to be here and now, eye to eye with Tabini, as Tabini laid a hand on his shoulder, a grip that bruised. "You are valued, paidhi-aiji. You are *valued.*"

"Aiji-ma, my value in this situation is my persuasion. I beg to try."

"Defend my grandmother," Tabini said sharply. "Thankless though the task may be, keep her alive, paidhi-aiji, her *and* my son. We want her back."

"Aiji-ma." Acceptance of his proposal—with all it meant. Persuasion. He was profoundly touched, and simultaneously terrified.

Assure the aiji-dowager turned from Eastern to western man'chi? Break the influence of her neighbors, if it was a factor—if, somehow, Ilisidi *was* in on this maneuver? Give her a politically safe turn-around if she was actually *behind* the kidnapping?

The boy being attached to his grandmother and not to his father . . . the boy might become a force in the East, a rival claimant, to shift the balance of power. All these things flashed across his horizon like summer lightning.

And he had no choice. "I shall do everything possible, aiji-ma. I shall do absolutely everything possible."

"Cenedi-nadi," Tabini said, and as Bren got up, Cenedi came close, not without Jaidiri's frowning and jealous attention.

"Nandi," Cenedi said. And if there was a man in the room at an unenviable focus of attention, it was Cenedi . . . *sent* here, in advance of the dowager taking action. He was, literally, in danger of his life, if Tabini had any suspicion at all.

Or not. Tabini, like Ilisidi, was capable of playing a very, very subtle hand.

"Go to the airport. There is no need for my grandmother to come to the Bu-javid. We *know* where one of those planes has gone, most surely, nadi. Do you dispute this likelihood?"

"One does not dispute, nandi," Cenedi said. And without *aiji-ma*. No acknowledgment of man'chi. *Only* Cenedi was, being in the household of the aiji-dowager, entitled to that familiarity.

"The paidhi will accompany you and the aiji-dowager: she may take command of the search in the East. One trusts she *will* act for the *aishidi'tat.*"

Cenedi, his face deep-graven by duty and the dowager's service, frowned. But this time he bowed deeply. "In her name, nand' aiji, and subject to her orders."

Tabini's hand shot out and seized Cenedi's forearm. "Return my son, Cenedi-nadi. And her, *and* the paidhi-aiji. Return them alive."

"Yes," Cenedi said: how did one refuse the force of that order? Bren froze, and remembered to breathe as Tabini released Cenedi's arm.

A second bow. Then Cenedi straightened and walked out. Bren hesitated a breath, a glance at the aiji. They were leaving Tabini—abandoning him to Jaidiri's competency, and to the attitudes and conflicted man'chiin of the court, all of which evoked the greatest misgivings. He wished, not for the first time, that Tabini's guard of many years had survived the coup, and that every resource Tabini had once had was around him now. . . .

But they were not. He bowed. He glanced from Banichi to Jago, and bowed slightly to Lady Damiri, and walked out, hearing Banichi and Jago fall in behind him.

Cenedi was outside that room. They went together, with Cenedi's two men, out into the outer hall, where Taibeni stood on guard.

"You will be welcome, nandi, one has every confidence," Cenedi paused to say, plain to be heard. "Her plane will be landing—one assumes it will get clearance."

"One is certain it will," Bren murmured; and Jago:

"I shall see to the packing." Leaving Banichi with him, and *not* leaving him alone with Cenedi, she went down the hall at a fast clip, and Banichi nodded to Cenedi. "We are ready."

"Nadi," Cenedi said, and with a nod of his head to Bren, "nandi."

And they headed for the lift, with no more than that.

No question that plane was going to stay on the ground any longer than it took to refuel, not unless the dowager was hellbent on an interview with her grandson, and one doubted that would happen until there was a definitive answer, one doubted it extremely.

"The hotel has been searched, nandi," Cenedi said after they were in the lift, after one of Cenedi's men pushed the button. "Caiti's party has indeed remained. And left in the night. One plane has turned east. One north. One south."

North was no problem. South, however, south was bad news. Scary news. If anything had moved south, it would likely be the Assassins' Guild, not the paidhi, who had to deal with that.

And a plane *happened* to go south when Caiti's party moved east?

Their mission might, by that fact, be in the right direction; or it might be following a diversion. . . .

No. If, at very worst, the dowager *was* involved—

God, dinner with the Kadagidi. Her great-grandson smuggled out of *her* apartment—

No. No, and no. He refused, emotionally, stupidly, it might be, to believe it.

It could not be their concern: they had to deal quickly with the target they were given, and the best chance of stopping events short of a bloodbath was the dowager's going back to her own region and knocking critical heads together, among her own neighbors . . . granted she was *not* behind this, God help them. If Caiti had made some deal with the south—the dowager knocking heads was not an inconsiderable force. The paidhi couldn't be everywhere. He couldn't *do* a damned thing if they had taken the boy south. He *could* do something in the East, with his connection to the dowager.

His own best use was as her support, and as a representative

of the aiji's confidence in her . . . and ultimately as a negotia-
tor, once he had the whole truth of what was happening . . .
whatever happened.

He was, he realized as the elevator plummeted toward the
train station, woefully short of staff, short of resources. These
Eastern conservatives would respect appearances. Force. A full
staff. He had no domestics: his personal staff was up on the station. Tano and Algini were at the coast trying to get his brother
back and could not join them in time to back up Banichi and
Jago. For servants—he would have the dowager's staff, at Malguri, presuming that was where they were going. But he had by
no means all the wardrobe; he couldn't even pack his needful
items. He had to trust Jago for that—and did. She would bring
his computer: that, he wanted with him, where he could at
very least wipe it, if things went wrong. He hoped there was
nothing else waiting in the wings, no other assassins aiming at
Tabini from within the dowager's staff—

God, God, when one stopped taking security for granted,
within a household, there were so many things to think of.

And priorities had suddenly shifted. He had, as best he
could, to rearrange the pieces on the board.

"It might be well if we recall Tano and Algini, 'Nichi-ji. One
assumes their assistance would be useful to you and Jago."

"If we can reach them at this point," Banichi said. "One will
try to contact them."

"Surely it was not Guild, nadiin-ji," Bren ventured to say, in
the company of those who sincerely were. "Surely—if it
were—"

"If it were Guild, the Taibeni boy would not have escaped,"
Banichi answered him—the one thing all of them could well
conclude. "Unless escape was part of the plan."

The car whisked past level after level, bound downward on
a high-level security key. Bren's stomach floated, in the precipitate drop.

And he clung to one hope. The kidnappers hadn't killed anyone. Their light-handedness argued for amateurs rather than Guild, argued for someone who feared bloodfeud that might well bring allies in against them.

But their being amateurs had its own particular dangers— not least, the possibility someone in their number would panic and all hell would break loose.

And, the other worrisome component of the problem, someone had let them into the dowager's apartment. Someone who was at this very moment close to the aiji, being either part of his staff or the dowager's, because, without that help, there was no way on earth they could have gotten in to reach the boy.

The lift hit bottom. So did Bren's stomach. Banichi, meanwhile, was on his small com before the door opened, issuing orders while he kept an unceremonious and surely distracted handhold on Bren's arm and pulled him along in Cenedi's wake: it hurt, and that was all but unprecedented. Banichi was entirely on edge.

Cenedi's two men meanwhile went ahead of them around the corner of the elevator bank, heading toward the trains that came and went in this heart of the Bu-javid complex. In better times, a small train had always waited in the event of the aiji's need—and one sat there, now, on a concrete-rimmed siding, an engine with three cars, the way it always had been, and the middle one a luxury special belonging to the aiji. There it sat waiting, apparently unscathed in the interregnum, and Cenedi's men, jogging ahead of them, split up short of the cars, one heading up to the engine, one moving to open the door of that middle car. That man went inside first, to be sure of it.

So they had clearance to use *that* train, *that* car. Bren now had no doubt where they were going. Banichi was moving fast, with Cenedi, and Bren kept up, dragged along, as it were. They reached the car and both of them, behind him, shoved him roughly up the atevi-scale steps.

They followed, and pulled the door to behind them. It shut with a thump.

Bren caught his balance against the transverse brass railing inside, near the bar counter. "Will we wait for Jago, Banichi-ji?"

"We shall wait, nandi," Banichi said distractedly, clearly listening to something else, and, thus assured, Bren worked his way among the padded red-velvet seats and small tables, and on to the rear of the car, the position he had always favored as simply less in the way of traffic.

They were as safe here as armor plating could make them. The windows were bulletproof and shaded in red velvet, affording not even the hint of a target.

Cenedi meanwhile spoke to Banichi in that shorthand the Guild used, half with handsigns. Bren caught enough to know that they were sure of the dowager's plane's security, and would have it or another plane fueled and diverted to their use, on their subsequent flight—likely a second plane, since the transcontinental flight needed a longer range. Cenedi indicated that the dowager was bringing all her security with her, leaving only Cajeiri's guards in the Bu-javid apartment, and that would reinforce them considerably.

Meanwhile, Bren thought he caught, via the conversation between those two, that air traffic control was reporting on the three planes that had already taken off. Directions had not changed: one eastward, one northward, and one bound to the hostile south. And he understood from that conversation, too, that Lord Keimi, lord of the Taibeni, had not been in the city, that he had gone back home two days ago, and that he now was coming in by train, to arrive by morning. That was a relief: Tabini could rely on Lord Keimi, absolutely, and to hell with critics trying to dictate the political composition of his body-guard and staff. Lord Keimi's arrival would take some of the pressure off Jaidiri, and that was to the good, within the staff.

But Lord Keimi had just had two of his own injured in this situation, and he would arrive with fire in his eye, bent on answers from someone . . . not to mention the youngsters' parents were probably coming in with him.

And, again, *who* had taken Cajeiri?

If the Taibeni boy had gotten to a security office phone, what had he reported, and what did Banichi know, by now, that Banichi was too busy giving orders to explain?

He sat gnawing his lip, wanting to ask, but Banichi and Cenedi leaned close together, talking urgently, and that must not be interrupted.

Who *could* have gotten through Ilisidi's security net—if not Ilisidi? Or had someone dared take service under her roof and betray her interests?

There'd be blood for that—if betrayal was the case. This wasn't the ship, and whatever staffer had double-crossed Ilisidi of Malguri had better be on that plane with the kidnappers, unless suicide was part of the plan—or unless that wasn't the picture at all. He just didn't know. And the reason Banichi and Cenedi were talking like that, so intently, so quietly, without him—could be Banichi trying to feel out just what the hell was going on, and even to learn whether Cenedi himself knew more than he admitted of what was happening.

It was like the first stage of entry into a gravity well, a little courage, and a little bit of confidence, until one had reached a point of no return . . . both in circumstance and in emotional context. They were sliding over the rim—the moment they boarded the dowager's plane.

Dangerous. Ilisidi always was that. That never changed. But there had to be a way for a diplomat to bend the situation. Any situation.

The train started into motion, a slow, inexorable sense of force.

And it was not supposed to move. Not without Jago. That brought him to his feet.

"Banichi-ji."

"Jago is in the baggage car," Banichi said quietly, diverting his attention from his conversation with Cenedi. "The plane will be ready for us." With the information came a direct look from Banichi, a look that, after all their travels, he could read as well as Jago could: don't interrupt, don't rock the boat. Sit down, Bren-ji.

"Indeed," he said, and sat, immediately, as the train rolled slowly, inexorably on its course downward. He found himself half-paralyzed with thinking—the only action he could take at present, and with precious little data to do it on.

But if he believed one person present, he believed Banichi, and Banichi thought they were right to be here, surrounded by Cenedi's men. He was at least as safe as Banichi could make them, and Jago had made it aboard. She was riding with the baggage, probably sorting equipment into order as they went, and probably eavesdropping on Banichi and Cenedi all the while.

Nor could he be a trusting fool, where he sat. Banichi might mistake the acuteness of human hearing. He could *not* hear what they said, not, especially, over the sound of the train. But clearly he was not welcome in the current conversation, which was, if he could make a guess, deeply Guild, and deeply dangerous, and possibly even that rare thing among atevi—completely frank.

Emotionally—he—that human word—*liked* Tabini; but that was not the be-all and end-all of his decisions. He wanted Tabini in power if Tabini could hold power, that had to be the bottom line. He wanted the dowager in possession of her habitual power if she could keep it . . . he wanted both those things not to become mutually exclusive.

His wits had to stay sharp, was what: if there was a word in isolation he had overheard, he still had not the pieces to put together any sane plan out of those words—east, north, south, and the dowager. He daren't woolgather once he left the train. He daren't think about anything but what was immediately at hand.

Meanwhile he sat in a rail coach rocking along as fast as a train could move within the curved tunnel, in company with Banichi, the two of them outnumbered by Cenedi and his men from the start.

If, God forbid, he himself had to choose loyalties between Tabini and the dowager—he had one, *one* overriding concern: what it would do when the kyo came calling, expecting to find a stable situation, the way they had described it to be—if Tabini couldn't hold his own grandmother's man'chi, something had to shake out.

It might, in fact, rest on him to straighten it out—*keep* her in the *aishidi'tat*. *Keep* the *aishidi'tat* together. Credit to Tabini, who more or less trusted him, the way he more or less trusted Tabini.

Not good, he said to himself, to the rhythm of the rails, not good, not good. Trust outside one's own household was a sure way to get into a hell of a mess.

Every turn of the track, every pitch and sway he knew—and they were three quarters of the way to the airport when one of Cenedi's men rose from a side bench, steadied himself with his hand on the bar rail, and announced, to Cenedi and Banichi both:

"A fourth plane, nadiin, has left southbound from Bedijien. Lord Wyndyn is the owner."

Damn. That was a smaller airpark, across town, where luxury aircraft underwent maintenance—at least that had been its role two years ago. And a fourth plane was in the air.

"Lord Wyndyn is himself in the south," Banichi said, from

the other side of the car, "having traveled by train. Why his plane is in this region at all is a matter for inquiry."

Wyndyn was a southern lord, neighbor to the Taisigin Marid, and not even in the capital, from the borders of which his plane took off. Murini was down there in the south, somewhere. At least they *thought* Murini was down there. Tabini's loyalists were out hunting for the usurper, and if he or one of his aides had instead been here in the capital, all along, and left on that plane—

No. If it *was* Murini's people who'd snatched the boy, how in hell could they subvert Ilisidi's staff, and why spare the Taibeni youngster? No. They had three planes aloft, four, *five*, now, with the dowager's inbound flight . . . and they were tracking all of them.

What in *hell* was air traffic control doing, allowing that takeoff?

Or had they allowed it? Had a flight crew panicked, seeing the airlanes closed, and themselves cut off from their homeland? If no one had physically blocked the runway, a plane could have done it. Once in the air, there was no way to stop them except flinging another plane into their path . . . and *that* didn't help the situation.

"The dowager's plane is landing, nandi," Cenedi said, for his benefit, as the train hit that long straightaway that led to the airport's outer perimeter. "A bus will meet us and take us to the ramp while they refuel. All aircraft are still under hold." Cenedi paused to listen to something. "The first southbound plane has been identified as a scheduled freight flight, departing ahead of the general ban. It says it will obey instructions to land in Omijen. Local magistrates will bring force to meet it. The other two, the northbound and eastward are also scheduled freight. One is registered to the district of Cie, and has made its turn east, according to usual plan. The fifth, a ten-seater, property of Lord Wyndyn, should not have taken off. No one at Bedijien, however, was prepared to prevent it."

Cie. Hell with Lord Wyndyn at the moment. It was *Cie* that rang like a bell.

Eastern. Upland.

And the largest airport abutting Lord Caiti's sprawling domain.

Look to the dowager's guests for damned sure. They had left their hotel in the middle of the night, and now they were headed out on a freight flight, unable to wait for daylight? People had used to travel that way, not so long ago, but not since there were dedicated airliners, and not since commerce had increased tenfold, so that they *needed* more freight runs, and freighters had given up installing the passenger section.

He cast Banichi a look. Banichi gave him one back, while Cenedi instructed his man and relayed a message.

Questions were unnecessary at this point. Caiti. Caiti became an exceedingly good bet.

8

The train pulled up at the security station at the airport in the morning darkness, and a van was waiting for them with dimmed interior lights as the coach doors opened. Bren, with nothing to carry, and Banichi going behind him, took the steps downward, with Cenedi himself waiting below to catch him as he made the last tall step to the concrete of the platform. Cenedi's men were one car ahead of the coach they had used, catching the bags Jago and one of Cenedi's team flung down at them, and two vans waited on the tarmac beyond the concrete, interiors dark, motors off.

They hurried to the van. Jago joined them there as Cenedi's men, taking the baggage, headed for the second van. Jago, Bren was glad to see, had brought his computer with her, and gave it to him with a direct and affirming glance in the slight light from inside the van.

Affirming what? That everything was all right?

That they had made the right moves so far?

Bren slung the strap over his shoulder and clutched the handle up close as he boarded—struggled for balance on the steep rise, and Banichi shoved him from behind as he set a hand on the dusty floorboards. He made it up in haste, and flung himself into the seat behind the driver as Banichi and Jago landed heavily on the bench seat behind him. Cenedi and one of his men had boarded, the man pressing past, Cenedi lingering to instruct the driver.

"We have not been able to reach Tano or Algini, Bren-ji," Jago said, leaning forward. "One left a strong request with Jaidiri to phone the estate, requesting they come after us as soon as possible. This supposes that the estate can achieve contact—but one also instructed them by no means to compromise nand' Toby's position."

Toby was as safe as he had been. At least that. And the safety of everything on the mainland was currently in doubt. He rested the hope of Tano and Algini joining them all in Jago's capable hands: and if he had to go with what they had, Banichi and Jago were enough. She had trusted Jaidiri with that call. Not Saidin, whose man'chi was to the Atageini. Did that tell him anything?

The van door shut, the van started to roll, and just then a desperate apparition showed at the door glass, hammering on the door.

He knew that face, in the sidewash of the foglights.

"Jegari!" Bren exclaimed, half rising from his seat. "Banichi!"

Banichi, outermost, was immediately past him, laying a hand on the driver's shoulder, checking the driver in his intention to pull away. The door opened, and Cajeiri's young attendant, in no more than trousers and a torn and bloody white tee, scrambled up the steps into the dim light inside.

"Away!" Cenedi instructed the driver—Cenedi was on his feet, too; and Banichi lowered the winded boy into a vacant front seat—Cenedi's, as happened. The injured youngster was clutching his left arm and bleeding on the upholstery, dripping blood from a cut on his forehead; and Bren dumped his computer to the seat and stood where he had a vantage.

"Nand' Bren," the boy gasped, looking up at him, blinking in the wash of blood. "They drugged us, I think. They took nand' Jeri—and Taro—one does not know—"

"Your sister is safe in the Bu-javid, nadi," Bren said, and the boy got a breath.

"But Jeri—one was not willing to escape, but one thought—

one thought, nandi—someone had to report back—if Taro were dead—no one would know where—one thought—"

"You jumped from the truck," Jago said shortly.

"Yes, nadi. I did."

"You reported," Banichi said, "that you saw them board a plane. What sort of plane?"

Two fingers. "Jet. Two engines, nadi." A gasp for air. The boy's teeth chattered. "One failed to see the emblem. The lights—were all where they were boarding—"

"Did you identify anyone? Did you see faces, or colors?"

A wretched move of the head. "No, no, nadi, one regrets extremely—one did not. But it—it was big. The number—the number started with nine."

"The plane to Cie," Cenedi said. "Caiti, for certain." The van hit a curve at that moment, and the boy slid in the seat. Banichi held him with a hand on his arm. The boy winced and all but fainted, and Banichi immediately eased his grip.

Banichi said, "This child needs a hospital."

"No," Jegari cried. "No. No, please, nadi. Does one know where they have taken my lord? One wishes—one wishes to—"

"The aiji-dowager is inbound at this moment," Bren told the boy quietly, holding to the seat as the van swerved and gathered speed. Jegari seemed justly due as much information as they had, given his help thus far. "We are joining her here at the airport. One expects to go after the young gentleman, as far as the Eastern Provinces, if that is where this trail leads. And what you say is good news—better, at least than a plane going southward. We shall find him."

"May I go with you, nandi?" The boy's face glistened with sweat in the reflected lights. "One asks—one asks—most earnestly—most respectfully—"

"I have no authority to say so," Bren began, but Banichi caught his eye and gave an affirmative nod, as if, yes, the paidhi did, in absentia parentis, in this cause, have that authority.

"Ask the dowager, nandi," Jago said. "This boy may well have seen useful things and his presence might be a resource."

"I should be forever grateful to go, nandi," Jegari said.

The dowager traveled, always, with her physician. On that plane, inbound with Ilisidi, there was medical attention.

And Jago was right. The boy was indeed a witness. Where the boy was now determined to go—answered to man'chi. And he was—dammit—not a human kid. There were obligations, questions of honor, of emotional ties in which he did well to take his staff's advice, for the boy's own sake.

He cast Jago a troubled look, all the same, then grabbed the seat back rail as the van made a turn, and dropped into his own seat rather than fight for balance. He wanted the kids in this wretched business all safe, not one more boy in risk of his life. He wanted a clear deck so people old enough to know what they risked could do what they had to do without more innocent parties getting hurt.

But he had clearly landed right in the middle of that territory to which atevi had never invited humans: the manner in which they dealt with their children. He'd had what he thought an intimate view with Cajeiri and the dowager on the ship—he'd winced whenever the dowager came down harshly on the boy, and he'd kept his mouth shut, and never intervened, though he had suspected it was just the dowager's way and she was never inclined to take prisoners . . . not when she expected perfection.

But how did he go back to Jegari's father and mother if they lost or crippled this boy? What would he say to them then?

Your son seemed useful to us?

Point of fact, it *wasn't* his decision. Not ultimately. He kept his mouth shut.

A floodlit building veered across their path, succeeded by dark, as the van swung full about toward the view of a plane parked amid fuel trucks. The aircraft was in a secure area, with armed Guild security dotted here and there about it. A second plane, smaller, taxied slowly to a stop as they braked.

That, he thought with a habitual surge of relief, that had to be the dowager's plane. She was down. Safe. They were one force again. Questions, doubts, seemed suddenly less reasonable. The unity between them was the way it had been, had been obliged to be, for the last two years.

Their van swung in toward the first, larger plane and began to slow to a stop. By the fact that no one shot out their tires, and that Cenedi was staring out the side door and actively using his com, the dowager's other security clearly knew their leader was aboard, and that their van was not full of lunatics bent on ramming the now-departing fuel truck.

That hazardous vehicle trundled across their path. They rolled near to the boarding ladder, and stopped, as their other van, that with the baggage, rolled past them and toward the cargo hatch.

Their door opened, and Bren gathered up his computer, waiting as Banichi and Cenedi took the boy between them and helped him carefully down the steps. The boy descended as if it was the last strength he had in him, his knees almost failing as he stepped down to the ground, but he stayed upright and walked between them.

Bren followed, as Jago inserted herself between him and the adjacent hangar, then seized his arm discreetly and hurried him on toward the ladder. He was surely one of any enemy's chief targets, a worry to his staff, and he applied all haste as Jago increased her pace and headed him up the steps to the boarding platform at a breathless rate.

Inside the aircraft, then, the dizzyingly ordinary sight of seats all prepared for passengers, as the ladder rang with footsteps behind them. He kept moving forward, with Jago. The compartment could be any airplane, with commercial seating, most of it vacant. He passed through that, meeting no objection from the two stern young men on guard at the bulkhead. He and Jago passed through a substantial door into the private sitting area forward of the wings, with its serving bar, and comfortable chairs. This was a transcontinental passenger plane. Lords traveled in such splendor, nowadays. The small adjacent accommodation, the bedroom nook that took nearly half the space, had private doors. Ahead of that, the pilots, behind their closed door. A lord's spare security enjoyed the seats behind the bulkhead, the galley and accommodation hindmost. He had reached a sort of privileged safety. Jago shut the door.

The boy had not made it through to this compartment. Bren disapproved; but *he* was not the lord in question, on this plane. He had no power down here on the planet, arranged nothing. Cenedi did, in the dowager's name, and Jago was probably listening to Banichi in her choices, in electronic communication—she had that abstracted look, one hand covering her ear to shut out noise.

Bren just stood, frowning, waiting while Jago ducked ahead to investigate the cockpit, and then, passing through, she ducked quickly back through the bulkhead door to check on matters back in the main cabin.

He had no desire to sit down while all this went on. The windows were shuttered. A glance at his watch informed him the sun was probably coming up now, just touching the horizon. A lord's dignity—and everything rode on that, far more than usual—precluded his going back and interfering in whatever Banichi and Jago and Cenedi were doing about the boy.

They were asking the lad questions, likely, sharp and difficult questions, maybe getting him bandages, maybe seeing to him after a Guildsman's fashion, very competent field medicine, making him at least tolerably comfortable. He hoped so.

He wanted to go over to a window and lift a shade to know what was going on outside, and whether his watch was right, but the lights were on full in the cabin, and he could make himself a target if there was any hostile presence out there in the dark. If there was—if there was—there must be quiet action going on apart from anything he would see. Guild in the dowager's service and maybe Tabini's would be moving out there, securing the area, dealing with anyone who opposed the plane taking off.

The engines whined into life. He sat down, waited. Listened to the sounds of activity on the back ramp. There was a small delay after what he took for an arrival aft.

Then from the bulkhead door Ilisidi walked in, in a dark brocade coat and with her cane in hand. Cenedi escorted her, and Jago came into the compartment and shut the door again.

Bren rose and bowed. Ilisidi walked to the centermost chair and sat down, both hands on the cane.

"Aiji-ma," he said—he had not planned how he would meet her. He had not even thought of the awkwardness of being assigned here by her grandson, under present circumstances. She sat now, grim and determined, and it seemed to be one of those rare occasions where staff had not passed word to staff as to what he was doing here or why he had inserted himself into a situation from which he had been—with considerable thoroughness—dismissed.

"Aiji-ma," he said, above the sound of the engines, "your grandson the aiji sent me, urging me to assist you."

"To assist me," she echoed him. "Assist me to do what, paidhi? To kidnap my own great-grandson?"

Anger was in her voice. Anger, and, apparently, indignation, in a display of emotion rare except among intimates. And he was shaken in his convictions, not knowing was that indignation an act—she was that good—or whether it was real. Either case was extremely dangerous.

"A plane has left the city, aiji-ma, forgive my forwardness, probably carrying your recent dinner guests Eastward. They had not left the city before now. They left their hotel in the middle of the night, and one believes they may have the young gentleman with them."

"Caiti," she said bitterly. "And who of my staff and my grandson's is dead, nand' paidhi?"

"No one that I know, aiji-ma."

"Yet my great-grandson is taken, nand' paidhi!"

"His young guards were struck down, aiji-ma. Jegari is out there—" He gave a shrug to the compartment at his right, beyond the bulkhead. "His sister they left. Jegari was taken along with the young lord and escaped, trying to get help. He very much needs medical attention."

"We are aware," Ilisidi said flatly. And in that moment the cargo hatch slammed shut, below. "Yet you came, paidhi-aiji. Good. Tatiseigi has returned with me from Tirnamardi, but he will not go East with us. He will resume residence in his apartments and support my grandson. He will assist in the investigation inside *my* staff."

"One cannot imagine—" he began, in that dreadful silence. And in the back of his mind was a surmise that Tabini's Taibeni staff would not take kindly to Atageini security asking questions: not to mention that Ilisidi's Eastern staff would be obliged to answer those questions under Taibeni witness. Fireworks were absolutely assured.

"One of my petty serving staff," Ilisidi said further, "has not answered to a summons. We assume this person is dead."

Assuming this person had died defending the house, that was to say—or it was possible that person *would* die, if they turned out to be on that plane with Caiti, aiding and abetting the crime. One would not at all like to be in that person's shoes when the dowager's men caught up. It had to be a powerful reason that diverted that servant to Caiti's man'chi.

The man'chiin. The connections. There *were* no likely ties from the aiji's Taibeni to Cei Province.

From the dowager's own Eastern-born staff, however . . . well possible.

"Who, may one ask, aiji-ma? Which of the staff?"

"One of Madiri's hand-chosen staff! *His* import from the province!"

It was grim. Madiri himself compromised? Maidiri was still in office—and in Tabini's household. But that chain of connection was exposed, and there were going to be questions: assume there would be questions.

He only had to explain why they had brought the injured boy aboard, if the dowager had not been informed.

"The boy Jegari, aiji-ma—his sister was knocked unconscious. Jegari avowed himself reluctant to escape, but he hoped to get help. He phoned to advise us and ran out—his actions seem above reproach."

"We are aware of all his actions," Ilisidi said in a chilling tone . . . not personal, he had that sense. This was not the dowager in a good mood, and there had begun to be a degree of abstraction in her eyes that one rarely saw, because one ordinarily saw the dowager with her mind firmly made up. She was thinking, thinking fast and hard, Bren decided, and he was not disposed to interrupt that train of thought.

More encouragingly—she was convincingly angry. He could not express how much that relieved his personal anxiety about her position in this.

Questions, however, were not a good idea at this juncture. He had asked all he needed to know, and he sat quietly, not willing to invade that privacy.

In a moment, Cenedi came in, and spoke quietly with the dowager, reporting, audible just above the engines. "There was intrusion into the young gentleman's premises," Cenedi said. "Jegari heard it. Antaro was sleeping in adjacent quarters. Jegari went out into the hall and something hit him before he could give an alarm. He waked in the back of a plumber's van: the young gentleman was also there, unconscious on the floor beside him . . . likely injected with some drug. There was one guard. Jegari laid hands on a piece of pipe and knocked the man to the floor, but he could not rouse the young gentleman afterward, and he was dizzy and disoriented. At this point he unlocked the back door from inside and jumped from the moving van, fearing to attempt to drag the young gentleman with him. He ran to a lighted office in the hope of raising an alarm and stopping the van: he asked to use the phone, after the officer in charge had used it to notify the officers on duty. The boy had significant difficulty phoning into the Bu-javid system. The airport security chief and his men did not immediately locate the van, or stop all aircraft from taking off. Several cargo planes were active, and there was an attempt to stop the last from reaching the runway, but it was too late—this we have from other sources than the boy, aiji-ma. Information came up the conduits too slowly, the boy not being Guild, and being under his majority. The Bu-javid operator did not cooperate with him. Two planes took off before they could stop traffic and the third, that bound for Cie, defied the tower and took off without clearance."

"Fools!" Ilisidi said, and one doubted she meant Caiti's lot.

"Airport security has now seized the van: they are processing it for evidence, aiji-ma. The boy stayed in the security office, refusing medical treatment in favor of staying in touch with Madiri in the apartment, evidently trusting someone from the house would come to get him—he maintains he had no word from Madiri that we were coming until the last. He ran out to intercept us on our arrival. He has a concussion, and bruised ribs."

"Madiri again," Ilisidi said grimly. Then: "The boy is a credit to his parents. And to my great-grandson."

"Siegi is tending to him." That was the dowager's own

physician. "The boy begs to go with us. We have no easy means to send him back at this point."

A grim, preemptory wave of Ilisidi's hand. "Granted. Nand' paidhi."

"Aiji-ma?"

"We are going to Malguri," the dowager said, and that was that.

He had already taken that for granted: if that one plane was registered to Cie, *they* would go to Cie or Malguri Airport, the only two with enough runway. There was nothing he could lend, either of advice or of information.

At that point the door at the rear of the plane shut with a distant, familiar thump. A wave of the dowager's hand dismissed Cenedi, and two of the dowager's young men came into the cabin.

The engines increased their power. The plane slowly began to move.

The young men assisted the dowager to swing a belt restraint across her shoulder. Bren belted in without a word.

Shades were still down. There was no view at all.

Whatever the dowager's physician might have done for the boy's comfort, one suspected more extensive treatment had had to wait until they were airborne. And if anyone had notified the youngsters' parents or clan lord, it had not come from the paidhi's staff. He hoped Madiri would. Or Tabini's staff.

Their plane navigated the taxiways to the strip, and swung sharply onto the runway, gathering speed.

Lifting.

No way back, Bren thought as they shot skyward. No way back now, right step or wrong.

9

The dowager retired to nap in her bedroom once the plane reached altitude . . . and, knowing the dowager, she probably would nap. Bren personally wished he could catch up the hour or so of sleep he had lost, but he knew himself, that *that* was not going to happen, not after the desperate race to get here.

Instead he sat pat, requested tea, along with information on the boy who, one hoped, was now being treated by the doctor behind the bulkhead door—the boy was, the dowager's staff assured him, in the best of hands, and indeed, being patched up by a real doctor. It was more surface injury, give or take the concussion. One suspected that, during the kidnapping, the boy had been administered a sedative, which had worn off—he was twice the young gentleman's age, and nearly of adult size.

Well, that was certainly as good an outcome as circumstances could make it. Bren felt better hearing that.

And, thinking of the breakfast he had also missed, he asked for whatever the staff might find. The young man assured him they were well-stocked, and proceeded to offer him three sweet rolls with jam, and warmed, to boot. He had those with the tea, feeling comforted.

He had one left when Jago came quietly into the compartment and sat down in the chair the dowager had left. He silently offered the remaining sweet roll to her, and she took it gratefully.

"How is the news, Jago-ji?"

"The plane to Cie is approaching the Divide, nandi." The sweet roll immediately diminished by half, and a cup of tea arrived at her side to wash it down, with the other half. "The boy is resting comfortably enough. Staff remains with him, against any maneuver the plane may need to make." The tea quickly disappeared. "He had a very limited view of the assailants, and still remembers nothing immediately surrounding the attack. He asked us more than once whether he should have jumped with the young gentleman in his arms. We replied that this might have been preferable, even lacking the skill to take such a fall. Broken bones would be a small price."

A direct, an accurate answer, to a boy who might plan to enter their Guild. He understood that. "No Guild planning, surely," Bren said, and Jago gently pursed her lips, grimly amused.

"No, Bren-ji."

The kidnappers had made a raft of mistakes . . . including leaving the unconscious boys unsecured, possibly mistaking the dosage on the healthy teenager—or having no medical expertise in the company.

"Yet they evaded all pursuit and got into the air," Jago said. "They were not total fools, Bren-ji, nor should we expect them to be."

"They had this planned, one thinks, before they visited the dowager's table."

Jago accepted another cup of tea, offered without request. "No midlander would risk this much, this recklessly. The fact that they have not involved Guild—this very strongly suggests Eastern politics, Bren-ji." A sip of tea and a darker frown. "Still one must wonder if there may have been some approach between south and East. That remains the most worrisome possibility."

The aiji's Assassins had not located Murini. And the fact of Murini continuing at large was now beyond worrisome. It was a terrifying thought, that they might be decoyed eastward by the appearance of a kidnapping going east, and all the while lose track of the boy, who might have changed hands.

"Is there any cause to think this could be a decoy, Jago-ji? That the Taibeni boy could have been *allowed* to escape?"

"Cenedi has made inquiries in that line, and reports that a delegation from the Taisigin Marid did visit the East during Murini's tenure—how those delegates were received, or even where they guested, was never clear. One suspects that there was contact between the southerners and certain of the Eastern lords. The aiji has made a Guild request at the highest levels."

With a new Guildmaster in office, one whose politics were uncertain, and Algini, who was familiar with those high levels, out on the west coast, thanks to him. The thought upset his stomach, upset it extremely.

"Was the dowager aware of this visit when she invited these persons as her guests?"

"She may have been aware of it. It was difficult *not* to invite them, nandi, since they turned up in Shejidan, requesting audience."

"A fishing expedition, perhaps, Murini's contacts with the East," he murmured. Jago understood that metaphor. And it was logical Murini might attempt to find a door into the East: the East had always been a chancy member of the *aishidi'tat*. One could well imagine Murini would wish to find sympathy for himself there among those opposed to Tabini; but the trick was that Easterners were not well-disposed to each other, let alone outsiders, such as Murini was, equally with the aiji—and navigating the rocks and shoals of Eastern politics was a matter of connections as well as skill. "The question remains whether any elements of Murini's man'chi might be directing this move—"

"Indeed," Jago said.

"Or someone who connived with him now feels himself exposed—exposed enough to take desperate measures, considering the dowager's return. One could be very uneasy, Jago-ji, asking oneself what the dowager might be walking into, returning to the East."

"The dowager's lengthy absence, rumors of her death, rumors of the aiji's death, these might have been persuasive among her neighbors while she was gone. Indeed, nandi, issues have surely surfaced, *since* the dowager's return from space— things that make particular sense to the East, and much less in the midlands."

"But her neighbors would be concerned with the heir," Bren said. Cajeiri's existence did many things—for one thing, it established Tatiseigi's influence as major, and therefore raised the Padi Valley's influence, Cajeiri being in their bloodline, too. It brought the Taibeni in.

And the dowager, meanwhile, being linked by fate, circumstance, and political necessity to that same Padi Valley region, might have stirred up certain individuals in the East, individuals who might not have been petted and cosseted enough by the dowager when they came to call—or who had seen reason to fear.

No, damn it, they had not cobbled a successful plot together on the spot. They had come in knowing what they planned and had used that visit to make contact with someone on the inside of Ilisidi's defenses. This was not an impromptu business.

And beyond that, damn, it was a very deep pond to probe. An outsider had no idea what moved in Eastern politics. It was bad.

And his security thought Jegari should have taken his young lord in his arms and jumped: that was how dangerous they thought Cajeiri's situation had become, how very dangerous it was to the aiji and the dowager and the stability of the *aishidi'-tat* to have the heir in Eastern hands.

Not to mention the opinion of their visitors from the depths of space. The East hadn't a clue what they were risking, in that regard, and would have no notion how to handle it if they ever gained the power they were after.

"Your computer is safe with the other equipment," Jago remarked, finishing the second cup of tea. "Such clothing as I brought, Bren-ji, is shamefully dealt with. Staff attempted to assist. There was no time. Staff at Malguri will have to press everything, but one can at least say that there are two bags of your clothes, with changes of footwear. More will follow, by tomorrow's plane. Cenedi assures us staff will retrieve it from the airport as soon as it arrives."

"Excellent, Jago-ji," he said. "One takes it the Guild is aware of this situation. Have we made any contact with the rest of the staff?"

"Regarding the Guild, yes, they are aware, nandi. Tano and Algini, however, remain out of contact."

He had hoped—he had earnestly hoped they could recover those two to his staff before morning. That somehow they would have accomplished their mission and headed in. "We do as we can," he said, and, entrusting her cup to one of the young men, Jago excused herself to go forward, back with Banichi and Cenedi and the rest of their security.

Time, then, to take what rest he could. He had never in his life been one to sleep on planes, always alert to any bump or thump in a flight, but having been waked out of his night's sleep, he thought that with some determination he could manage. He put the footrest of the chair up and settled, at least until the sun coming through the shaded window had become a mild, pervasive light.

★   ★   ★

It was a long, anxious trip thereafter, the flight across the continental divide, and on across a sizeable expanse of wilderness. The dowager slept through lunch. The boy slept. Bren went back into Guild territory to check on the youngster's welfare—Jegari was resting well, injuries eased with ice, the doctor rousing him periodically to check his alertness, considering the concussion—and Bren detoured to have a look out the unshaded windows there.

Hills lay behind the wing, below them, in front of them. They were flying over an immense expanse of snowy, untamed land, a wilderness cut by rivers, but not by roads, except only one: the transcontinental rail, and they were following that course, not visible from this height and with the sunglare, but, knowing the general routes planes took, he was sure it was down there.

From the Divide, the land rolled down toward the Kadenamar, a vast river drainage, an immense fault that probably followed an old plate boundary—at least the experts had advanced that theory. In that wild, game-rich territory, still far ahead of them, the Kadena River's ancient plateaus descended step by step to a wide and sudden lowland, a region of lakes in the north—old glaciation, the same experts said—with an expanse of boggy land to the south, a natural barrier which had held the East from the sea.

That geological fact had meant no ports, no seacoast trade. Every resource the East used was consequently bottled into a tract of habitable and rich land along the Kadena, the hills rich in minerals, the plains rich in game, the river margin rich in arable soil.

It should have been a paradise—if not for the history of equally bottled-up feuding clans, mostly situated in the lake country, above the fever-belt to the south.

And—invading that paradise—came the railroad, after the

epic struggle of its builders, through tunnels and across bridges. Once across the Divide, the rail began to follow an easier route.

The greatest tributary of the Kadena, the Naijendar, started as a modest stream and a high scenic falls in the snowmelt of the Divide. It wove in other streams until it became a torrent, a whitewater flood that steadily gained volume and violence on its eastward plunge. The Naijendar had cut the route the rail followed, that, nowadays, planes followed for a guide—because civilization had followed that route, too, in the earliest regular trade between east and west, the ancient mountain trail, a precarious track rife with bandits and legends of buried treasure.

Malguri had gotten its early power by controlling that route—as the one convenient access to the mountain wealth of ore and, later, of water power and electricity. Malguri had begun as a medieval fortress perched high in the hills that overlooked the Naijendar, the lake it filled, the eventual railroute—and now ran the modern airport that met the railhead.

In fact, planetary geology, ancient trade routes, and the hard-handedness of the ancestors had conspired to put the supreme power over Eastern politics into the hands of the latest Lord of Malguri, namely Ilisidi, grandmother of the aiji in Shejidan.

Oh, there were rival centers, dotted about the various lesser lakes and flatlands. They never had managed to get the better of their local geology, a few growing rich off trade, but that had to pass through Malguri. And the East had generally opposed the determination of the western atevi to get a railroad from coast to coast, to get that wealth of ores and game from the East to their factories and their tables. Not Malguri, whose lord had seen it would pass through *his* hands, going and coming.

The west, already carving its tunnel and laying track

through the mountains on a collision course with Eastern culture, had started playing high-stakes politics with Ilisidi's father.

The aiji of Shejidan had ended up not conducting a war, but marrying his way into that trade route.

The aiji in Shejidan had brought his bride west, probably hoping for her to keep enough of a claim on Malguri to prevent the East from falling apart, but never expecting her to become a force in western politics—or possibly—rumor had it—to aspire to rule the *aishidi'tat*. She had come damned close.

Ilisidi had been no fool, in anything. Her sojourn in the west had never loosened her real grip on Malguri—Malguri the province, not just the ancient fortress itself. Her neighbors knew who was in charge. The aiji in Shejidan had gotten a son of both bloodlines, and that son had gotten a grandson, Ilisidi's grandson Tabini, who had yanked the southerners into the *aishidi'tat*. Now Ilisidi had gotten a great-grandson—who wove even more of the lineages of the *aishidi'tat* into his person, by bringing in the Padi Valley. And then she had gone off to space with that great-grandson, and if all the world had wondered if she or the boy would come back . . . the East had the greatest reason to worry.

The paidhi had seen Ilisidi's Eastern establishment in action: he had visited that ancient heart of Ilisidi's power, not half understanding at the time either the history or the current state of affairs . . . how Malguri was *not* only the fortress, with its handful of staff, but was the whole widespread holding, villages, towns, establishments, alliances—and control of the primary railhead *and* airport for the whole eastern subcontinent. He had not appreciated the commercial power and wealth that lordship over Malguri entailed. Now he did.

Not to mention the import of certain advantages out of the west into the East, like Guild support for the aiji-dowager. It was never in the interest of the Assassins' Guild, the Messengers' Guild, the Makers' Guild, or the Merchants' Guild or any other guild, for that matter, that anything should ever disrupt the hold Ilisidi had on Malguri and that Malguri had over the whole of the East . . . because *she* controlled the one point that kept the ore coming into the western manufacturies and held the rest of the East in check.

Damned right that the dowager's two-year-long absence in deep space could have encouraged certain ambitious parties in the East to think that Malguri might finally be leaderless, that with Murini-aiji overthrowing Ilisidi's grandson Tabini—the whole world might change shape. Even people who would never want to overthrow her authority might have started making precautionary alliances, when the west, for its own reasons, started going to hell in a handbasket.

Damned right that Ilisidi's unheralded return might have caught a handful of her neighbors by surprise, some of them with potentially compromising recent histories, others vastly embarrassed to be in the company her agents might have reported they were in.

Her neighbors had come west to have dinner with her and welcome her home?

My God, how *had* the paidhi been so dim?

Damned sure that the aiji-dowager had not been overwhelmed by sentiment and gratitude that evening. She had had all her connections on display.

Now he waked to the currents that had been running at that table. He saw the whole pattern below them, in that thin white gash that was the Naijendar and the railroad, leading like a missile track to Malguri and all it meant to the aishidi'tat.

Stupid human. He'd been so preoccupied with the dangers in space. He'd taken Tabini's power for unshakeable until he saw it shaken, and taken Ilisidi's power for granted even after that example. Even Tabini, blood of her blood, had had to fight back the immediate western atevi assumption that Ilisidi herself, the mysterious Easterner, had the greatest motive to orchestrate this move, and the theft of her own great-grandson.

One could so easily think that, standing on a balcony overlooking the maze of roofs that was Shejidan, with all its convolute politics.

Looking down on the Naijendar, however—one found other perspectives that slammed western suspicions sideways.

Malguri had always played for power. It would do that now. It absolutely would. And Ilisidi's neighbors hadn't done what they'd done without the notion they could get something out of it and get away with it.

What? A share of power if they helped her hold the heir for ransom?

It was no more than what they had—a small range of political power for their transport-dependent little provincial centers. One could not even say capitals—provincial centers.

Provincial networks. Mines. The tradition-bound East would not even smelt the ore it mined. They were not industrial, like the west. They refused to be. They made choices that stemmed purely from the desire for raw resources, and the power to move them—or withhold them.

And they had that. If they left their province, they had nothing—nothing that *they* valued. So what did they want, that could let them deal with Ilisidi and make bargains?

He raked through memory, recalling what mines, what products, what raw resources the several lords shipped from their districts. And unless there was more to the move than three lords, there was no way in hell they could arrange an embargo against the west if things went down to the trenches. Rival lords, their neighbors, would break it, and it would all fall to pieces.

More, Ilisidi could have gotten her great-grandson to the airport herself without breaking eggs, as the proverb ran. She could have snatched him off to the East with his two Taibeni attendants and used *them* to mollify the wrath of the Taibeni Ragi, who supported Tabini. Such a plot, with her involved, would not be running the way it had, half-assed and losing Jegari out the back of that truck.

Hell, no.

So back up. Retrace. There was no way this effort was going to win Ilisidi as an ally.

But what did the conspirators stand to gain? Overthrow Ilisidi? Embarrass her?

That was about the most dangerous course he could think of.

Lure her East?

They were certainly doing that. If Ilisidi *hadn't* been visiting Tatiseigi at Tirnamardi, the kidnapping would have—

—*might* have involved Ilisidi as well as the heir. The plotters would have had to take on her security, or incapacitate them. They had *not* gone into the other wing of the apartment to take on Tabini and *his* guards, who were not a known quantity. They'd gotten in, and out, with some facility they shouldn't have had, damn it.

Consider: if Ilisidi were no longer in the picture—the East fell apart, it bloody fell apart. That could have been one objective. Chaos. And who benefitted from that? That thought led to some very bad places . . . mostly in the south.

Except, if, down in that hotel, waiting their chance, the conspirators had heard through their sources that Ilisidi was leaving, and leaving behind the boy—who was heir to—

Malguri itself, as it happened. Cajeiri was not only his father's only heir—he was Ilisidi's ultimate heir, the one who would have to succeed her—there was no other choice, since it was damned sure she was not going to cede her power to her grandson Tabini.

Damn, the boy not only united the bloodlines of the west—

and stood to become aiji in Shejidan—he stood to inherit the keystone to the East, to boot.

Some of Ilisidi's neighbors weren't going to like that idea.

And that—God, that didn't augur as well for the boy's safety. If negotiations went wrong, if things started sliding amiss—it wasn't good, was it?

Events were tumbling one after the other. They were in virtual hot pursuit, as it was. There had not been time to analyze everything. But was it possible the west—even Tabini—had been looking through the wrong end of the telescope?

He left his window, moved quietly to settle on the edge of an empty seat by Jago and Banichi.

He said: "The boy, nadiin-ji, is heir to the *aishidi'tat*. But from the Eastern view, he is heir to Malguri."

"Indeed," Banichi said.

His staff had a way of making him feel as if the truth had been blazoned in neon lights for everyone to see—and he always, always got to it late.

Still, he plowed on. "They would have wished the dowager dead, or in their hands. But whatever traitor there was on staff would have advised them she was in Tirnamardi. That left—"

For once, once, he saw a simultaneous recognition go through their eyes. It was a dire little thought they had *not* had. He had no idea what thought, but it evoked something.

"They would have learned that the paidhi had relocated, as well," Banichi said, "and that the aiji had moved in. They would have been fools to take on *the aiji's* precautions. His own staff was around him."

"While Cajeiri's was mostly the dowager's," Jago said, "like the traitor herself."

"You know specifically who it was, nadiin-ji?" Bren asked.

"A maid. A member of the staff," Banichi said. "Pahien. The paidhi may remember her."

"One remembers her," Bren said. Indeed he did: a woman who found every opportunity to hang about the young gentleman's quarters. Ambitous, he'd thought, someone who wanted to work her way up in the staff of a young man with prospects.

"She is probably on that plane," Jago said darkly, and Banichi:

"If they controlled the heir to Malguri—and anything befell the aiji-dowager—"

"The dowager may be in greater danger of her life than Cajeiri," Jago murmured. "It is entirely in the interest of the kidnappers that he stay alive, in that theory. And the dowager is going to Malguri. One does not approve."

It was not the conclusion he had drawn from the same facts. "Possibly they wish to coerce the dowager to take certain measures they favor, nadiin-ji."

"That would be a dangerous move on their part, Bren-ji."

To attempt to deal with her . . . damned certain it was. She was a knife that turned in the hand—her husband had found that out.

"If *she* were dead, on the other hand, the lord of Malguri would be a minor child—in their hands."

"Balking the aiji in Shejidan as well," Jago said. "If the aiji were to disinherit his heir, it would have calamitous effect in the west, and no effect at all in the East. He would still inherit Malguri."

"Has Cenedi advised her against going? Will she remain inside Malguri?"

"Advised, yes, but by no means will the dowager leave this matter to her security, nandi," Banichi muttered. "Cenedi cannot persuade her. Our Guild is already in Malguri Township, moving to secure various of her assets, but it is not even certain that our landing at Malguri Airport will be secure. One hopes to have that news before we land."

He had not thought of that point of danger, but it was good

to *know* the old links were functioning. "Can Guild possibly intercept that plane on the ground?" he asked.

"If Caiti were only so foolish as to land at Malguri Airport," Banichi said, "it would be easy. Cie, however, will take time to penetrate. And one regrets we will not have time. Planes fly faster above than vehicles or mecheiti can proceed in the weather there."

"Then they will land unchecked, nadiin-ji?"

"Very likely they will, Bren-ji," was Banichi's glum assessment, "for any effective purposes."

"Is there any chance of *our* going in at Cie?"

"They will surely take measures," Banichi said. "We cannot risk it, Bren-ji."

The Guild was not given to suicide. Or to losing the people they were trying to protect. Almost certainly there *were* Guild resources in Cie or moving there, but Banichi was not going to say so: the only inference one could draw was that there were not *enough* Guild resources there to protect the dowager or to effect a rescue. He nodded, quietly left his staff to their own devices, and returned to the dowager's cabin.

There he sat and brooded, among shaded windows, with only his watch for a gauge of time or progress. Eventually, after a long time, the young men moved to rap on the dowager's door, doubtless by prior arrangment.

Cenedi entered the cabin, then, glanced at that door, then said to Bren: "The plane we are tracking, nandi, has entered descent, not at Malguri's airport, nor even at Cie, but at a remote airport up at Cadienein-ori."

"Still Caiti's territory, nadi, is it not?"

"And a short runway, nandi," Cenedi said. Cenedi did not look in the least happy, and must have heard something on the com, because he left for the rear of the plane immediately.

The dowager meanwhile emerged from her rest, and settled in her chair.

"The plane will land at Cadienein-ori, aiji-ma," Bren said.

"One is not entirely surprised," the dowager muttered. "They must trust their pilot."

It was a scarily short airstrip for that size jet. Bren knew that much.

He imagined that if the Guild had scrambled to get assets as close to Cie as possible, they were now moving upland by any available means, to get to that small rural airport. One was not even sure roads ran between Cie and Cadienein-ori: in much of the rural East, lords had roads between their primary residence and a local airport, but freight might move entirely by air, these days, and the configuration of the roads was more web-work than grid. One often had to go clear back to some central hub to go to a place only a few miles across a line of hills from where one was.

Cenedi returned after awhile, and bowed. "They have landed, aiji-ma, at Cadienein-ori. They undershot the runway, attempting to use all of it, and the plane seems damaged and immovable. There is only one runway. And it was iced, with heavy snowfall."

No way for anyone else to get in, with a large plane blocking the runway. No way for them to land, certainly, except at the regional airport, in Ilisidi's territory: their going in at Cie was no good, now. And whatever the Guild had just revised their plans to do was now blocked by a disabled plane.

By accident or arrangement, Caiti had gotten farther out of their reach, and out of reach of Guild intervention. It was not to say that the non-Guild protection the lord of the East had at their disposal was unskilled. Far from it. And now how did anyone get in, with the weather closing in? One hoped that *they* could land.

"So," was all the dowager said to that news, except, "Would the paidhi-aiji care for a brandied tea?"

"Indeed," he said, agreeable to anything that pleased the dowager and settled her nerves.

So he waited, full of questions, knowing he would not be the one to ask them, and believing that the dowager herself might not have all the answers. Caiti had most of them at the moment. And at this point they *hoped* the young gentleman was in Caiti's hands.

"Thank you, nadi," he murmured to the servant, and accepted the glass. He took the merest sip and waited for details, if details might come.

In a moment more, Nawari came in, and bowed.

"Nand' dowager," he said, and with a second bow, "nand' paidhi. Three cars met that plane. The emergency slide had deployed. But there was some further delay to remove the luggage from the plane and take it with them in the airport bus. All passengers seem to have left."

"Effrontery," was Ilisidi's comment, regarding the baggage. "Was there sight of my great-grandson?"

"Not that was entirely certain, nand' dowager," Nawari said. "Members of the party were shaken up in the landing. And precisely where that car went afterward, there is as yet no report. It left southward, as one would going to the Haidamar *or* the Saibai'tet. One small bus pulled away from the column, its whereabouts and direction seeming to the southern route, as one would go to the lowlands. It may be Lord Rodi leaving. Or Lady Agilisi."

"Pish," Ilisidi said. "We know. We have every confidence my great-grandson is wherever Caiti is."

"Indeed," Nawari said, "aiji-ma, it seems likely that he might be. The majority has gone on eastward."

"Tell Cenedi we will go to Malguri as planned. Tell the staff prepare. Have that car tracked."

"Nandi," Nawari said, and went back to deliver that instruction. It might or might not be a diversion . . . but the dowager's strength had its limits. They had to believe the boy was there, that he had not been taken off somewhere else. The dowager chose to believe it.

At least, Bren said to himself, that plane was safely on the ground, and if the car had gone south—the direction of either of Caiti's domains from that highland airport—at least the plane was down, and there had been no ambulances.

Under present circumstances, however, the Guild was not in position to act, and no one could be surprised that the occupants had simply driven away, no one preventing them. There were three minor airports besides that in Malguri province. Cadienein-ori was not the largest, not by a hundred feet of runway . . . not unless they had improved it since the last time he had sat on the Aviation Board.

So effectively Cadienein-ori was shut down at the moment, with that very large airplane stuck in the snow somewhere on the only runway that would remotely accommodate any airplane bringing Guild to address the problem.

And if the Guild intervened with too much fire and smoke and failed—it would alienate the very people most likely to be of use getting Cajeiri out alive: the neighbors and rivals who most naturally would cooperate to Caiti's disadvantage. In the East, there were always rivals. Shejidan had grown up in the west and gathered provinces around it, an anomaly of politics and centrality and old history of associations, but it was not a pattern the East had adopted, not to this day.

And one didn't get anywhere good in the East by forgetting that. If either Rodi or Agilisi had left the party, it might be because that lord had gotten cold feet. And that might be an asset, a chink in the conspiracy that might be useful. Or it might mean something else, including even spiriting the boy away elsewhere. It needed observers in place to know that.

Would Tabini be moving his own agents into the situation in greater force? Was there a second plane behind them?

Maybe. But Tabini had already made his opening move, in sending him in with Banichi and Jago. *They* were the aiji's eyes and hands in this situation. Aside from them, one reasonably expected everything would work through Cenedi and his men, men who operated here because they came from here and knew the rules. If the aiji did send Guild out under the Shejidan seal, things they needed on the ground would mysteriously break, fail to appear, go missing, or simply fail to reach a destination . . . that was the way of things. Even Ilisidi would make no heavy-handed moves of Guild in the East, and the few other lords who did employ Guild employed them mostly quietly. Getting her great-grandson out—no lord alive would deny her the right to try, and nod quietly and move to her side if she proved she could do it without annoyance to themselves.

But it was all very delicate. Power rested in the will of a very loose confederation of lords, and she was one of them, but there was no council in the East. There was no legislature. There were no widespread and unifying laws. Every estate of every lord of every province was a feudal holding without an acknowledged central overlord, except the ancient dominance of Malguri. Certainly not all the neighbors would have agreed with someone kidnapping the heir of the lord of the West, as they called the aiji in Shejidan—and if someone disturbed their local way of doing things by bringing war to the region, the ones who did it would gather ire upon themselves. But it was not guaranteed they would get help from anyone at all.

So that plane was down safely. People had left it alive. Good hope to this hour it was not a diversion, and the boy *was* where they thought, and not handed off via that mysterious car to some plane bound for southern territory. In that, the weather became their ally. Getting anything in or out was not easy.

In the meanwhile he sipped his brandied tea, and Ilisidi gave orders for a light meal all around. Her young men hurried about business in the galley, and soon food issued forth from the galley, going fore and aft. The presentation for him and the dowager was immaculate, the linen spotless, and the sole topic of conversation during what amounted to an extravagant teatime was the weather and the reports of snow at Malguri and across the uplands—much as if they had been planning a holiday, nothing more strenuous in the trip.

One complimented the young chef—who, indeed, was also part of the dowager's security team: one complimented his choices, one enjoyed tea, and really wished not to have had the earlier drink—fatigue had the brain fuzzing, the ferment of emergency and impending crisis proving just too much after a night short of sleep. They were not that far from Malguri. The paidhi had to think; and he still had no idea whether something was proceeding on the ground, some Guild operation to rescue the boy, or how Jegari was faring, or what Tabini might be up to while they were suspended between heaven and earth—

Or what they were going to do next, if somehow they had missed the boy at the airport, followed a lure instead of the real thing and let Murini's faction get its hands on Tabini's son—

The dowager held a conference with Cenedi, after tea, one that named names, notably those of her dinner guests, and inquired about transport, and the reliability of the service at Malguri Airport.

"A bus will be waiting, nandi," Cenedi assured her.

The bus. God. The bus up to Malguri: that was one tidbit of information, that they were indeed going to the dowager's stronghold and not the long way around the lake to the other airport—a long trip in; but he had forgotten the upland bus, and that road.

He excused himself aft, looking for more substantial information.

Jegari was sitting up—had had a sandwich, being a resilient

lad, though he was a little subdued, and probably muzzy and confused with concussion. Banichi and Jago got up from their seats and proved amenable to questions.

The answers, however, were simply that they knew no more than before—not unlikely, if a Guild operation was in progress, and still short of its mark. They would not radio it hither and yon about the country, nor would this staff. Their own plane was, indeed, about to start descent toward Malguri Airport, near the township, and somewhat below the fortress that ruled the province.

"We do what we can," Banichi said. "We have taken precautions."

"When we leave the plane, Bren-ji," Jago added, "stay with us. Nawari and Tasi will see to the boy. Cenedi will be with the dowager."

Meaning he was to move quickly and not encumber his staff; and that they did not take for granted a safe move between airplane and bus. He entirely understood, and went forward again, where the dowager was busy putting on her coat.

He did the same, no time to be wasted.

He had hardly finished that operation before the nose of the plane began that gentle declination that warned they were going down. He settled in a chair, as the dowager did, and falling into her mood, he said nothing at all as the plane descended, asked no questions and expected no answers. The plain fact was, staff believed they were going in to a landing in which the dowager theoretically controlled the ground, and from which presumably Cenedi had had satisfactory responses, but they took nothing absolutely for granted.

Nor, he told himself, should the paidhi delay a moment once his feet hit the ladder.

The plane arrived in a gentle landing and with a slight oddness on the runway: snow, Bren thought; but with the sound of the tires as they came to a full stop, he thought, in some dismay— ice here, too.

They stopped, eventually, and taxied back and around. When the plane came to rest and the dowager got up; Bren got up, taking his computer with him. Meanwhile the thump of doors and hatches advised them that the crew was scrambling to get the plane opened up and the passengers needed to move out at all deliberate speed. He led the way back into the central aisle, and picked up Banichi and Jago.

"We shall go down first, Bren-ji," Banichi said, and he made no objections: the dowager was too precious to risk drawing fire, in the case something was wrong here—one hoped some of Ilisidi's people were in place outside. He felt the cold waft from the door as it opened, and they went back to the rear, where Ilisidi's young men stood. The ladder had pulled up to the plane in an amazingly short time, considering it was not located near the terminal; and he drew in a breath and exited, sandwiched between Banichi and Jago, moving fast to get down into the shadows below the blinking running light from the nearer wing and the tail.

A half-sized bus arrived out of the darkness and stopped with a squeal of tires. Two uniformed Assassins bailed out and held the door open, and Bren climbed the steps. A clatter on the ladder above announced another party debarking, which, by the time they had gotten into the back of the very small bus, proved to be Jegari and his two protectors.

Last came the dowager, to be settled into the front seat, with Cenedi and the rest of the crew, which filled the little bus. There were no headlights. There were still no headlights as the bus pulled away and headed away from the plane, gathering speed, across the unmarked snow.

They crossed what might be the bus's own tracks, passed a wire gate at high speed, skidded on ice on a shallow turn, banged a curb, and then the headlights flared on.

Bren exhaled a breath, realized he had the computer clutched in both arms like a panicked schoolboy, and studiedly settled back into the bench seat, with the fever heat of his bodyguard one on each side of him. The side of the terminal loomed as a gray stone wall in the headlights, then vanished sideways as they swerved again.

Malguri's regional airfield was nothing like the metropolitan surrounds of Shejidan. The whole assembly was a huddle of stone buildings, a garage, a freight warehouse, snow-veiled and capped with white. Snow was piled on either side of the roadway, and the snowfall was gaining on the most recent scraping. Malguri sat at altitude, and winter was in full spate here.

They reached the outer road, and took the fork that led to the highlands. Breath frosted the windows. Wipers beat a frantic time against falling snow, and the engine hiccuped and growled alternately as it struck deeper snow—God, he knew this vehicle. They had never replaced it. They had gone to space. Traveled to the stars. And this damned bus lived.

"Have we heard from staff at Malguri, nadiin-ji?" he asked his bodyguard.

"They are waiting for us, Bren-ji," Jago assured him. "There will be food, and a bed tonight."

Food and a bed was not the sum of his worries. "The young gentleman—have we learned anything, nadiin-ji?"

"Guild is pursuing the situation in the north, nandi," Banichi said.

Upward bound, then. They whined their way through a drift, made it onto the road, bumping and jouncing.

The drive from the lowland airport to the heights of Malguri had figured in shipboard nightmares—it was still that potent. And that had been in good weather. He had repeatedly seen the view of a particular chasm and felt the vehicle tip under him, one of those edge-of-sleep falls that associated itself most firmly with folded space, the terror of losing oneself in nowhere.

It couldn't possibly, he told himself, be as bad as he remembered it. And the driver would be more cautious with snow on the ground. By no means would Cenedi tolerate any real risk to the dowager. It was simply the memory of an islander grown too spoiled, too used to paved roads. And they had the injured boy with them tonight—his injuries now well-wrapped, but by no means should he be jostled.

The bus bucketed fairly sedately along the first snowy climb, headed up small canyons, along reasonable curves. He ought, he thought, to be ashamed of himself—hell, he knew mountain roads: he'd grown up with them, well, at least on holiday. In that long-ago day he'd been anxious about his situation, was all. He'd transferred that anxiety to the bus . . .

The vehicle suddenly swerved, bringing empty air and distant scrub into his view beyond the headlights, as the bus tipped. He'd swear the wheel had found a road-edge gully under the snow. And ice didn't improve the situation. He heard the wheels spin as they made the corner.

"God!" he muttered, and heard Cenedi sharply caution the driver and threaten his job—unprecedented.

Things settled markedly, after that, a number of sharp curves, but nothing so alarming—until they veered off on the Malguri road and nosed up toward the hills.

Bren's foot crept to the stanchion of the seat in front, braced hard. Banichi, beside him, had a grip on the rail of the row in front.

They hit ice. The driver spun the wheel valiantly this way and that and recovered, then *accelerated*, for God's sake. They rubbed the snowbank, and in a bump and a shower of snow they plowed through a small drift, with empty, snowy air on the left hand.

Cenedi leaped to his feet and, very rare for him, actually swore at the driver.

He could not hear the driver's response; but one began to think that perhaps the driver had a reason for anxiety, in the dowager's unannounced return.

Not to mention his own presence. The paidhi-aiji was as popular here as the plague.

The bus slacked its speed, however. Cenedi stood behind the driver, and one of Ilisidi's young men had gotten to the fore of her seat, braced between her and the windshield.

There was something wrong, something decidedly wrong. Banichi, too, got up, eased out and went forward, leaving Jago behind, as the bus reached a slower and slower speed, proceeding almost sedately now.

The driver, whose eyes Bren could see in the rearview mirror, looked wildly left to right.

"Down," Jago said, beside him, and suddenly flattened him to the bench seat. "Bren-ji, get down."

Ilisidi's guard was, at that moment, shielding her with their armored bodies.

The tires, Bren thought, flattening himself on the seat, were highly vulnerable. Welcome home, was it?

Jago slipped down and squatted down in the aisle next to him, her hand on his back. "We have contacted Djinana," Jago said, naming one of the chief operatives in charge of Malguri Fortress, where they were bound. "He has contacted Maigi, and others of the staff, and other staff at the airport. They have the road secure. They met traces of intrusion onto the road, but these are now in retreat. None of us believe that Caiti would be such a fool. This was a local piece of banditry."

"Banditry!" Welcome to the East, indeed. That a handful of individuals severed man'chi and set up independent operations— my God, he thought: the mental shift, if not psychological aberration, that *that* act required— And in Malguri District, itself, no less . . .

"Very ill-considered on their part," Jago said.

"Against the dowager, Jago-ji . . ."

"One doubts they are from Malguri itself. More likely, they emanate from among the neighbors, and have taken advantage of the dowager's absence."

He took her reading of the psychology on faith, faith that it would not be wishful thinking behind that assessment, not from Jago, who could at least feel the undercurrents she met. He was all too aware at this precise moment of missing a critical sense, being totally blind to what others read. He tried to figure their situation, lying there with the possibility of shots flying over his prone body, trying to reason where such bandits would come from—from among the neighbors, some overambitious second nephew with no prospects? Or some wildcard from among the reasonable neighbors, who just wanted to wink at such activity in a neighbor's domain and gather profit from outright theft? That might have worked in ancient times, when there was open land. One did *not* move in on the vacant lordship of the aiji-dowager and expect to prosper, not even when Guild affairs had been in a tangle and a usurper had overthrown the dowager's grandson. . . .

But anachronism was the heart and soul of the East. If it was going to happen anywhere, it would certainly turn up here, where modern plumbing was still controversial.

"The driver has heard rumors in the township, almost certainly," Jago said. "Your staff puts no great credence in these threats of banditry—if such there be at all, Bren-ji. There may have been mutterings. Some associations may be greatly disturbed by the dowager's return."

"One understands so, Jago-ji, but—to come on her land—"

"Once the dowager is home, there will be phone calls

among the neighbors; and there will assuredly be apologies
from the bus company."

About the wild driving, perhaps. Or about not advising the
dowager's security that there might be a hazard, and forcing
them to get their information from the dowager's estate—after
they might well have run into an ambush.

They were still all crouched on the floor—except the driver
and dowager, except those physically shielding the latter. The
boy Jegari was kneeling in the aisle with the rest, supported
and protected by two of Ilisidi's young men.

"The driver is operating on rumor?"

"We do not know the accuracy of his fears," Jago said. "That
will be determined. Certainly he should have stated his misgivings to the dowager's security at the outset, and did not.
That is a fault. That is a grievous fault." The bus swayed and
skidded slightly outward around a sharp curve. "Instead, most
charitably, Bren-ji, he hoped to get us there alive without be-
traying certain individuals—so that the issue would never
arise. One would surmise these people talk much too loudly,
and the driver has gained at least peripheral knowledge of ambitious behavior in the district."

Ambitious behavior. Not banditry. So he guessed right in
one particular. "So what the driver heard might lead under the
certain doors, do you think?"

"It will certainly be interesting to know. One doubts the
company will get its driver or its bus back for a number of
hours, Bren-ji—possibly Cenedi will send it back to bring
your wardrobe, when it arrives on the next plane. Perhaps one
of the house staff will drive it. The driver may need protection. One will attempt to determine that before sending the
man back."

The dowager had been away for two years, completely out of
touch, while the district around her estate thought they had
found a power vacuum, that was what. The realization that she

was alive, and resuming her old power, had tipped a balance back to center, leaving some, possibly including Caiti, caught in an untenable position. The noisiest of the rest had now to decide whether to try to pretend nothing had happened—a dangerous course—or they had to make a move to become powerful.

And how that meshed with the overt action of Caiti and his companions—that was a serious, serious question.

And if certain of the neighbors, namely Caiti, thought they could make no headway with Ilisidi, and if they *were* still operating on their own, the dowager's strong responses might drive them to more desperate actions, like linking up with Tabini-aiji's opposition, specifically the restless south, Murini's supporters—if they could demonstrate they had Tabini's heir, and were willing to play that game—

Dark, desperate thoughts, with one's face down against the seat cushion, and the bus tires spinning in a drift of snow.

If the kidnappers could demonstrate the dowager's power had declined, it might, for one, tilt the ever-fickle Kadagidi, the clan of Murini's birth, Tatiseigi's near neighbors, right back into the anti-Tabini camp, at the very moment the presumedly anti-Murini faction in that clan was in charge and negotiating with Tabini for a political rapprochment. And at the same moment, the East might start to disaffect and join the association of the south, the *aishidi'mar*.

It could break the whole damned business open again and create another armed attack on the aiji's authority.

Not to mention that Cajeiri was at the present in hostile hands and they had quasi-bandits in the neighborhood.

Oh, this was not good.

He saw Banichi move farther forward, encouraging the driver, whose progress was far more sedate than before. Turn after turn, an incident or two of spinning wheels and a slow climb, and Jago looked up, and got up onto the seat.

"Malguri," Jago said, and as Bren lifted up and tried to see the gates, Jago's hand pressed him right back down.

"Let us clarify the situation first, Bren-ji."

He stayed put, deprived of all sight of what was going on, until the bus slowed and turned on what distant memory read as the very front approach to the fortress.

Then he made another move to get up, and Jago did not intervene. He sat up, seeing, like a long-lost vision, a place that had been home for a brief but very formative time in his career, the nightbound stones just as grim, snow-edged, now, the upper windows alight—there were no lower ones, in this house designed for siege and walled about with battlements. Ilisidi stood up as the bus came to a halt, her security parting so she could have the view from the windshield. The front doors of the house opened, and staff came outside, bundled against the cold, as the bus opened its door and let Cenedi out.

Ilisidi came next, Cenedi offering his hand to steady her steps. The boy Jegari got to his feet, with help, and managed to get down the aisle as Bren worked his way forward behind Jago.

Down the steps, then, in the dark and the snowy wind, a breath of cold mountain air, and carefully swept and deiced steps. The inside gaped, with live flame lamps.

Malguri, heart and soul. Yellow lamplight and deep shadow of centuries-old stone, nothing so ornate as the Bu-javid, or Tir-namardi. If there was color on the walls, it was the color of basalt, red-stained and black, rough hewn; or it was the color of ancient tapestry, all lit with golden lamplight. A table met them, bearing a stark arrangement of dry winter branches and a handful of stones, underneath a tapestry, a hunting scene. The air inside smelled of food, candle-wax, and woodsmoke. Servants met them, bowed. This was Ilisidi's ancestral home, her particular holding, and the place in the world she was most in her element. She accepted the offered welcome, and walked in, and up the short interior steps.

Bren recognized those servants who welcomed them, and pulled names out of memory. He stood while Banichi and Jago surrendered some of their massive gear to servants— they would never do that in another household, not even Tirnamardi—and then turned back to deal with some issue that had occupied Cenedi as well, diverting their attention from him, as they would in no other house but the dowager's. Other servants had taken Jegari in charge, fussing over the wounded and now wilting boy and taking him immediately upstairs—straight to bed, one hoped, after a little supper. Bren meanwhile followed the dowager to the formal hall, where a fire burned in the hearth, and more servants stood ready.

Ilisidi sat down in her favorite chair before a roaring fire, a chair set precisely where it had always sat. Bren shed his coat into a young maid's hands while another servant dropped to her knees and applied a towel to his boots—just short of the antique carpet—all deftly and quickly done. He took his own seat by the fire, afterward, settling his computer by the chair leg, and accepted a cup of tea, as the dowager had done.

Safe. Behind walls. Cenedi was out in the foyer attending some necessary business, Jago and Banichi were with him, and one could imagine they were supervising the removal and handling of heavier luggage, and possibly the removal and handling of the bus driver, who clearly knew things he had not told them.

Ilisidi meanwhile enjoyed her tea in decorous quiet, in her first moments home, then asked the staff about the weather reports—snowy, nandi—and the snow pack in the mountains—very deep, nandi. An excellent year.

"Good," she remarked, and there was no question from staff, not about her missing great-grandson, not about her precipitate arrival, not about her wounded young guest or the company of the paidhi-aiji, or even gossip from the township and the very things that Cenedi might be asking the driver. Information had doubtless already passed—or would, behind the scenes, to Cenedi and his staff. Tranquillity settled like an atmosphere, that bubble of not-quite-blissful ignorance that surrounded lords of the land. One anticipated a briefing, and a thorough one when it was ready, but one sat and drank one's tea like a gentleman in the meanwhile.

"We should advise the neighbors we are in residence," was all the dowager said on the matter of business. And when the tea pot was empty: "Join us for supper, nand' paidhi."

"One would be extremely honored, nand' dowager." He took it for a signal to depart for the while, and picked up his computer, rose and bowed—no question of when supper would be, but he clearly was not dressed for the occasion, and needed to remedy that. He bowed a second time, received the dowager's gracious nod, and took himself out, across the foyer and up the stairs, attended from the outer door, not by Banichi or Jago, who were conspicuously absent, but by the trusted staff that he had known before at Malguri—Djinana and his partner Maigi, both welcome faces, somber in the grim news that doubtless had already run through the household, and concerned about the business that had brought them here, but clearly glad to see him.

He had not, he noted, heard the bus start up outside.

The assigned rooms upstairs were, he was glad to see, his old ones—the cozy little sitting area, the historic bedroom with its snarling hunting trophy, and the bed in which historic murder had been done. He longed for that bed. Oh, he longed for it. He had left his own somewhere in the small hours before dawn.

But he had to dress for dinner instead.

His was a string of rooms, all in traditional order, the short hall beyond leading to the bath and the ancient accommodation, as the word was. He did reasonably hope for a bath before dinner. He settled on that as his ambition, and set his computer safely against the wall, next to his modest luggage that sat in the bedroom, already emptied—staff would be fussing his abused and meager wardrobe into respectability. He had both Djinana and Maigi attending him personally on a tour of the remembered premises.

"One has never forgotten, nadiin-ji," he said earnestly. "One recalls your excellent care with great gratitude. The consolation of this unhappy circumstance is the chance to see you and these premises again."

There were deep bows, several times repeated, and Djinana took the lead, indeed offering him the chance to bathe after his journey—he was very glad to agree, and shed his travel-worn clothes in favor of a bathrobe.

"How is the young man who came with us, nadiin-ji?" he asked, and Maigi assured him Jegari was abed, warm, and sound asleep after his ordeal . . . a good report, a reassuring report. The boy was a hunter, a woodsman from birth—he would bounce back with more vigor than a slightly worn diplomat and translator might do under like circumstances.

Said diplomat and translator sank into the stone bath. Staff had remembered exactly the way he liked it; and he rested his head on the rim, soaking away, and wishing Banichi and Jago were able to enjoy the same.

They were not. They likely would not even stop for supper, whatever reconnaissance they were about, which might even entail leaving the grounds: he earnestly hoped not.

But to his surprise Banichi and Jago were waiting for him when, wrapped in a warm robe, he exited the bath to prepare for supper.

"Is there news, nadiin-ji?"

"None firm, Bren-ji," Banichi said. "Cenedi is still talking to the driver."

"Regarding the dowager's neighbors," Jago said, deliberately cryptic, and he pressed no further. He was at least advised where the minefield lay—what topic might be bad taste in a civilized dinner. Hence the warning. The dowager owned the house, the dowager had the neighbors: the dowager would receive a report while it was still rumor and make the estimation—it was not his business, nor his security's business. He only had his advisement.

Meanwhile his dinner attire, pressed and pristine and rescued from his luggage, was laid out neatly on the dressing bench, and Djinana and Maigi stood by to assist. He dressed as far as his shirt, his trousers and his boots, and Jago came and offered him his coat. The pockets of that coat, when he put it on, were heavy on both sides, and very fortunately, it was stiff brocade, which did not collapse under the weight.

One burden was his gun, he expected: he hated carrying it, but it had been useful before; the other thing, a small unit like a pocket-com—he felt of it, not recognizing what it was.

"Keep it with you, one begs, Bren-ji," Jago said, regarding the contents of that pocket.

"What does it do?"

"It locates," Banichi said.

Well, damn. One of the mysterious units. And for dinner in Malguri. Cajeiri had been snatched out of his bed, and if he guessed correctly what this was, it was a means of location. If Cajeiri had had this about him—but what the hell did they expect inside Malguri's fortress?

"How does it work?" he asked. "What am I to do?"

Jago held out her hand, and he brought it out of his pocket. It had a small, glowing screen.

With a dot.

"Like the one on the ship," Jago said. "You are here."

"The satellite reaches it," Banichi said, the man who once upon a time had not cared whether the earth went around the sun or quite the opposite. "Keep it with you."

Ship-tech, let loose on the planet, when the planet had swallowed all it could take, as was, a choking lot, enough to have overthrown Tabini and plunged the whole world into chaos.

He didn't like it. He didn't like the other little gift, either, the one with the bullets. He didn't at all like machinery plummeting out of the heavens and landing in atevi orchards he was responsible for protecting from such intrusions.

But that was the situation they had to work with—that or see chaos and overthrow in the *aishidi'tat* far ahead of any disturbance modern tech might make in the atevi culture. The *aishidi'tat* was still suffering aftershocks—

And the boy's welfare—Cajeiri's—outright overrode ordinary precautions, workaday rules, even major ones. The paidhi was supposed to mediate and rule on the introduction of tech, not have it in the hands of his staff before he had a chance to study the question. He ought to forbid it. He ought to tell them shut it down, let it alone, let them solve the problem without it.

Things were too precarious, advantage too important.

He took the gear. He didn't order any curtailment of its use. Any advantage they could get: that was his thinking, now, right or wrong. Speed in settling this business. News. News would do.

"There was that baggage delay at Cadienein-ori," Banichi said darkly. "It may have involved the young gentleman."

Shocking notion. They had the boy in a trunk? "Guild has gotten there?"

In force, he meant. And that was a truly stupid question and Banichi failed to answer it. Guild never mentioned where allied Guild was, not on a mission.

"We should go back downstairs," Jago said. "Are you comfortable with that situation, Bren-ji?"

"Absolutely," he said. Into the matter with the driver, and the source of their information—he did not inquire, having asked his one stupid question for the hour. They might tell him, but he decided his mental energy was better spent on the dowager, and on readying himself for dinner. If there was information to be had, it would properly come to the dowager before it came to him—and the dowager's staff was not resting at all at the moment.

He looked forward to supper . . . and not at all in anticipation of the food.

10

There were appetizers and preserves, there was a presentation of game of the season, with triangular heaps of vegetables of varied colors—not to mention the sauces, the breads, the crackers and soups—there were three of the latter, each in small cups, the whole dinner service at a modest portable table set near the fire, just the dowager for company.

It was, Ilisidi remarked, snowing heavily out. The bus was still parked in the drive, and the driver was still in interview with the dowager's young men.

And, exhausted by the mere sight of the pile of food, one had to sit waiting and hoping for what else the dowager might have learned, or guessed, or understood, besides the weather report. It was absolutely impossible to breach etiquette with a superior even at such an intimate supper.

But Ilisidi could do so, if she chose. After the formal compliment to the cook, and well before the after-dinner brandy, a message came, which was simply, in the words of the young man who delivered it: "It is Caiti's summer house, nandi, in the Haidamar."

"Well, well, well," Ilisidi said, seeming to taste the words when she said them. She looked up at Bren, then, and gave a decidedly unpleasant smile. "My great-grandson is indeed with them, nand' paidhi, and the name of the villain is indeed Caiti."

That—however grim—was the best news of the day. They

had guessed right. They had followed the right movement. "Whatever the dowager wishes to do," Bren said, "the paidhi-aiji supports."

"A visit, one thinks," Ilisidi said.

To Caiti's domain? Bren wondered in alarm, but the dowager took a serving of sweet berries, seeming unruffled.

In a moment more she remarked: "We shall call on my neighbor. We have so seldom spoken in recent years." After yet another bite she added: "Your presence is requested, paidhi-ji."

The neighbor?

Which neighbor, of several?

That was the likeliest cause of the driver's apprehension—trouble in Malguri's own district. At least two pieces of information began to come together.

"Tonight, aiji-ma?"

"Tomorrow at first light," the dowager said, and added: "Overland."

Cajeiri had a bad, bad headache.

In the dark. Smelly, musty dark.

It was somehow and very surely not Great-grandmother's apartment. That much was clear in all the overset of things that had been true when he went to bed. It was none of the confused sequence of places he had dreamed. Somewhere, he knew he had heard Jegari tell him he was going to leave him and would try to bring help, and the whole world had been roaring and moving, but a slit-eyed attempt to see where he was now produced no Jegari, no information but a cold, black space, the hard-padded surface he was lying on, and a thin wool blanket without a sheet or a pillow.

That was not Great-grandmother's apartment.

He felt further, opened his eyes more than a slit, and felt an attack of nausea, not to mention the widening of the splitting headache, right behind the eyes. It was utterly dark. There were no sounds. This place was cold as the ship could be cold, but it smelled of age. Age—and what mani would call very bad housekeeping.

The silence around him was as curious. He had never been in a place this quiet. No Jegari, no Antaro, no staff. Just a drip of water. Plink. Plink. Plink.

Well, it was scary. But it took more than dark to put him in a panic. He had been in the deep passageways of the ship, in a section with no lights, where it was colder than this. He had found his way through, had he not?

He heaved himself up to sit, hugging the blanket about him. He was as naked as he had gone to bed, and the blanket was scratchy, nothing of quality at all, besides smelling musty. His stomach felt more than empty: it felt as if it would like to turn inside out and his head was going to implode if it did. He had to concentrate for the next few moments on breathing and set-tling that feeling.

He was, he decided, about to be mad instead of scared. But being mad was going to hurt his head. So he tried not to be that, either. He tried to think instead. That by no means helped his headache, but he needed to know where he was.

It was certainly no place he knew, that was foremost. Ship air was filtered and had its own smells of plastics and heat and humans, besides that the ship had no way to reach down and snatch him up. Great-grandmother's apartment smelled throughout of fragrant woods and spices and dried herbs. This place smelled of cold damp stone and things decaying and dusty. And dripping, cold dripping.

It was a place few people cared to fix up. It was where they put things they did not care much about, either, that stood to reason; and they put him here. Unless it was the best they had, nobody he trusted would possibly bring him here for any rea-son. It was a dungeon, that was what. A real dungeon. Like in nand' Bren's movies.

Had not Jegari talked about getting help? But when had Jegari been here, and where had he gone?

He just could not remember. He thought he remembered a vehicle, but that was getting away from his memory the longer he stayed awake. And there were legs, dark legs, several pair, and more steps, and there had been a place that moved, and one that roared, and right now his mouth told him he was thirsty and his stomach told him he still wanted to be sick if he moved too fast.

But sitting still was no good. Just waiting for somebody bad to show up was no good.

A foot off the edge reached stone floor and knocked into what proved to be a wooden stool. Something fell off it. Feeling on the stool and beside it he found a metal bottle and a heavy hand-sized cylinder with a switch. He moved that switch, and light stabbed out at bare stone walls and a growth of something dark and nasty on the rock.

The room was cube-shaped stone, top to bottom, and there was a wooden door—a door that looked very solid. The little stool held one other item: a sandwich, and the metal bottle was a can of fruit drink. He might trust the can. He by no means trusted the sandwich, the thought of which turned his stomach anyway. Fruit juice—he might get that down.

Where were Antaro and Jegari?

Where had Jegari gone? For help. But he could not remember when.

They had been three, safe, comfortable, Fortunate Three, and now, wherever this was, wherever *he* was, he was One.

Alone. He never had been alone in his whole life.

And upset. And hurting. And sick at his stomach. And mad. And scared.

One was a Unity. One could not be divided. One could not be made into anything. It just was.

He wrapped the blanket around him, hugged it close to his

chin for warmth and swept the beam about. There was cloth in one corner. There was a kind of a pit in the opposite one. There was a bucket, a red bucket next to the pit. He was lying on a kind of a bed, with a thin, worn mattress.

He got both feet on the icy floor, stood up, still dizzy, and investigated the door, the obvious way out. It was, no surprise, locked.

The bucket against the other wall was cheap plastic, with a metal handle. The pit in the floor was dank and foul-smelling—very foul, like the recycling tanks aboard the ship. He guessed what that was for, in the absence of other accommodation. It was like—it was like *The Three Musketeers*. It was like *The Count of Monte Cristo*. Only he had not guessed how bad the Chateau d'If would smell in real life.

The cloth pile he found was clothes, new and clean, and fairly well his size at least, and with them was a light coat and a pair of light, cheap boots, used ones. He dressed and put the coat on, warmer, and feeling a little safer, but it was cheap woolen clothing, and it was all a little too large—the long-sleeved shirt hung past his hips and the light coat covered his knuckles. The pants wanted all the tabs taken up as far as could be, and even then tended to drift downward. The cheap leather shoes—those were too large, too: the socks were at least heavy and warm. And all of it smelled musty, as if it had been stored somewhere and never washed.

There was no light in the ceiling. There was no switch by the heavy door, which proved to be locked from the outside. There was no window, nothing but a beamed ceiling that had collected ages of dust.

A dungeon, for sure.

Maybe on the other side of the wall was some other prisoner. Maybe he could dig his way out.

Or maybe he could find a way out through the pit in the

floor. He leaned over it and considered it, and it was just too foul down there. More to the point, there was no updraft that would indicate it led anywhere but down into bottomless and unspeakable filth.

There was, however, a little trap at the bottom of the sole door. But it wouldn't lift. The opening was smaller than he was at his smallest. And he couldn't come at any hinges on it: they were all on the other side.

So were the door hinges, to his disappointment: the door opened outward. And he tried the pull-tab of the fruit juice can to see if he could reach through to lift, say, a latch on the outside. It was not long enough.

Disconsolate, he sat down and had a quarter of the sandwich, deciding there was no need for poison, if they could just shoot him, and drugging him hardly made sense if he was stuck in here for hours and hours. But he kept it to a quarter, not knowing when they might feed him again, and he drank only enough of the room-temperature fruit drink to make the sandwich go down. He had been mad. Now he was, in fact, swinging a little back toward scared. He hoped Assassins had not killed his father and mother when they kidnapped him. He hoped Antaro and Jegari were still alive.

They would never get away with killing his father, if they had done that. His great-grandmother would come back from Tirnamardi with Uncle Tatiseigi—they would take over, and anybody responsible would be very sorry for that.

They would be very sorry, too, for putting him in this hole, once he got out.

He had the drink can, which could be valuable. And he had the metal pull tab. And then he looked at the metal bucket handle, but he thought that if they were halfway smart, they would miss that when someone came to do something with the bucket. He dared not go on using the flashlight, running the batteries down, so he took a careful survey of the place, got up and ran the beam down into the hole (horrid) and along the door seam, and looked even under the bed.

There was a shadow around a stone, gap in the mortar right in the middle of the wall, at the foot of the bed—a little stone, where it seemed there had never been any mortar, or maybe it had just eroded away, the place looked so old.

He didn't know what might lie behind that rock, or how big the little stone might prove to be, but it was something to start with. He took his blanket to sit on, and his can key, and started scraping away at it, hoping, as it wore out, that the people in charge would go on giving him fruit drink in cans.

So what would the Count of Monte Cristo do?

He switched off the light to save the battery. He could feel the spot without it, and he started chipping away, getting rid of the last bit of mortar, chip by little chip. The Count had spent years trying to get out. He was willing to, if that was what it took, so long as they went on feeding him.

If there was dirt on the other side, he could sweep it into his blanket and dump it into the hole in the corner of the room. He could dig and dig under whatever building he was in until he could hope he was outside.

Surely it would go a lot faster once he got one stone out.

If it was another room it let him into, that other room might not have its door locked.

At very least, it was a plan, and it was something to do, rather than sit in the bed and be scared.

And when he got out, oh, some people were going to be in trouble.

11

It had been a long, long time, Bren was well aware, since he had been in Malguri's stableyard. His own mecheita, Nokhada, had nearly forgotten him.

Or she conveniently pretended to have forgotten. She towered aloft, a winter-coated, snaky-necked, and supercilious creature with jaw-tusks the length of a man's hand. Her clawed feet ripped the straw of the stable-aisle, and she threw her head up, pulling at the restraint of two handlers.

The dowager was already safely aboard a younger creature, Babsidi son of Babsidi, a handsome mecheita of high breeding and elegant line, new to the dowager's service.

Bren had the crop. He was in no patient mood himself, on a short breakfast and in frigid morning air, and, as it happened, he had refreshed his riding skills between their landing back in the world and their taking up residency in the Bu-javid. He took the rein, he targeted the stirrup he had to reach, whacked Nokhada wickedly on the shoulder, and gave the command while he was in motion.

A good thing two of Ilisidi's young men were holding on: she squalled and tried to disembowel the foremost of the two, who was fast enough and strong enough to keep that head out of play. Bren popped the shoulder again with the crop, and a third time, hard—he could make a move for the saddle, and even get aboard while the young men held her, but if he let her get half of her way now, she would try for it with him for the rest on the ride.

And the shoulder dutifully dropped. The head shook, rattled the harness, lowered. Bren got a foot in the mounting loop and hit the saddle, rein in hand.

Nokhada gathered herself up then, a powerful surge, a deep sigh once she stood, and then she obeyed the rein, after he touched the offending side lightly. He was not fooled: he kept her under close governance. Nokhada had gotten the better of him on their very first ride, and forever hoped, after any hiatus, that she could do it again to a person of his size, never seeming to recall that he had since learned to ride.

Banichi and Jago were up on two of the same herd. They had four of the dowager's young men, the dowager, besides Cenedi, nine in all, but the herd numbered twenty, and would go with them, four of them under packs, with portable shelter, considering the weather and the length of the trip and the rest just because splitting a mecheiti herd was more trouble than any handler wanted. They were prepared against a cold night in the open—or for a formal dinner and an overnight stay, if their intended host, who did not acknowledge having a telephone, proved reasonable after all.

They were bound, so the dowager said, to pay a social call . . . on Drien, the lady who *hadn't* come to dinner in Shejidan. And after flying all day yesterday, they were up before the crack of dawn, kitted out and equipped for a minor expedition.

One gathered the lady in question had no desire to be contacted. One gathered Ilisidi had a point to make and intended to make it unmistakably.

Why? he might have asked his staff once upon a time. Now he had a very solid notion that it *was* a good idea—just serving notice: letting the nerves that reacted to man'chi *feel* that the aiji-dowager was no longer light-years removed from the East. Getting up in people's faces, as the saying went. A demonstration of who feared whom . . . and who needed to fear whom.

And sometimes such a meeting meant the judicious removal of an obstacle or shifting an association: earthquake, in the interlinking pattern of associations.

The paidhi didn't need to ask, not after years of experience with the aiji-dowager. The paidhi didn't say a thing, or provoke conversation, not with the dowager in her present mood. She was not reacting: she was thinking all the way, he was well sure of it. She was thinking, and whatever she was thinking, the best the paidhi and his staff could do was exactly what Tabini had sent them to do—keep the Eastern Association intact. Keep war, that least likely of atevi interactions, from breaking out between districts.

Get Cajeiri back. That was only the first step.

Stable doors opened. The young men quietly let the restraining loops slip through the bridle rings. Free, Nokhada threw her head and swayed, blowing steam in the frosty air, and they surged for the door, to the peril of timbers and posts

They rounded the corner for the outer pen gate: handlers swung it open, and in that very moment, in mid-stride, one short, brass-capped tusk gleamed in Nokhada's lower jaw as she snaked that head around to stare at her rider from one dark, calculating eye.

Pop of the quirt and a retensioning of the rein: Bren didn't even think about the choice.

Nokhada blew, threw her head and, raking and shoving Banichi's mount, fell right in where she belonged, next to pale Babsidi and Cenedi's black mechieta, and with Banichi and Jago riding right behind. Fighting for position in the herd. It was like atevi politics—it didn't give a damn for anyone in the way.

God, he wished he'd tucked that last breakfast roll into his pocket, but he'd been afraid it would shed crumbs on the gun.

Snow came down on them, a sifting off the eaves three stories above. It was scarcely morning even so, a gray glimmer of dawn as they rounded the end of the building. Clawed feet gained scratchy traction on the occasional icy bits and sent the snow flying. Nokhada, always ambitious, but aging, nipped a too-forward unsaddled youngster at the turn around the ell of the building, and the interloper dropped back in the order as Banichi and Jago moved up.

The bus still sat in the front drive as they passed, its roof bearing a thick blanket of snow. Its driver was a guest of the estate, so he had learned over such morning tea as the servants had brought in—which meant that the bus sat here rather than at the airport, and *that* meant that their spare baggage, and his clothes, would not make it up when they arrived. The driver had reportedly feared for his safety last night—with some reason, had been Banichi's word on it. But Ilisidi would surely make it clear to the district that the driver was detained and threatened, and that would keep him safe from reprisals—who knew?—reprisals possibly from the very lady they were on their way to visit.

Jegari, who had not been informed everyone else was leaving, was still abed, probably still asleep, and Maigi and Djinana vowed to be sure he stayed there if they had to sit on him. It was a dirty trick to play on the lad, who now was a virtual prisoner in the estate, but the boy had told them all he knew, and there was no good dragging him along in a rough, cold ride.

This is an investigative and diplomatic venture, Bren had written Jegari in a note, to be given him when he waked. *The aiji-dowager and the young gentleman alike will be best served if you remain in the house to await or relay messages. There may well be such and they may well be of extreme urgency. As a member of the young gentleman's staff, you have a certain authority to answer.*

The outer gates opened by remote, and let them out onto the same road the bus had used. The snow made quick going at the mecheiti's long, clawed stride, with the mecheiti fresh and full of energy. But they didn't follow the road all the way to the bottom, where it had branched off from the township road. Not too far along the downward course, they took a small downward spur that led off under a rock wall of frozen springs.

The trail, if honest trail there was beneath the snow, then led them down past evergreen and scrub: at best it was a path not often used, not in any season, by the look of it. The mecheiti's clawed feet broke down barren winter brush, gained a sometimes chancy purchase on the ice near streams that made frozen exit from the rocks, and went where, very clearly, no bus had ever been.

It was at least four cold hours on that trail, with several very chilly breaks for rest, before they hit a service road, and two more with no sign at all of any dwelling or estate boundary. But that was the way in the East: civilization had large gaps, and roads passed through long spaces of empty before they got anywhere at all, not necessarily with convenient interconnection. Roads were historically nonexistent where there had never been association; roads were poor where association was loose, broken, or in name only.

And the two estates in question, Malguri, which was Ilisidi's ancestral holding, and Cobesthen, which was Lady Drien's, had, as one could well see, no well-established roads between them—no ties, no polite connections socially, not for a century and a half. The lady of Malguri and the lady of Cobesthen were cousins, legatees of a historical breakup, from a time when the two estates had been one power, centered at Malguri. The association had fractured—the murder in the bedroom at Malguri was not unconnected with this event, though in exactly what particular Bren was a little hazy—and the cousins, the only living relatives of their generation within the district, did not routinely speak, though sharing a common boundary.

The current lady of Cobesthen, Cenedi informed them, used

a phone for outward communication, like ordering up vegetables or items of clothing from Malguri Township, but refused any message that came by way of such a device.

Drien did Tatiseigi of Tirnamardi one better in stubborn ecological conservatism, Bren thought glumly. One got the picture, one got it quite clearly . . . and one would have wished to ask the dowager why the human in the company was being asked along if they were facing an Easterner with a particularly strong loathing for modernity, humans, and all that came from them.

Because Banichi and Jago were damned good at what they did, was one answer, and they would not leave him behind in Malguri at any order. The dowager surely wanted all the help she could get in this venture, and would therefore risk her neck and his to get it. That was the conclusion he drew on the matter. He could not foresee any good he could do—his camping outside in the foyer for the duration of the interview might be a good move, once they got where they were going, except that Banichi and Jago would not leave him alone out *there*, either.

A highland lake lay off the eastern face of Malguri, down a gentle slope. That vast lake, remnant of some past glaciation and an eons-old fracture and uplift of the world's crust, divided them from Cobesthen, which held the southern lake shore. They were short-cutting a jagged peninsula of the lake, as Bren remembered the geography, to get to Cobesthen, choosing the mecheiti rather than going by boat from the very beginning—from Malguri Fortress itself.

"Why ride?" he asked Banichi and Jago, during one of the rests. "Why not take the boat across? What is the plan, nadiin-ji?"

They stood near the mecheiti, an isolate knot of warm bodies in a cold winter woods. Banichi lowered his head and answered quietly, "A boat, Bren-ji, could be prevented from landing. And recall Lord Caiti holds land across the north shore of the lake. Almost certainly he expects intrusion. The land is wider and affords cover. The lake while wide—is very flat."

That was a thought.

"Do you think he would continue to hold Cajeiri there, within the—"

—within the dowager's reach, he had been going to say. But he said, instead. "Bait?"

"Very possibly, Bren-ji. Continued proximity would make it irresistible."

And would offer the greatest possible embarrassment to Ilisidi. Caiti's holding there was named Haidamar, the summer retreat on the northwest shore. Caiti's lowland and more frequent residence was down in the lowlands to the west, the Saibai'tet. But the airport at Cadienein-ori served the northern territory, and, by extension, several mining concerns near the north end of the lake and downward—was there, in fact, even a road between Malguri and the Haidamar?

By his memory, there was not. Not on *this* side of the lake. But, God, he thought, looking out toward the snow-hazed lakeshore, dim through the trees—were they that close to the boy? Was holding him there meant to draw Ilisidi into a trap, to get her to attack across the lake?

She, in effect, had little choice but to move first, move fast, and try to do something; and that meant crossing another lord's land, by a route that *had* no roads.

"*Are* we actually calling on Lady Drien, nadiin-ji?"

"If she will open her gates," Jago said. "One believes we are, Bren-ji."

They had, besides him and the dowager, Cenedi, Nawari, Banichi and Jago, and the dowager's young men, having, one hoped, called in Guild to their assistance and relying on staff to protect the house back on the heights from a flank attack.

And were they going to pay a social call on their way around the lake's far shore, possibly as a base to move against Haidamar?

Possibly.

And phone or no phone, he would lay a bet that Drien knew they were coming: a stubborn aristocrat who wouldn't acknowledge messages that came by phone, wouldn't respond, and hadn't communicated with her cousin in the years when they had been close neighbors . . . would not be caught by surprise. The lady would know if something moved on her land, even in the dead of winter. Her guard might not be Guild, but they could not be that careless, or that lacking in modern abilities.

The question was whether the lady had used that grocery-ordering phone to call the Haidamar and advise Lord Caiti she was being trespassed upon, by a certain number of persons intent on reaching Caiti's land.

And had it been Drien who had set so-called bandits on the road to Malguri last night? Or might they have been instigated from Caiti's side?

Ilisidi was uncharacteristically silent and cheerless as she rode, speaking only with Cenedi, and Bren let that situation be. Nokhada typically kept pressing to the fore, but he kept her back, out of the dowager's way, figuring that if she wanted him, she would signal so. She didn't, which said worlds.

The sun made a midafternoon appearance through the lowering gray cloud, a small patch of sky as they passed along the lake edge, where a snowy beach and a rime of ice afforded easier going than the woods. That was the warmth in the day, short-lived as it was. By the time they reached the end of that beach, the gray had wrapped the peaks behind them and erased half the lake, giving the false illusion of a low, endless plain under a misty sky.

That icy mist rolled in off the lake with a sifting of snow, and, leaving the shore, they rode in fog, among ghostly shapes of winter trees, down a local road blanketed in snow. No vehicles had crossed here. The mecheiti's feet turned up no ruts of wheels beneath the new fall. Even Jago remarked on that fact: they might have stepped back centuries, when mecheiti *were* the only transport in this district.

It was a lonely, lonely place, Cobesthen. It was isolation, failed prosperity. Ancient anger.

Eventually, around a snowy rock outcrop, they came on an iron grillwork gate, between two lowering and massive towers. Cenedi leaned from the saddle to ring an icicled bell and announce their presence—and one could almost hope the notoriously contrary lady of Cobesthen would open those gates and let them in, unpleasant as the encounter was bound to be. They had been in the saddle all day. They had their gear to camp out here, but one gathered that the aiji-dowager did not intend to camp in tents outside the lady's gate . . . not without taking some action for it.

Time passed. They waited, mecheiti shifting restlessly, nipping and shoving as they tended to do while, incredibly, finally, on the other side of the gate, a band of men rode mecheita-back toward them, a reciprocal force that might have ridden right out of the machimi plays.

Bren let go a long, long breath, facing these messengers, the East at its most obstinate. It was a wonder, in fact, that the lady had not stationed guards out in the old tower, to freeze winter-long on a lonely, outmoded duty.

But the fact she hadn't said there was more modernity out here than met the eye.

They sat, they waited. The mounted group arrived, the leader asked their identity, and, receiving the reply from Cenedi, "The lord of Malguri," that leader signaled a man of his who quietly got down and unchained the gate. It ultimately took the help of two others, who dismounted, forced the snow-blocked gate open barely enough to let them through . . . no, Bren said to himself, that gate had not seen many comings and goings in recent days. The snow was up over the footing, and carved itself a deep arc when they moved it.

They passed that gate, with their pack train and their spare mounts, and the several locals afoot pulled the gate shut and noisily ran the chain back through, ominous sound in the foggy surrounds, before they got back to the saddle. They had wanted in. They *were* in. Who else the lady of Cobesthen thought she was keeping out was uncertain. One hardly liked the feel of it.

And if one disliked that, the silence of the guards and the general demeanor gave no better feeling.

The other side of the wall protected a small, youngish forest, well-kept, actually, though fog obscured the details and snow covered the ground. The lake should, perhaps, have been visible to the left, where the wall came up against a snowy rock outcrop, but fog had obscured everything into a dimmer and dimmer sameness as the sun sank and the snow came down with increasing vigor.

The house materialized out of that haze as they moved, a towered old mass of stone sitting on the lake shore, low-lying, with some sort of stone structure beyond it, on the shore itself. It was reputedly coequal with Malguri in age, or nearly so, older than that wall they had just passed. The only sign of warmth in all the scene was the glow of light in two windows on the upper floor: like Malguri, being built for seige, it had no lower windows, not a one. Its doors, when they approached, were deep-set within that nasty trick of mediaeval architecture, a shooting gallery on either hand, the only apertures in the lower floor being sniper-slits.

That particular feature could still operate, with guns instead of arrows. But it was undignified to look up in fear. They came to a halt in front of the shadowed front door.

The dowager, helped down by her young men, straightened herself, took a firm, gloved grip on her cane, then walked, on

Cenedi's arm, up the icy steps. Bren slid down, finding his weary legs like stumps underneath him. Banichi and Jago alit, and Banichi shouldered a heavy bag from their gear.

Well, Bren said to himself, with a slight glance at Banichi and Jago, whose faces were impassive. Well, here we go. He walked the icy steps after the dowager, all the while conscious of the gun in his right pocket. He had no intention of giving that up. His bodyguard would let no one lay hands on him.

The doors at the top of the steps slowly opened. Inside, there was firelight—live flame, in lamps from a century before electricity, illumined the hallway. Brighter firelight from an open inner doorway cast a live sheen over the irregularities of slate flooring in the hall, and the austerity and appropriateness of the single hanging and the single, horizontally-mounted spear above it were downright chilling in their lack of mitigation or welcome.

One. A Unity of One was the declaration here. *Kabiu* at its simplest.

Arrogance. Solitude. Again, isolation from the world.

And absolute power at least within these walls. Malguri made a far, far different statement in its foyer, with stone and winter branches, a porcelain vase and a scatter of river stones: diversity, balance, harmony.

Bren read the arrangement, treading deliberately at the dowager's back, and had the very clear realization that no human foot had ever sullied this floor.

Did the lady know by now that he was with the dowager?

If she knew there were visitors at her gate, and knew they were not the egg delivery from the lowland farms—which doubtless did not rate an armed escort—she indeed knew that detail. He did not expect a welcome.

But then this lady was not only scantly disposed to accept humans, as he recalled. She had been scantly disposed to recognize the fact that Ilisidi had married a westerner, more than

half a century ago. This lady was still scantly disposed to recognize the existence of the *aishidi'tat* and the aiji in Shejidan,
let alone welcome a stray human.

A maidservant met them inside that further door, and
bowed.

"The lady wishes me to show you to your rooms."

"We are not here to tour or dither about," Ilisidi snapped,
and the cane tip struck the floor with the sound of a rifle shot.
"Where is my cousin?"

The maid looked as if she had rather be almost anywhere
else. "If the dowager would be so good as to take cognizance of
the offered rooms . . ."

"We are *not* good!" Ilisidi said. A second time the cane hit the
ground. "We are impatient and out of sorts! Our great-grandson
is in the hands of idiots! We assume our esteemed cousin is
more intelligent than to abet this nonsense by delaying us in our
search, and we assume she is not ignorant of the proceedings and
the perpetrators! Shall we draw other conclusions?"

The maid opened her mouth, hardly looking up, then shut
it, bowing deeply. "One will relay this sentiment to a superior
immediately, nandi. Please wait."

The maid fled at, for a decorous household servant, a very
fast pace. They stood in silence, melting small puddles onto
the slate floor.

A second servant, an old woman, came from the lighted
room, and bowed. *This* was likely the major domo, who should
have been the one sent to greet a guest of high status. Mark
that down in the score.

A deep bow. "The house is distressed to report, nandi, that
the lady is indisposed. She will see her guests at breakfast."

Wham! went the cane. The old woman flinched, not raising
her eyes.

"Cenedi," Ilisidi said, and quietly, smoothly, Cenedi moved
forward, oh, about half a step.

"We are at the dowager's orders," Cenedi said, and lifted a hand. His men moved in the indicated direction, right toward the open door. Three set themselves in place to guard that door. Two more moved down the hall to take possession of that.

My God, Bren thought, and did not stare about to see what Banichi and Jago were doing. He had the nape-of-the-neck sense they were paying attention round about, not looking at him or at Cenedi at the moment.

The major domo, give her credit, stood her ground, though deferentially.

Ilisidi hardly paused to notice. She headed, with Cenedi, right past the woman, right toward a further lighted doorway, and Bren found nothing to do but follow her, with Banichi and Jago one on a side and very much on the alert.

They passed Ilisidi's guard. They met another, inside the room, two women not in Guild black, but wearing firearms.

In an ornate chair by a fireside, the chair one of a set of three, sat a thin, aristocratic woman enjoying a cup of tea. A book lay face down in her lap. Her hair was liberally streaked with white. She wore half-moon glasses, slid well down on her nose, and looked up with a flash of golden eyes.

"Well," the lady said, "one is hardly surprised at such behavior."

"Where is my great-grandson?" Ilisidi asked, the cane in both hands.

"How should I know?"

"By various sources!" Bang! went the cane, end-on. "Neither of us is a fool."

"What is *that?*" The lady took off her glasses and waved that object generally at, Bren feared, him. He decided it behooved him to bow courteously at this point, and look as civilized as possible in a slightly damp padded coat and outdoor boots.

"This *gentleman*," Ilisidi shot back, "honors this house, as do we."

"Guild guards and a human," the lady scoffed, looking down her nose. "You dare dispose your hireling guards under my roof!"

"Your roof by tolerance, cousin. Your grandfather—"

"Leave my grandfather out of this, nadi!"

Ilisidi marched over to the other chair and sat down, damp traveling coat and all, cane braced between her knees. "Tea," she said to the servants.

There was a lengthy pause. Lady Drien sat still, and sat, and finally lifted the slim, jeweled fingers of the hand that rested on her chair. A maidservant bowed, turned and walked to the large standing tea urn, an impossibly ornate thing that looked like a silver dragon with brass belly-scales. Bren followed the motion only with his eyes, watching hands as the maid prepared and filled two cups, and brought them back on a cinnabar and blackwood tray.

Ilisidi accepted. Drien accepted. There was a space of decorous silence while the two sipped and thought.

Drien set her cup down first, click. Ilisidi's followed, click. There was another moment of silence.

"Remarkably early snow," Drien said.

"It makes searching inconvenient."

"Gods unfortunate! Impatient even at your own disadvantage!"

"There is a boy, your own cousin, badly handled by the likes of Caiti and other fools, and you are prepared to be tolerant of this circumstance! We are appalled, Cousin!"

"I had no part in your decision to bed down with western barbarians! Anything you got of that error is not my concern!"

A small pause and a dark stare. "My great-grandson remains your cousin, Drien-daja. Blood is blood."

"Unwillingly!"

A longer pause. "Your neighbors came under my roof presenting compliments," Ilisidi said. "They entered under our residence. They sat at our table. They complimented our cook. They spoke disparagingly of you, in particular."

Drien's nostils flared. "So cheap a ploy."

"But true, nandi. They said nothing *specific* against you—certainly nothing quite accusatory. But one is certain they were perfectly willing to do so, had we indicated we were at all willing to hear it. They later suborned a maid of our staff, a woman with ties to the lowlands. Perhaps they threatened the woman or her relations to gain her cooperation. She breached the doors. She admitted them by way of the servant accesses."

"Perhaps she was a lowland scoundrel."

"Ah. Indeed. Perhaps she was. Or perhaps she harbored an honest grudge against us. We only fed and housed her for four years, for very little work. During the last two, with Murini sitting in authority in the Bu-javid, perhaps she began to form other man'chi."

"Then back you come, like an old bone, several times buried."

Ilisidi laughed silently. "We are extremely hard to bury, cousin. You know that. You declined to come visiting with them. Why?"

Drien seemed, reluctantly, in better humor. She snapped her fingers, and the maid collected the cups for another round of tea.

The whole room stood still while the two indulged in yet another cup, and the cups went, click and click, down on the side tables.

"My great-grandson," Ilisidi said, "is faultless in this dispute, Drien-aba. I have ridden a snowy road to enlist your understanding in this matter."

"And you bring *this* under my roof." Drien made a flick of the finger in Bren's direction, almost without a glance, as if she were disposing of lint on her sleeve. "To sleep here! How dare you?"

"One relies on your adventurous nature," Ilisidi said dryly. "Nothing affrights you, Drien-aba."

"Nothing *affrights* me, nadi, but this abomination offends me."

"Bren-paidhi." Ilisidi moved her hand, and indicated his place beside her. He walked over to the side of her chair. He bowed to her, moreover, with perfect understanding of the degree of inclination requisite.

"Well-trained," Drien said. It was the word one used of a mecheita.

"Drien-daja." Bren offered a second bow, perfectly impassive. "One is honored to address the lady of Ardija." That was the district name. "If my presence offends the lady, I shall lodge with the servants."

Provocation. Deliberate, and he could all but feel Ilisidi gathering her moral force should Drien take him at his word. Ilisidi would have him in her own quarters before she sent him to Drien's staff: he was sure of that.

"Sit," Drien said sharply.

That was a thunderbolt of protocol. He bowed a third time in courteous deliberation and took the third chair. Ilisidi, in the tail of his eye, simply signaled to the servant herself for another round of tea.

It came. They all three drank.

"So," Drien said. "Was it for amusement, cousin, that you brought this foreigner under our roof?"

"It was for your edification, cousin."

"Indeed." A brow lifted, rousing an architecture of wrinkles. "Mine? You go traipsing off to the heavens and associate with humans. You mingle in their affairs at their behest, and they reward us all by picking quarrels with still other foreigners—after which, my esteemed cousin returns to the world to cry alarm and take up habitation with—what is the lord's name?"

The chairs were set in a triangle. Bren had a fair view of both ladies, and sat still and tense. But a hint of wicked still humor hovered about the dowager's mouth. "Which one?"

Drien's eyebrow lifted. "Oh, come now, nadi. There can be no such abundance of midland lords."

"Your gathering of gossip seems at least adequate." A sharp frown came down between Ilisidi's brows. "Where *is* my great-grandson, Dri-daja?"

"Why apply to me?"

"Because there was a reason you did not join Caiti. What was it?"

"Recognition of fools in action."

"So you knew what they were going to do."

"One had not the least notion. Foolishness has every direction open to it. Wisdom is much more limited in choice."

"Well? What direction does our wise cousin take now?"

The lady held out her cup for a refill. Her arm hardly reached full extension before tea was in the cup. She sipped it thoughtfully. "Perhaps not a direction. A position. Caiti was born a fool, lives a fool, will likely die a fool. And *you* let him to your table. But then you allow humans, too." A small silence, in which Ilisidi said nothing. "Were you not aware, cousin, of Caiti's ambitions? Perhaps if you visited your estate more often, you might become aware."

"The thing of which we were not aware," Ilisidi snapped, "was the corruption of my staff in my absence."

"A child stolen right under your roof," Drien said sweetly. "And whisked through the heart of the Bu-javid and the whole width of Shejidan. You are not yourself, cousin."

"Where *is* he, Drien-ji?"

"One believes, with Caiti."

"Where?"

"In the Haidamar."

The lady, Bren thought, was extremely well informed—for a lady using live flame to light her front hall. And they had been detected at the front gate, quite readily: hell, they had been detected *approaching* the front gate—it took time to saddle a herd of mecheiti.

"One rather suspects," Drien added, "that my neighbors fear Caiti."

"Do you fear him?" Ilisidi shot back.

"That depends, 'Sidi-ji, on which side I take."

"You call him a fool," Ilisidi said.

Drien's brow lifted. "He is. But there are more sides than two."

"Consider mine," Ilisidi said.

"I do," Drien answered. "I choose to answer your questions. He was in the Saibai'tet, in his winter home, before he and his associates went to Shejidan. He takes residence in the Haidamar. He knows you will come. And look to your safety if you do."

The Haidamar, the fortress of Caiti's domain, held the other end of the considerable lake. It sat on one of the rivers that fed into the north of the lake, had historically suffered from its easy access to the flatlands just beyond and had proved a soft target many a time, where it regarded forces coming up from the plains, but that meant, in the modern age, fairly easy access to an airport—and communications.

A schemer with allies, Bren said to himself, needed communications, and dared not bottle himself into a dead end like the Saibai'tet, which nestled on flat land eastward, where the foothills gave way to wide plains . . . agriculture had been Caiti's forte. Until now. Now it became something else.

"You think my great-grandson is with him in the Haidamar, nandi?"

"Possibly, cousin. One certainly might be very suspicious."

"We have grounds for discussion, Dri-daja."

"Do we? Perhaps we might manage a late snack. Will this join us?" With a wave at Bren.

"The Lord of the Heavens will join us," Ilisidi said firmly.

He had had better invitations in his life.

The stone came free. It proved to be about hand-sized. Cajeiri turned on his light for just a moment to have a look at his progress, which had created a little spot of darkness in an otherwise unbroken wall under the bed, and he lay flat on his side to look into it.

Inside, to his probing fingers, was more rubble, more crumbling mortar. He saw how it was, set it in memory, and cut the light off to save the batteries.

He had hoped to meet dirt right off, but it was still a start. And there was no use tearing his hands up getting straight at the rough rock inside. He had traded the bit of aluminum from the can for the metal bucket handle—that had been a struggle, getting that off—and he dug away at the next stone over, to widen his gap. He tried wiggling it. Nothing yet. He kept digging, raked out rubble, and it gave.

His backside was cold, his hands—he alternated using them—were miserable and approaching open wounds. But work and hope kept him warm, and he had made progress. Where the hole was going, he had no idea. How long it would take, he had no idea, but he had learned—Great-grandmother had confined him to his room no few times—that it did no good at all to pitch a fit or wait for relief. What did count was to find a job and keep at it, and to be just blithe and cheerful when summoned out and try to better his situation—he doubted he would get such an offer from people who had lodged him with a scratchy blanket and a single sandwich.

He could do what he set his mind to: Bren-paidhi was no bigger than he was, and Bren got along, and made people listen to him, and got through where bigger people failed. It was just technique, that was what Banichi would say. Just technique, and keeping one's mind centered right on the job at hand.

So—putting Banichi's lessons together with great-grandmother's—he was making progress of some sort; he meant to get things on his terms. He was hungry by now. That hardly mattered.

And, much faster than the last, the next stone wiggled in its mortar jacket, ever so slightly.

He heard footsteps, the first sound of life he had heard in this place. They were coming. He shoved his rock back into place. He scrambled back out from under the bed, lay down under the blanket, kept his grimy hands under the covers and looked distressed and sleepy.

The lock rattled to a key, and opened. Someone came in with a potent flashlight.

He shielded his eyes with a blanketed elbow, squinted up pitifully at two men, one of whom had a tray. Servants, clearly, but he was going to remember those faces.

"Is he ill?" one wondered, and the other said, "Only sleepy."

The man with the tray set it down. Cajeiri coughed and looked as pathetic as he could manage.

"My medicines," he said. This was a ploy he had seen amply demonstrated in the human archive. "I need my medicines."

"We should report it," one said. And for just a moment Cajeiri thought of making a break for that open door, but he had no idea what lay outside. They were believing him. They felt of his face.

"He has no fever, nadi."

That was a problem. Cajeiri thought of the biggest, most uncheckable lie he could fashion. "I was in the heavens, nadi." A cough. "One has to have medicines, for years after. One will die without them."

"What sort of medicines, boy?"

"One has no idea," he mumbled. "The doctor gave them to me." He doubled up, still under the blankets. "My stomach hurts. Oh, it hurts."

They wrapped the blanket around him. The door was still open. And perhaps it had not been too smart—if they got a look at his hands. Or looked to see where he had gotten all that dust. He rubbed it off as he clutched the blankets, rolled over, and he could see a very barren, rock-walled corridor outside, uninformative except that this was not a very fancy hallway.

"One begs, eat your supper, boy. It may help."

"It makes me sick. Oh, it hurts."

"We had better tell the major domo, nadi."

To his disgust, one stayed with him while the other ran that errand. He continued to hold his stomach, and took only a sip of water when offered, even if he was starving.

"Where is this place?" he ventured to ask the sole servant.

"We are not to answer questions, young sir."

"It is a very poor place, clearly."

"It is by no means poor, young sir!"

He had stung the man's pride. And consequently he learned something, at least. Not a poor place, indeed, a place with a major domo, and servants. Something else occured to him. The food smelled a lot like a dish Great-grandmother liked, spices from her side of the world.

"I think it is very poor," he said. "And clearly you are not Guild."

"The Guild has no power here."

That was the East, and the servant was a fool, or thought *he* was. He remembered Great-grandmother saying that in the East, some lords refused to employ Guild, but that the Guild infiltrated them anyway: it took just a bit more work.

"My great-grandmother will know what to do," he said, and doubled tighter. "Oh!"

"Lie down. Lie still."

"It hurts to lie down, nadi. And when my great-grandmother finds out you failed to give me my medicines, you will wish you had Guild to protect you. She will be very put out." All the while his mind was racing. If there were Guild, the man'chi of the Guild to his father might say that his father's son was not to be kept in a basement—for that matter, the man'chi of the Guild might argue that this was an illegal action, and Guild could not support it. It was one thing to kidnap someone. It was another to kidnap the aiji's own son, a minor child: he had studied the law. Mani had thumped it into his head.

But nobody had caught Murini yet, and there were definitely people who wanted to kill his father.

The Guild had pulled support from those people. That was a scary thought, that there was one other group of people besides the Easterners who might not use Guild these days, or who might employ Guild who were no longer following the rules. It *could* mean that he was in the south, and that the household cook had just bought Eastern spices imported in. Maybe these people were tied to Murini-aiji, and rogue Guildsmen were out there somewhere: nand' Bren's people had killed the Guild leader who had tried to subvert the Guild into backing Murini—but there were definitely some of that man's followers loose.

The man had said—had he not—that the Guild had no power here. That was hard to parse: it could mean either thing. But the spicy aroma was a vote for Eastern. And a stone dungeon? That was more Eastern-like, too. In the East people hated human conveniences—like bathrooms with real toilets and electric lights that ran without a local generator. He knew about Malguri. If they wanted electricity, like for the Guild to run some of their equipment, they had to fire up the generator, because no wires came up from the township. He had that from Great-grandmother. He had been appalled, hearing it. She had been making the point that he was too soft. Maybe he was, but one reasonably expected lights to work when one flipped the switch. And they had a plastic bucket, and used flashlights instead of candles. *That* said this place or these people were not *that kabiu* . . .

Footsteps came back. The first servant came in with a man of some authority, and they felt of his forehead and checked his eyes and felt his pulse.

"He says spacefarers have to have medicine," the man who had stayed with him reported, and the other two asked all the next questions, concluding with: "He says he has no idea what he takes."

"Move him upstairs," the authority said.

Well, that was certainly a disappointment. Not at all what he wanted. He *wanted* someone in authority to turn up so he could worry *them.* Instead they gathered him up, blanket and all, and took him out into the hall, letting him walk, which he did slowly, marking every detail of what was surely a basement.

They went up a short stairs, and into an electric-lit, inhabited hall, the plain sort of hallway that said servants' quarters, and maybe kitchens, a place with modest items of *kabiu.* They brought him to a door, and inside what was someone's room, which had a single glaring electric bulb in the ceiling—the room belonged, he gathered from what they said, to a junior servant, who would double up with one of the others. They set him on the bed and carried out the little dresser, which, besides the bed, a portable toilet, and a small straight chair, were the only items of furniture.

They brought his supper up, and set it down on the chair. They brought a metal water pitcher. That rated a little interest. But he tucked up on the mattress under the bedclothes and feigned misery.

He simply had to start over, was all. And up here the rooms were closer together, and he knew where the next room was.

And here there was electric light, but the switch was not in the room. Damn.

There was no window, either. That was not good. The walls were plastered. There was probably stone underneath.

They called a workman to reverse the lock in the door. That took a while. The food would be cold, if he wanted to sneak a bite or two. They brought him another couple of blankets and piled them on, so he was too hot.

They left, finally, leaving the light on. He got up, took the spoon from the tray and had a couple of cold, disgusting bites, which helped the hunger, nonetheless.

They might not miss the spoon. It was, he thought, silver. That was a conductor. He had electricity. That was a good thing. The switch was on the outside of the room. That was a stupid arrangement, if it was regularly a bedroom. But probably it had been a storeroom of some kind before it had been a servant's room.

But he had a chair. A bed. A spoon. And a portable toilet, which was a disgrace and an embarrassment.

Besides that, he had the bucket handle, which he had kept under the blanket with him.

He was locked in.

But electricity and light: that was certainly looking up. The air was warmer. And the bare overhead bulb, far up out of his reach, at least worked.

And he was ahead by one other thing. He had a reasonable glimmering where he was: the East. And he wondered why the East, and he thought of the mysterious dinner guests. Which led him to think of Great-grandmother, and he remembered how Great-grandmother was with Uncle Tatiseigi, since right after that dinner party. Then his father and mother had moved in with Great-grandmother's staff, and Bren-nandi had moved out, and things had gotten boring and disgusting, but then—

At that point his memory of what had happened had a big hole in it, one in which Jegari and Antaro disappeared, and he found himself here, in what smelled and tasted like the East, which had no tie to anything in his recent life except that dinner party.

If Great-grandmother had wanted to bring him here, she could have just done it, easily.

So it was definitely somebody Great-grandmother would not approve of, and possibly something her recent guests had to do with.

Something could have happened to his father when they took him out, but he thought not, somehow, because these people were locking him in and being very careful not to tell him anything.

That meant they were afraid of somebody finding out.

And that probably meant his father was all right, and that Great-grandmother was, and that they would be looking for him, and so would the Guild in their employ.

Well and good. The Guild getting involved was a good thing. That would be Banichi and Jago, and Cenedi and Nawari, none of whom would take his disappearance lightly. And he would enjoy seeing them take these people to account.

This level of the place was much more occupied. People came and went outside. Voices reached him. It was harder to know when someone might come in. What he really, really needed was a wire. A nice long conductive wire that might reach that door latch. He might almost manage it with the bucket handle, but it was not long enough. And there was no other metal available but the dinner spoon.

So in the meanwhile he got down under the bed and took the bucket handle to the plaster of the adjoining wall. It wasn't too bad a place to be changed to.

Plaster was a *lot* easier than mortar.

It was not the servant's quarters Lady Drien provided them, nor yet was it Ilisidi's degree of housing, one could well imagine. It was a modest, though gentlemanly room that allowed a man and his staff to dispose their baggage and settle, at least enough to dress for dinner.

"The staff, Bren-ji," Banichi informed Bren, while Jago rebraided his queue, "is by no means Guild and resents our presence, conceiving us a threat to their lady. This is a house belonging to the *aishid'itat* only by convenience, and only as long as convenient. They fear us, one can reasonably surmise, and very much hope not to be set against us."

"There is, however, news," Jago said from behind him.

"News, yes, Bren-ji," Banichi said, folding his arms in an attitude of thought. "We are not at the moment in communication with this staff. But we have heard, since being here, a small item or two which persuade us that Caiti tried to enlist the lady, and failed. At least he came here and was rebuffed. This we find encouraging."

Particularly encouraging, seeing that he prepared to share the lady's table, in an absolutely classic machimi situation. Or it could be a tidbit the staff had intentionally let fall— Banichi and Jago would not be off their guard in the least, nor should he be. "One certainly hopes not to be poisoned tonight, nadiin-ji."

"They know we would take revenge," Jago said. "And that, Bren-ji, is why your staff does not share the table."

They had brought their own rations, in the baggage. Prudent, Bren decided. He wished he personally had that option.

But he had delayed about dressing as long as he dared. He had washed off the grit and scent of the trail, had arrayed himself in a fine lacy shirt and a good coat, not to mention the soft house boots. He headed out and down the hall, looking fairly splendid, all things considered—he caught his reflection in the antique mirror at the landing, pale individual flanked by two looming shadows, Banichi and Jago, in their polished Guild black and silver.

He was a little behind the dowager. She and Cenedi were in the process of admittance to the dining hall as he arrived downstairs, and the major domo, who had escorted her to her seat, came back and gave him a curt wave of the hand—not quite sure of the protocols with a human guest: that was at least the most charitable interpretation of the gesture.

"Thank you, nadi," Bren murmured, the old woman having been moderately polite, and took his chair opposite the dowager at a table that probably, with other leaves installed, could have served twenty: the room was of that scale, and a host of spare chairs stood about the walls.

Drien was not much slower in arriving. Her formal dress was neither in fashion nor out of it—rich, and dripping with lace, and sparkling with small stones. The dowager almost out-glittered her, in a rich green sparked with small diamonds, but, for the dowager, it was modest, calculatedly so, the paidhi could well guess. His own attire was plain, pale, and moderately fashionable, give or take an unfashionable abundance of lace. It could not have given offense in the East, where fashions always lagged Shejidan by a decade.

There followed the initial service, the offering of drink and the opening course of seasonal items, preserves—those items were usually to avoid, and Bren picked his way through the al-kaloid minefield of atevi cuisine without the usual assurance that the cook knew better. It was not polite nor politic to mention his sensitivities. Staff should have taken care of that—if they listened: perhaps they did, since poisonings outside policy and purely by accident were a very embarrassing event in a dinner.

He didn't bet on it, however. He set himself to be hungry only for items he was relatively sure of and knew that the real danger attended the main course, which there was no dodging.

There was a good deal of small talk: Ilisidi caught up on neighbors' births and deaths, endured a few small barbs with remarkable patience, and generally remained in fair humor—which meant, Bren thought, that Ilisidi thought there was a very great deal to be gained here.

The main course turned out to be *adichara*, a fish recognizable in its presentation, the head and dorsal spines set on one side, the tail on the other, in a bed of autumn berries. He was vastly relieved, and took a child's portion, with no berries.

"The paidhi-aiji hardly eats enough to keep alive," Drien observed, and Bren bowed his head.

"At my size, nandi, I forever leave too much of my servings. It is by no means a slight to the cook, whose skill is extraordinary. One will remember this dish, indeed."

"One is hardly sure that is a compliment," Drien said, looking at Ilisidi. "Do you think his taste can judge anything good?"

"The paidhi's own table matches any lord's," Ilisidi said. "Even mine."

"One is extravagantly grateful, nandi," Bren said with a little bow of the head toward Ilisidi.

The small barbs went back and forth, right into dessert, which was another variation on autumn berries—Bren declined, professing himself full, and wondered quietly to the server if there might be *co di suri*, instead, a white, sweet liqueur he knew was safe.

It appeared, duly served. The one attempt to poison the paidhi-aiji fell aside, whether a test of his aplomb, or his knowledge, or whether it was the mere mischance of an unaccustomed cook. He sipped, and the dowager and their hostess ate, and got down to brandy. Then talk moved to the salon, the room with the fire, which was blazing high this wintry highland evening.

All this time Banichi and Jago had stood by, as Cenedi had, with Nawari, this time stationed outside the salon doors, which a servant shut. The room was the very essence of the East: the beamed ceiling, the ancient hangings on ancient stone, the wooden floor overlain with carpets which had seen at least a hundred years of wear: the sitting-group, of carved wooden chairs with rich cushions.

"He does persistently go with you, Sidi-ji," Drien remarked rudely.

"He certainly does," Ilisidi said with a tight smile. "And will go where we go."

"Perhaps he might stay *behind* when you go. He has a certain interest."

Bren's heart did a little jump. The last time Ilisidi had gotten him involved with local lords, he had ended up with a broken arm. It did another jump when Ilisidi answered:

"Perhaps. Why would you wish it?"

"Curiosity," was Drien's answer. "Mere curiosity." She sipped her brandy.

"We were speaking of my great-grandson, nadi," Ilisidi said sharply. They had not been speaking of him since before dinner.

"One has no idea, nadi," Drien said.

"We did not ride all this distance for dinner and a dance, cousin. Out with it! You have an opinion. Let us hear it!"

"My opinion. Now when has Malguri asked that?"

"*I* am asking," Ilisidi said in a low voice. "I am asking, Dri-aba."

Drien drew a long, slow breath. "Perhaps there have been exchanges of letters to the south, nand' 'Sidi."

Bren's heart sank. He had hoped they could dismiss that fear. It was the worst news.

"And?" Ilisidi asked.

"Distraction," Drien said. "Distraction serves the southerner. That fool Caiti did have the sense to hold apart from him while he ruled. Now, seeing your absence, your preoccupation with affairs in the west, one suspects he has ambitions . . . not favoring Murini, no. But favoring his own agenda."

"One *suspects* he has ambitions." Ilisidi's tone was contemptuous.

"One has no proof except his actions. He has made a move which he alone cannot sustain. What profit to him, if he must invite more powerful allies? He has offended the Ragi and their association. Of what profit is this to him?"

It made an unwelcome sense. Caiti had made a move that could only draw Ilisidi here, that could only alienate the Western Association, and that could only serve to divide Tabini's attention and divert it from pursuing Murini.

Only one thing made sense in that context—that the most likely target was Ilisidi herself. Take down Malguri, and Caiti had the heir to Malguri in his lands. If Tabini attempted to intervene, the East might fall away entirely, and Caiti would rule the East, a situation that would make Murini court him for an ally.

Murini had already spent all his credibility with the west, and might not gain power there. That left . . . of potential aijiin of the entire *aishidi'tat* . . .

Caiti.

"It is aimed at you, nand' dowager," Bren said out of turn. "By this account, it is aimed particularly at you. With you dead, Caiti has the heir to Malguri. And a great deal of leverage with the south."

"Well," Drien said with a little astonishment. "It speaks. And it is not stupid."

"No," Ilisidi said, "nand' Bren is not stupid. Nor are we, aba-ji. You knew they were about to move. A letter would have been courteous."

"And dangerous, nand' 'Sidi. Your power here has grown dim, and we have no man'chi to the West. You have not bothered to visit here. How should *we* know you remember us?"

A direct statement, and on the surface, rude. But Ilisidi nodded slowly. "You wish us to inspire you."

"Astonish us, nand' 'Sidi. Prove you are what you were. Get the boy back. He is with Caiti, and he is, one is certain, in the Haidamar, not the Saibai'tet. I have said what I would say to a guest under my roof. I ask you nothing, until you have the power to promise something."

Ilisidi gathered her cane before her. "Then we shall not linger to distress your hospitality," Ilisidi said. "We shall ride back tonight."

"Folly, cousin! The snow is coming thick out there."

"We have no time to lose," Ilisidi said. "And you will help us, Dri-daja, you will communicate to us anything you learn. Cenedi will leave you the technical means, and despite your distaste for western ways, one would advise you take advantage of a resource your neighbors would not expect you to possess. Use our secure communications, Dri-daja."

"Western nonsense."

"Like nand' Bren, you are not stupid, Cousin. You are far from stupid. One would even suspect you are better equipped in this household than rumor has it, though not with a secure line. Every call your household makes is doubtless overheard. Yet these conspirators still fear you. They have not coerced you into their company despite my absence. They made a particular effort to slander you at my table. In very fact, you *want* Malguri to succeed. You have every reason to wish that, and you know it."

Drien's nostrils flared. "Give us our independence, nandi, signed, sealed, and sworn to. *That* is my ambition. Freedom from your man'chi."

"What, we should cede all claim to Ardija?"

"What is better, Cousin? Man'chi held by force or man'chi won by performance? Promises will by no means suffice with me. Malguri must win this challenge, and free us from all claims. This duality of man'chiin has always been unfortunate, in more than numbers. Now you think we should help you recover this son of the western aiji."

Ilisidi stared at their hostess a moment, a flat, uncommunicative stare. "Your cousin, Dri-daja."

"None of mine!"

"We have spent two years aboard the ship educating my great-grandson in finesse and tradition—"

"In a spaceship run by humans! And contacting more foreigners beyond the horizon!"

"In finesse and tradition, I say! That boy can parse the tribes and the rights of the East, yours among them! He knows the heraldry and the machimi—I taught him! He knows the law of rights and the law of succession, the law of land and the law of usage. He knows the worth of bringing these principles into the west, and he is his father's heir, undisputed, blood of mine, blood of yours, Dri-daja, blood of the Ragi and the North. And any rumors of our disaffection toward the East are utter fiction!"

A small silence followed. Drien folded her hands in her lap, and Drien's nostrils flared, a deep, long intake of breath. "Ardija. I will have Ardija, and this estate, and I will not bargain for it."

"You wish justice, Drien-daja," Bren said, entirely out of turn, and in the next instant not knowing what had possessed him—it was one of those downhill moments, when for a flash of a second he saw the course through the rocks, and in the next blink it would be lost, irrevocable. He spoke out of turn, and saw in slow motion the dowager's glance and the lady's astonished stare.

The lady said nothing for a moment. The dowager said nothing. The silence went on, over the crackling of the fire in the hearth.

Bren cleared his throat—anything to fill that deadly, downward-sliding silence. "Nand' dowager, one begs to say, there is kinship here. But an unfortunate number exists, an Infelicity of Two. If that were adjusted . . ." The dowager was no more superstitious than she was gullible. But the language of numbers conveyed the situation. Two. Divided. Never one.

"Independence, Cousin," the dowager said then, and Bren's heart quietly resumed its beats.

"At his behest?" the lady cried, indignant. "When we have sued for centuries?"

"No," the dowager said. "Not at all at his behest. At his reasonable explanation."

"Explanation! What was never clear? *What*, fortunate gods, was never clear?"

"He rarely objects. He does so with careful thought. Clearly, we make an Unfortunate Two in this situation. We would need a third to complete us, and one has no notion where to find that third, in the East as it is now."

"Apparent! But why should I join you?"

"We are survivors of our age, you and I. We are old, old adversaries. And if anything of the gracious old way is to continue, the tradition will not lie in the south. It will lie with us. Ardija is yours, by my grant . . . while I live."

"Damn you," Drien cried.

An actual smile spread on the dowager's thin lips. "But nevertheless, I stand by my word. You are free. Take your own course. And we shall go on to the Haidamar and free my great-grandson."

"You need help," Drien said, "you stubborn fool. By no means should you go! Stay and let my staff make inquires. No good will come of your killing yourself!"

"You will make yourself trouble, Dri-ji."

"You are the trouble in my life!" Drien reached beside her and picked up a small brass bell, which she rang vigorously. Doors at either end of the room flew open, and the one from the hall, where their own staff waited: Cenedi and Nawari were there; so were Banichi and Jago, on the alert.

"Beds for our guests, nadiin-ji!" Drien ordered, and waved a hand. "Kasi, ride up to Malguri and advise them our guests are staying."

"No need for your staff to trouble itself for such a journey, cousin," Ilisidi murmured. "Proprieties aside—"

"You have your cursed radios," Drien said in disgust, and in that moment, in that fire-crackling stillness, every ateva clearly heard something. Motion stopped. People listened. Then Bren heard it, in such a deep quiet, remote from all hum of electrics, the faint, faint sound of a laboring engine.

Drien's face held utter disapproval. "Is that yours, Cousin?"

"Mine?" Ilisidi asked. "Malguri has no such."

The room and the house waited, hushed, and the sound was clearer, as if the source had passed the cliffs and come onto the road.

"That infernal machine," Drien muttered.

"The airport?" Ilisidi inquired, logically enough: airports and train terminals were the usual source of transport connections. "Are you expecting anyone to arrive tonight?"

"By no means. That is a bus. That is a miserable bus," Drien said. "One knows that motor. That wretched vehicle! What delivery has civilized business arriving at this hour!" She addressed her staff. "What does it require for our privacy, nadiin? That we shoot the driver?"

"One would hardly counsel that, on this night in particular," Ilisidi said with a grim look. "In our present circumstances, one wishes information, of whatever source. And the Malguri bus sits at our doors at present. It may be some visitor from the airport or from Malguri itself."

"Go," Drien ordered one of her staff, "and discover what this intrusion wants, nadi."

It was a cause for anxiety. Bren looked at Ilisidi, and Ilisidi remarked, "Perhaps Banichi might investigate, as well."

Bren nodded, and Banichi left. Jago did not. There was no way that any bus could negotiate the final part of the road: whoever it had brought would have to walk up to the gates.

"Well, well, well," Drien said comfortably, "we sit, and we wait. A brandy to pass the time?"

12

Banichi was gone a lengthy period of time. Possibly he reported in the interim to Jago, who had resumed her watch at the door. For his own part, Bren had far rather be in on the Guild's information flow, but that was not the available choice. He fretted, keeping his ear tuned meanwhile to the conversational tidbits that fell during the wait—Lady Drien discussed her neighbors, discussed the doings of Ilisidi's staff during her absence. It seemed that Djinana had at some point personally ejected a member of Drien's staff from the gates of Malguri, in a memorable confrontation over a rowboat that had come unmoored in a storm . . . the boat had been, one gathered, eventually repatriated to the Cobesthen shore through a neutral party down in Malguri Township.

"Perhaps," the dowager said, regarding the complaint, "we may, nandi, improve feelings between our staffs. We would never doubt your claim of ownership of such a boat if we were in residence. It would not have happened."

"Who but the rightful owner would ever know a boat had drifted?" Drien had a gift for pursuing a quarrel far past any useful boundaries. "Are they fools, that they think we would claim some other person's boat?"

"We do assure you to the contrary, nandi." Ilisidi's tone grew just a little icier. "And one will assume my capable staff might have responded differently to your visitation had there been any communication in advance of a party intruding onto Malguri grounds."

"The common lakeshore!"

"We do not concur! That is Malguri land!"

"The common lakeshore, I say!"

"Nandiin," Bren said, desperately seeking to head off renewed warfare. "Ought not Banichi to be—"

Back by now, he had meant to say, when there was, indeed, the sound of movement on the snow, that crunching of crusted ice that heralded multiple people arriving on the outside steps.

"Well," Drien said, still ruffled, but she dispatched servants to the outer hall.

There was some little to-do outside, by the sound of it.

Then came the sound of the outer door opening, a cold draft that sucked at the fire in the grate, attended by a stamping of feet and Banichi's deep voice overlain by servant voices.

Banichi was giving orders out there, regarding something. It was a peaceful arrival, or there would have been more noise than that, Bren told himself.

And a moment later the lady's servants returned to the doorway. "Lady Agilisi has arrived, nandi," the servant reported.

"Indeed?" Drien looked rightfully surprised. Bren was, himself. Ilisidi, however, had that formal face on, and no emotion at all escaped, beyond an arched eyebrow—which was to say . . . the dowager was on the alert.

"The lady wishes to present her respects to the house, nandi," the servant said.

"Admit her," Drien said. And a moment later the door opened its left half to let in a snowy lady in heavy boots and too much cloak, a graying lady who looked quite undone, her hair coming loose in wisps about a cold-stung face. That face showed dismay, distress, all manner of turmoil.

"Nand' Agilisi." Drien did not rise. "Come in."

"Nandiin." The lady bowed. That was the plural, acknowledging the second presence. And, thin-lipped, she bowed again to the dowager. "Nand' dowager."

There were reciprocal nods.

This was that lady from Ilisidi's dinner party, the lady who had, during the dinner, seemed somewhat in charge. Right now she looked thoroughly done in and windblown.

"We come here," Agilisi began, and could not get the rest out.

It was not the paidhi's place to stay grandly seated while an elderly lady struggled for breath. Bren rose to stand behind his chair, at least, in respect to the lady's age, rank and distress. It was the host's prerogative to offer her a seat. Not his.

"Will you take a brandy, nandi?" Drien asked. "You do look very out of sorts this evening."

"Nandi." Agilisi cast about a heartbeat as if looking for a chair, any chair, and a servant quickly moved one into the circle, a stiff, straight antique. Another servant took the lady's snow-caked cloak and gloves, and the thin figure that emerged, wearing a rose brocade coat, was far from the ramrod straight carriage of the banquet night. Agilisi reached the chair and sat down, heavily, as if her legs would no longer hold her. A servant brought the brandy service, and another poured, and offered the little glass to the lady, before making the rounds of the rest of them, a de rigeur gesture which all of them declined.

That left the lady with one glass of another house's brandy, and the necessity to drink it—or not.

"One regrets," Agilisi managed to say, the brandy as yet undrunk, and with a look at Ilisidi: "one regrets extremely, nand' dowager . . ."

"Where is my great-grandson? What do you know? Out with it, woman!"

"Caiti," Agilisi said, and took a largish sip of the hazardous brandy, dissolving into a coughing fit. She took a second sip and wiped her lips with a hand gray-edged with cold—or terror.

"Caiti has gone entirely mad. One had no notion, no notion at all what he intended. One hardly knew—"

Thump! went the cane on the carpeted stones. *"Where is my great-grandson?"*

"In the Haidamar." Agilisi said. "In the Haidamar Fortress, by all evidence."

"Were you on that plane, nandi?"

Astute question, Bren thought, and held his breath. In the days before they left the world, there had been one passenger flight daily to and from the East, and unless Agilisi had miraculously hired a plane that had preceded the kidnapping and left the city before the airport shut, she had shared the plane with the kidnappers.

Agilisi was caught with her mouth open. And shut it to a thin line, knowing she was caught, clearly. "Yes, nandi," she said faintly. "One did. And left. One hoped you would follow."

"Nonsense!"

"One hoped, I say!"

"Liar."

"You deserted us! You went to the west, you went to the heavens, you went on this human's business, while our own affairs languished! One came to Shejidan in hope—one came to learn whether humans had had all their way, or whether there was still a power in Malguri!"

"And concluded?" Ilisidi asked dangerously.

"One saw too many things, too many changes. One had no idea what to think."

That, Bren thought, might be the truth. And if ever a woman had better tell the truth, Agilisi was in that position. The lady was in a leaking boat, as the proverb had it. In a leaking boat and paddling hard for shore—any shore, and possibly without assurance that her own house was a safe refuge for her, given her recent moves. Her ties to Caiti had become life-threatening under this roof . . . granted Drien wasn't in on it.

Which one did not automatically grant.

"Go on," Ilisidi said quietly. "What did Caiti say, after leaving his neighbor's table?"

"One can hardly say—I had no idea, nandi, no idea of the plan. I had no idea of traffic between Caiti and your house—I had no idea of the things afoot . . ."

"No idea at all. And now you come here, tonight, so opportunely."

"To an ally."

"An associate, a remote associate, and by no means invited!" Drien said.

"Your independence in this matter," Agilisi said. "Your historic independence, Dri-daja—but I had not expected the aiji-dowager to be here . . . one hoped for your help, Dri-daja, to know whether the aiji-dowager had come home . . . whether she *would* come home, or had the power to come home—"

"You doubt it?" Ilisidi asked ominously. "And, leaving Caiti, you came dashing *here* instead of to me at Tirnamardi, or even more convenient a trip, to my grandson in Shejidan, who was simply up the hill from your hotel!"

"What would one expect there but doubt and arrest? One came *here*, for one's dignity, for the dignity of one's own—"

"Dignity!" Down went the cane again. "Dignity! What of my great-grandson's dignity, woman?"

"There was nothing one could do—I had come to Shejidan with half my staff. They said—limitations on the plane. Which in no wise proved true, nandi. The lie had started before we ever left the ground for the west. I was slighted. My house was slighted! One does not take that lightly!"

"You were at best a damned *key*, nandi, a piece of social stage dressing, all my lakeside neighbors save one, and their people are *in* your house, do you deny it?"

Agilisi's mouth opened and shut. And opened again. "There

are ties," she confessed. "There are ties of marriage. As there are ties to your own household, nandi!"

A bit of cheek, that. A muscle jumped in Ilisidi's jaw. "A tie that will not long survive," Ilisidi said.

"Nor in mine, nandi. Caiti—Caiti has to be stopped."

"Does he, now? And what sent you flying here, Agilisi-daja? What sudden burst of understanding informed you it was time to run here? —Or were you sent, woman?"

"Not sent. Not sent here. The convoy formed—by the plane—and we dropped behind—my guard and I. Saein stayed, my seniormost, he moved to lead them off. Toward Cie. They know—Caiti knows—" The brandy glass went over, dislodged by a motion of Agilisi's hand, and she failed to catch it. It landed, intact, on the carpet, but no servant moved.

"What does Caiti know? And what does he intend with my great-grandson?"

"Caiti, nandi, Caiti has contacted the usurper. Murini."

Bren's heart skipped a beat. Likely several hearts present did.

But Ilisidi only resettled her fingers on the head of her cane and stared straight at Agilisi. "Remarkable."

"One had no idea," Agilisi cried. "One had no idea there was any such aim in this venture. He plans—he plans to have the heir of Malguri in *his* hands, and to fling the usurper into war with the west, to keep your grandson occupied in his own lands. And if you join them, nandi, they say they will deal, and if not, they will still have the west at war and the heir of Malguri in their hands."

There was a heavy, heavy silence. "Is that his message?"

"No! No, nandi, that is not his message, that is his plan. He knew you were likely following. He wants you dead. He wants the heir in his hands. He wants Malguri. And we will not back him in this: there is no aiji over the East, and if there is ever one it will not be Lord Caiti! He has lied to us, he has misled, he has drawn us into a plot without consultation, and brought in the south without any authority—we do *not* consent to this, we do *not* bow the neck to this damned bully!"

"A pretty, pretty speech, nandi. And where is Murini?"

"Coming here, if Caiti told the truth—coming to ascertain Caiti *does* have your great-grandson."

Ilisidi rolled her eyes up to the ceiling and down again, a gesture of exasperation.

"The truth, nandi, the truth this time!"

"Caiti *is* a fool!" Agilisi cried.

"So he will invite Murini under his roof, and demonstrate he has my great-grandson. And Murini, in awe of this astonishing fact, will obligingly *leave* my great-grandson in his hands while he goes off to become a target for my grandson's forces. What do you think we are, Agi-daja? *Equal fools?*"

"Nandi, so he told Lord Rodi and me! And Lord Rodi went with him to the Haidamar, but I slipped back and my guard got me away—to come here, to consult with Lady Drien, to find some middle ground—some means to unite the independent neighbors in protest of this lunacy— Clearly, neither I nor my people were respected, to be brought there ignorant of all plans, to be confronted with this—we are innocent. I and my people are innocent!"

"A fine story. And all this plan was to get through our door in Shejidan, to make face-to-face contact with a traitor on *our* staff, carry out this monstrous idiocy, and we, of course, were to come rushing obligingly into ambush in the Haidamar."

Across the lake, Bren thought: the image leaped up of a force from Malguri coming in by water, instead of overland, all exposed, and vulnerable. The dowager would not have done it.

Murini would have known that. Murini had some sense of tactics. But did Caiti, whose people had faced Malguri across the haunted lake and quarreled about its isle for generations— did *he* think the dowager would be where she was at present, not at Malguri plotting to sail across, but overland, and past the jut of the south end cliffs to make peace with a splinter of Malguri itself?

Without that peace, Malguri might have found difficulty to cross that land quietly. There might have been alarms.

Certainly it was noisy enough to have drawn Agilisi in, claiming she had come to appeal to Drien.

And Drien, fresh from her acquisition of the disputed land, had said not one word to back her. *That* had to worry the woman.

"How can I prove my favorable disposition?" Agilisi asked—in truth, in a desperate situation. "How can I make Malguri understand that my district has nothing to gain here?"

"How indeed?" Ilisidi said darkly. "Except you tell the truth, every particular of this truth. When? How? Why? And with what force does this southerner invade the East at Caiti's invitation?"

"Caiti plans to double-cross him, one believes." Agilisi's lips formed the syllables carefully, distinctly. "Nandi, we are *betrayed,* we are all equally *betrayed.* "

"Oh, one doubts *equally,* Agi-daja. One very much doubts *equality* in this treason. So you dared not go home. Who are his people in your household? Name them."

"My nephew," Agilisi said faintly. "But one pleads for him. He is young. He is associated with a Saibai'tet girl, a young fool. The one—the one to fear is his mother, Saibai'tet and resident with my brother. That one . . . that one I freely give to you."

"Your brother? Or the Saibai'tet woman?"

"The woman, nandi. My brother's wife. My brother is in a sad state of health, incapable of knowing what she signs, what she appoints, what staff she brings in to attend him."

"Is this an accident, this indisposition? And do we attribute it to the wife—or his sister?"

Agilisi's mouth hung slightly agape. She was not, Bren thought, a very clever woman—or her fabrications were not.

"One would justly have been suspicious," Ilisidi said. *Bang!* went the cane. Cenedi moved up beside her chair. "I think this lady should have been far more suspicious. One needs more fingers than the gods gave us to count the betrayals. *She* fears to go to her domain. Clearly, she is in want of protection— granted we find out the truth in the next quarter hour."

"Nandi!" Agilisi cried, looking from left to right. "Dri-daja!"

"This boy whose welfare is at issue is my youngest cousin," Drien said coldly, "and has been shamefully treated by associates with whom you have willingly sat at table and connived, nandi. And now you bring your difficulties under my roof? We are offended."

"The lady's guard is resting below," Cenedi said quietly, "nandi."

Stripped of protection, her guard incapacitated, and the dowager as coldly angry as one was ever likely to detect—the unfortunate lady darted glances from one face to another, quick, reckoning, fearful glances.

"The truth, woman!" Ilisidi snapped. "Your ailing brother, indeed! *You* are the lord of Catien! *You* have permitted or not permitted this infestation of Saibai'tet servants *and* this woman under your roof, am I mistaken? Talk!"

"We were threatened!" Agilisi protested. "Malguri has done *nothing* for our region since you left! Who was there, nandi? Who was there on whom we could rely to sustain our independence? The aiji in Shejidan was lost—there was *only* the Kadagidi and the Taisigin! There was *only* them! I never chose to accept a Saibai'tet wife under my roof—but I had no power to resist, I had no great store of weapons . . ."

"And Caiti did?"

"Caiti had the backing of the Kadagidi!"

"Ah," Ilisidi said, and indeed, in that, a certain number of things made sense. "The backing of the Kadagidi. And was this maneuver Caiti's idea—or Murini's?"

"Caiti—" The woman seemed short of breath, as if there was not enough air in the room to get out what she had to say. "One suspects Caiti intends to double-cross Murini. Clearly—clearly—Murini is fallen and falling fast. He will surely go down. But with his help—" She ran utterly out of breath, and drew in another. "Caiti means to take the East out of the *aishidi'tat*, build an Association here, holding the child—the child hostage against his father. He intends you should come there. He knows you will never negotiate, nandi."

The plane that took off simultaneously for the South, the lord with the convenient excuse, a diversion, Bren thought, ticking off one southern lord who needed dealing with.

But they had plenty on their hands where they were.

"We shall not negotiate," Ilisidi said quietly. "Nand' Bren."

"Nandi? We shall go wherever we need go."

"One has no doubt," Ilisidi said.

"Can either of these ladies open those gates?" he ventured to ask.

Agilisi glanced at him, clearly taken aback. Drien looked disapprovingly down her nose at his impertinence. Ilisidi, however, had raised that dangerous brow.

"Answer the Lord of the Heavens," Ilisidi said, leaning chin on fist. "You can find your way back into Caiti's good graces, can you not, lady of Catien? One is certain you can at least get the gates open—if only for their desire to know what sudden turn of events brings you back."

"One might venture it," the lady said. Gone, all her prim assurance. It was a straw, and with whatever motivation, she grasped at it. "One might, with your favor, nand' dowager."

"We shall hold my *favor* in abeyance, woman. You have walked into it and you know your life is sinking low, low indeed, in my present plans. Redeem it. And rest assured this is your one chance."

"Agilisi is my associate, cousin," Drien said, "and courted

by lords Caiti and Rodi, as was I, as *all* the lords of the lakeshore and eastward. Her house was, indeed, infiltrated."

"Is yours?" Ilisidi asked bluntly.

"My people have been with me all my life, Cousin. As yours."

That, Bren thought, might be a frank and honest answer. A small silence persisted in the room, and Agilisi's life quite literally hung on that silence.

"Our man'chi," Agilisi said. "Rescue my house, nandi. We need your help. We appeal for your help. We *quit* this madness when we knew its intentions . . ."

"Do you know the premises of the Haidamar?"

"Somewhat." A tremor possessed the lady, who was not, herself, young. It might be a chill. Her boots showed waterstain, the snow having melted. But again, one doubted that tremor was in any sense chilled feet. "I have been there. I was a guest there, before this venture. Nandi, I had no knowledge . . . I appeal for protection of my house, my associates, nandi. I am putting them all at risk in turning to you. These are innocent people, my staff, my guard . . ."

Ilisidi lifted her hand, stopping the torrent short. "Their safety now depends on our success and my great-grandson's life. Provide my staff a diagram."

Getting through that gate. Getting the gate open, Bren thought. That was all they needed—the bus that had brought Agilisi to Cobesthen might be able to break through, but finesse—finesse was going to get the boy out alive.

Agilisi looked about to wilt altogether, trembling visibly as she lifted a hand in protest. "One hardly knows," Agilisi began, and then Drien:

"*We* know those premises," Drien said, the infelicitous dual augmented with the mitigating article. "And they will admit *me*, cousin, with my neighbor. Let me intercede for my neighbor. She may stay here. *We* shall ride to the north shore."

It was gallant of the lady. It was downright grand, considering the peril of her association and the dowager's outraged anger. There was still the remote chance Lady Drien was in with the kidnappers from the beginning—she had certainly been named; there was the remote chance Lady Drien had sought the promise of title to Ardija from Caiti, which could mean she was trying to lead them all into Caiti's trap—

But if a dozen years of reading atevi faces and manners was any guide, she had every appearance of telling the truth, and every reason for peace. Ilisidi as a neighbor was assuredly more stable than Caiti's hare-brained effort to rip the East out of the *aishidi'tat.*

If they survived it.

"I would go," Agilisi protested in a faint voice.

"Yes," Ilisidi said, "but you *shall* not. Rely on my cousin for your survival. Become indebted to *her.* And expect your brother to lose a wife!" To Drien she said: "Cousin. You will find we remember debts."

So they sat, with the same fire crackling away and all the players the same but one, and the whole East changed. *We've landed in a damned machimi,* Bren thought, not letting a wisp of expression to his face. He could even put a name to it: *Kosaigien Ashai,* as ancient and tangled a nest of pieces as existed in the dramatic repertoire. He had studied it, and never made thorough sense of the moves and the motives.

But there it was, the grand gesture, the acceptance, the realignment which had challenged human students for decades—a revised set of man'chiin . . . the principal's own, and everybody else's.

And blood to follow. A lot of it.

Neither Agilisi nor Drien had Guild help, as such—and the thought came through clear as a lightning strike: Cenedi and his men, Eastern themselves, would be recognized in a heartbeat. Banichi and Jago might not be . . . but Jago had been at the dinner party.

Banichi, however, had not been: Banichi had not yet returned from the Guild that night. He meant to mention that fact to the dowager, at the next opportune moment. And he wasn't sending Banichi and Jago off into a desperate situation without him, no way in hell.

"Where," Ilisidi inquired further, "Agi-daja, where is the bus that brought you?"

"At the base of the hill, nand' dowager. The very last of the road. There is no driver. Your man took us at gunpoint—"

"We shall need that bus. Nand' Drien, you may go with us."

"In that infernal machine! Overland is the sensible way, overland or at very least by boat. . . ."

"Come, come, Dri-daja, straight into ambush? You need new experiences. You are not too old. We *need* you."

"Then overland!"

"We cannot dither about riding there, not with my great-grandson—your cousin thrice removed!—at issue! The bus may need to go further, but it goes faster, and does not wear us down."

"I am far too old for that rattletap!"

"If I fare well in a bus," Ilisidi said, "you may survive it. And *your* staff, Dri-daja, can bring the mecheiti overland. *You* shall ride with us and arrive ahead of them, I wager you on it."

"One has never agreed to this machine!" Drien cried.

"One has not written down the disposition of Ardija, either," Ilisidi said primly, and called for pen and paper.

Three quarters of an hour later Ilisidi had signed and sealed a note ceding Ardija, the lady Agilisi and her sole retainer were confined to a comfortable though chilly room in Cobesthen Fortress, and the rest of them were on mecheita-back, with the entire local herd *and* the Malguri herd together, all riding down toward the intersection and the waiting Cadienein-ori airport bus.

It was a whole damned cavalry, Bren thought, and the two herd bulls were not in the least compatible, Drien's and Ilisidi's. They raised a bawling complaint all the way down the road, prime reason to take the bus and not have *that* all the way around the lake shore, announcing their presence.

And having hastily having thrown on his warmer coat and trousers and having left all but his most essential baggage under Drien's roof, Bren tried to keep that shorter coat spread out over Nokhada's warm, winter-coated body, holding as much of her heat near his body as he could. The bus itself was not going to be comfortable, he was damned sure.

It sat, dark and dead, right amid the one-lane road, with snow piling on its hood and top—a stubby half-bus transport. A delivery van might have been more commodious. It said, on the side, in large letters: *Cadienein-ori Regional Transport Authority.*

It offered no sign of life as Cenedi's men investigated it end to end and underneath. Two bundles went out, unceremoniously, likely Lady Agilisi's luggage, right into a snowbank. One of Cenedi's men started the engine, and reported a half a tank of fuel.

"Enough to get down to the depot," Cenedi said, getting down.

Nawari slid down and held Babsidi's rein, urging him to kneel. Ilisidi got down, and Drien followed, helped by her own people, while the squalling between Babsidi and the other herd leader went on and men strained to keep snaking necks out of play.

Bren secured the rein, slid down to the snowy ground and got out of Nokhada's way in a fast move to the side of the bus.

Cenedi himself elected to drive; and all of them, Banichi, Jago, Nawari, and all the rest of the dowager's men took to the bus in haste, except the one of the dowager's men assigned to handle Babsidi, and go with Drien's men and the herds overland to rendezvous with them at the Haidamar.

There was no loitering, either, with mecheiti involved. "Go!" Nawari told the men with the herds, and Drien's men headed off into the dark, down the road ahead and off it, in short order.

Ilisidi had meanwhile appropriated the front seat, Drien was, one could see through the small back window of the cab, compelled to the second row, and Bren jammed himself up close in the fifth with Banichi and Jago: cold, poorly padded seat, cold metal floorboards underfoot, and a draft from the ill-framed windows, but that was minimal discomfort, all things weighed against a long cross-country ride. A lone, relatively thin human was very grateful to be surrounded by atevi that gave off heat like a furnace.

Weapons were everywhere. The bodies around him were armored, another good thing, in the paidhi's estimation. The engine growled, and the bus got into motion, backwards. Bren stayed very still, with his hand on the gun in his coat pocket, as a last two shadows climbed up onto the bus bed, both the dowager's men, dim silhouettes bristling with armaments, and made their way down the aisle to the rear of the bus.

The bus kept backing. Would back, until they reached a turnaround, and Bren could not readily remember how far back that wide spot was.

So they were off, and Agilisi waited the outcome. The lady had arrived expecting to politick with Drien and now had an unenviable refuge in Drien's upstairs, doomed to wait, and hope it was not the other side that showed up. Her man, not Guild, and vastly outnumbered and outgunned, had no part in the dowager's party, or in Drien's, but one had to remember that unfortunate man had a partner somewhere, and that partnership would not be split, not by anything less than death or

highest duty. Consequently, the household staff, such as remained, was under Drien's orders to admit no one of that
man'chi.

"Is there," he asked Banichi and Jago finally, while the bus
was still, in reverse, navigating the track downhill, "any remote chance she knew the dowager was here?"

"No one at Malguri would have given out that information."

"Drien's staff *does* have a telephone."

"Tapped, Bren-ji," Jago said with what seemed a certain personal satisfaction, "and no message went out or in."

The virtues of having a *lot* of Guild security staff about
one's person. Efficiency. They lacked Tano and Algini, who ordinarily managed electronics *and* explosives, but things got
done.

And *that*—besides Drien's sudden self-interest in seeing the
dowager win—gave one a certain notion the lady with them
had told the truth . . . the ink might be hardly dry on that pact,
but it gave Drien a powerful motive; and Agilisi could only
hope they got back in one piece and that it was the dowager's
previously negotiated mercy she had to trust. Drien's household was there to swear to what she had said and done.

But it was a good situation. Not an enviable place to be.

And damn, could the woman not have come with a full fuel
tank?

The bus reached the wide spot, executed a precarious turn-
around, then picked up speed.

They had to go clear back down to the airport road. But they
did as they could. It was what they had. And they moved as fast
as a vehicle of this vintage could manage . . . en route back to
the valley, to clearer, less winding roads, and, ultimately, a fuel
station. The lake sat in an old crater—Malguri on the highest
side, with its impregnable cliffs; Cobesthen to the south and
the Haidamar to the north of it; and they were headed down, if
not on the flat, at least on flatter ground, *between* Caiti's two

holdings of the Haidamar and the Saibai'tet Ami, and very much within his domain for most of their trek, verging on Catien for a small part of it.

And if Caiti made a run for it—could they possibly get intelligence of such a move, which might be designed to carry the heir to some other prison? Could they get between him and the Saibai'tet? That depended on where the roads lay, and he didn't know that answer.

But Murini, Agilisi had said, was coming to the Haidamar, likely from the airport at Cie, judging that Malguri Airport would not be a good landing spot. Murini meant to take the heir in hand and would gladly take on the aiji-dowager and any force she could bring to bear, presumably while Caiti sat and watched, basking in this new and favorable alliance.

Ilisidi was moving as fast as she possibly could to get ahead of this train of events. She had not threatened war. She had not called in the Guild, unwelcome in the East. She went directly after her great-grandson, and went after him in the dead of night, in a snowstorm, and maybe that was the best choice, and maybe it was not.

Get through the gates, and hope to God they were the first to do so.

Once Murini got his hands on Cajeiri, there was no question of Murini leaving the boy in Caiti's hands, no hope of that, as he figured it, not unless Caiti was a damned sight cleverer than any of them thought he was. And what Caiti had tried, never mind he had succeeded this far, did not encourage them to believe that he was all that clever.

Bren found dinner sitting very uncomfortably as the bus lurched and tilted on the narrow road, rocketing downhill, all but out of control on an unfamiliar road. Everyone swayed. A few had heads down, against hands braced on the seats. If he were at all sensible, Bren told himself, he would try his damnedest to sleep while they traveled. It was going to be a long night, a long way around. The Guild with them knew it. The Guild took its rest where it could.

But he doubted he was going to be able to.

He heard certain of Ilisidi's young men debating the wisdom of trying to get through to Malguri, whether their satellite phones were help or liability in this situation—he heard frank discussion of other Guild being sent in, if Tabini-aiji got the straight word on what was happening, and about the likelihood of Eastern disaffection, and the plain fact they were just that far from help.

This, as the bus hit the lowland road. It assumed a roaring fast pace for about an hour, and then slowed and pulled in—the fuel depot, Bren thought, where the road passed through a finger of Lady Agilisi's district of Catien—or he was thinking that, when Banichi and Jago flattened him to the seat.

The rest of the men scrambled out. Bren stayed down as Banichi and Jago followed. It was very quiet outside, and then came the distinctive sound of the fuel cap going off the bus and the hose going in.

There was such a thing as trust, that of his bodyguard toward him, a contract of obligations. He obediently stayed flat the while the refueling went on, not satisfying his curiosity, not even lifting his head from the seat. Banichi and Jago didn't need his help on this mundane task, not in the least.

He heard voices, quiet ones, against the side of the bus. One mentioned something about the attendant being in the cellar.

That was informative.

The cap went back on. Everyone boarded again, Banichi and Jago among the first in, and wanted their seats, which he supposed gave him leave to sit up.

Jago set a hand on his shoulder as she eased in.

"Cenedi has called Malguri on the depot phone, Bren-ji. They are aware. They will get word to the aiji."

"Good," he said. Well that Tabini at least be warned what

was happening. He had the most amazing disposition to shiver. "Are we all right?"

"A plane has landed in the north," Banichi said. "At Cie."

"From?" he asked.

"No one is sure of its origin," Jago said. "It may be scheduled freight. It may not. It is worrisome. Planes are entering Eastern airspace again. Malguri Airport itself is back in operation. Guild may have come in. We did not inquire."

They wouldn't. They wouldn't raise the question for fear of blowing cover. Malguri had seen fit to tell them that was going on, but there was no telling what else was.

Which meant they could be neck-deep in a shooting war by morning. It didn't help the chills, as the bus started up and began to accelerate away from the fueling station.

"Did we kill anyone back there?" he asked. He didn't know why he asked. He didn't want to know, except that he wanted some sense of how far the dowager was holding off the people of Catien, whose lady was locked in Drien's upstairs. He hoped there was still a modicum of civilization in this district, that there was still some sense of restraint governing the lords

"No," Jago said. "They were very wise, and respected the sight of the lady of Catien's ring."

So they had that—by force or by gift: Agilisi's seal on their use of her goods.

"They are locked in the storeroom," Banichi added, as the bus reached its traveling gear, "where there is no telephone, nor radio. They believe someone will come along before noon tomorrow."

13

Chip and chip and chip.

The outer halls were quiet now. The light was off out there. The light had gone off in here, too. One had no flashlight: that had gone, with the other cell. One could no longer see what one was doing. And Cajeiri's fingers hurt. Probably they were bleeding, but one could ignore that when one was mad. And Cajeiri was mad by now. He was damned mad, and tired, and grew madder the more it hurt.

He was, however, well through the plaster coating. He had come up against a bare spot of what felt like thin boards, which he could just get the thin, flat end of the bucket handle into. He pulled. Repeatedly. He said bad words to himself, in shipspeak.

One thin board broke with a snap like thunder, and took plaster with it.

That was good. He got much of his hand in. He pulled another board. He began to grin, partly from the effort and partly from the success. He wriggled around and applied both hands, which broke more boards and brought more plaster onto the floor where the bed ordinarily rested. Beyond that was a gap. And rubble. He ripped out pieces, rocks, some fist sized. None of them were mortared in, or if they were, it was entirely haphazard.

He began to get the picture of a neat plaster facade and some sort of rubble fill between. Cheaply done, mani would say, and sniff at it. A quickly done wall in a building this old. Maybe dividing something off, on the cheap. That was interesting. It was not at all how they built on the ship. He could *do* something with this.

He started scraping the opposing wood with the use-sharpened flat end of the bucket handle, scrape, scrape, scrape. His knuckles bled. That was no consequence. Temper kept him warm on the cold floor. Temper kept him going when they might expect him to be asleep.

He wished he had Gene's help. Artur's. He imagined that they worked beside him, Fortunate Three, and that made matters better. He ought properly, he knew, to think of his Taibeni associates. He belonged to them. He feared they might even be dead because of those people who had carried him away from his bed, a thought which roused a keen and proper pain in his heart; but when he really, seriously wanted help, he naturally thought of Gene, who was always ready for a scheme, who thought of things, really clever things, instead of looking at him for help.

Gene and Artur had no idea where he was now. They could never imagine the trouble he was in at the moment. If they did know, they would be trying everything to get to him—if they were not separated by space and authority and adults. And that, when he got out of here and if he got to grow up, *that* was going to get fixed.

They were his first associates, the first beings in all the world—or above it—who had ever come to him, as persons of his own age and rank— Well, at least they were all of them passengers, and so they were equals in that way; and they were still his, in a special way.

Gene and Artur. Their coconspirators, Bjorn and Irene, he let into their company for felicity's sake and to please manima, so they were at least a Completion of Five, which was very solid and respectable, like a social group. But increasingly he kept forgetting Bjorn, and now in desperate case he began thinking just of Gene and Artur and Irene, his Felicity of Three. . . .

Because he was gone from them. He was gone from them and unless he could get back or get them down here, they would go their own way and be human, and he would be atevi—

Damn it.

Granted he lived through this.

Scrape and scrape and scrape. The spoon kept bending, but the bucket handle held out. It was slick with sweat or blood, he had no idea which, in the dark. It made a gritty paste with the mortar scrapings and the dust, and one end had sharpened. It made it a better tool.

Damn them. Damn them, Bren-nandi would say. He was by no means sure what that meant, but Bren was careful about saying it, so he figured it was potent.

He did hope he still had Antaro and Jegari, if they were alive. And he knew beyond any doubt in his very core they would want to find him—if they were still alive. He really, desperately hoped they were. And in between imagining Gene and Artur, he imagined Jegari and Antaro going to his father, and telling his father what had happened.

Oh, then all hell would have broken loose, and they would call his great-grandmother, was what, and they would tell nand' Bren. The whole world would be looking for him by now. . . .

Granted his father and mother were still alive. Granted the Bu-javid was not back in the hands of Murini and his associates, which was the thought that scared him most and made him stay awake and keep digging.

He scraped a knuckle, gritted his teeth, and scraped away, which necessarily hit the knuckle over and over and over.

He wanted them all to be alive, and looking for him. He

wanted his father and mother to be alive. He wanted mani to come and get him. He had complained about their discipline, and never thought he would miss it, but now he wanted them, he wanted their rules and their law around him. He had never been alone in his life, not alone like this, and if he stopped fighting long enough, he could be scared, which mani's great-grandson never could be. So he kept at it.

Scrape and scrape.

Damn!

Something resisted. He got fingers into it, and found something like—

Wire. Two or three strands of it. He pulled, popping it past boards and plaster, and pulled, bracing his feet.

It might be part of the construction, some sort of recon-struction. But the more he pulled it, he began to think it was really wire, metal-centered wire, electrical wire. *Somebody* had made a very inelegant repair when they plastered up the wall, was what.

He was by no means sure he could get the mess loose, but he wanted it. He wanted it out of his hole, for one thing; for an-other—

For another, an idea was coming to him, even if the light switch was on the other side of the door.

There was a light socket in the ceiling.

He braced both feet and hauled, and hauled as the wire re-sisted. One end came out, and he tested it gingerly with the bucket handle.

No spark. Dead. Entirely dead.

But it *was* metal-centered. It was old and dusty and twisted, but he had a lot of it and it was metal. And if he could cut it off or bend and break it and get it into his hands . . .

He tried breaking it. Hauling on it. Got out from under the bed and hauled on it until it cut his fingers.

Plaster popped. He felt along it. More wire had come out of

the wall. He had no way to see what he was doing, but he hauled hard, feet braced, the wire wrapped around his hands, and suddenly, as if it had been twisted around something, it just came loose and came out, pitching him backward.

He had his prize. A lot of it. But it was only a prize if it had no breaks in it. And he picked one wire and ran it through his fingers, sitting there in the total dark.

Intact, until one got to the bristly, prickly end. He tested the other pieces. And he began to put them all together, until he had one *really* long piece of somebody's very sloppy work on an old wall.

All useless, however, unless he could get up to that light socket in the ceiling.

He got up. He found the chair in the dark and moved it over. The light, in the picture his memory gave him, had been a little off from dead center of the room, a little more toward the door. He put the chair there.

And he climbed atop it. The ceiling was out of reach. He was just that much too short to reach anything but the tip of the bulb.

Damn again.

He thought of things he had. And climbed down and hauled the mattress off the bed, wondering if he could do anything with the bed frame—close call, then. He nearly upset the metal water pitcher. He saved it, in the dark, down on one knee.

Then he had a thought, dragged the mattress over to the chair, and laid it midway over the chair bottom, and climbed back atop it all. It made queasy footing, but the thickness of the mattress gave him another little bit, if he balanced very carefully.

He could reach the ceiling. He unscrewed the darkened bulb, got down and got the conjoined wire and his bucket handle and climbed up again, with the wire wrapped around his arm to hang onto it.

This was the anxious part. He felt the inside of the socket, identified the contact as best he could guess, then used the bucket handle to try to pull the whole socket apart and get at the wires that connected to the socket.

That proved harder than he thought. He peeled a corner of the socket, peeled more of it, but there were screws involved, and he could not get at the wires themselves. Instead, he folded metal over, punched it onto the contact, cutting his sore fingers, and rammed it down hard. Then he stripped the covering off his insulated wire, got down to paper lining, and stripped and spat, balanced precariously there the while, and hoping no one came.

Somewhere far off he could hear doors opening. He could hear the sound of a vehicle, a bus or a truck, somewhere outside. People were coming and going and that was not good, if somebody was leaving and might mean to take him with them, or maybe if they had gotten a doctor—that would not be good at all.

He spat paper, took the stripped part of the wire and just wrapped it into the wreckage he had made of the socket, finding no other way to secure it, and, worst of all, having no way at all to test his construction to see if it even worked. He got down, shivering from long effort, and from the cold, and carefully, gingerly, took his dangling wire past the chair back and over to the door.

Big metal door latch there, a lot of metal. He stripped more wire, starting it with his teeth, and stripped it way up and wrapped bare wire around the door latch.

So the light switch was on the outside of the door. If somebody flipped it on and then put his hand on the latch—

Then he thought of something else he knew about electricity. He found his water pitcher by the bed and he brought it to the door and made a puddle just right where someone had to step.

That was the first part of his plan. But he did not, as Bren would say, put all his eggs in that basket. Or try to eat dinner before he caught it, in mani-ma's proverb. He got back onto his bruised knees, started to move the bedframe to cover his escape hole, and, on inspiration, and seeing how it rattled without the weight of the mattress on it, decided to see if the bedframe and the wire underpinnings came apart.

The frame readily unsocketed, no question. He took the thin, linked-wire frame that constituted the mattress springs over to the door and laid that metal framework down right over his puddle in front of the door.

But he had derived something better from the disassembly of the bed frame. He had the metal side rail, a pole longer than he was, with a flat end where it had hooked onto the other end. And when he applied *that* to the hole he had made in the wall he had started, he was able to lever out pieces of wood and chunks of plaster one after another.

Now if somebody tried to walk in on him and turned on that light, they would be busy with that watered metal gridwork.

There was a lot of racket outside. A lot of coming and going. He heard doors slam. He kept digging, hammering the interior of his hole in the plaster until the rail went all the way through the wall.

Free for an instant. Then it hit something on the other side. Thump.

Dammit!

14

Big bump. The bus bounced, swung, skidded. And clawed its way onto an uphill climb.

They'd made the time they could on the lower road. They were headed up again. Everyone in the bus had waked including Banichi and Jago, and now heads sank again, experienced security getting rest where they could.

Bren lowered his head back to Jago's shoulder. She hugged him a little closer, maybe seeking relief from his weight, maybe just for the warmth. As resting places went, he couldn't complain of it.

And he tried his best not to think. Thinking did absolutely nothing for sleep. He just listened to the tires on the snow, tried to make himself believe they were just going up to Malguri, peaceful vacation . . . breakfast in the morning . . .

Damned lie. But he kept telling it to himself. Reason wasn't working outstandingly well. He was so tired he was glitching in and out despite everything else.

Eyes shut. Another dark space, and a turn. Another dark space, and another turn, consistently upward, and at an uncomfortable grade, the winter tires grabbing for purchase.

God, don't let us get stuck in a snowbank.

Lurch. Then the bus accelerated, on the level.

The lakeshore, he thought, which jarred him right back to the immediate moment, a desperate race, the bus now fueled for a long haul, for the north rim and the north shore.

Possibilites started crowding in. Contingencies. Resources. Calamities.

He gnawed his lip and started calculating. Again. And knew nobody up front was going to ask him anyway.

Through the wall. But blocked by something.

Cajeiri braced his toe against an irregularity of the slate floor behind him, shoved the long pole through the hole with all his strength and felt whatever-it-was scoot a little.

Furniture, maybe.

Then he thought if there was somebody next door it was certainly going to be suspicious-looking when plaster started cracking and the wall started going. He got down flat and curled around to get his eye up to the hole.

There was no glimmer, which only meant it was pitch-black if there was a crack in the other side at all, and there was no way to tell whether he was getting anywhere.

The hell with it. If he heard them coming, they would run into the boobytrap first.

So he swiveled about again and started thumping away at the plaster. He bent double, lying sideways, braced his feet and got hold of the thin boards that backed the plaster, where the wires had been.

It definitely gave. Cracked, with another heave.

He had a wide enough escape hole on his side of the wall. He lay as he was and simply kicked. Hard.

Two and three more kicks, and his toe went partway through the other side, trapping it in thin boards. It took work to haul it out. He got the bed rail in, took aim, and rammed it.

Crack.

That was encouraging. He swiveled about again and looked. Then he turned about again and went on kicking it until his whole foot could get all the way through.

Then he started kicking just above it, and broke the plaster and boards in on his side, and out, on the other side. By now his foot hurt and his knee hurt and his arms were tired from holding himself still, but he was finally getting somewhere. He kept after it, kicking it and ramming it with the bed rail, and eventually he could get his whole leg through if it wanted to. It just needed a lot more kicking in.

He rolled over and changed feet, and battered away above, and when that leg got tired, he sat down by his hole and pulled at the boards behind the plaster, and took out rubble fill, and shoved that aside. He pulled and pushed again for all he was worth, until he was sure his hands were bleeding, and he had splinters in every one of his fingers.

But it was bigger. It was nearly big enough. There were ways to get through really narrow grates and conduits—he had learned that on the ship. You got one shoulder up, and made your ribs small, and you just lifted this side of your ribs and then the other side the same, and you could do that every time you breathed, just a finger's width, maybe, but he might make it through. His shoulders were the widest part of him. If he practiced the ribs-lifting, he thought he could get there, if he just took off his coat and his shirt.

He took off his jacket, and took off his shirt and put that through, to be sure it didn't snag on the edges. Then he started after it, right shoulder, whole arm, folding inward, ribs, and all, in time with little, helpful breaths. It was like smothering. It scraped his ribs—bloody, he was sure. And it was dangerous to stop, because one lost the rhythm if one stopped, and if one lost the rhythm, muscles could freeze up and then one would be stuck for sure and maybe not able to breathe if one's associates failed to pull him out by the feet—which had happened to him once, in the conduits on the ship.

And then they would find out, and if somebody got shocked getting in the door he would be in far worse confinement, not to mention—

His right hand came up against something, a barrier, whatever thing had stopped the rail from going through, and it was too close. He shoved against it with all his strength, and it scooted, and felt like a cardboard box.

He kept moving, all the same, breathe and wriggle and lift and move. He kept the movement going, and shoved with his toes on the other side, which, besides his scraped ribs, was a very useful leverage.

His head had emerged into a place as black as the one he was leaving. His arms were both through, now, and he shoved, and butted his head against the stupid cardboard box, and with repeated efforts, he got one elbow down onto the dusty floor and began to drag the rest of him through, alternately shoving at the obstructing box and heaving forward.

Now his bare stomach scraped over debris. Ragged edges of board and plaster and rubble had scored his shoulders and ribs, and the air was icy cold. But his front half was through, into a whole other and unguarded room. The rest of him came fast, feet and all, a last scrape over the rubble, and he could stand up.

If there was a door, it was likely to be to his right, the same orientation as the room he had come from. He gathered up his shirt and coat in a wad, then felt his way through chaotic stacks of boxes, bumped into a shelf and, after that shelf, found the door.

Not locked. He moved the latch downward, his heart beating hard.

He stopped, then, put his shirt and coat on for warmth, even tucked the shirt tail in—for luck, everything the way mani insisted. Coat on. Proper young gentleman. Time to go and leave this place.

He pushed down the latch just to test it, so, so relieved that it moved. He ached. All his scrapes stung, and all his bruises hurt. And he really, really hoped there was no guard out in the hall. He could hear some to-do somewhere in the building; but that was all the more reason just to be out of here. Fast.

The latch moved down, and bumped just slightly, moving the latch mechanism, and the door came open a crack, letting in a dim light. At that point, looking back, he saw he was leaving a room full of unspecified *stuff*, that was Gene's word for it: *stuff*. Cans on the shelf. Food. Drums of flour and sugar. None of that helped him.

But there were packets with a label he recognized, a sun figure. And that was always dried fruit, and packets of dried fruit were good. He got into the box and shoved handfuls of those into his shirt and his coat pockets.

Then he cracked the door wider and slipped out into the hall outside, shutting the door after him to keep everything as ordinary-looking as he could. Down the hall to the left were what might be servant rooms, and a dead end. At the end of the hall to the right of his door was a dimly lit stairs going up, and there was a door up on the landing, on the opposite wall, that could go anywhere, outside, or to another hall. The landing was where the hall stopped.

But just before that set of steps was—what might be an archway. Another hallway.

Servants' quarters was indeed where he was. *Kitchen* storerooms, to boot, given the flour and the fruit, and it must be that hour or two in which kitchen staff might be asleep in rooms all up and down this hall. House serving and cleaning staff, and any night watch on duty, would be upstairs, two levels or so above the lordly rooms.

Kitchens, now—a thing he had learned from mani, and not from Gene and Artur and Irene—kitchens of a big house tended to have their own section, and tended to be in the basement, or just above it, the basement being mostly storage. The machimi he had had to read talked about *kitchen stairs* and *kitchen doors*.

And in those machimi mani had made him read, assassins notoriously got in by those low-level routes, so smart houses had alarms on them. You had to switch them off at some station somewhere in the house.

Well, but sometimes you just did what you had to, and took a chance.

He had seen how Banichi and Cenedi moved when they were on business. Quick and quiet, and stopping now and again to listen.

He always tucked away that kind of information. He remembered now, and had it in his head just how to go: whatever was going on up above meant the masters of the house were awake and about something, which meant at any moment someone could decide they wanted something that would send staff running down here to rouse up the kitchen folk.

His own room—he knew his trap could kill somebody; maybe one of the innocent servants; and he worried about that, now that he was out and slipping past that harmless-looking door.

Well, let it, he thought.

And then he hesitated.

And then he went back, and flipped the light switch on, so if somebody was a dolt and failed to notice the switch was down, he would get a fast shock from the door handle before he really closed down on the lever.

Which was maybe too obliging, but he felt better about it, not knowing who it might catch.

And the kitchen itself—would have a way out.

Mani had told him that the layout of noble houses tended to date from way back. Houses had used to get water from a well, and the strongest kitchen servants had had to carry it, until someone invented hand pumps and then electric pumps and brought the water inside, which was why kitchens were traditionally never upstairs.

And a well court might be where that stairs and that doorway led, the reputed outside door that was usually also near the storerooms. Mani had thwacked his ear and told him pay attention and not get bored when she was talking, and he had listened, even through the parts that had never made sense—why had people not thought of making pumps in the first place and piping water inside instead of carrying buckets? He had asked that question—and now the answer paid for all those thwacks.

Because there must be a well court. In old houses, there was always a well court.

It was not, however, a time to get careless. Banichi had taught him about wires, that could take your feet off, and about interrupt alarms, that could spot an intruder—if the house had systems up, and it might, with all that fuss in the upper halls, the systems could well be armed.

The hallway that intersected just short of those steps, however, looked more promising—looked like it might actually hold the kitchens themselves halfway down, a big area of arched openings where there were no doors, and down there was another closed door, on *this* level, and—near it, better than anything, oh, wonderful sight! a row of plain outdoor coats on pegs, with heavy boots arranged beneath them.

That must be the outside door. *That* must be the well court, right on the kitchen level.

He ran as lightly as he could, stopped, grabbed a coat off the peg, and saw something else hanging on the same peg: a flashlight, and a set of keys. He took that, just in case, and maybe to cause trouble, if they needed the keys. Then he bundled the too large coat about himself, stepped into men's snow boots that fit right over his indoor boots, and headed for the door, using the flashlight to look that door over top to bottom.

No wires. But a simple magnetic interrupt alarm just stuck on as an afterthought, of all things, and without even any concealment: it had just been tacked onto the ancient woodwork. It was so simple, he looked it over and over again to try to find some hidden trap, but that seemed to be just what it was.

Steps sounded on the stairs at the turning. The door up there opened, and he froze. People were coming down, guards, by the look of them in the hall light. His heart started beating doubletime, and he edged back into the cover of the hanging coats. They were headed down for the room he had been in.

He had no choice. He pulled the magnet right off, keeping the tacks with it, and, never breaking contact, jammed it against the main part of the unit, where it would stay, preventing the alarm from sounding. He was about to open the door.

And about that time there was a yelp, an oath, and the whole hall went black.

He flung down the latch, yanked the door open, and—

And the whole world out there was white, lit with floodlights from the left, where a bus was, and the ground was white—just white, with white puffs falling out of the sky, cold, and the most startling sight . . .

Snow, he thought. He had never seen snow. But that was it. He took a step.

Hit ice and his feet went out from under him, faster than thinking. He landed at the bottom of the steps, half winded and backward, staring up at the door he ought not to have left open.

Suddenly an alarm was going off, wailing into the night.

He rolled, and scrambled up and ran in utter panic, half-blind from the jolt, stumbling in outsized boots. He made it to the stone wall—defensive wall, outer wall, just like in the movies. And of all things, there was a bus parked up by the big gates, and lights, and people stalking about in the floodlights, so the place was on the edge of swarming.

But the big wrought iron gates up there were shut.

Iron gates with big wide bars, and beyond them—beyond

them, who knew? It was better than being trapped and put back in a worse room.

There were people running about everywhere in the light of what looked like the house's front door, and the alarm was still going, but that gate was where he had to go, and there was that bus with its back end right up near it.

So he did what Banichi had always told him was the best way to avoid suspicion: walk, walk as if he knew exactly where he was going; and he walked right up near the middle of the bus, and then walked back to the iron gate, and the bars.

The bars might stop a man coming through. Not him. He squeezed through, saw a second gate, metal and solid, that might really stop something, but it stood wide open—just the barred gate was shut behind the bus.

He glanced back. People were clustered around the front steps of the house. People with guns. He saw no one he knew. He had the bars between him and them, now, and he turned and just kept walking. He hurt, where he had hit on the steps.

So he scooped up a handful of ice and clamped that down on the back of his head, and just kept on walking along the wall, where it climbed up and up the hill. There was the road the bus had used, but if he went that way, there might be more people coming along, and that was no good. He wanted to get back beyond the road. There were trees, and brush covering a lot of rock, and if they got mecheiti out tracking him, he knew they tracked most by air-scent, and the wind helped, if he just didn't touch things, and if he just got onto rough ground where mecheiti could not go.

Move faster, he said to himself, and tried to run. It was dark, and the snow was coming down, and that had another benefit: it might cover his tracks. He had pockets full of food. He was out. He was away. He was probably somewhere in the East, and if he could figure out where he was, he might get to a fuel station that had a phone . . .

. . . if he knew what land he was on, and where their man'chi was.

All of a sudden the lessons mani had thwacked into his skull were life and death.

And if he had no precise knowledge where he was, except the East, up in the mountains.

And the mountains and down to the plains was where those guests of Great-grandmother's had come from.

And they were her neighbors.

And if they were her neighbors, if he just kept going upland, if he just got up high enough, he might reach the lake, and if he got to the lake, he had to get to the shore and keep walking, keep ahead of any riders, because that was the worst thing, that was the thing he had to worry about.

He had no idea which one of the three that had come to dinner had done this, or in whose house he had just been. But it had to have been one of them, or somebody they knew. There was Lady Drien at the south end of the lake, there was Lord Caiti who lived in the east and had the estate at the north end of the lake, and Rodi farther north and Agilisi farther east in the lowlands of Cie . . . he had no clue, none, where he was, but he knew it was Caiti or Drien. If Drien, south would take him around the lake to Malguri. If it was Caiti, north would be the direction.

And his stomach hurt from running, and he slipped and stumbled in the big boots. Finally, he stopped for breath and took the heavy boots off and just carried them, because he knew from the ship that if you stopped where it was cold, you were going to want heavy clothes. It was hard even to carry them; but the top of the ridge both encouraged and dismayed him.

There *was* a lake. It had to be *the* lake—it was just as mani had described it . . . except it was far down the slope, not near, and it was . . .

Huge.

He could not see how big. There was supposed to be an island out there. An island that had ghosts, and where a bell sometimes rang for no reason. But the gray water just went on and on into the haze of falling snow, until it was all one gray nothing.

He heard voices in the distance.

Then he heard far-off gunshots.

And sucked in a breath and took off running, north, for no particular reason, and without looking back.

Run and run and run. He clutched the wretched boots to him, and slipped over the edge of a snow-covered ridge, never even seeing it. He skidded to a landing at the bottom, closer to the lake but still, so, so far away, and now, down here, he thought, anybody chasing him had to have a good view of everything below.

But there had been the shots—he knew they were shots, and somebody was fighting up there.

And it could be mani, with Cenedi, come after him—it was the only person in all the world he would think would get here that fast and know where to look.

But even if it was, he dared not turn back to find out, and if they were shooting up on the ridge, he had a small window to get himself clear.

And that meant run.

The snow was coming down. That meant he left tracks. That only meant he had to be fast, and keep going, and maybe get somewhere he would not leave tracks.

He ran until he was out of breath, and fell on the damned boots, just sprawled. There were trees ahead, old gnarled trees, and a spooky looking place, but it was cover, at least from being seen.

Run and run. He stumbled on roots and rocks, but found a place beneath the evergreen branches where tracks were not evident, and that meant he just had to push himself and go by twisty ways and not get caught.

It was quiet behind him now.

He leaned against a tree to catch his breath. He could see all along the slope he had crossed, above the lake shore, and it was white out there, and he was in shadow.

He saw a flash of light, a starlike flash where no flash ought to be.

They were looking for him. Somebody was, with a flashlight. He had no guarantee that somebody behind him was of mani's man'chi. He would believe nothing and no one until he got clear to Malguri, and he had chosen his direction.

Shortest to go low, around the lake itself, and he drew as much cold breath as he could suck in and veered off lower as quickly as he could, toward the lake, toward the shortest route.

Best he could do. Only thing he knew to do.

They had never taught him this on the ship.

And here it was no game.

15

Bren had indeed slept. He waked against Jago's shoulder, aware that the bus was climbing steeply, and that everyone around him was stirring.

Slept like a child. He felt Jago shift her weight, lay a hand on his shoulder.

He rubbed a face gone rough with stubble. Not exactly set for a formal visit, atevi finding this human characteristic, as they did, passing strange; but his personal kit was back at Drien's abode and there was no help for it. They had to take him as he was, scratchy and chilled and in a parka and outdoor boots.

The bus tires slipped and skewed, and it clawed its way upward, steadily. It was far from a noiseless approach they made, but it was not intended to be. First they got in.

And that, even with Drien's help, might be easier said than done.

Banichi got up, rifle in hand. It was the plan that he would go in, accompanying Lady Drien, asking admittance to the grounds. They would be seen. The rest would keep in the shadows.

"Bren-ji," Jago said. "Things may move quickly. One requests, stay close."

"One can manage. One requests you do not look back or divert your attention for my sake. One will not be a fool in this."

"Yes," she said.

She moved to speak to one of Ilisidi's young men. Rifles were much in evidence, and one had to remember the metal shell of this bus was very little protection. One hoped there were no snipers, or at least that they would wait to see who arrived.

They reached mostly level road, and ground and slid to a stop.

Gates. *Open* gates appeared in the headlights, through the front windows—when they had had every apprehension it would take Lady Drien's presence to get through those gates. And the house doors themselves wide open, scattering electric light out onto the snow.

That was no scene of tranquillity. People didn't leave the doors of a great house open in the middle of the night. The yard held one bus. But there were a lot of tracks, recent, in the snow of the yard.

The bus stopped. Banichi and Lady Drien got down, and a trio pair of Ilisidi's young men with them.

The dowager stayed, with Cenedi, and with Jago. Bren moved up closer, to have a vantage out the front window.

Banichi and the lady crossed ruts, deep tire tracks where either that one bus had been backing all over the yard, or where other buses had come in. There were all sorts of footprints out on the snow where they stood.

Banichi had put on a heavy coat, a coat lacking the spark of silver that distinguished the Guild. A heavy down coat, likely, of the sort Drien's own guards wore.

Damn, Bren said to himself, eyes riveted to that sight, one of the two individuals he most cared about in the world walking with the diminutive lady, across that footprinted bare expanse of snow, and up the trampled, icy steps. He took faster and faster breaths, expecting—something. Any sort of thing. Gunshots.

They reached the top step. The young men went inside. Came back out.

And at that point, Banichi turned and signaled "come ahead."

Come ahead wasn't in the plan. But none of this was.

The dowager moved, with Cenedi's help, to descend the steps. Jago went next, and Bren came closely after, caught Jago's arm to keep his balance as he landed and saw the dowager and Cenedi heading in. He went at the dowager's deliberate pace, crossing that exposed expanse of rutted snow.

The house steps were icy and lightly snowed over, atop a lot of footprints. Banichi and Lady Drien had moved inside ahead of them, and when they reached the shelter of the front hall, there they found Lady Drien had stopped, waiting for them, and Banichi had gone on.

"Go," Bren said. "Jago-ji, go." More of the dowager's men were at their backs. They had firepower all around them, and Jago let go his arm.

"Protect her, nandi," Jago said, and was off in an instant. The dowager, snowy from the transit, stood with them in that hall, and Cenedi gave rapid orders to two men, then headed inside on Banichi and Jago's track. Immediately two of the dowager's guard took out down two side hallways that led off the small, mud-tracked foyer.

And not only mud. Bren's eye picked out a ruddy stain in the mix—blood. Someone had quit this place in a hell of a hurry, leaving the doors open to the winter air, and he was very much afraid that there had been a falling-out among their enemies, maybe not to Cajeiri's benefit. Someone had left the front doors open, and that would be someone who cared little for the fate of the house that belonged to Caiti.

Someone else whose name, he very much feared, was Murini. And their own plans were changing by the minute, trying to adapt, but behind the events now, well behind them.

Hurt. Hurt awfully to keep running, but mani would expect— mani would expect him to keep going; Cajeiri could all but hear her saying it . . . You can do it, boy. A great-grandson of mine can do it . . .

The forest gave out ahead. He was losing his cover. Tracks would show, and the snow out there beyond the trees was unblemished. Open. Shining in the night. There were trees, but they became regular as if planted. They *were* planted. It was somebody's orchard.

He leaned against a tree under cover of the woods and caught his breath, his heart pounding against his ribs. His mouth was dry. His whole body ached, and his feet were numb with cold in their light boots. And if he went out there, whoever might follow him would track him easily in that open space between those widely spaced trees.

Then an idea came to him. He had kept the damned boots. He had clutched them all the way he had run, thinking that it would be the only means to get his feet warm again—and now he thought—they were a man's boots. And whoever was tracking him would be tracking a boy.

He looked for bare spots among the trees, carefully eased over a ways from where he had been standing, setting his feet carefully. He worked over maybe the length of mani's dining room, and then, leaning against a tree, put on the boots right over his own boots.

They were warmer from the start; he wanted to pull off boots and stockings, and enjoy dry boots as well, but he might have to run again. It was only a temporary thing, this trick, until he could get through the orchard, and best not have the others slipping around and wearing blisters.

So he walked out under the trees of the orchard, under thin branches edged with snow, and tried not to touch any of them. Just—north, as best he could, and west to the lake shore, as close as he could get, as fast as he could get there.

*   *   *

The com in Bren's pocket beeped. He fumbled after it, more nervous than he had thought, in his wait in the foyer.

"Nandi." It was Jago's voice, scratchy, on unit-to-unit function, and with a lot of interference. "You should come. The dowager should come, too."

"Yes," he said, and he flipped the com closed. "Aiji-ma, nandi, we are urged in at this point."

"We shall go," the dowager said.

Drien, thin-lipped, looked less determined to venture anywhere, but they went, all the same, up the three steps, through the arch, and into a broader hall, where there was a conspicuously open door and a brightly lighted room.

The bullet hole in the plaster near that door was a forewarning.

And there was a reason to fear boobytraps and wires, but that was why Guild had gone in ahead of them, being sure nothing of house defenses or hostile setups remained live. If Jago said come ahead, he came ahead, to the heart of the house, where Jago and Banichi and Cenedi were gathered about a man on the floor, a man in house dress. Another, to the side, lay like a heap of laundry, where blood had soaked into the antique carpet. A third and a fourth lay about, dressed like house security.

The man in the middle—Lord Rodi—was still alive, leaning on a footstool, his elbow on it; and seemingly missed in all this bloodletting.

Their security stood up, gave a little bow at the dowager's arrival, her assumption of authority in the room.

The cane thumped the carpet. "Where, nandi, is my greatgrandson?"

"A good question," Rodi said in a thready voice. "A question he could not answer." This with a nod to the dead man by the grouping of chairs. "The boy escaped."

"Escaped." Few things drew such startlement from the dowager. "How, escaped?"

"That was never clear," Rodi said, and gave a wave of his hand, gathering breath. "Murini-aiji arrived with his staff, and the boy had disappeared. One has no idea."

"Where?" Drien asked. "Ro-ji, answer!"

"Dri-daja?" Rodi blinked up at the lady of Cobesthen. "Odd company you keep."

"Answer," Ilisidi said, "and you *may* survive this."

"Oh, I think I shall not survive," Rodi said. "I know I shall not survive."

"Poison, aiji-ma," Cenedi said. "He had taken it before we arrived."

"Damned slow," Rodi said. "Too damned slow." He drew his knee up, and winced, as at a cramp. "Caiti believed he had the answer, believed he could take Murini. But that depended on having the boy for a pledge. On persuading Murini." Rodi's knuckles showed white, where they clutched the top of the footstool. "Hold the boy for Murini, assassinate you, and rule all the East, while Murini took on the aiji in Shejidan. But he could not produce the boy. So Murini shot him."

"I say again, where is my great-grandson? What happened here?"

"Murini arrived . . . to negotiate with Caiti . . . he was supposed to. But he came in force, to take the house."

"Did Caiti expect otherwise? *Where is he?*"

Rodi was having difficulty holding his head up. One hand had begun to shake. "One did not expect—one did not expect—he would attempt this . . ."

"Fool, then! Which airport?"

"Caidienein-ori."

"And has taken him there?"

"If he has caught him."

"Caught him."

"Murini expected—expected Caiti had double-crossed him—tried to get from Caiti—from me—where Caiti had taken him. No knowledge. Murini ordered—all in pursuit. Bus—bus to go—"

"Where, damn you?"

"The north road—to meet him overland. One decided not to wait—to be shot. Your landing—in Malguri Township—is known. I took my dose—damn the man. Damn Murini and damn Caiti and that woman."

"Agilisi," Bren muttered, out of turn.

"She left us. She ran. That was the beginning of unraveling. We knew she had gone to Malguri."

"She did not," Ilisidi said shortly. "The bus, the bus, Rodi. Did they leave that way? Did they find my great-grandson?"

"One does not think— Caiti's men—Caiti's men went in pursuit—leaving the house. Murini arrived—believing Caiti had taken him away. Not believing—the escape. They shot Caiti. Went to track—went to track where Caiti had hidden the boy. But it was a lie from the start. All a lie. Murini meant to take him away. Never any negotiation. He was smarter than Caiti."

"There was a room on the next level," Cenedi said. "A great deal of digging, and a wire rigged to the light socket . . . one assumes the young gentleman . . ."

"Nand' paidhi," the dowager said sharply.

"Aiji-ma."

"Send your guard. Find him."

"Banichi," he said. Aiji or not, it was impossible to order another lord's guard. He had to do it. And he had his own conditions. "Jago. Let us go."

Banichi looked sharply at him, at the dowager, as if hoping Ilisidi would order otherwise.

But the dowager was on one agenda: finding the boy before Murini did. And anything less was not acceptable.

Bren, for his part, headed out of the room, for once ahead of his bodyguard. Ilisidi had Drien's men and her own headed in, on mecheiti. If there was any attack from Murini's lot, *they* had help coming, not to mention communication with Malguri, from this house.

He and his staff were the most experienced in tracking the heir, no question about that. Two years of practice, tracking the boy through the bowels of the ship.

"You should stay, Bren-ji," Jago said. "You will slow us. Protect the dowager."

"She has Guild to call on and Drien's lot besides. Where does the trail start?"

Banichi and Jago were on the same area link as Cenedi. They knew. They headed down the hall at their traveling stride, and a human had to exert himself to keep up even before they reached the stairs.

Two of Ilisidi's young men were in the lower hall, by an open door. "The young gentleman was held here," one said, and pointed back down the hall, the way they had come. "Tracks in plaster dust, one smaller and many larger, go down the side hall."

"The aiji-dowager is upstairs, nadiin," Banichi said, already in motion down the hall in the indicated direction. "We shall find him. Lock this door after us."

Down the side hall, then, out into the dark, and into a view of the courtyard, and icy dark steps. The traces inside, in plaster dust, were faint. Out here it looked like a mass exodus, down the steps and out across the snow, obliterating any trace of the boy, but giving clear evidence of very many men exiting the building and heading out across the courtyard, straight for the gate.

Banichi headed out at a jog, Jago with him—trying to dissuade him from going along, Bren said to himself, and sucked in air and outright ran, as hard as he could, keeping pace all the way to the open gate.

There, a second set of tracks came clear, where a man had

gone through the bars. The rest of the pursuers had opened the gates, and headed out on foot, trampling the trail beyond.

Bren stepped through the bars of the open gate. Banichi and Jago looked at him.

"The young gentleman," Banichi said. "In thick boots."

They had to go to the end of the gate.

"Five, ten men," Jago said, as they rejoined him. "A bus left here."

"Down to the north road," Bren said, still hard-breathing. "To rendezvous with the others. Overland. To get back to Cadienein-ori Airport. With the young gentleman. Agilisi leaving—so scared Lord Rodi—Caiti. Murini shot Caiti to finish off—untidy business. Left Rodi to his suicide." He ran out of air. "Can that be what happened?"

"It would seem reasonable that it did," Banichi said. "Bren-ji, go back now. One asks you go back."

"One asks," he said, trying to ignore the pain in his side, "that we make all safe speed from here, nadiin-ji. I shall *not* slow you down. Caiti's men—are likely out tracking—Cajeiri. Murini's, too. Your Guild does not negotiate. I can. I may help."

"We cannot carry you where we may go, Bren-ji," Jago said. "You must keep up."

"Shall," he said, and gestured the direction the tracks went. "Go!"

Banichi and Jago lit out at a ground-devouring run; and then he was glad he had the jacket on and not the coat, glad he had zipped pockets, too, and good boots, because the broad trampled trail lay uphill, along a ridge of evergreen and up among the rocks, rising, constantly rising, a long, long climb in which he began to think, no, they were right—he could *not* do this, he *was* a detriment to everyone's safety. Including the boy's . . .

His feet slipped on snow. Jago grabbed his arm and bodily hauled him up, shoved him up, hand on his backside, to the next ragged level among the rocks, and said not a word doing it. He put his head down and just ran, making up time, whatever time—God knew. They hadn't asked Rodi how long since the boy's escape, how long since Murini left. Possibly a dying man wasn't that sure of schedules. Possibly Banichi and Jago knew that detail. There was no leisure to ask questions. No use in it either. Not his job, to catch them. Just to talk.

By the time they reached the high rim, his ribs ached and his vision blurred. He caught sight of the lake below, water half-glowing with the snow-light, and on his next step he nearly went down the slippery rock.

Jago got one arm, Banichi the other, and if that was not humiliation enough, they set him down on that rock, and dropped down themselves to reconnoiter—

Their keener night-vision. One forgot that, one tended to forget that, in the safe hallways of the Bu-javid, in the corridors of the ship—but they saw what he could not, out here, and so did their enemy, and he was, comparatively speaking, blind.

More, he had just come over that ridge silhouetted against the sky, and risked all three of them.

He was utterly embarrassed, resolved to be smarter than that.

Come, Banichi signed, and he got up, not escaping Jago's hand under his elbow, keeping him low, and they started the descent, down at an angle toward the lake.

Long climb down. The trail down was plain, even to his eyes, wending down a rocky, little-grown slope, where old fumaroles made spires and provided cover for ambush. It was not a comfortable place to be, but the trampled trail led them, and they kept to it.

On to lower ground, and a ridge which might have marked an earlier lakeshore—along that, then, and down again.

"Traveling fast," Jago commented, "with a clear trail in front of them."

Damn, Bren thought. He hoped the boy knew he was followed. Cajeiri could have no idea by what, could not have an inkling of the worse danger tracking him; and the three of them, alone, were fewer than they needed against what they might run into, he was well sure of it. Cenedi was likely calling for reinforcements from Malguri, which might come straight across the lake—to reach a road meant going clear down to the township and around, and there was no way to come from Malguri Fortress except overland, by mecheiti, no way to reach the north road, that between the Haidamar and the northern airport, except to come over by water, or clear around the lake, as they had done, a journey of hours.

He hoped for boats. That was the likeliest. And the most help.

But none showed. The vast lake was snow-veiled, icy around its rim, and placid below them. And if they were very lucky, neither Caiti's men nor Murini's lot had a clue they were being tracked by a third force.

His side hurt. Calisthenics on the ship was no substitute. He gained a coppery taste in his mouth, as if he were bleeding inside. And now the ancient beach played out in a rock slide, and the track descended again, on a tumble of rock.

The footholds Banichi and Jago took were increasingly too far apart for him as his side seized up. He put hands down and clambered and outright slipped in spots, determined to keep up. Ripped a hole in his trousers and nearly broke his neck making one step, but he kept the pace, down and down, and at the last, he let himself slide and relied on Jago to catch him.

She set him rightwise about on the path and immediately headed after Banichi.

Way out of breath by now. It was a mad, a reckless speed, by his lights, but it was what they had to do. His legs felt like rubber, his left side was afire, and now lights began to dance in his eyes, step after step. He wasn't seeing where he was going, now, he was just following, keeping up, sweating as if it were a summer's day—

His foot skidded into a brushy hole and his reach after balance snagged his sleeve on a branch.

He went down, hard, hit the rocks and thought that was all the damage. Then he began to skid, slipping helplessly over an edge, impact onto a slope, and a rock-studded slide all the way to the bottom, leg wrenched, head banged, stars exploding in his eyes, and a keen pain in ribs and elbows—thank God for good boots, which let him get his feet again, and for heavy tread, which let him stay there and negotiate his way to level ground.

Not, however, up again.

Banichi and Jago were up above, stopped for him, facing the need to leave the trail, all to go down and recover a fool.

Go on, he waved them furiously. *Go on!*

Banichi did that. Jago hesitated half a step. He waved her off, and then started moving himself, reprised his jog along the lower, flatter shelf he'd reached, and with a glance up, he saw Jago departing at a run, on Banichi's track.

They had to. Right set of priorities. The boy was in danger. The fool paidhi had a sore ankle, nothing broken, and the fool paidhi could run, by what might amount to a shorter route. The old caldera reached a point of ancient blowout at the north end, a place where the rim was virtually level with the lake, and the ground grew flatter, and, dammit, he had a map, if he was lucky and the station's web of satellites included this end of the continent . . . damned right there should be a map of the place, and the road.

He leaned for breath against a rock, hauled out the locator from his zipped pocket, turned it on, and waited while it went through a small search. Satellite, damned right. *Several* satellites up there. And a map, a magical, detailed map. The lake.

His position, with the haunted island out there mid-lake and invisible in the snowfall. He clicked out on the zoom.

And saw the road from the remote hamlet of Cadienein-ori to the Haidamar, the same road that, skirting Cadienein-ori, crossed the hills to Cie. The road made a slow sweep close to the lake, right up ahead, and topography showed a low spot. If Murini and his lot were going to intersect the immediate pursuit, it was going to be there. If Murini, who might be on that bus, was going to get personally involved, it would be there.

He left the unit on, not knowing all its functions, but knowing Banichi and Jago had the same item in their possession, and that they had that map and were going to draw the same conclusion as he did. There was a small depot or some sort of building up there in that low spot. The map gave no indication what it was, just a square. Possibly it was a fueling station, maybe belonging to the Haidamar.

But it was a place, and people who were meeting a search party indicated a place to rendezvous, and worse, far worse, a boy who was running for his life might mistake a place for a refuge.

The land got steeper, directly after that small square: the topology showed a sheer rise, right where the ancient eruption had blasted through a wall of sheer rock and all sorts of geologic mayhem had gone on—sheer cliffs, and rough land, after that. He and the dowager had ridden the uplands, from Malguri, once years ago, and the dowager had said, had she not, that there was only *one* approach to the lake from Malguri, and that was her boat dock?

Did the boy know, did he possibly know, that there was no way out from where he had gone *except* the north road? That there was no beach to let him around to safety, only sheer cliffs? Could the boy even have any idea that it was Malguri land, just beyond that sheer wall?

He hurt. But he ran, all the same. He dared not trust the

immediate-area function on the pocket com. What he had just reasoned out, he was well sure Banichi and Jago damned well knew, and everybody else in the world knew. They were coming to the bag-end of the course, the place where everything stopped.

16

The shore itself, a flat, treacherous strand, lumpy with rocks, offered no sure ground under the snow. Water lapped up against the icy edge, ice in the shallows along shore, in some places under a film of newly-fallen snow, that gave warning it was water only where the slight surge lapped up through the ice like lacework. Bren stayed away from that, skirted it at the fastest pace he could make—had to stop now and again to double over and catch his breath, and then reprised the effort, run and run and run, with no idea how far ahead of him Banichi and Jago might be, or whether the dowager and Cenedi had made contact with Malguri, or asked for help, or what.

He passed signs of habitation—the regular geometries of an orchard situated in the blowout gap, and that might be the reason for the box on the map, the indication of structure. That might be all it was. And hope so. Hope that the boy had not gone to any definite Place that would give his pursuers any help finding him.

Hope that surprise would give them a marginal advantage over Murini's lot, at least until help could get to them—and *they* had taken the mecheiti Malguri had in stable, mecheiti which might have carried help to the dowager by now, and help *might* be coming overland toward them, maybe down the north road itself, to try to catch Murini's lot *before* they laid hands on a young hostage.

* * *

It was impossible to run fast, shod in oversized boots. Impossible to make any speed. Cajeiri kept walking, just trying to get far enough through the orchard that the branches might screen him off from anyone following him, and hoping they might mistake the boots for one of their own. He walked wide-striding, trying to keep a man's gait through the snow.

Then something different hove up through the veil of snow and branches, something solid, like a building, a rustic kind of building.

No lights showed. Nothing gave any sign of life. He walked on, and as he walked, saw a snow-covered roof, a native stone foundation, stone walls . . .

It was a house, was what. A house out here. Maybe there was an orchard-keeper, but it was winter, and maybe nobody lived here in the winter.

At the edge of the orchard stood a second thing, a great big hulk of a thing that he thought might be a wrecked storage shed, but it was a very odd-looking shed, if that was what it had been . . . it was all smooth-sided, and nested among folded-up girders, and it looked as if it had stood taller and then just collapsed down on one side.

Maybe it was a bin for the fruit or something, just toppled by age or weather, if nobody used this orchard . . . the orchard _looked_ like a working orchard—there was no overgrowth sticking up through the snow—but who knew what it looked like without the snow? Maybe the trees were all dead. The house looked completely deserted. And in winter, the orchard-keeper could have gone to live in town.

Maybe—maybe there was stuff left in the house, stuff he could use.

Maybe there was even a door open—mani said country people rarely locked doors, in _her_ district, and if people locked doors it was odd, because sometimes a neighbor just wanted to borrow something, and did, and would hike over and pay it back when the owner came back. That was a country tradition. Only the fortresses and the lordly houses kept their gates locked, mani had said, and whoever came there could not just walk in, and that was just the way things had always been, because there were historic things and firearms and, besides, always staff—but any country person who had business with the lord could still turn up at the gates and ask for help, and know he had a right to go in and talk to the lord. That was the way a proper lord's house had to be . . . always ready to open, the same as any farmer's or herder's.

Mani had said—mani had said that, after her, he had to know these things, because he would be lord of Malguri.

And he would be neighbor to these people who had locked him in the basement.

He had a score to settle with them now. He knew mani would do it. But he had his own, once he came into his own. *His* staff, the same as mani-ma's, *his* heritage, and if the neighbors had gotten together to treat him the way they had, *they* were the ones who had to be worried when he got to Malguri.

This orchard *might* even be a Malguri orchard. He had no idea how far toward Malguri land he had come—not because he had not paid attention, but because he had no idea of distances in this place. That pale grayness between the trees to the left might even be the lake itself—but he was not sure. The whole scale was more than he had ever thought.

But if the lake was coming closer and on his left on this trek, *that* meant it was Caiti's summer house where he had just been, and *that* meant he had turned the way he ought and was skirting the shore, at a distance.

And *that* meant, in turn, that he was sooner going to come up around to the other cliffs, those on which Malguri sat and still have to skirt around a long, long way before he could get to Malguri's boat dock—because those cliffs were as good as a

defensive wall. The slot in which the boat dock set was the
only way up to Malguri from the lake shore. Malguri had held
out in the wars because there was no real way for a lot of people to come at it except from the south, or way up over the
mountains, or fighting their way through that gap in the cliffs.

And he was going to be forever getting there, a very cold forever. He had food in his pockets, and he had eaten a little of it,
just to try to stay warm. But he was so tired, and his feet were
still so cold, and he had nothing but the oversized coat and the
stupid boots—

And this place might have stuff in it. It might have coats,
and blankets, and dry socks, for that matter, if whoever was
the gardener had not packed everything, and set everything
ready to come back in the spring.

But it was a scary-looking and neglected place, with that
broken *thing* out in the yard, sitting in the middle of broken
trees, and others all tilted. It looked as if something had blown
it up, because there had been a stone wall, and part of that was
down. It looked as if there had been a battle here—

So maybe it *was* Malguri land. And Caiti had attacked it.

No light, no light at all, and one of the windows was broken.
All of them were dead and dark.

The window beside the door was broken, too. And he got up
on the porch, which was mostly clear of snow, and looked in,
and there was furniture—he could make that out. There were
things lying all over the floor, maybe because of the wind, or
maybe because of people searching here.

He tried the door latch. It gave, and he pushed the door inward, very quietly. There might be a kitchen. There might be
a knife or something. A weapon.

There was much better than that. There was a phone on
the wall.

He went straight to it and lifted the receiver. It was dirty,
old, it had no buttons inside the handle—he was scared it

might be an intercom with somewhere he might not want to talk to, but in a moment more he heard a man's voice ask:

"What number, nadi?"

He hung up, he was so startled. He had no authorizations.

But it had not challenged him. He decided—maybe it was authority, some sort of security station. He picked it up again and listened.

"What number, if you please, nadi? Is there a problem?"

"Who are you?" he asked.

"This is the Malguri switchboard, nadi. Whom do you wish to call?"

He hardly knew what to say, he was so startled. But he knew where to start—where mani had gone. "One wishes to speak to Lord Tatiseigi in Atageini Province, nadi, if you please."

"In Atageini Province." That seemed to startle and perplex the person. Maybe it was impossible from here. Or he had given something away. *"One moment, nadi."*

They could be tracing the call. He knew about that from nand' Bren's movies. He knew every second he spent on the line was dangerous. But he heard clicks and some discussion, perhaps among the operators, and then, just as he was about to hang up, came a ring at the other end.

And someone picked up. *"This is Tirnamardi night staff."*

"Nadi!" he exclaimed. "Is my great-grandmother there?"

"No." There was a pause. *"Is this nand' Cajeiri? Is this our lord's grand-nephew?"*

"Find my great-grandmother immediately, nadi. Or Great-uncle. Either. One is in utmost need, nadi! It is extremely urgent."

"They went together to Shejidan, at the report of your kidnapping. Please stay on the line . . ."

"Impossible! There are people shooting here, nadi. I need my great-grandmother, I need someone to come to Malguri District!"

"Just stay on the line, young sir! Just one moment. Just one moment. I am calling Lord Tatiseigi, as fast as I can."

Authorities did that when they were tracing a call. That was as old as the movies with no color. He hung up. Fast.

Maybe, he thought, he should try to get the operator to call Malguri itself, the fortress. Maybe the staff there could help— could just drive down the road and pick him up, easy as that.

But that was right in the district. If he started giving particulars about where he was, then the operator might know, and if the operator was not to be trusted, the operator might call somebody, and it could be the wrong side. It was just too dangerous to give out his location, supposing someone was tapping the lines.

Banichi and Cenedi would not sit here just waiting, either, after making a phone call on an unsecure land line. He had to go. He had to. He made one detour back to the kitchen, threw open drawers and took three knives, then looked in the pantry, but it was too dark to see anything useful and he was getting scared. He went out the back door.

And right from the back porch, he saw shadows in the trees, shadows moving across the white ground out in the orchard.

He dropped right off the small square of the back porch, right down into what might have been a flowerbed, and pasted himself to the side of the house, down low.

Men afoot, those were. At least there were no mecheiti on the hunt—mecheiti could have smelled him out, but they might not have made it down the climb he had done. There was no hue and cry at least, no indication they had seen him step out the back door. He had a little time, while they were stalking the house, and maybe spending their own time wondering what had blown up the tower or shed or whatever it was.

He could not help leaving a few tracks: he knew there were some on the back porch above his head, but he could stay out of the open. He edged along the foundation, turned the corner, and kept against the foundation about halfway back up the outside wall of the house.

Then he turned around and walked backward—another thing he had learned from the human Archive—to the low stone wall that divided the orchard-keeper's yard off from the high rocks and the wilderness beyond. He vaulted it, and ducked down low.

Best he could do. He might climb the brushy rocks that rose beyond the wall, but that would bring him into the view of whoever was advancing on the house, and besides, he had no idea whether that massive rock went on for a long distance and became flat above, or whether it stopped there and went down sharply on the other side. If he climbed it for safety, there he might be, sitting on a stupid crag, while they climbed up after him and surrounded the place on all sides.

The same rocks ran right down to the lake, and more even jutted out into it—he could see spires that rose right out of the water. There was no shore beyond, at least not here, just the rock and a narrow strip of land, and if you meant to get beyond it, you had to wade, or worse, swim to do it, in freezing water.

And if he ran down to the lake shore to get a better look, they would see him for sure.

There was one virtue to an oversized coat, and far too big boots. They could keep him warm if he just stopped moving and tucked down. He found a nook in the rocks, deep in a drift, behind some brush, and burrowed into it, and put the coat entirely over his head as he sat tucked up into a ball, with just a slit to look through. He could stay there. He had food. He could stay there past breakfast, or until the people chasing him decided they had lost the trail.

The dicey part would be when they traced those footprints to the wall backward, and tried to make sense of it all. They would be all over the wall, up and down the little drainage channel, up and around the rocks.

But the snow was still coming down. And the more the better. He had become a rock, and the snow sifted down on him. All he had to be for the next number of hours, was a rock deep in the leafless brush. He would stay there, not moving for as long as he could, and they could take the house apart and not find him.

If only, if only, *baji-naji*, they believed those lying footprints.

Breathe. Breathe, as much wind as he could get, and try not to cough, try not to make noise. Bren had no idea where Banichi and Jago were, except he'd bet, ahead of him, considerably, though his was the shorter route, along the lake shore.

Run and run. If help was coming, there was no sign of it, and when, in a moment he had to stop to ease the pain in his side, he snatched a shielded look at the locator, he saw he was closer to that box on the map, the structure, the fueling depot, whatever it was.

And thus far no shot fired, no sign of parties stalking one another, and he hoped to heaven Banichi and Jago were in fact ahead of him, not veering off to try to make immediate contact. He left it to Banichi's sense whether to try to use the unit-to-unit function on the pocket com: if Banichi or Jago called him, he'd use it, but not trust it otherwise. He only kept moving, watching the woods and the orchard edge carefully for any sign of life, and not, as yet, seeing anything. He would be unwelcomely silhouetted against the lake if he grew careless and took the fastest, smoothest course. As it was, he climbed over snowy driftwood and skirted around brushy outcrops, terrified as he did so that he could himself fall into ambush—whoever was tracking Cajeiri would be almost as happy to lay hands on the paidhi-aiji, for revenge, if nothing else, and he was determined to make a fight of it if he had to, but to avoid all chance of it if he possibly could.

Bare spot in the woods, something, for God's sake, akin to a private yard, and a set of steps and a boat dock, such as it was, a mere plank on pilings, and a rowboat turned over and beached on the shore, up on blocks for the winter, as might be. He got down by it, said, quietly, foolishly, "Cajeiri?" in remotest hope that the boy might have taken cover in that shell, and the snow have covered his tracks.

No answer. Nothing. And there was no way Cajeiri could mistake his presence. He edged away, keeping low, and filed the location of that boat in memory.

Escape, for him and the boy, if he could lay hands on Cajeiri first. A way out. He formed a plan, if Murini's lot was still rummaging about the area . . . if that bus was not out on the road, if Banichi and Jago were up there somewhere reconnoitering the situation.

And if shots were not being fired, either they had not made contact with their enemy, or, most terrible thought, they were altogether too late to intercept that bus out on the north road, and Murini and company had already laid hands on the heir and spirited him off toward one of the two airports.

If *that* was the case, it was going to be damned messy at the other end, and they had to hope that the dowager had gotten Guild into position up—

He stopped, froze, with a brush-screened view of an ordinary house in the middle of that yard, the answer to why there was a rowboat up on blocks on the lakeshore.

A country house with two figures standing on the small back steps. He very carefully subsided into a crouch behind a log edging, trying to stifle his breaths, keep them small and quiet.

That wasn't Banichi and Jago. Not a hope of it. That was Guild, plain and simple, that segment of the Guild, southerners, who had supported Murini's takeover once, and had declined to come in and bow to new leadership.

So the house was occupied. Plain and simple. An enemy was in it, and one could assume it was the same they had been following.

He didn't think Banichi and Jago were going to go blithely up to that door. He hoped to God they didn't have Cajeiri in there, but he couldn't bank on that hope.

The log that he sheltered behind lay, snow-covered, on the edge of the yard, as if it and the ones beyond it, all in a row, had been put there to make a fence, or stop erosion—lake waves must have gnawed this edge in storm; or rain had washed the earth down. It gave him cover. He could see the men on the porch, standing out there, as if deliberately to advertise their presence, or to draw fire, and one could bet they were wearing body armor.

Beyond the house, through a veil of light snowfall—

Beyond, toward the front yard of the house, was the damnedest thing, as if there had already been a battle there, ruined trees where the orchard abutted the yard, and a structure that might have been some round bin, maybe a water tower, all down in a welter of girders—

The men on the porch went back inside, and others appeared at the edge of the front porch, just visible.

Damn. Swarming with people. And no clue about Cajeiri. No movement from Banichi and Jago, either. He could *not* have outpaced them, no way in hell, and there had been no shots fired. They were out there, seeing what he was seeing, laying plans of their own, he had no doubt in the world.

What he had, while those men were in the house, was a modicum of cover, which might let him get a vantage here, from the edge of the lakeshore, that Banichi and Jago were not going to have, to set up a crossfire, and maybe convince the southerners that there were two forces, and that it was time to run for it.

He edged along, downright crawling on his belly, under the

cover of the log and its neighbor, to the small gap that allowed shore access, and a worn path out to that flimsy dock and the rowboat. God, if only—if *only* Cajeiri had gotten this far . . .

There was, edging the yard on the other side, screening it off from brush, a drainage channel, that let out right onto the shore, with an eroded, snow-filled gully, at the base of a low stone wall that edged the yard—he could see it, a low, inconsiderable wall that mostly blocked the brush that grew there, and just beyond that, a huge rock face, that ran right out onto the beach, the start of the cliffs that rose to Malguri's height.

The rowboat was only one place a person his size could hide. A brushy ditch was another.

He made a fast crossing of that eroded path, and crawled on along the line of logs toward that ditch.

Footprints there, men's footprints. They'd been down this way, searching. They'd been all the way up and down the shallow, stony ditch. And with the overgrowth of brush, the last thing he needed was to disturb the brush overhead and have it seen from the house.

Just—

Mechanical whine. A sound from the ship. An out of place sound that scared hell out of him and froze him in mid-move. It went on, from the far front corner of the house, and imagination replayed the wreckage up there, the destruction. What in hell? he asked himself, and then memory sorted out the lines of that collapsed tower, and replayed Lord Caiti at dinner, arguing about—

—landings.

God only knew. *Something* was going on. The occupants of that house were likely distracted—it was a chance to move, was all, whatever else was going on, and he crawled up into the ditch and kept crawling, while the hydraulic whine went on and shots broke out, wholesale firing.

Crawl like mad, trying not to disturb the brush. He was out

of breath. And the hydraulics reached a rhythmic, interrupted regularity, thump, thump-thump, as he hung up on a branch and tried to free it.

Hell with it, they had to be busy. He forced his way past, never mind the shaking of a branch, and moved faster, faster.

Crash, splintering of wood, firing like crazy, and he could hardly stand it, but he kept crawling, his elbows sore and his knees and feet frozen, face scratched from branches. He was hopeless if they came back this way—he was trapped between the rock and brush of the cliff and the rock of the stone wall. It was a stupid thing he had done, but it might lead him up to the road, where if they had Cajeiri, he might get a vantage to pin them back into that house until help could get here—there *must* be help coming. The dowager would see to it—she would turn out the whole of Malguri Township to help them. It was not just himself and Banichi and Jago . . .

Hydraulics kept up. Thump, thump-thump—interspersed with fire and voices. He reached a nook in the cliff on his left, a snowed-over spot where brush was thick, and there was not even storm-light to see farther down the ditch. He took advantage of the dark area and an overhang of brush to put his head up and try to get a look at the house and what was going on.

A whisper of movement behind him. He spun flat against the wall and made a foolish grab for the gun in his pocket.

"Nand' Bren!"

Boyish whisper. His heart thumped, heavy as the thing in the yard.

"Cajeiri? Damn, Cajeiri?"

"One is very glad to be rescued, nandi."

Rescued. Rescued, in a ditch, pinned against a cliff, with a firefight going on and something on the loose out there.

He managed to breathe. "Get over here," he said, rude outright command, and the brush moved, and a figure no bigger than he was came wriggling out from the roots and the rocks.

His immediate impulse was to grab the boy and hug him; he restrained it, contented himself with laying a firm grip on the boy's parka-clad shoulder to be sure that young head stayed down.

"Banichi and Jago are out there on the other side of the house," he said, and thought of that boat, down at the other end of the ditch and along the shore. "Go ahead of me. Hurry. Down the ditch."

Probably, he thought, no damned oars. People took that sort of thing into storage for the winter. That was a flaw.

But the boy moved, crawling along in front of him. And the shooting came their way, and that *thing*, going thump, thump-thump. The boy crawled for all he was worth, and he did, never minding disturbance of the brush.

Now the thing was closer, and the shooting was. It came right up against the wall, a towering dark shape flashing with lights, blotting out the sky.

Lander, hell! he said to himself, and Cajeiri reversed course as stones fell off the wall, a tumble of the first tier of masonwork, before the thing made its turn and simply limped away, thump, thump-thump. Bren levered himself up for a hair's breadth glance over the wall as it lumbered on its way, and Cajeiri got up beside him. He put a hand on Cajeiri's head and shoved him down, seeing, God, a monster, a mechanical monster, a cylindrical tower on three legs, a fourth one clanking and bent askew as it headed past the house. It misjudged, lurched, and took the corner of the front porch, which came crashing down in a crack of broken carpentry.

Stay put? Make a break for it down the ditch? He had no idea what to do.

His pocket com vibrated, like electric shock.

He grabbed it out of his pocket, flipped it open, and ducked low, back against the wall. "Who?" he asked.

"Btayi! Aeit eiga posii!"

It took him half a second to realize that sharp, clear tone was Jago's voice and a heartbeat more to recognize and translate the out-of-context language. Kyo. Uncrackable by the southerners.

"Aeit makki." Vocabulary eluded him. Wall. What the hell was *wall*? And how was she coming through that clear? *"Topik!* Aeit topik! Punjo'kui. Uwe aik haeit!"

"Kaie."

She knew now where they were. We're all right, he'd said. And: Don't come here! because he and Cajeiri were safe where they were and man'chi would surely pull her and Banichi to risk their necks to get to him—Guild-instilled discipline might dictate something else, which was why they'd kept going when they had gotten separated, but come to him, they would, if he called, and he didn't have any such—

Something exploded, out beyond the front yard, an eruption of fire through the trees, illumining the orchard, highlighting the damned lander that was still thumping about in the wreckage of the porch as if it had gotten completely confused. *That* was their relay. *That* might even be driven by the station.

Then something major blew, and a fireball the size of a bus ballooned up, casting the far end of the yard in light, illumining the trees, and the wreckage. Pieces of metal began to come down, one heavy lump slamming down like the fist of God, right in front of their position.

Cajeiri popped his head up. He grabbed the boy and held him flat as a piece of sheet metal fell down right over them, providing cover, but near deafening them with the impact on the rocks.

"Ow!" Cajeiri breathed.

"Are you all right, young sir?"

"One is crushed. My leg—"

"Some vehicle blew up on the road," he said, out of breath, and, hearing shouts and gunfire break out, he got up on one knee, struggling around past the piece of metal to get another look over the wall.

A dozen or so of someone not theirs was coming toward them, and in the light of fires touched off by the explosion, he saw Guild uniforms. He fumbled into his coat pocket, laid his hand on his gun.

"Get out," he hissed at Cajeiri. "Get down the ditch to the lake, go left, and keep going."

"Left, nandi! *Right* is—"

"Gods unfortunate, go!" No time. He opened fire at the one in civilian dress, the only one not going to be armored, as Cajeiri scrambled to do as he was told. That man dropped, the on-rushing mass balked, several moving to retrieve the fallen man, and the lot veered off to the back yard, dammit, in the very direction he'd just sent Cajeiri. He fired three times more, at legs, which also weren't armored, and hoped to God he was right which side was which.

He scrambled down the flagstone ditch, gun in hand, as fast as he could, while shots blew chips off the rocks and the stones of the wall over his head.

Second heavy explosion. He heard the lander thump, thump-thumping down the yard, and fire pinged off something.

"Halt!" a voice yelled, amplified and echoing off the rocks. "Halt!"

Fire redoubled. He reached the end of the ditch, and just slid off the eroded end of the drainage, trying to make speed and just get the hell wherever Cajeiri was.

Hands grabbed his coat, hauled at him. Cajeiri had found *him*, and he flung an arm around the boy and dragged him up and behind a jut of rock, while fire and light exploded—the whole damned house was afire, now, and the lander stood outlined against the surrounding woods, blinking with lights and threatening.

"Shall we run?" Cajeiri asked.

Good question. Dive out there and risk getting spotted, or continue to try to be part of the rock? He didn't know what to do.

"Nand' Bren!" Cajeiri exclaimed, and grabbed his sleeve and tugged him around to look at the lake.

There was a boat coming in. There were two boats. Three. None of them were showing lights, and they were coming hard.

"There is the greatest chance," Bren said, as calmly as he could, "that they may be from Malguri, young sir, but it would be foolish to rely on it. Stand still. Let them come in. We may find that ditch a good retreat after all."

"Yes," a tense young voice answered, very properly, and Cajeiri stood like the rock itself as those boats came close, and veered off toward their end of the icy edge, and with a roar of the motor, ran around. Men in Guild black got out, and one, shorter, faces of all of them lit by the blaze of the burning house up the slope.

My God, he thought. My God. "Tano? Algini?" he called out. And most improbably: *"Toby?"*

They came running, all of them with rifles, Tano and Algini with a deal more gear than that, and Bren patted arms, that irrepressible human impulse, and outright hugged Toby, atevi witnesses or not, hugged him for dear life.

"God, Brother! What are *you* doing here?"

"Message said you were in the soup again," Toby said, a return embrace nearly crushing the breath out of him. "They weren't wrong. Who blew up?"

"I don't know." He changed languages, or meant to, but Tano and Algini had already headed off, likely on unit-to-unit with each other, and, he hoped, with Banichi and Jago somewhere up above. He put the safety on his gun and tried for his pocket com, hoping to find out.

"Hi, there!" Cajeiri said to Toby. "I know you!"

"That you do," Toby said. "Glad you're safe, nandi."

He got the pocket com, held it to his ear, heard, blessed sound, *Banichi's* voice telling Algini and Tano they were a shade late, but they could come in on the yard.

Then Jago's saying, *"Murini is dead. His man'chi is broken. A bullet found him, and the Guild attending him wish to withdraw."*

"They will report to Headquarters," Algini said then. *"They will leave all weapons and turn up at Guild Headquarters, or be hunted."*

"They wish to take Murini to the Taisigin Marid," Jago said.

Not even to Murini's own clan, the Kadagidi, Bren thought. That said something.

The last throw made. The final try. The rebellion was done.

"We need to notify the dowager," Bren said. His heart rate, which had hammered away for the last hour, began to slow, the strength to run out of him, and he was aware of knees battered and bruised, palms not much better, and a keen desire to sit down right where he was and not hear anything explode for the next while.

"We've got a radio in the boat," Toby said.

"What in hell are you *doing* here?" he asked.

"Well, Tano and Algini had found *us*, and then the message got there, about the aiji's son, and you going after them, so they just gave orders at the airport, refueled in Shejidan, and we came straight ahead from there. Too late to overtake you. But when the dowager's man phoned Malguri for help, we went down to the boats. They've got help up there in the other fortress—"

"The Haidamar. The riders got there?"

"The whole lot, help from the other neighbor on the lake—"

"Lady Drien. So they're all right?"

"Seems they are. But the boats were the quickest way

across, and I figured I might be useful. If there's one thing I know—" "

"It's boats," Bren said, and became aware of a pair of young ears following all of it, but not necessarily understanding every word, in a world that was no longer the ship. "Nandi," he said in Ragi, "your great-grandmother seems to be safe. Cenedi called Malguri and got help across the lake. We are safe. We can take the boats back to Malguri dock."

"We would very much like supper," Cajeiri said. "And we would be very glad if Great-grandmother came across the lake, too."

17

A glass of wine for the grownups, and tea for the young gentleman. Malguri staff, at full strength, having drawn up additional servants from the township, bustled about breakfast, which looked to be an all-out affair, on short notice. Cajeiri and Jegari had gotten together, Jegari with his arm in a sling, which had gotten considerable respect from Cajeiri . . . and an enthusiasm from the young gentleman which had thoroughly embarrassed Jegari and gotten a reproving Look from his great-grandmother.

Bren just held his cup in newly bandaged hands and was very glad of the ice bag on his right knee, the foot propped on a footstool, and both his worlds being very hale and well this morning. Toby—the odd man in the scene—had brought along his fishing-trip best, a clean khaki coat and clean denims, but another plane had arrived in the last confused hours, finally bringing the luggage out from Shejidan, so there sat Toby, looking a little uncommonly short-haired in a gentleman's proper lace shirt and morning coat, but very proper, all the same, and very much cosseted by the maids. Tano and Algini were huddled in a corner conversation with the rest of the Guild present—Banichi had gotten off with a sliced hand (hand to hand with another Guildsman) and Jago with a sore shoulder (falling debris from the explosion), while Cenedi and his men had gotten off entirely unscathed . . . but all of them had tales to tell. Jegari had been determined to stand and attend his young lord, wobbly as he was from concussion; but Cajeiri had ordered him to sit down and have a cup of sweetened tea; and now the two boys chattered away in lowered voices, with animated gestures from Cajeiri as he told his young attendant all the gruesome details he had missed.

Murini was confirmed dead, of small caliber arms fire, uncommonly small caliber. Bren took a deep swallow of wine and tried not to think about aiming at a man in that oncoming line of attackers, but he would do it again, he knew he would. He was sure Banichi and Jago knew exactly who had done it, and whether they told anyone, he left to their judgment: he needed no deeper personal feuds with either the Kadagidi or the Taisigin Marid.

Lord Caiti was also dead—had been dead when they entered the Haidamar. Lord Rodi was dead, the poison having had its ultimate effect about the time the company holding the Haidamar had reached Malguri by phone. Lady Agilisi had gone home to her lowland residence in Catien, in no high good favor, but alive, and now needed to restore herself to the dowager's good graces by a thorough house cleaning.

While Lady Drien—

Lady Drien had come to Malguri to capitalize on her new relationship with her cousin, to sit, looking a little travelworn, but refreshed. She sat, starched and ramrod straight, awaiting breakfast, and quite proud to be participating in the exchange of experiences and timetables. Staff from Cobesthen had arrived by boat, and would take the lady home after breakfast, by which time, Bren presumed, all of them would be very content to collapse into bed and let breakfast settle. He tried to count when he had last seen a mattress. It seemed a while.

The dowager herself had spoken on the phone to Tabini, shocking event. The dowager was not inclined to use telephones.

And then Cajeiri had gotten on the line and blurted out a wild adventure involving digging through a wall, trying to electrocute the guards (but changing his mind) and then watching a giant robot wreck a house. . . .

As usual, with Cajeiri, it was all, all true. Bren figured Tabini would come to appreciate this tendency, as the rest of them did. Always take Cajeiri's accounts seriously, that was the way to manage the young rascal. Never assume he wouldn't, couldn't, or hadn't.

Bren found himself with a phone call of his own he had to make, once he got a secure line, one on which he could pose a few plain questions to Jase—questions like: what in *hell* have you been dropping all over the continent? And why?

He'd shed the gun, the locator, all of that, when he'd had a warm bath—which had nearly put him to sleep—and changed for breakfast. "We knew where you were," Jago told him, "and we believe that Jase-nandi did."

Now didn't that say something of that thing's capabilities, too? He recalled how Jago's voice had come through the com quite clearly all of a sudden, when they were in proximity to that robot, and so had everyone else's voices, at the end.

Relay station, hell. Juggernaut. A lander that could get up and walk.

That sort of gift from the heavens had stirred hostilities in the East, and led Lord Caiti and Lord Rodi to try to deal with Murini instead of supporting Tabini's party, almost certainly contributing to everything that had gone on.

And if Murini had been a leader of better qualities, and not as suspicious, and not expecting treachery out of Caiti and most anyone else he dealt with, he might not, in fact, have gotten treachery served to him in the end.

Murini had been preemptively fast on the trigger when he thought he was betrayed: Caiti had been acting suspiciously from the moment Murini, arriving from the airport at Cie, had wanted to see the kidnapped boy—who turned out to be gone, to Caiti's great distress.

And in that confusion of Caiti's fear at having lost the boy, and Murini's suspicion of Caiti's motives, someone had moved first and shots had broken out—the great disadvantage when Guild met non-Guild security. If any of the participants had been of any better character than they had been, affairs might have gone better for the conspirators than they had gone—but they were not, and things had gone very ill indeed the instant Murini had incorrectly concluded he was in a trap. Caiti had reacted, so Ilisidi had gotten from Rodi before he died, by actually attempting to assassinate Murini on the spot. But his guards had been in no wise up to the deed, since half of them had been out desperately chasing Cajeiri.

So Caiti had died, the staff had all fled or died as Murini's people had gathered from Lord Rodi that the boy really had been there and escaped. They had clear tracks to follow—those of Caiti's men tracking the boy—so Murini had taken out in pursuit, intending to find the boy and link up with their bus on the road—an airport bus from Cie, as they had guessed, a vehicle which was now in pieces, thanks to Banichi. Lord Rodi, realizing he was left behind in a considerable embarrassment, and faced with explaining either to Murini or to Ilisidi, had swallowed poison which had turned out to be a miscalculation: Ilisidi had been quite willing to let him live. So he died with that knowledge.

And on one other point Murini's intelligence had badly failed him: he had not been informed the Cadienein-ori runway was still blocked and that Guild out of Shejidan had by then taken control of it—a force now modestly and quietly withdrawing now that the heir was safe, a force vanishing back into the woodwork and pretending it had never, oh, *never* operated in the East. So Murini would have been trapped there—and been trapped with Cajeiri for a hostage, right in the middle of a firefight.

This had not, of course, happened.

So Murini was confirmed dead, along with most of his Guild bodyguard, two staffers from the Haidamar had gotten back alive, of the five who had gone in pursuit, and it looked very much as if the northernmost district on the lake was now up for inheritance, regardless of whoever Caiti's heir might be down in the plains. Bren had not tracked the heredity of the Eastern lords as precisely as he knew those of the west. He thought Caiti's likely beneficiary was a third cousin, and there was a niece, in the case of Lord Rodi.

But the question was very much whether Malguri was going to allow the summer residence in the Haidamar, which it might consider strategic and of interest, to be inherited along with the Saibai'tet—Caiti's main holding, down in the low-lands, neighboring Agilisi and Rodi. It might claim the Haidamar, if the dowager was in a mood, and she was, and the lowlanders might whistle for their rights to it.

One could grow quite dizzy trying to map the associations and bloodfeuds involved, or that might become involved. But Cajeiri was safe and the two boys were, perhaps a little too noisily, sharing their respective adventures with the Malguri servants. . . .

And thank God for one more thing, Bren said to himself. Toby had left Barb at his coastal estate—to keep up the boat. She would assuredly make demands of the servants. She would naturally botch up the few words of Ragi she might figure out and that would certainly amuse the staff there—at least, one hoped she would amuse them, and do nothing outrageous or insulting. He rather hoped she would stay on the boat, and not accept the natural and courteous invitation to move into the house. God, she would leap at the chance to be lady of the manor.

His eyes drifted shut. Just for a moment. His whole world being in tolerably good order for a change, he decided he could just rest for a moment. No one would notice if he rested scratchy eyes.

He realized then that someone was shaking his arm. He looked up, blinked, to find the whole company on their feet and generally trending toward the dining hall. On one side of him, Toby was leaning on his chair back. On the other, Jago loomed above him, a shadow against Malguri's yellow lamplight.

A shadow with a sober smile, who at the moment had a hand on his arm.

"Nand' paidhi," she said. "Hold out just one more hour, Bren-ji. Then we can all rest."